Under
Fishbone Clouds

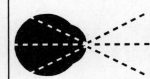

This Large Print Book carries the
Seal of Approval of N.A.V.H.

UNDER
FISHBONE CLOUDS

SAM MEEKINGS

THORNDIKE PRESS
A part of Gale, Cengage Learning

GALE
CENGAGE Learning™

Detroit • New York • San Francisco • New Haven, Conn • Waterville, Maine • London

GALE
CENGAGE Learning

LIBRARY OF CONGRESS CATALOGING-IN-PUBLICATION DATA

Meekings, Sam.
  Under fishbone clouds / by Sam Meekings.
    p. cm. — (Thorndike Press large print core)
  ISBN-13: 978-1-4104-3582-8 (hardcover)
  ISBN-10: 1-4104-3582-2 (hardcover)
    1. Married people—China—Fiction. 2. China—History—20th century—Fiction. 3. China—History—Cultural Revolution, 1966–1976—Fiction. 4. Large type books. I. Title.
  PR6113.E29U53 2011
  823'.92—dc22   2010049185

Published in 2011 by arrangement with St. Martin's Press, LLC.

Printed in the United States of America
1 2 3 4 5 6 7 15 14 13 12 11

For Noah

1:
1946
THE YEAR OF THE DOG

Beginnings are always difficult, especially when you have lived as long as I have. I could start by telling you that this is a simple story about two hearts and the way they are intertwined. But that won't do. The Jade Emperor would not like that at all. I think I will have to go a little further back.

In a small border town huddled at the furthest reaches of a northern province, there was an old teahouse. It was winter there, thousands of years ago. And inside was the owner, his face flushed despite the frost that had turned his windows into rivers of curdled milk. He bolted the door at the end of the night and ran a wet rag through his hands. As he moved, sweat slipped between the folds of his shirt. He had been pacing between the tables since morning. Lukewarm tea sat in a squat clay cup on one of the dark wooden tables, the leaves sunk to the bottom like broken lilies given up on light.

The teahouse was situated at the end of a

long, narrow street that looked as though it had been sculpted out of ice. It was one of the last buildings before the city trailed off into tracks darkened by the reach of the mountain's misshapen shadow. Since winter began, the owner had not had enough customers to afford to keep his tattered lanterns lit. Even so, he had not become accustomed to waiting. Instead, his eyes had taken on a furtive quality, as though at any second he would be ready to reach for the taper and strike the small room into life. He sat and sipped his drink, almost dropping it when he heard the timid taps at his door.

On the other side he found an old man who appeared to be at least a head shorter than himself, although this might have been due to the way he stooped and held his body at an angle, looking like his left side was weighing his right side down. He looked to be at least double the owner's own age. The owner ushered the man inside, anxious to keep the cold wind from sneaking in, and guided him to a chair. He turned to light two of the thinner lanterns, which hissed at him as the oil caught. The old man's face was sunburnt and as lined as if it had been whittled from oak; his beard was like a bird's nest flaked with ash. One of the mountain people, the owner muttered to himself as he heated some water. Definitely from the mountain — probably hadn't even set eyes on a coin in years.

Seeing no need for the swan-necked pot perched proudly in the centre of the room, the owner filled two cups straight from the pan, adding a stingy pinch of dried leaves to each. He sat down at the same table as the old man, and both of them clasped their hands round the cups.

'From the mountain?' the owner asked.

The old man nodded slowly, not taking his eyes from the steam rising off the tea in front of him.

'Bet it's cold up there this time of year. Streams must be frozen up.'

The old man nodded again. They sat in silence for a few minutes. As the owner rose from the table, the old man spoke. 'Do you have anything to eat?'

The owner looked back at the old man for a moment, considering the scraps in the kitchen. He was embarrassed with himself, but he asked anyway, 'Can you pay?'

The old man traced his hands across his grubby jacket and shook his head.

'It's all right,' the owner sighed. 'I'm about to eat anyway. Just some rice.'

Soon he returned from the kitchen with two bowls. They ate. By the time they pushed the bowls away darkness had settled like dust between the tables. Yet before the owner had time to suggest setting up a makeshift bed in the back, the old man had got up from the table.

11

'Thank you, but I must keep moving. I've still got a long way to go.'

The owner did not try to dissuade him. Old men can be stubborn.

However, instead of heading for the door, the old man tottered toward the opposite wall. He ran his hands across it, as though it was a giant page of Braille, and then fumbled in his pockets. The owner watched him with the strange impatience of those who have nothing better to do. The old man pulled out a grubby piece of cloth and unwrapped it to reveal a small lump of charcoal, which he raised to the wall. He began with a small arc, which became a beak, and from there the rest of the bird was born: a dark smudge of an eye; ruffles of soot above the brow; feathers; and, finally, long slender legs ending in water. Neither of them had any idea how long he sketched for, as the minutes had become tangled and lost in the movement of his hands. By the time his arm dropped there were five proud cranes sketched on the wall. He folded the cloth back around the stub of coal, then wiped his hands on his trousers.

The owner inched closer to inspect the parade of birds lined up on the main wall of his teahouse, unsure of what to say.

'Cranes,' the old man said. 'No one seems to agree on the strange paths their flight follows, or the distances they cover. In all my studies, I have never found a common consensus on this matter. They are my thanks. For the tea, and the food.'

He bowed his head and walked to the door. The owner opened his mouth, but was still uncertain of how to speak to the stooped man.

'Have a good journey, old uncle.'

The old man started down the street without looking back. The owner watched him leave. It seemed that it was the distance moving to meet him, rather than his slow and awkward steps, that gave him motion. The owner bolted his door for the final time that evening. On his way to bed he looked at the cranes staring down at him and shook his head. I would like to say that he dreamed of scores of graceful journeying birds, or the top of the nearby mountain that he had never ventured up, but the past is one thing, and dreams are quite another, so we will have to leave those to him.

The next afternoon three tables were full — the most since the evenings had begun stalking back into the days. One, a musician, was a regular; since the owner was in a good mood because of the increase in trade, he urged him to play. The musician gently waved his hand in front of his face. It hardly seemed worth it. The owner tilted the swan-necked pot, refilling the musician's cup to the brim. The musician exaggerated a sigh and bent down, pulling the rectangular box up from between his feet. He took out the *zheng* and gently placed it on the table, running his hands across the bamboo before suspending his fingers over the silk strings that travelled across its raised bridge. It was unclear whether he paused for dramatic effect or because he was searching the corners of his memory for the beginning of a certain tune. He must have imagined himself a magician, his left hand bending the strings while his right began to pluck and swim between them, drawing up notes as if from some invisible depth.

For a few seconds as he started to play the other customers fell silent and listened, only to resume their conversations moments later, and it was a while before anyone looked at the wall. Then they saw it. Only the musician, halfway through the song and humming along as he picked, did not turn with the gasps. The charcoal cranes were moving across the wall, in time with the music. They had begun with slowly dipped and nodding heads, then the raised arch of tentative steps, and, as the tempo increased, the birds unfurled their wings. A shiver of feathers seemed to shake the whole room as the cranes started to bob and strut. The owner looked at them, scratched his head and smiled nervously. In the muddle of clapping hands, whoops and singing, the dark lines of water shifted into splashes, the wooden frames of the windows

14

rattled to the tap of swaying beaks, and chairs and tables groaned like weary beasts as they were nudged across the floor toward the boisterous mural.

By evening the next day customers were crammed in two to a chair, with others squatting on the floor. The owner barely had room to move between the babbling crowd, so the long neck of his teapot preceded him around the room. Despite the snow piling up outside, the teahouse bristled with heat as the gathered musicians bustled and sweated, each trying to outplay each other with increasingly wild flourishes. Everyone was watching the birds dancing and darting for fish where the flaking wall met the sloping floorboards. They drove ripples across the water and sent shudders through the finely etched lilies as they shifted from leg to leg. It seemed that the birds could do anything but stop moving. The thudding music was drowned out by shouts as one launched itself upward in flight. It pushed itself higher with frantically fluttering wings, and then it began to soar: tucking its legs under its plump form as it flew across corners and looped over window frames and above doors, conquering the whole circumference of the crowded room.

The owner soon had more coins than could fit under the wonky floorboard in his small bedroom. As he drifted to sleep that night his face was lit by a broad grin, which did not disappear despite the cold winds creeping under the door to interrupt his dreams. Was it that he believed the world could be changed by a single act of kindness? With hindsight he would consider himself naïve, and curse himself for investing meaning in possibilities that usually belonged only to stories told by old ghosts like me. One thing was certain: he did not question what had happened. Why would he? His pockets were full and his arms sore from brewing, stirring and pouring. If the birds did dance as he slept, to the un-schooled music of wind-rattled cups and creaking chairs, then he was happily unaware.

Months passed, and every night was the same, with locals as well as people from distant villages huddled in the now famous teahouse to watch the dancing cranes. Late one night, as he was mopping up small streams of spillages, the owner heard some-one banging on his bolted door. He opened it, half expecting to see the old man returned, but instead found himself face to face with two of the city guards. They were stocky men, proud of the uniform they were always dressed in as well as the power that went with it.

'As of today this establishment has been requisitioned by the city government,' one of them said.

His eyes scurried over their hands, looking for an official document, then above their shoulders, searching for the local magistrate. He saw neither.

'You have two hours to vacate the property. We'll be waiting here.'

'But why?' he stammered. 'I don't understand. I've paid the taxes. I . . .'

His words trailed off. The guards stood silently in his doorway. He understood, and slouched, deflated, towards the backroom. Once there he took his bedsheet and lay it on the floor. Within an hour he had filled it with his things — his winter fur, a rice bowl, the precious swan-necked pot and the handful of coins he had managed to stealthily extract from under the floorboard. He bundled it up and hauled it over his shoulder. I should have been expecting this, he thought. There was no point waiting around. He did not consider fighting, bribing or pleading with the impassive guards as he slunk past them onto the street. Neither did he yet believe, as he would come to years later, that the teahouse walls were skin peeled from his back, rubbed raw beneath the weight of his possessions as he wandered further from the city, into the winter.

The governor was a pot-bellied man not much given to smiling. He appointed his gangly nephew as manager of the newly acquired teahouse, and, after dismissing the guards, sat and pushed the wooden beads of his tall abacus from end to end, attempting to solve an impossible equation in which the variables continually shifted shape to elude him. His nephew arranged for posters to be hung up around the city, depicting in bright colours the fabulous dancing cranes.

On opening night a trail of lanterns led to the freshly painted door. The gangly manager welcomed all the new patrons to the refurbished teahouse, bowing to his uncle who sat sullenly in the corner flanked by two visiting mandarins, a specially summoned court musician and a local general. Thin and tanned waiting boys poured jasmine tea, and coins began to clink. The musician played. The cranes seemed for a moment to be staring back at the expectant faces studying them. The water at their feet dimpled, and they raised themselves up, their proud necks extending and their feathers a blur as, one by one, they pushed forward and flew. From their slender throats calls burst out, spurring each other on as they ascended. The new customers cheered, and even the restrained mandarins laughed and clapped.

It was the governor who first noticed that they were shrinking. His mouth opened but he did not speak. Everyone began pushing toward the wall, and in the crush the musician dropped his instrument. The music splintered into the sound of broken strings and reproachful shouts. The cranes got smaller and smaller as they glided toward the horizon line, the brink of sight at the top of the wall. They were scribbles, then thumb-print smudges, and then they were gone. For a while nothing happened. Soon, however, the teahouse was empty except for the gover-nor and his tearful nephew, who sat listening to the mumbles of the crowd as they filed down the street. Neither of them moved, nor gave voice to their doubts and recriminations. Outside the cold wind blew a blank poster onto the roof and whipped the door closed. They did not bother to bolt it.

Bian Yuying had been thinking about the story of the dancing cranes all morning — how so much can turn upon a single act of kindness, how so much might depend upon the whims of history. How nothing is ever as you expect it. She thought of her husband ly-ing in the hospital, then picked up her bags and started moving again. Cranes are a symbol of fidelity, she thought; they mate for life. She could not recall how many times she had heard the story of the dancing cranes, half sung by storytellers in teahouses to the rhythm of squat drums when she was a child, then in the confines of the stone-walled bedroom where her husband had told it to their children, and later their grandchildren. Each time, the story changed a little, though this had never bothered her. It was in the dif-ferences that she located the tale's restless heart, which, like the cranes, would not allow itself to remain still. The cranes represented karma, the delicate balancing act of the universe that rewards good acts with rewards and evil acts with punishment. Everyone gets what they deserve in the end. Yet after all she had been through, Yuying was not sure that life was ever that simple.

Her back ached from leaning against the wall for so long. She enjoyed wandering through the older, narrow streets, on her way back from the hospital. They reminded her of the house she had been born in seventy years before, the house where she was married, the house she fled from and returned to, the house where her father died, the house her mother was thrown out of after the revolution. A house of hopes and hopelessness. She always had to remind herself to turn left towards the main road, to head back to her daughter's third-floor flat near the massage alley instead of wandering on towards the courtyards and houses guarded by stone lions, deeper into the past. Yuying soon came to the bridge over the murky river which sliced the city in two. It looked to her like the discarded skin of a huge water snake, shimmering where the light fell with the flow. She was nearly there.

Climbing the stairs was a slow and precise operation, and when Yuying first reached the apartment her hands were shuddering too much to direct the keys into the lock. Finally in, she sat down on her grandson's bed and stared out of the window. She pulled open the wooden drawer, and, from beneath her neatly folded winter layers, extracted a small album. It fitted perfectly in her lap. Only a couple of hours to kill, and then she would return to the hospital, with a plastic box of fresh dumplings, to resume the bedside vigil. She pushed the door closed and flitted quickly through the album to the penultimate page, on which there was a black-and-white print no bigger that her palm.

Around three thousand years ago, the Shang kings turned to their dead ancestors for help at times like these. The dead, they believed, were powerful. Evidence of this was all around them — storms gathered from frothy clouds, drooping and meagre crops, victories in vicious frontier wars: all could be attributed to the unpredictable justice of the dead, moving between the seen and the unseen. To appease their ancestors, the kings offered sacrifices, slaughtering scores of convicts and slaves, and transforming fields of oxen into seas of cloying blood and wild flies. Yet this did not always solve their problems, and, when rains continued, battles stalled and queens became barren, they sought to commune more directly with the dead, to ask them how much sacrifice was enough. They turned to animal bones in order to learn how to tame the future. Their questions, for which one of the first written examples of Chinese was created, were inscribed on these oracle bones and were answered by the cracks that appeared in the bones after they had passed through fire — for everyone knows that the dead do not speak the same language as the living. These writings have survived them, and so another exchange with the dead has been achieved, though even today it's impossible to fathom answers to their dark and blood-soaked questions.

Hou Jinyi, his cropped mass of curly black hair plied into a messy side-parting over his horsy face, scrubbed up and shaved and dressed and smiling especially for this, his first visit to a photographer, stared up at Yuying. She traced a finger over that familiar lopsided smile. She too talked to those who could no longer answer, though she did not expect a reply. This is how she wanted to remember him, not as the wrinkled thing wheezing fitfully in the busy ward. She leaned forward to study the small portrait, and slowly let her memories carry her back to where she always travelled when she was alone, to the summer of 1946.

By now you may be wondering who it is telling this story, who has been listening in on this old woman's thoughts. So let me get the introductions out of the way. I have lived a long time amidst woks and greasy chopsticks, beside chicken feathers and plump dough ready to be fisted down into dumplings. In short, I am a god. But not the storm-bringing, death-doling type — rather a common household deity: the Kitchen God.

The truth is, however, that being immortal has its drawbacks. The almost infinite pleasures of the many heavens begin to lose their appeal after the first millennium or two, and no matter how much they try to resist, most gods find themselves creeping back down to earth whenever they get the chance. We cannot help ourselves. I am not alone in returning time and time again, although I have not as yet disguised myself as a white bull or a swan, or started whispering in the ears of would-be prophets. My powers do not stretch much further than being able to dip into people's thoughts as easily as you might trail your fingers through the lazy flow of a river. And until lately I was doing this as much as possible. In fact, I could have been starbathing by the bright rapids of the Milky Way or attending the most lavish of celestial soirées over the last fifty years, and yet instead I followed Bian Yuying and Hou Jinyi, trying to understand what it is that enabled their love to survive the separations, the famine, the Great Proletarian Cultural Revolution, and even death.

It would be easy to say that I did this simply to win a bet I made with the Jade Emperor about the workings of the human heart. However, that would not be quite true. As soon as you glance into a person's thoughts, you're trapped. If I stayed with these two people for so long, it is because I once had a heart myself, although I never learnt how to keep it from destroying me. But we will come to that later — once again, I seem to be getting sidetracked. After all, this is not my story: it's theirs.

'Bian Chunzu — come here! Quick! I have something for you.'

She heard her father's shout rumbling through the house. She was sixteen, and he was the only person who still called her Chunzu. Everyone else called her Yuying, the name her Japanese teacher had given her and which she had recently decided to take in place of her own. Chunzu — 'spring bamboo' — was too pretty, too artifical, too delicate. When I am an adult, she thought to herself, I will be a suave Japanese translator and no one will think me delicate. Her Japanese teacher was a petite woman whose every word she had hung on to for the last few years; the last time Yuying saw her, however, she had been placed in a wooden cage after the other Japanese had left, and the locals were shouting about revenge for the occupation. Yuying tried not to dwell on this image.

Her father called again, and his hoarse voice rattled through the large house. It was the type of place where echoes were still heard days after the words were first uttered, slowly winding through the cold stone corridors. She fought the urge to shout back. I am not that type of daughter, she told herself as she placed her pen in the book to save her place. By the time she would return to her bedroom, a dribble of ink would have spread from the stunted nib and blotted out an intricate point of advanced Japanese grammar. As she passed her servant outside her door she blushed, knowing that she too had heard the shout.

Yuying had once overheard the two younger servants whispering about her father's nocturnal journeys to visit one of his many other women in the city. They had giggled as they recounted how they had heard him slipping past their rooms late at night. Now, when she could not sleep, Yuying's imagination conjured up the sound of padded slippers gently slapping against the stone hallway, the bamboo in the courtyard rustled by the breeze his creeping form created.

As she reached her father, she pushed these thoughts from her mind and chastised herself. She loved her family more than anything she could imagine.

'Father.'

'Sit down. I have found a way to grant both

our wishes, Chunzu.'

She stole a glance directly at her father as she sat. He looked exhausted. Below his pug nose, his thin moustache twitched like the bristly mane of a regal dragon, and, when she dared to raise her head to look more closely, she saw that his pupils had melted to eclipse the rest of his eyes. She had no doubt as to where he had spent most of the day: the Golden Phoenix, the priciest opium lounge in the city.

'Come on then. Take a look.' He let his hand fall to the slim bundle of papers on the table between them. 'I have made most of the arrangements already. The rest should be simple enough,' he said as she slowly furrowed through the bundle to find a small grey photograph within a milk-white frame. It showed a wild-haired young man.

'In a little under one month, this will be your husband.'

She felt her throat tighten.

'He has agreed to let you continue your studies. You will both live here, of course, and so our family need not be broken. He will even take our name. Well?'

She tried to stop the tears slipping down her face. Her father banged his fist on the table.

'Ungrateful daughter! Everyone told me that educating a girl was the most foolish thing a father could do, but did I listen? No,

I heard only your pleas. And now I have worked so hard to find a suitable match, and you do not even give me thanks! Get your tears out now, then, but be sure your eyes are not red in one month, when we will have a joyous wedding. Do not bring shame on your family, Bian Chunzu!'

She sniffed and nodded.

'Leave me now. Go tell your sisters.' He waved his hand towards the door.

She stood, hesitating. For months she had looked over photos of prospective grooms, sending messages through matchmakers and her father. Yet their unusual demands had meant that the family had already turned down a large number of young men. If one finally agrees to everything, her father had reasoned, there will be nothing else to consider. She would soon be seventeen, and no one would want to marry an old woman.

'Can I keep it?'

He said nothing, but stared across at where dust swirled in the solitary slice of sun falling in from the window. He tapped his fingers lightly on his temples.

'Thank you, Father.'

Yuying left him studying a fly that had found a way into the room but not yet a way back out. She was never quite sure what he was thinking. She stepped over the mute's large black dog dozing in the hallway, and tried to concentrate on the dizzying image of a swelling red wedding dress snug against her skin, suddenly transforming her into someone else. She did not dare look at the photo again, but instead held it tight against her side.

Yuying could already see her life forming, fluttering out from this photograph. Her mother, in her more bitter moments, had told her that a woman is a receptacle into which a man pours his dreams and his desires. Yuying did what she did whenever the world seemed at odds with her own hopes — made herself small, made herself a stone that rivers might rush over without uprooting. I wish I could have told her that although it is easy to make yourself stone, it is difficult to turn back. But us gods have a policy about interfering with humans, so there was not much I could do.

Let me tell you a little more about Yuying in the summer of 1946. Already others mistook her shyness for superiority. Already she had begun to bite her bottom lip when the world seemed to veer beyond her control. Already she had picked up her father's stubbornness, and her mother's superstition that if others talk about you too much you will become the person others think you are. Already she had learnt the one thing that would keep her alive in the years to come — that sometimes silence is a kind of love.

Yuying's room was in the east wing with her siblings, though after she married she would move to the north wing, to the large empty room just before the mute's chamber and the servants' quarters, to have some space with her new husband. She shuddered at the thought. Yuying had never considered it strange that her mother slept in the east wing while her father usually stayed in his study in the central compound, next to the entrance hall and small shrine, so that he could hear people coming and going (or, as the servants whispered, sneak in and out himself more stealthily).

She stopped, hearing laughter. Inside the next room her two younger sisters, Chunlan and Chunxiang, were playing *weiqi*, although they had learnt to call it Go, just as the Japanese did. Each had a handful of slate and clamshell pieces, tar-black and dirty white, and were stretched out over the floorboards, leaning down to surround each others' imaginary army. As they threw down the pieces, tactically trying to trap each in ever increasing circles and squares, Yuying could not help but picture the armies that until recently had swooped through the city, outside the schools, through the restaurants and around the park. Every little victory for one of her sisters made it harder for her to open her mouth. She hung back in the hallway to watch them play. Within an hour everyone in the house will know anyway, she thought.

By the time of Confucius, Go was considered an art form, ranked alongside painting, poetry and music. Old stories said that an ancient emperor invented it over four thousand years ago to educate his dull son. In the newly unified Japan of the seventeenth century, four Go houses were set up and subsidised by the government, schooling students in the strange and divergent probabilities of its play. Since the careful strategies implicit in the game ensure that the occurrence of two identical matches is a virtual impossibility, the game took on an intellectual aspect to complement its martial application. Scholars debated its relation to cosmology, physics, consciousness and infinity, sipping blossom tea while watching stubbornly long matches. The idea of infinitely changeable empires, conquered, reclaimed, conquered again and continually swept clean, must have appealed to the warlords of the early twentieth century, who might have recognised in the game's shifting patterns the possibility of rewriting whole maps according to the formation of different colours. When the Japanese invaded the north of China to proclaim the state of Manchuria, how many people spotted the first throws of a handful of black pebbles?

'Hey, little devils, come here. Guess what?'

Her sisters scrabbled to their feet and ran to her. The middle one, Chunlan, was bony and sharp, right down to her fierce eyes and her pursed lips that were always ready to sting. The younger one, Chunxiang, was tall and awkward, with a spirit-level fringe and thick black-rimmed glasses, her round face always breaking into blushes, her shoulders slouching to try and hide her height.

'I'm getting married.'

They made twittery noises, like morning birds.

'Who is he, Yu? Where did he come from? No, I mean, what's he like?'

She held out the picture hesitantly. They huddled close to study it.

'Well, he's kind of handsome . . .' Chunxiang ventured.

'When's it going to be?' Chunlan asked.

'I'm not sure. Soon. Pa has arranged it all, I think.'

'Wow. Just imagine it, Yu. I bet we'll have pig's trotters, and goose eggs, and spicy pork, and well, of course, more dumplings than you've ever seen!'

'Do you always have to think with your stomach, Xiang? It won't be like that. It'll be romantic, and we'll be too busy looking beautiful in Ma's best jewellery and new silk dresses to want to go too near all the food,' Chunlan chided her sister.

'So, you'll be leaving, Yu?' Chunxiang asked.

'No. Pa said he'll come to live here. And I can keep going to college.'

'Well, it's great you get to keep your precious books, but when I get married, we'll live in a big place that's all our own, and I'll be the lady of the house, and everything will be different to here. We'll visit, of course. Come and see you and your husband and your pile of papers.' Chunlan giggled to herself.

Yuying pursed her lips. She didn't have the energy to argue with her sister, not now. 'I'll be able to finish my degree, and then I'll be able to do anything I choose,' she said.

'So, who is he? Is he from the city? Did a matchmaker find him?' Chunxiang asked, cutting through the tension between her two sisters.

'I don't know,' Yuying conceded. 'He could be anyone.'

'But he's not. He's your husband.'

Her sister could not know how, in the years to come, those words would catch like swallowed bugs at the back of Yuying's throat, struggling and beating wings to draw back the dark. Her youngest sister — who would disappear into the smoke of the steelworks and iron forges that dotted the frosty plains of the furthest north — stared at her and grinned.

'There's so much to think about,' Yuying said, and, though for a moment the sentence seemed serious, the three girls suddenly burst out laughing.

'At least you know he won't be old and ugly. Remember what happened to Meiling from down the road? Her new husband looked like he'd been hanging around since the last dynasty. If only he'd had half as many teeth left as he had bars of gold stashed away! And what about Ting from school — do you remember how her lanky husband stuttered his way through the ceremony?' Chunlan set them laughing again.

A shadow poured through the open doorway. It sloped up into Peipei, their auntie, holding a single finger up to her lips. She was not really their auntie, though as she had nursed each one and calmed them through countless night terrors, they did not think to lose that familiar term of address.

'Sshh. Your father is working,' Peipei said. 'Do something useful, like some needlework.' Peipei still believed, despite their schooling, that the girls should not bother themselves with too much thinking. Educating girls is like washing little boys: all well and good, but they only get dirty again, she told anyone who would listen. 'Come on, you know what your mother said.'

'Where is Ma?'

'She's resting.' All four of them knew that this was not true — they had never known their mother to be anything but busy. Peipei scowled, pulling her trio of hairy moles further down her face. She then shooed them from the room, Yuying to her Japanese and Chunlan to her etiquette essay. Chunxiang was left to sweep up the Go pebbles and pile them into the two boxes. She didn't bother to separate the colours, and in the quickly brokered armistice the armies became inseparable.

As she passed the study, Yuying peered in through the half-open door to see her father throwing three silver coins to the floor. She knew his temper well enough to realise that she should not stay and risk being caught. Yet she longed to see what he would find out, for she was sure that he was asking about her wedding. He would count up the number of heads and tails and convert them into either a straight line or a broken line (old or young, yin or yang). When he had done this six times, he would have a hexagram with which to divine the future. He would find the corresponding hexagram in his private, battered copy of the *I Ching* and read from the obscure explanations first set down more than two and a half millennia ago. He would then change each of the lines in the hexagram to its opposite and read the verse that described the resulting hexagram — for there are two sides to everything, and always at least two ways to see the world. The book describes everything and nothing: it is a little universe which you must immerse yourself in to find any kind of sense from the answer it gives. Yuying carried on back to her room as her father finished tossing the coins. Who knows what he found?

Yuying opened her Japanese grammar book and discovered the ink stain, which she dabbed at with the back of her hand. The rest of the day was blotted out like this. At dinner her mother's exhausted eyes stared for a while at the birthmark-like blotch that the ink had mapped onto Yuying's hand, but instead of speaking she only arched a carefully tweezered eyebrow.

With the news of the wedding, everything seemed suddenly different to Yuying — the lazy Susan's slow orbit, her sisters' chopsticks pecking at the plates like hungry beaks scrapping in the sawdust of the yard, the servant girl's awkward manner when bringing the dishes; even her own sluggish chewing and swallowing seemed out of place. She looked up to see her mother staring at her. Will I still be your daughter, when my husband comes? she wondered. She imagined her home turned upside down. Will you still visit me, or will it be my children everyone comes to fuss over?

Yuying watched her mother, and wondered when it was that she had been young. She looked old, older than her forty-something years. Her husband, Yuying's father, had already reached forty before he was pestered to take a young wife from outside the city. Her cheeks sagged under the weight of her eyes. Not enough pigment left to call them anything but black, her daughter noted. They were darker even than her chopstick-knotted hair. She was shorter than her daughters, with tiny shoes and terrible looks that could stop vines growing and silence anyone in the city — even her husband, though he sometimes pretended not to notice.

Old Bian did not often eat with them, and today was no exception. More than once, in barely audible whispers, the sisters had joked that he might be a ghost, neither eating nor moving much till night welled up, though they would never have said this if they thought anyone might have heard them.

'Listen, girls. Tomorrow you can start preparing for the wedding. The three of you can begin by sewing the pillows. Oh, Yuying, remember: a smile makes you ten years younger. It will be the happiest day of your life. Your father has found you a wonderful husband.'

'When will we be meeting his family?'

Her mother's tongue skirted over her front teeth, like a pianist's hands grazing the ivory. The girls recognised the movement — she always did this when she did not know how to answer.

'There's no need to worry about the details. You girls just make sure you're prepared, and your father will do the rest.'

Her puzzling dismissal clouded the table. Yuying suppressed a shudder. A few picked-through scraps sat between the four of them. She looked at her sisters looking down at their laps, and knew she must ask.

'Ma,' she said, 'have *you* met him?'

Before her mother could reply, they were interrupted by the sound of the mute's dog barking, signalling his return from the restaurant. The nervous servant girl jumped, and their mother quickly rose from the table. She bent down and kissed her eldest daughter, her lips like breeze-borne embers, almost branding Yuying's cheek.

'Of course I have. Now, best to get some rest,' she whispered. Although her steps were small and stunted, as she rocked forward tentatively on the balls of her feet, she still gave the impression of retaining an untouchable grace. After she left, the girls wandered to their separate rooms, the youngest two no longer daring to tease Yuying.

Yuying flopped down on the hard wooden bed, which would soon be given up to her youngest sister. It was now that she should have retreated to the loft to mourn her separation from her family and curse the go-between who had arranged the union which would usually prise apart a family. She should have been singing strange laments with her sisters for the things she could not know that she would lose. She had not learnt these songs, had not yet heard the music of departure and its bittersweet arguments that

37

bubble and blister on the tongue. All her friends had drifted into different stories, scrabbling new beginnings from little rooms. But she was going nowhere. She imagined herself aged a hundred, moving from corner to corner of that same house, sharing space with spiders' webs and her precious retinue of books, with their perfectly cracked spines and pages whose reek of must and ink rubbed off on her eager fingers. Yet, in the years to come, when the books were stoked up in the fire or buried beyond the back of the garden, she would not even shrug.

Unable to rest, Yuying got up to look once more at the photo her father had given her earlier that day. Just as she never imagined that the Japanese, present on every corner since she was a toddler, would ever leave, she could not imagine being a married woman. The world was becoming alien to her. The streets seemed empty without the Japanese soldiers, and the wild celebrations of the end of the occupation had quickly faded into more local squabbles. And now a wedding. She did not dare to consider the half-lit rooms in which her father might have found him. The photo slipped out of her fingers.

She slumped down amid the piles of copious and useless notes for which her sisters mocked her so unremittingly. The declensions and tenses and equations would be replaced by tea-making and babies as soon as her four years of college were finished. Trying to think any further than this seemed to cause the future to retreat and contract to a hazy vanishing point. She flicked through a couple of books, knowing she would not read them now. In the tinny light of dusk the brush-strokes floated from the open pages, a sea cast over by shadows. Her head thumped like a kitchen orchestra of pot-and-pan percussion.

These were the last things she remembered of that day more than half a century ago: silver streaks sneaking in under the door, snoring and moonlight and tiptoeing foot-steps at the threshold of sense as the whole house slipped toward sleep.

Did she dream about the future? Don't ask me — I've already told you, dreams are off-limits. Did she dream about how her heart would be forged in the furnace of her marriage, and come out welded to another, hot and heavy and inseparable? Or did she dream about me, scuttling along behind her and Hou Jinyi, trying to figure out why they kept going?

Let me tell you a secret. Even us gods have trouble predicting the future, let alone dreaming it. Look around at the city of Yuying's birth if you want proof. Who could have guessed that the sun-starched plains attacked by plough and hoe and ox would give way to squat apartment blocks and offices littering the landscape like insatiable insects? Would anyone in Old Bian's household have had the imagination to predict that Fushun would sprawl outwards from those few ancestral courtyard homes into skyscrapers and chimneys churning out smoke that would leave the sky the colour of scratched metal? That old men who ought to be revered and welcomed in each house, as custom dictated, might end up foraging through the bins in search of plastic bottles and cola cans which could be sold at factory doors for a handful of change?

Anyone who had said as much in the summer of 1946 would have been laughed out of the room, and their sanity called into question. So let's leave dreams and predictions to those that want to make fools of themselves, and get back to the wedding preparations.

The newspapers of June 1946 were still filled with talk of the surrender that had been forced the year before and its aftermath, while the civil war crept back across villages, distant cities and everyone's lips. As the preparations for the wedding become more frantic, Yuying tried to ignore the fact that the usual pre-wedding gifts of cakes, liquor, mandarin oranges or notes from the groom's family had not appeared. Instead, as the day grew closer, she focused on her studies, scribbling away in her notebooks and deriving philosophical speculation from the shortest of essay questions, until each night's candle had burnt down to its scaly stub. Both her sisters and her classmates took the view that she was nervous about the wedding night, but this did not explain the gnawing curiosity that wriggled inside her chest. Her father had been out of the house most of those days, like a magician trawling props behind the sheet of some cheap street theatre to produce increasingly wild tricks.

The day before the wedding, the children of friends and family were invited to climb on the marital bed, to scrabble for the dates, pomegranates, lotus seeds and peanuts that were scattered across the sheets. In this way it was believed that something of their spirit would be left behind, making the bed more receptive to the possibility of conception. Perhaps it is true, Yuying thought, that we leave something of ourselves in every place we visit, in every thing we touch. And if the world around us retains such memories, then it is in this that we survive death.

That night her sisters tiptoed to her room, each clutching an — orange — the smallest of stolen gifts to exchange for something they could not name. Scattering peel and pith over the furniture, they gossiped about classmates and shared the rumours they had overheard from the servant.

'It'll be strange, tomorrow, with a man in the house. I mean another man, not just father and the mute pottering around — though he doesn't really count since he can't speak,' Chunlan said.

'Don't talk about Yaba like that! He's our friend!' Chunxiang said.

'You don't think it's strange? That my husband is coming here, and I'm not leaving?'

Her sisters exchanged glances. No one they knew had had a similar experience. According to their father's wishes, her husband would even be giving up his family name to take hers. This was the antithesis of centuries of formal tradition.

'Have you seen your new room yet, or do you want it to be a surprise?' Chunxiang asked.

'Hey, I know,' Chunlan spoke before her sister had a chance to answer. 'Why don't we go have a look now? I'm sure no one will be nearby. Father is out somewhere, and Ma is probably working. Let's see what a real wedding chamber looks like!'

The two smaller sisters giggled and took Yuying's hand to lead her across the house. She quietly consented, not wanting to spoil their excitement by telling them that she had already been in there to witness the blessing of the bed. She was suddenly aware of the years that separated them. Chunxiang reached out and pressed a clammy hand over each of her sisters' mouths as they wandered through the echoing corridor.

After taking a shortcut through the little garden, past the servant's quarters and the small room where the mute lay rasping in his sleep, they found the brightly garlanded door. When they had worked up the courage to push it open, they were surprised to find their mother sitting in Yuying's new room, her small frame perched on the bed that had been hauled in the day before.

Yuying's mother shooed the two younger girls from the room. A bed is a butterfly, and a couple are its wings, she explained. This is how we learn to fly. She mentioned nothing of the possibility that a butterfly's beating body brews hurricanes. Yuying shivered when she touched it, and, for a second, thought that the next day might never come, that if she really believed this, time might stop.

Her sisters were waiting for her outside the wedding chamber. They took her hands and wandered with her back across the house to her childhood bedroom, then settled themselves to sleep on the old rugs laid loosely on the floorboards beside her bed, to share her last night as a girl. Their conspiracy of midnight whispers quickly turned to muted snores.

Yuying woke before dawn and lay for a while listening to her sisters breathing, one faintly echoing the other. She soon heard the proud birds begin to strut and call out in the central courtyard, and pulled herself out of bed. Her sisters sat up slowly as Auntie Peipei and another servant girl flitted to and from the room, carrying large pots of warm water to fill the old wooden tub in the corner.

'Do you think if you sleep in the same bed as someone else that some of their dreams spill out and get muddled with your own?' Chunxiang said, as she rubbed her eyes and watched her eldest sister disrobe before the tub.

The smell of pomelo and orange blossom floated between them. Yuying slipped into her reflection and disappeared. From under the water, the murmuring voices sounded like the music of a celestial zoo or a long-forgotten war. She could not keep still in the bath and pulled herself out after only a few minutes. As she dried herself, she eyed the wedding dress now laid out on the bed. A phoenix drifted across the red silk, moving toward some invisible point. Phoenixes feed on dewdrops, she remembered, and are wedded to dragons. Beneath its sharp beak and snake-scale neck, its feathers seemed to stir and rustle like leaves in the rain.

Peipei sat down behind her, and began to arrange her hair. This was where the transformation should have taken place, the long loose black strands combed out, looped and tied up tight into the inflexible marriage style.

Yuying fiddled her fingers on her lap. To calm her nerves about the unusual reversals of her wedding and to show Yuying that the breaking of tradition did not have to be a cause for sorrow and worry, Peipei began to tell her a familiar story, that of the only empress of China.

Peipei's version of the legend of Wu Zetian's ruthlessness gave more space to the legends and old wives' tales than the historic achievements of the empress's reign, though she was careful to omit mention of the countless young men who were said to have shared the imperial bed. Yuying, however, was only half listening. On top of a small pine cabinet was the black-and-white photograph, face down.

Once her hair was finished, she turned to her sisters.

'You look lovely Yu. Just like a queen. I'm so jealous . . .' her youngest sister began.

'I know you're lying. But thanks. Are you sure it's fine? I feel like I've suddenly become Ma.'

'No, Chunxiang is right. It suits you. Stop being so nervous, you're not doing half the scary and boring bits anyway. A couple of hours from now and we'll all be at the banquet, eating and laughing and everyone will be looking at you swishing about in your expensive dress, so enjoy it.' Chunlan said.

'I will, I will. Now go, you've both got to

get ready too.'

Yuying playfully shoved her sisters and they filed from the room. She peered out of the window and found herself unexpectedly disappointed that the courtyard was still empty. In the past, the groom's family would have left their house at dawn to the sound of firecrackers and worn drums and marched to the bride's house where the front door would be blocked by tearful relatives, making a show of not wanting to lose a daughter, a grand-daughter, a niece, a sister. After performing acts of reverence before the bride's family, the groom's party would then have carried the bride in a small sedan carriage to her new home. In this way a bride would be torn from her childhood home and begin life in a new household, often miles from her family. Yuying knew that this would not happen to her. She would not be carried into the distance, toward servants that might spit in her food behind their master's back, or to a husband's spoilt siblings suddenly under her confused command, or, worst of all, to become the latest of a line of envious and warring wives. She had yet to hear any mention of the groom's family — it was he who would slip into their family and be trans-formed. He had even bartered off his name for hers. For a brief second she imagined herself an empress, and her name that of dynasties, unchangeable and craved; but as she turned she stubbed her toes on the corner of the bed and these thoughts were lost among her weak curses.

Her family had gathered in the dining room — her father on his wooden chair, a thin cigarette in his tight lips, her mother seated beside him looking at her feet, and her sisters standing as demurely as they could manage. Next to them stood the balding mute, Yaba, who had cared for her since she was a baby. He looked awkward and out of place. Everyone was dressed in a high-collared silk suit or neck-to-toe dark silk dress, each displaying a web of finely stitched patterns.

'The guests have begun to arrive. Almost all the family is here. They are waiting in the garden. You wouldn't want to be late,' her father said.

Her mother clasped Yuying's hands tightly and whispered something inaudible in her ear. Outside, the sun was threatening to sauté the leaves upon the lanky trees. From the branches hung rows of red paper lanterns, which, by evening, would throw their light across the grass and plants, making them look as if they were dancing in a strange and heatless fire. At Yuying's entrance, the murmurs of the crowd of family and friends mixed with the purr of the crickets and cicadas. This suddenly changed into an excited hush as they heard the clip-clop of lazy hooves against the rough stone cobbles of the adjacent street. A horse announced the imminent arrival of its rider with a loud snort.

Years later, Yuying would tell her grandchildren how she had been tricked by the photograph. At first she doubted that this short man, with a mess of hair resembling a muddy mop, could be the same figure as the one in the picture, and suspected her father of having simply hired someone else to sit and pose in the studio. The man in front of her was thinner, with none of the stocky exuberance that the picture hinted at. She would go as far as to ask Jinyi, once their marriage had moved from the nervous unfamiliarity of its beginnings into the knowing, casual ease that only comes with time spent close together, if it really was not some handsome friend who posed in his place. Yet, for all this, there was no mistaking the lopsided smile that frequently sneaked across his face. A photograph presents a simulacrum of real life, but it is always one we cannot fully trust, for it seeks to give life to things that are already irrevocably altered.

The mahjong tables that had been rattling with the moves of the waiting guests were silenced, the half-finished games abandoned as Hou Jinyi moved to Yuying's side. She tried her best not to blush as the wedding began; she had never had this much attention focused on her before. She felt the phoenix wriggling across the folds of her long dress as the crowd surrounded the couple, judging how each was changed by the proximity of the other. She tried to push the fact that he was inches shorter than her from her mind, and they turned, moving under the arch through the main door into the house.

When a bride arrived at her husband's house on the morning of her wedding, she would have expected to stay there until her death. Hou Jinyi measured his steps, trying neither to walk ahead of his new bride nor to fall behind and admit that he was ignorant of the layout of the sprawling house. Yuying, as she had been taught to do since birth, showed no emotion in her fixed expression. She too was reluctant to acknowledge the fact that they were acting out a strange reversed image of ancient customs, as if they had stepped into the other side of the mirror. In the main hall, they bowed together to an effigy of me, to heaven and earth, and to the stone tablets which contained the spirits of her ancestors. They offered prayers, which melted into the air, mingling with the smell of the roast suckling pig and the uncorked bottles of liquor lying offered and untouched on the altar before them. From the kitchen they could hear fat sizzling in hissing woks as the servants prepared for the banquet. The carefully crafted ancestors watched their every move.

Her parents were seated solemnly in a pair

of high-backed wooden chairs facing the doorway. Bian Yuying and Hou Jinyi sunk to the floor in unison to kowtow to them.

'We wish you both a future full of joy and understanding. Let your love learn from the cypress, the gingko: let these little roots spread, nourish, grow and endure against the wild. Take this name and fill it with life. Bian Jinyi, welcome to our family.' Her father clasped his hands together as he finished speaking. Yuying and Jinyi then turned, not quite identically, and knelt before each other.

The couple rose and poured dark and sweet-smelling tea from a delicate pot into two white china cups emblazoned with paintings of blue-bearded dragons. Each one knelt to present the cup to a parent. As she served her father, Yuying slyly studied the dark crescents under his eyes — it had been years since she had been that close to him. She remembered her sister's teasing words, and that she would have to spend her life tied to her husband's shadow as he got older and uglier. This is how the world works, though, she assured herself; why should I resist something so natural? After serving the heads of the household they turned again, and each of them waited on older aunts and uncles in return for gifts of money folded up in small red envelopes. Eventually they came to her siblings and poured a small cup full of red tea for each of them.

Buddhist myths recount that an ancient Buddha, determined to gain enlightenment, left the city and climbed to an empty mountain plain. However, instead of meditating, he soon fell into a deep sleep on the sun-parched grass. He ended up sleeping for seven years, his snores drawing seedlings from the ground as birds nested on his gently thrumming chest. When he awoke, he was so disheartened at his lack of concentration that he ripped off his eyelids to stop himself from falling asleep again. Where they fell, the first tea bushes grew. Secular stories claim that an ancient Chinese ruler discovered how to brew tea when dark leaves blew into his boiling water. The caffeine consumption of the Asian Buddhists who first adopted tea-drinking as an integral part of the monastic day was motivated by their desire for clarity, to rid their vision of the world of their lingering dreams.

During the tea ceremony, Yuying continually stole glances at her new husband. From the familiar pattern and stitching of the long granite-blue silk robe, stiff at his neck and loosely hung about his wrists and ankles, she correctly guessed that it had been picked out, ordered and bought by her father. He lowered his head before her relatives, and never once seemed to look in her direction. Is he even interested in me, she wondered, or has he struck some kind of deal with Pa? What is it

51

he imagines he has traded his name for? As she put down the tea-tray loaded with envelopes, she conjured up a probable past for him, but not yet a future.

Outside the guests were laughing and eating, the men on one side toasting and congratulating each other, the women giggling discreetly about topics that, if overheard, might make their husbands or fathers choke on their food. Chopsticks dived and glided above, below, around and between each other as if they were sparrows dividing a busy sky. These were the foods Yuying imagined: shark's fin soup, crisp layers of duck rolled into wafer-thin pancakes, chickens stuffed with black rice and dates, whole fish sitting in spicy sauces slowly plucked bone-thin, green beans and whole chillies, broccoli swimming in garlic, sour soups, hot soups, spicy soups, noodle soups, lucky four-season meatballs, spring rolls, peanuts and sunflower seeds, and scores of empty plates whose previous contents were unidentifiable.

The truth was more prosaic; even for her rich family, there was no way to get those delicacies, even now that trade was no longer controlled by the Japanese. The liberating Russians had only recently left, and, although many thin prisoners had returned home after years of occupation, hunger had not yet surrendered or been bombed out. A few dishes had to suffice. But still Yuying thought of feasts. She was in the couple's new bedroom. The bride was not allowed to eat, nor speak. Only wait. Her new husband, meanwhile, was making the rounds between the tables, receiving toasts and playing drinking games. She knew how it would progress, although at other weddings she and her sisters had always been forced to sit silently, demure and shy with their mouths hidden behind intricate paper fans. They had always been packed off in rickshaws or the shiny new automobiles of family friends before the real fun had started.

As they raised the clear liquid in the ornamental thimbles, several of the older guests already appeared red-faced and sweaty. These were her father's associates, men whom Hou Jinyi had never met before and would never see again. Yuying pictured them from her room — those few who had been in collusion with the Japanese, now denying everything; judges, officials and warlords in hiding with their many young wives; Manchu men who lost out in the republic and headed north; shopkeepers, brothel-owners, opium importers; the few other restaurateurs in the city who were not her father's sworn enemies; and, of course, her father's most trusted ally, Mr Zhu, one of the richest men in the province, downing drinks and slapping backs, no doubt. She had heard it whispered that he started off as an executioner for the republic, providing quick and clean decapitations.

Since everyone knew that the only cure for tuberculosis was to eat a piece of dough soaked in human blood, he soon amassed a fortune by providing that delicacy for the choking children of rich, worried parents. By the time the Japanese arrived, he had found that buying and selling secrets and allegiances was just as lucrative.

As the banquet progressed and the shouts and songs spilt in under the closed door, Yuying pressed her finger into the starched white sheets to trace words and faces into the folds. Her sharpened fingernail mimicked the slow brushstrokes used in the classroom to produce the ancient ideograms. As she drew, she tested her Japanese, stretching simple characters into ever more complicated constructions, then trawling backwards, unwriting them, and beginning again, from the same few strokes, in Chinese. She noted where they overlapped, merged, converged and parted. But this was as far as she allowed the thought to go. She would not bring to mind her childhood friends, the rattlebag of kids she used to play skipping and marbles and imaginary war games with, whose parents had now been lost in the unmentioned world of mines, railways, factories and prisons, all under new command. Those would not be suitable thoughts for her wedding day. Nor would the whispers she heard about the neighbours' boy who, feverish from hunger in the difficult days soon after the occupation began, stole some rice from an unguarded store. People reported that, shortly after having gulped down the forbidden meal that he must have cooked quickly with dirty river water, soldiers spotted him and, when he had finished, cut his stomach open as an example to others. She practised grammar and advanced form, and wondered how soon after the wedding she could get back to college.

Soon Jinyi was wishing the older guests good-bye. Yuying smoothed the sheets down, and plumped the pillows. She was unsure what she should do with her wedding dress. She undid a button and seconds later did it back up. She knew something of what was to come, but the details were vague, blurry, and made up of instructions she had never felt interested enough to pay attention to. It must be something akin to the doubling of every-thing in the room, she thought to herself. Everything in there was paired, from the two pillows and two blankets on the new bed to the matching wooden chairs. The carefully drawn character for happiness was joined with its double and hung on the wall for good luck, and on the dresser stood twin candle-sticks, on each of which was an etching of a solitary crane. Cranes live for a thousand years, she thought. She stood to light both candles.

'Everyone's gone home.' Jinyi was hovering hesitantly at the entrance to the room, unsure of whether or not to enter. His accent was coarse, rough, slipping at the ends of words. She tried to pretend that it did not bother her. 'I hope you're not disappointed. I don't know if I'm what you expected. But your father told me a lot about you, and I promise you I'll always be proud to call myself your husband.'

She smiled, and he smiled too.

'I brought you some food.' He unwrapped some sweet dumplings from a handkerchief. 'Just leftovers. I know it's against tradition. But, well, all of this is a bit topsy-turvy anyway, so I decided it wouldn't matter — as long as no one else sees. I just thought you might be a bit hungry.'

She laughed at him, and he laughed at himself, still propped awkwardly in the doorway.

'So can I come in?'

The single nod was enough for Jinyi to close the door behind him. And as it would be rude to intrude upon a couple's wedding night, we must content ourselves to wait outside the closed door. Meanwhile, the servants began their nocturnal work to ensure that no trace of the sprawling party would remain the next morning. Yuying's sisters had fallen asleep while fantasising of their own wedding days still to come. Their mother lay in bed alone, no longer expecting to be visited by her husband. Old Bian had led out a number of friends to continue the celebrations elsewhere, to while away the rest of the unusually long summer nights of 1946 with opium, liquor and one of the many madams he was on first-name terms with. Outside the windows, bamboo rustled, as if grazed by the lingering whispers lost in the old corridors and courtyards, and slowly the house fell silent. The twin candles in the wedding chamber burnt down to waxy stubs above the delicately painted cranes that had not yet learnt how to fly.

There were great silver moonfish, platters of fiery sea slugs, ruby-encrusted tureens over-flowing with starfish soup, oysters in egg batter and plates of sautéed donkey. Most of the guests, however, simply nibbled or nodded in appreciation, having little need for food. Many went straight for the tall urns brimming with three-thousand-year-old rice wine. I had helped myself to a drink — it would have been rude not to — and was preparing to yawn my way through another of the Jade Emperor's heavenly banquets, pushing through the crowd of fox spirits and day-out demons, when I was approached by one of the smaller dragons.

'I do hope you have been keeping yourself entertained up here,' it snuffled in a sonorous baritone. 'All these soirées and this enforced joviality can be tiresome, and if you have the misfortune to be cornered by Confucius, well, he'll talk at you until your brain melts.'

'I'm all right,' I replied. 'I keep an eye on things down on earth when I'm bored or lonely.'

'Oh. I pity you. I gave up interfering with that lot years ago. What is it now — floods, famines, wars?'

'Well, yes, but there's a bit more to it than that —'

'I thought so.' The dragon nodded and curled its supreme whiskers. 'Any chance that there is a capable emperor keeping everything in line?'

'Well, they don't call him that anymore, but —'

'Hmm. Sounds like a terrible mess,' the dragon drawled.

'It is. I reckon even I could do a better job of sorting everything out down there than the Jade Emperor is doing. Maybe he's just lost interest in humans.'

The dragon nodded in sage agreement as I gave my practised critique of the human world, as I understood it. Soon something of a crowd had gathered. I should perhaps have shut my mouth right then, but I was just getting into full flow, and once I begin talking I find it hard to stop. I was perhaps also more than a little flattered and encouraged by the nods and glances of a number of bird-people, unicorns, Lao Tzu and his motley gang of disciples, immortal toads and a couple of the angelic (though of course untouchable) daughters of the Jade Emperor.

The rest of the banquet was filled with the usual miracles — fountains of stars pulsing up from the floor; bodhisattvas recounting the highlights of their countless incarnations;

prayers in a thousand languages and prayers in tiger skins and ineffable symbols; whole galaxies fading and dying all around us in the transparent walls.

It was only when I returned to my home as a silent presence in the many kitchens on earth, carried back down on the tail-end of a rushing cloud, that I thought about the consequences of what I had said.

I was not naïve enough to think that word would not get back to the Jade Emperor, for, just as on earth, the citizens of heaven love only one thing more than gossiping, and that is snitching on others. Still, for a while I simply wondered how he would respond to my indiscretion. I had heard stories of people reincarnated as mosquitoes for less. And if you think being dead limits your fear or the number of punishments that can be inflicted on you, then you lack imagination.

2:
1942
THE YEAR OF THE HORSE

From where the white wig (made from human hair, of course, and recently powdered with lavender-scented starch) was fixed to his scalp, streams of sweat trickled down to collect on his blotchy jowls. Lord George Macartney mopped his face and prepared to head back to the palace. It was late summer, 1793, and he and his mission had been travelling for over a year — nine sunburnt, brine-blistered months across a series of knotted seas followed by another four months spent weaving north along the craggy borders of this shape-shifting country toward the capital.

For this diplomatic journey on behalf of George III and the East India Company, Macartney had been offered an earldom as well as a handsome salary. He was beginning to wonder whether that was enough. Despite, in the past, having been captured by the French, and having governed parts of India, he was unsure what to make of the surreal turn of events of this mission. Their transla-

61

tors had deserted them, and a newspaper in the northern port town of Tianjin had proclaimed that the Englishmen had arrived bearing such gifts as a cat-sized elephant, a giant coal-fed songbird and a party of scholars barely one foot tall.

That was not quite the case. In order to open trade between the glorious British Empire and China, Macartney had brought an array of more practical gifts from George III to the Qianlong Emperor. These included telescopes, globes depicting both the earth and all the known reaches of the universe, a spring-worked carriage and a number of barometers, all designed to demonstrate the scientific prowess of the technologically advanced nation. They would, however, be dismissed as trinkets and toys, a small and somewhat useless tribute offered to the celestial ruler of the earth's only heavenly kingdom. Wandering through various ports, Macartney had been taken aback by the strangeness of the country: dark women darting nimbly through the streets as if unconstrained by the foot bindings he had heard about; sailors barking and singing in a birdlike language that only his twelve-year-old pageboy had been able to decipher; the elaborately woven colours of the gowns standing out against the uniform black of the angular masonry; and, everywhere he turned, naked children running, squealing, scrapping, shitting, playing and slipping between every-one else's feet.

Macartney, as the representative of the most powerful empire in the world, had expected to be received with much fanfare. Instead, eunuchs spent days trying to per-suade his party that they would all need to kowtow before the elderly emperor. Macart-ney would return to the English crown hav-ing achieved none of his stipulated goals. There would be no British embassy in China, no ports opened up to British residences, and no trade agreements. The heavenly emperor would decide that the English had nothing to offer the already advanced Chinese and would consign their impractical gifts, un-touched, to an empty shed. Yes, I was there too, eavesdropping as ever. And yes, my pow-ers of mindreading extend even to foreigners — you may be surprised to learn, as I was, that they also have souls.

My point is this: history does not always turn out how you expect. In fact, it seems to me that it sometimes goes out of its way, like a crafty wasp, to sting you as soon as you're not paying attention. If history can take something from you, it will. This was to be Hou Jinyi's motto, repeated time and again to his family in the later years — at least until history came along and stole his memory too.

Hou Jinyi had only a single, blurred memory

of his parents. He saw them as if through an empty bottle, their features at once both exaggerated and indistinct, and, as time passed, their faces increasingly woven and patched with flickers from dreams. He had been too small to understand the seriousness of the sweating illness which stole both of them within weeks of each other and sent him toddling to his uncle's farm, where he spent ten cruel years that he was now trying to put behind him. He knew his parents, then, only from what he had overheard from others. Before the pen, this is how all tribal histories travelled, from burning mouths to burning ears.

Jinyi had also waited, like Macartney, between two possibilities. He had left home at the age of fifteen, as the 1930s were shivering to a close. And on that fateful day, he had been slumped at the side of the road, sitting on top of an old sack in which was stuffed another pair of trousers, a worn and dirty shirt that may once have been almost white, and a short and weathered kitchen knife. He was barefoot and bare-chested; bruises floated upon his back like murky autumn leaves bobbing on the surface of a dull stream. For the past two days he had been following dirt tracks, skirting round the edges of long fields of bowed cereal, oilseed and tea plants, and had finally returned to something resembling a road.

Some hours had passed since he had sat down to rest, though he could no longer tell how many. He heard the pebbles rattling into life somewhere behind him, and he lifted his head. A haggard mule was pulling a rickety cart, on which a weathered man was half sitting, half squatting. It was hard to tell whether the mule or its master was the worse for wear — a cloud of flies flittered around the pair of them. They were moving so slowly that Jinyi was able to climb on without the cart stopping. He settled back to back with the middle-aged driver. The older man's sun-beaten skin felt like a worn leather hide, his heavy breath swaying his body in time with the mule's stubborn steps.

Jinyi did not bother to give his name, and neither did the middle-aged man. They were a day's walk away from Baoding, the nearest city. And if the middle-aged man did not ask anything of his new passenger, this was probably because he was not surprised to see people wandering, lost, between lives. It was Hou Jinyi who spoke first, after sitting silently back to back with the older man for an hour, watching the sun meander across the distant slopes, slower than the twitchy mule.

'Where are you going?'

'Not far. Few stops to make. Won't get there by dark though.'

'What do you do?'

The man laughed — a laugh like a large

dog's bark segueing into a harsh cough. He turned to have a good look at the boy behind him.

'What do *you* do?'

Hou Jinyi did not reply. They lapsed again into silence. The cart wobbled through creeks of ochre slate and chalk, only occasionally passing peasants whose gender was indiscernable under their wicker hats and brimming baskets. Every other minute the driver hocked up from phlegm from the depths of his throat and spat.

'I'm not a runaway.'

'Fine.'

'And I'm not someone's servant.'

The driver shrugged. Jinyi did not mention the fact that he had left his aunt and uncle's house twelve *li* back. Why should he? He did not plan to return. Ever. They will forget me soon enough, he told himself, and then they can take their anger out on the mongrels instead. He thought about the three dogs that slept outside and how they sounded at night, howling at the ghosts in the chimney while the tattered wind tugged at their chains every autumn until spring. He bit his nails, one by one, closer to the grubby quick.

'You won't get far.'

'Fuck off.' He went back to biting his nails. Then, 'Why?'

'I'll tell you why. You're short and scrawny and look like you'll bolt any minute. You're too like city people.'

'Fuck off.' I am nothing like city people, he told himself; though, having never seen a big city, he could not be sure, and was unsettled by the driver's remarks. He had not even seen a school: the furthest away he had travelled before he left was to the market in the next valley. He wanted to go wherever it was the cranes went each year. 'I've worked every day I can remember. I'm not good for nothing. I'm not like city people.'

In his mind cities were fantastic and impossible; opulent, yet indolent. They were places where idle men played games of mahjong with bronze and jade tumbling blocks, betting houses, wives, slaves, daughters, fortunes, mountains, rivers and armies on each round. Where the birds in the lush trees whispered to you the secrets of the local lottery; where palaces grew up from the ground like leisurely weeds while your back was turned, and dead men's treasure might be found under any floorboard; where rich men slept until noon, and where even their chefs and messengers and Pekingese wore diamonds for teeth. To create these imaginary cities, Jinyi had pieced together scraps of fairy stories and conjured the opposite of everything he hated about his own life in the country: waking before dawn to chop firewood and grind flour for his aunt to cook, feeding the trio of bedraggled dogs, furrowing with chilled or burnt hands in the short field every afternoon till the sun descended, and, most of all, being thumped by a fist or thwacked with the handle of a rake for every word out of place, as well as for some never even spoken.

As they crept along, Jinyi closed his eyes and drew a future on the inside of his eyelids. He had lain awake all night for months working up the courage to run, trying to decide where he would go. Then one afternoon a neighbour had told him an anecdote about the scores of sunburnt labourers setting new train tracks straight through someone's field. Since sneaking out of the house two days ago while his uncle, aunt and gloating cousin slept, he had had only one destination. He would go to a station. And from there, the world would open like a clamshell prised apart in his fingers. He had thought of engines roaring out like the call of a circus. He had envisaged metallic dragons with crushed wings condemned to slither between provinces, of trains hollering in a language that might drive listeners to the edge of sorrow, their winding bodies glinting silver. Even then, half asleep behind the driver, he imagined the endless paddies cleaved by huffing locomotives.

The idea of trains in a country of fields and mountains had already provoked desperate reactions. In 1876, China's first railway was built by foreign businessmen who bought up hundreds of family plots and navigated round graves marked out on the principles of *feng shui* to connect the nine miles between Shanghai and Wusong. At first the locals flocked to the free rides, awed and fascinated by what was, for the imported British engines, a laughably short journey. The Qing government, however, was not impressed. After a soldier committed suicide by waiting on the line for the train to hit him, the railway company ran into difficulties with the official bureaucracy. In the end, the government negotiated to purchase the railway from the businessmen at a high price. Meanwhile, the trains continued to run, gaining in popularity while the government made its series of payments. The day after the last transaction completed the purchase, the government had the tracks dismantled, inch by inch, and sent away to gather rust. They had not considered, however, that inventions live apart from us, willing their own future from the depth of ideas.

It was railways, too, after the exoduses of the gold rush, that consolidated many one-way journeys across the Atlantic. By 1865 the Central Pacific Railroad Company, two years into laying tracks for the transcontinental line snaking east from Sacramento, was in desperate need of labour to complete the joining of the railways across terrain that quickly shifted between sea-level and an altitude of 7,000 feet. They turned to the mass of Chinese immigrants around California. Despite an aborted strike, the fact that the Chinese were whipped and worked longer than the white labourers, and the high number of casualties from harsh winters and even harsher conditions in the tunnels being drilled, the last ten miles needed to join east with west were laid in a single day, 28 April 1869, by a joint Chinese and Irish effort. Imaginary borders are constantly redrawn behind cartographer's backs, with sweat, with words, and, it hardly need be said, with dollars.

The miniature labyrinths that blossomed in the shadow of America's bigger cities, the ubiquitous Chinatowns, were not simple copies transposed to an alien continent, but chimeras capable of changing form at any second — towns which, if you were to walk in them for too long, would shift their streets beneath your feet and become other places. It is not just scaled-down cities, but all ideas and fantasies that are reproduced, daily, with varying differences, until it becomes unclear which is the original and which the facsimile. The facts remains that, if there was an original, it is irretrievably buried beneath the successive smudges and alterations of an ever-thickening palimpsest. And, in this junk-shop of history, cities learn to wear their wounds like prizes, knowing that this is how they survive, like those tree frogs in the rainforest canopy whose colouring, rather than camouflaging, alerts the world to what might lie behind.

So I know what you're thinking. Why on earth am I following this mangy-looking runaway from the backwaters? Well, it's pretty simple.

Let me tell you what I learnt about Hou Jinyi from those early days. His body was a bag of jigs that he spent most days trying to master. He never knew what to do with his hands, and had learnt from a young age that speaking about their feelings only made men weak. He was driven equally by a desire to find somewhere that would finally feel like home and the lurking suspicion that he would never find it.

One other thing — there was a restlessness in his heart common to all orphans, a deep-seated fear that if he ever let himself love something it would be taken from him. Perhaps that fear was not as foolish as it might seem.

I do not just tell stories — I am a part of them too. Take a look around and you might find that the same could be said of yourself, regardless of whether you are immortal or not. And so, I would like to think that, in some way, I had an influence in Jinyi's choice of a job in a small kitchen.

'You're going to burn your whole bloody hand off if you don't quit daydreaming, mate. And I'm not going to put my balls on the line for you again. You've been doing it for weeks. Just watch me.'

'All right, I know what I'm doing — you just concentrate on your own side. You know yours always gets overcooked. No one wants any of that burnt bitter sugar; it sticks on your teeth and you can taste it for days,' Hou Jinyi replied, mocking his colleague to hide that he had been momentarily far away. He leaned further forward over his vat.

'By the devils!' The elder boy continued as if Jinyi had not spoken. 'I haven't got a clue what you're daydreaming about. Now, if you'd come out with us last night to the Celestial Gardens, you'd have something to remember — they treated us like gentlemen, you know. Not like the old women in the barber's backroom on the corner. Worth every extra *jiao*.'

Hou Jinyi raised his eyebrow and looked at his friend for the first time during his speech and then laughed. 'One week's pay, just for some girl. You can't tell me she was worth that much, whoever she was.'

'Worth every extra penny,' Dongming said again, and grinned to himself as he stirred the glowing vat of bubbling sugar. 'You'll understand one day.'

Though he had only recently turned nineteen in that warm spring of 1942, Dongming attempted to assume the air of worldly teacher to Jinyi, who was only a few years younger and stood nearly a foot shorter than him. Despite the monotony of heating, stirring and pouring from the vats all day, Dongming gave the impression of never keeping still, his body alive with shrugs and twitches even on the rare occasions he stopped chattering. Jinyi, on the other hand, did his best to keep to a small rhythm of careful movements. These movements even extended to his face, where his lips occasionally twitched as though formulating ideas not ready to be spoken aloud. Dongming, despite his jokes, was too polite to point these out.

On the wider streets of this small town in northern Hebei children were gathering with their grandparents. They crowded round a seated figure who was dripping strings of caramelised sugar onto a cold surface to produce crisp images of animals from the Chinese zodiac. Small sticks were thrust into these sticky webs of animal-shaped sugar so that they could be picked up and eaten.

The work done by Dongming and Jinyi required little of this artistry. In the heat of the stone room where they melted the sugar before adding water and spice, they stood naked but for their rolled-up trousers. The steam that rose from the sugar matted their hair to their heads. A third worker had come and gone, having sustained disfiguring burns from the wild bubbling and spitting of un-watched caramel. Their days were spent stir-ring, topping up and pouring the caramel into metallic moulds, which they then set to cool in the courtyard to await inspection from their doughy-faced boss, whom they had only once seen sober. He mostly stayed in the house next door doing the accounts and discussing philosophy with a collection of caged birds, which, with hooked nods and heavy flutters of wings, feigned interest in his ramblings.

Each batch of candies was sold for more than Dongming and Jinyi earned together in a day. They worked, like everyone else they had ever met, from sunrise until the last shred of light had scurried from the sky, between six and seven days a week.

After work Jinyi followed Dongming home, not because he had nowhere else to go (though this was indeed the case), but be-cause the elder boy's endless gibbering diverted him from his own thoughts. As their bare feet slapped against the dusty streets, Dongming kept up a rambling monologue that was only interrupted when the two of them spotted the Japanese soldiers or trucks.

'Every year there's more of them. Vicious bastards. You heard what happened to Little Ying, right? Brutal. Absolutely brutal. I reckon there must be some factory somewhere churning out Jap soldiers, because they can't all come from those poky little islands, can they?' Dongming looked around to make sure that they were neither near a checkpoint nor being followed. 'You know what, I'd follow my brother right now and join the Nationalists if I thought that would swing things. It won't, not while we've got the commies stabbing us in the back. You know everyone says they went into the country, gathered up and packed off somewhere to regroup, right? Unlikely, if you ask me. They've probably just given up. About time too. Let them disappear. We don't need a bunch of cowards following Russia like fawning dogs.'

'Oh, come on, Dongming. You haven't got a clue. You've never lived outside this city. It's different out there,' Jinyi interrupted. Dongming stared at him, neither offended nor shocked, but with the pursed smile he always gave while formulating a suitable reply. 'What I mean is, shouldn't we be working together? We're all Chinese. That's all most of us have got.' Jinyi bit his nails, and looked down at his feet as they walked along the narrow road.

'Well, sure, but what does that mean, Hou Jinyi? Does that mean we're going to get mansions and feasts everyday like the warlords in Beijing or the merchants down south? Fat chance. It's an illusion. A rotten illusion that's stealing sense from people, when we should be making ourselves stronger. Of course we all ought to fight the Japanese, but how can our armies work together when a man can't even trust his bunkmate? How are we supposed to get stronger and fight the Japanese if we end up sharing everything we have with incestuous and inbred dopes from the dirt fields? You explain that to me!'

The civil war had been raging since both of them were tiny children, when the figurehead and binding personality of the young Republic, Sun Yat-sen, had died in 1925. The brief Kuomintang and CCP alliance had quickly collapsed into purges and guerilla warfare. It had taken a rebel general's desperate action back in 1936 to provide a united front against the Japanese as they began to spread out from the puppet-state of Manchuria. The general kidnapped the Kuomintang president Chiang Kai-shek to force him to join the Communists in resisting the Japanese. For this patriotic action, the general, Zhang Xueliang, was arrested and imprisoned by the Kuomintang for the next forty years.

Since Jinyi did not reply, Dongming returned to his favourite theme, the future. But his colleague was no longer paying attention. Jinyi was back in the house from which he had escaped — coal clogging his pores and his aunt berating him for the paltry vegetables he had worked from a patch of the garden.

He was back where his uncle glared at him whenever the sound of his rumbling stomach could no longer be muted, where the damp crept through his bones, where the wind whistled demonic melodies. Where, at night, the four of them in the crumbling shack in the deserted valley slept the sleep of the shivering, repentant dead. Where each day had begun with a headache, sore muscles, sweat clinging to unchanged clothes. How was it that the years since he had left had passed in the same way as those hard years — thrown aside with the same practised movement of busy hands?

Soon they came to the single-floor house, its brick walls tightly squeezed together in a lane barely wide enough for a bicycle. On either side, the neighbours' petty squabbles could be overheard. The house consisted of two joined rooms backing onto a small courtyard where all the families on the street shared a fire for cooking and boiling water. As they crossed through it, Jinyi glanced at a young girl washing her knee-length raven hair in a wooden bucket. Though they were now used to Jinyi visiting, the family had still swept the house and gathered together some wrinkled vegetables so that they would not lose face.

They ate in a muddle of noise, with the younger brothers tumbling across each other as they grabbed at the few dwindling dishes, the sisters attempting to disguise their gauntness with what they falsely conceived as grace, a grandmother asthmatic and nibbling like a giant wheezing caterpillar, two unmarried aunts, and the patriarch ever more distant as the dusty bottle of liquor came closer to emptiness. Only in conversation about the missing brother did the family begin to raise their voices.

'He'll be having it rough now, sleeping with his eyes open, what with the Japs heading further south now —'

'No . . . the Japs are cowards at heart, everyone knows that. It's fighting alongside the commies that he'll have to worry about. He'll need to watch his back —'

'He'll be back by Spring Festival, you'll see.'

'You're crazy. There's plenty of work needs doing before anyone can pack up and pull out the firecrackers —'

'*I* don't see what the fuss is about. We were fine before, we'll be fine now. We've seen darker times than these. He ought to be thinking about marriage, a boy of his age. Nothing is going to change by —'

'How can you even say that? The Japanese are carving up our country while the rest of the world looks the other way. It's people like you —'

'Quiet. All of you, eat your food and thank the dead that you've got your family and a loyal brother and a warm bed.'

The Kuomintang was just one of the refuges of the family's meagre hopes; Jinyi was happy to be ignored and, for once, not asked his opinion. Not because he disagreed, but because he still saw himself as an extra out of place in this strange and unconvincing scene. His world began and ended with glimpses of girls, scraps of food and fantasies of a pocket full of loose change. Later, as he lay in the cloying room shared between all the men of the family, on an animal skin bunched up over the cold stone, Jinyi counted the days since he had left home, weighing them up against the days ahead. In the midst of this melancholy mathematics he fell asleep.

That night more troops rolled into town. The slow but steady crawl of vehicles and quick-stepping black boots continued their push south, overrunning town after town. It was faceless, this army, gliding across the maps like the sullen shadow of a low-hanging cumulonimbus. Each month, its numbers multiplied. It had swarmed down from Manchuria in the north, and every day issued new edicts from the capital of occupied territory that had been established (after a massacre to end all massacres, or so the rumours said) in Nanjing. Even the dead were buried quickly, outside the town, dotting the nearby hills with little mounds. If one were to suggest, to the starved, the exhausted, the executed, the maimed, the coughing-up-blood, the excluded, the bug-eyed big-bellied small-limbed kids, the battered, the paper-thin and the dry-mouthed that by the time their children came of age the country would be so populous that the government, worried there would soon be no room to house the blossoming population of the dead, would enforce cremation over burial, you might expect to be laughed at, or, more likely, pitied.

Jinyi was used to the combat and fatigue uniforms on every street corner, as well as to the short sharp barks of an unfamiliar language filling the air around him. The schools had been emptied out for barrack space, so children now ran in the narrow lanes between the passing troops. The restaurants were closed and empty except for those in which the invading soldiers claimed meals on the house. The few Chinese still wandering the main streets walked quickly — but not too quickly — with their heads bowed.

Within a month the candy business closed — the Japanese had placed tigher restrictions on the sugar ration. Dongming said nothing when they were dismissed by their drunk and bloodshot-eyed employer, and stayed silent as he and Jinyi sauntered down to the river to sit on the bank, unsure where to look for another chance.

'There must be corners of this country where no one knows anything of history, of the present, of war, of Japan. Where no papers or messengers or troops reach. There must be,' Jinyi mused.

'If there was such a place,' Dongming said, 'would you go there?'

Jinyi picked up a stone and threw it a far as he could down into the sweep of the river. They watched it sink, neither bothering to pick up another.

'No. But what I mean is, where are the places from all the stories? You know, the places our elders always talked about, where monks destroy whole buildings with the tap of a finger, where snakes and fish change into beautiful women, where dark-faced gods come down and dabble in all the difficult bits of life, or where lucky cooking pots double everything put into them? Where are those places? Anywhere's got to be better than here, right now.'

'That's an easy thing to say,' Dongming replied. 'But then you've never said where you came from in the first place. You've seen our house: my grandfather helped build it when my dad was a child and the backyard was full of fields.'

'You're lucky. No one goes anywhere they don't have to.' Jinyi picked up another stone and rolled it between his fingers, studying the way its surface jittered in the slats of light between the clouds.

'So, I was right. You are running away. It's

81

not that easy, saying you've got no history and suddenly making it so, is it? I was born here. And if I'm born again, I'll be born again in the same house, by the same crooked table and tame fire, amid the same stink of coal and sweat and mothy fur. That's just how it is. You're crazy if you think it's going to be any different anywhere else.'

'But how can you know anything if you never leave this place?' Jinyi said.

'The next town will be the same as here, probably worse. You think all the people passing through looking for work have found it? They don't just head one way, you know. There isn't work anywhere, and that's not going to change with all this fighting. If you ask me, the only option is to just get on with life. That or join the war. Oh, Jinyi, stop thinking about yourself. You think life's difficult? You don't know shit. A few starved corpses and executions in the schoolyard. That's just the beginning. Haven't you heard about what they do to people up north? There's only so far you can run, you know,' Dongming said.

'I'm not running away.'

The older boy snorted contemptuously. But he quickly checked himself, and turned to his friend. 'What do you think you're going to find? What is it you want? No, wait. I don't really want to know. All those daydreams — I'm not sure it can be right, giving in to all those fantasies.'

'What else is there?' Jinyi said.

Dongming grinned, then spat. 'You dig your heels in, and live.'

Jinyi shrugged, still rolling the stone between his fingers. He rubbed his thumb over its rough edges, then put it back down.

'Look, let's go to a restaurant,' Dongming said. 'I've still got enough change to get us drunk enough to at least believe we're in another city. Not that it'll take you much to get that way. But someone's got to teach you to drink before you run off somewhere else. Come on.'

Streams of dirt were collecting between the crooked paving stones, so the two boys slipped into the first dingy restaurant they came to. There was no menu — they got what they were given, and paid with the last of the coins dug from their pockets. The liquor was sour and stank of long-rotten cereal (only the Japanese were now allowed to eat rice), but they sipped it regardless, sitting with the potato-nosed man who was owner, chef, waiter and tin-bucket dishwasher rolled into one. All three of them drank in silence.

The rain began to fall, a thousand spiders shimmying down translucent threads. Neither of them had had enough to drink to restart their conversation. Instead they watched from the window as a young woman walked shakily down the street, every few steps putting a hand out as if to steady herself against an imaginary wall, or raising the other to push back the stray wet hairs stuck to her forehead. Her left eye was dark and swollen, and a thin cut tugged at the top of her mouth. Recognizing her from the Celestial Gardens, Dongming turned away and poured another drink into each of the three chipped glasses.

'If you ask me, there is only one way out of here,' Dongming said. He waited, and then looked at Jinyi, who, not used to the liquor, had his eyes half closed and his thick dark eyebrows sloped together above his pale face. Dongming was repeating himself, and he knew it, pitching himself towards the distance to see if his thoughts would carry his words that far.

'My brother, he was a stupid bastard. Lazy too. The whole house used to curse him for keeping us awake with his snores. I swear they made the walls shake. My dad once threw a bowl of water over him to shock him out of it. He woke up all right, but he just wiped his face with his sleeve, turned over and started snoring again. My dad used to get so mad with my brother that he'd lash out at the lot of us. But now that he's gone, no one remembers any of that.'

'So?' Jinyi said, unwilling to consider the fact that his own uncle and aunt may now be missing him. He sipped at the liquor and shuddered as it burnt the hollow of his throat.

'So, why shouldn't I follow him? He's not the only one who can do something. Something real, I mean,' Dongming slurred.

'Real? What about your speech — digging in your feet and getting buried in shit?'

Dongming laughed, rubbing his fingers round the swollen rim of the glass. 'That was for you. There is a difference between leaving with a purpose and leaving because you have no idea what your purpose should be. Most of those people we passed out there on the streets, they'll be gone by morning, and we all know why. They've got no choice, but you have, yet you still haven't said why you want to leave. Do you really think you'll find work and food and riches in another city? Do you really think other towns have more crops, more machines to work, more coins to spend? Perhaps they do, but what if they don't?'

'That "perhaps" is enough for me. It's the biggest word we've got. You've noticed it hanging on the edge of every sentence, like vultures over the shacks of the starving. Maybe. Perhaps. There are whole worlds inside those words, you've just got to prise them open,' Jinyi replied.

'No, Jinyi. They mean "No, not a chance in hell." That's all. They're just a way of saving face. If we can beat the Japs — even just force them back up north — then we'll have the whole place right in no time. Then there won't be any *maybe* or *perhaps.* Then every-

one will say *is* or *for sure* or *without a doubt.*
If you ask me, it's either fight or watch the
city get washed away by dirty rain and rusty
guns.'

'You could always come with me.' Jinyi
looked at the table as he spoke, and the older
boy turned away too, for this was the furthest
this point could be pressed.

'I can't run away from my family. I either
stay here and rot or go the same way as my
brother, wherever he is. I'm not even sure
what it is you're expecting to find.'

'When I get there, I'll know. And then I'll
be able to come back, and hold my head up
a little higher when I do. Places chew you up
and make you part of the scenery. You're not
yourself: you're just someone's uncle's
cousin, or someone's grandson. There must
be places where there is just half a *jin* of opportunity — that's all I'm looking for. A place
where you can write your own story instead
of getting stuck in a web of memories.'

'But this country is made of memories.
Even if a man can't read or write, he still
knows the name of his great-great-
grandfather's uncle's half-brother and everything he did in his sorry life! You could come
with *me,* Jinyi, and turn those memories
around, like my brother.'

'Can you see me with a gun in my hand?'

The drinks were almost finished, and the
streets outside were strangely peaceful in

their evening glow, despite the hiccupping engine of a military truck skirting the outer walls.

'You're going to end up part of one of those stories, whatever you do,' Dongming replied. 'So you'd better choose a good one. Places make stories out of whatever they can. Think of my family sitting mulling over my brother every night. Or think of Old Li — you know, that thin businessman with the face full of ink-stain birthmarks. He spends all his time wondering if his wife will ever return, and, every time he looks into people's eyes, he sees that no one else has forgotten it either. Look at the trees, the river, everything. I must have heard a hundred different stories about things that used to happen in the forest before it got torn up, and how people swear the river changed course after that girl threw herself into it. Oh, what was her name?'

'Stories are like that. People bend their memories into stories to make themselves feel content, or to disguise the horror of everything around them. I don't want to be like that. That's why I left home in the first place.'

'So we'll both go.' Dongming looked at the younger boy as if for assurance.

'You're suddenly serious. I was waiting to see what that looked like,' Jinyi said.

Dongming showed a fake smile, all yellow teeth and embarrassment. 'Yes, I'm serious. If my useless brother can rewrite his story, then I can too. At least then there'll be something to come back to.'

'All right. Let's stop talking about it and do it.'

'All right. Sure. We'll both leave this shitty little town.' They raised their glasses and sank the scummy dregs of the bristly liquor.

Neither dared ask exactly where the other planned to go. There were gaps and holes in everything Jinyi took for granted, and this, he felt, should be no different. When they left the shop a couple of hours later night had nuzzled up into the nooks and corners of the way home. The restless calls of the cats crept over the eaves above them. The two boys eluded the pair of soldiers on night duty by skirting through deserted courtyards, steadying each other so they didn't trip over broken stools and empty chicken coops. When the time came to part, they were awkward, the alcohol wearing off into tiredness and despondence. Finally they bowed to each other. Both suddenly embarrassed by this, they turned and walked until they could no longer hear the lazy beat of the other's feet against the soggy stones.

Before the year was out Dongming and Jinyi's former boss would jump from the highest stone bridge into the river, having never learnt how to swim. The same day his brightly feathered birds escaped from their cages and lived in the town's trees until winter, when they suddenly departed. No one was able to explain how they continually managed to evade the Japanese's persistent attempts to catch them, or why the birds, which had spent all their lives caged in a stuffy room, should survive so well in the wild. Both would eventually be attributed to the fact that, unlike every other bird known to the city's inhabitants, they never emitted even the smallest sound, neither morning song nor warning squawk.

It was the men in Dongming's family who would die first, starved and exhausted, working for scraps on the building sites the soldiers had taken over. The asthmatic grandmother and the unmarried aunts survived in their papery skin a little longer. No one was left to witness them mixing sawdust into their stingy bowls of millet after the little sitting-room Buddha was requisitioned by troops as they took it to the town centre to be pawned.

Dongming would head south, hiking through villages the Japanese had not bothered with, and circling down toward Chongqing, the Nationalists' capital since they fled Nanjing in the wake of the invasion. Chongqing was then a city divided in half by the fast-flowing Yangtze river, the longest in China, and buffeted between the mountainous plateaus of Tibet to the west and south and the Japanese-controlled areas to the east.

Even seventy years later the stretches of grassland amid the hills would remain cordoned off because of the amount of mines laid by the retreating army to protect their last base.

Perhaps Dongming died crossing the expansive minefield, something even the Japanese did not dare to attempt. Perhaps he joined the ranks of the Nationalists and, when both the world war and the civil war were finished, fled with the rest of the higher-ranking officials to Taiwan. Perhaps he worked in one of the prison camps that sat at the top of some of Chongqing's mountains, collecting mist and guarding the Communist prisoners until their executions. Perhaps he was imprisoned by the Communists when the People's Republic was created, and was re-educated, sent to the fields or shot. In all likelihood, he never made it as far as Chongqing. But because Jinyi did not hear from him again, he must remain as a ghost to us, on the other side of knowledge. There are some things that even I am not allowed to tell.

Jinyi followed the thin river which skittered beneath the mountain ranges. On the high ridges, stretches of the Great Wall had already crumbled into a few decayed teeth stubbing out of rocky gums. He had decided to head north because south would be back towards his uncle, his aunt, the dregs of his family.

North was the edge, the wall; where the past spilt over into today. Besides, it would be madness to follow the Japanese south, and, if there was to be no escape, why not go against the grain, towards the eye of the hurricane: Manchuria, which grew closer and closer each day.

Occasionally he strayed close to the train tracks he had once longed for, but he always backed away, so as not to be mistaken for a deserting railway worker. The only things that seemed to rush past him were goods trains, carrying coal. Some days he passed villages where rickety stalls served watery dumplings and dried-flower tea brewed from warmed-up rainwater, villages too small for the invading troops to have bothered stopping at as they marched through. Half starved, he would eat until he felt ready to retch. He stole sleep on porches and in railway storehouses. Just a bit further, keep going, I'll get there soon, he told himself.

He stopped in small cities, towns, villages. He worked as a servant, a childminder for a rich family, a farm hand, an oddjob man on building sites, a carpenter's apprentice. Yet in every place his feet would begin to itch, his hopes would carry him on. He kept walking. The seasons changed from bracken to jasmine to gingko. His bare feet blistered into hooves.

His seventeenth birthday snuck up on him

and yet he kept on pushing north, pursuing that part of him he could not yet name, following dirt roads etched through the granite and long grass by the stubborn steps of driven mules. Wheat fields, barley fields, whole days spent longing for his parents.

And as he walked, Jinyi thought of those snippets of conversations he had heard in the backrooms of restaurants: that the Communists would bring the country a new beginning so that getting a job wouldn't depend on knowing someone's uncle or brother or providing them with a fistful of cash; so there wouldn't be any more foreigners squeezing the marrow out of the country; so rice would be shared equally between everyone. Jinyi's stomach whined, moaned. He found these ideas hard to believe, knowing, after all, that with a little rice wine and the promise of better things people can get carried away. If it were possible to swap lives, he reasoned, the whole world would already have become an electric storm of flitting souls.

Walking is hard work. I should know, I trudged behind him most of the way. Why did I bother? I know what it is like to spend your life chasing an elusive dream. And since we've got a little time, on the long trek between Hebei and Manchuria, I may as well tell you how I ended up here too.

My real name is Zao Jun, and before I was the Kitchen God I was an ordinary mortal, just like you. I assume you are already familiar with my face, my finely curled moustache and long black goatee, for there was a time when every house in the country kept my likeness above the stove, and quite a few are now doing so again. There are many who wish to slander me for reasons I cannot quite fathom — if they envy the gods then they have no real idea of what we do — and have put about a story that depicts me as a horny old fool. They assert that I abandoned my wife after falling in love with a beautiful young woman; that I was then visited by bad luck, and lost the young woman, all my money and even my sight; that I stumbled starving through the forests until I was finally taken in and fed by a sympathetic woman who I confessed my sins to; that in doing so I cried such remorseful tears that my eyes were healed and I saw that the woman who had treated me so well was my old ever-loving wife. They go on to say that I was so overcome by shame that I then threw myself into the stove. However, let me tell you that there is no truth in this tale — its only purpose seems to be to tarnish my reputation.

I would never have abandoned my wife for someone else, for my wife was the most beautiful woman in our village. I loved her the first moment I saw her, following her father to the market where her family would trade corncobs for some of the plump red chillies my family laid out on our flat roof. Sometimes I would lie up there myself in the dusty sun of those long childhood afternoons among the peppers. From there I could watch her bag-laden family, the stooped father and his three daughters, as they made their way down the rocky path toward the fallow stretch where everyone would gather to haggle every month after the new moon. Her long plait used to swish down to the small of her back, a smile always flittering around the edges of her lips. She had inch-long eyelashes and tiny feet, and every time my eyes met hers in the market I would blush, despite being five years older than her and nearly a full-grown man.

Yet my feelings would have come to nothing had her father not been the worst gambler in the province. He left his daughters when he fled his debtors and, thanks to the local matchmaker, I got married only a few weeks later.

When I think back now to the early days of our marriage — the shy way in those first weeks that my new wife always looked at the ground when speaking, or the way she would cling onto my body at night as if I was a raft in a storm-churned ocean — I am never sure whether to smile or cry. For those first, innocent days did not last long.

We married in summer and kept each other

warm through the long, bitter winter that followed. Our field was covered in frost until close to halfway through the next year and, after only a few weeks of sun, rainstorms washed the soil and the half-grown seeds away. We resorted to gathering shrubs and firewood in the forest, but in that second winter my mother died from the shortage. After the next short summer when the field was attacked by clouds of tiny green aphids, sucking the juices from the chillies and leaving them shrivelled and inedible, my sister followed her.

We took to scavenging for food, hunting for hedgehogs and mice in the forest, making soups with leaves and grasses. My brother became so desperate that he tried to steal from our landlord's house up on the mountain. He was caught and disembowelled, and we were turfed out of the house I had been born in.

For close to a year we traipsed around other nearby villages, tending to my maddened father as if he was our child and searching for a second cousin he was convinced would help us. We did not find him; instead, after three hundred days of drinking murky puddle water and eating mushrooms and unripe fruits pinched from vines, after a miscarriage and countless days in which we would wash away each other's dirt and sweat in the salty brine of our own tears, we had come almost full circle, and arrived at a town on the same mountain range that overlooked our former home. We could go no further.

A man who is not a good son cannot be called a man. He will be forever tormented by the spirits of his ancestors, his soul immersed in shame. My father was frail and sick; he needed rest, warmth, care. I left him in a cheap room, swearing to the owner that the rent would be forthcoming, and while he rested my wife and I visited every shop, every farm and every landlord in the whole town, imploring them to take pity on us and help us find work. At each door we met with the same response. That is, until we arrived at the house of the man the locals referred to as The Nobleman, the richest landlord in the whole miserable county.

His mansion was vast and incomprehensible; we passed through courtyards that led to galleries opening onto patios and gardens, corridors that spiralled into porticos and antechambers. When the slave guiding us eventually left us in the waiting room, my wife and I both prostrated ourselves before the haughty figure of a bearded man dressed in the kind of rich, colourful silks that I had previously only seen in the strange and malleable fabric of my dreams.

Seeing us so nervous, he began to laugh. 'I hope you do not mistake me for my master. I am Bei, the head servant of this household. I believe you have come to offer your services to my illustrious master. Please, do not waste your breath. As you can see, my master has no need of further servants, and considers charity a base affront against the gods of fate. Yet he is by nature a generous man, and he has a proposition for you. Please be seated, and enjoy some tea, for you must have been travelling for many days.'

We did as he suggested, surprised and confused by the extent of this servant's knowledge of us. He disappeared from the waiting room for a few moments, and we were left to study the statues that adorned the altar by the main wall, the many-armed gods who seemed to be weighing up our chances. The servant returned carrying a small pouch, which he opened to reveal five silver coins. He placed the pouch in my hands.

'My master is prepared to pay you these, on the condition that you leave this house and never return.'

I nodded eagerly, garbling words of gratitude, and my wife and I both rose to bow to the servant. He shook his head and put out his hand.

'You have misunderstood. The offer applies only to you. The woman is to stay here, and join the household as one of my master's wives.'

'What?' I shouted. 'But she is my wife! Your

master has never even laid eyes on her! Why should he want to tear us apart?'

The servant produced another pouch of silver coins, which he added to the first. 'You must make your decision now.'

Both of us knew that we had no choice. Can love feed you, keep your family safe, stave off death? I have since learnt that it can do all these things; but I learnt too late. Before I could even open my mouth to say goodbye, my wife had followed the servant from the room, not even daring to look back at me. I took the ten silver coins and returned to my father, my heart blistered into a black scab.

A doctor with his many putrid medicines and high-pitched incantations took two of the coins, the owner of the room another for all the trouble, and the rest were spent on bribes to various local officials until we had managed to procure a small plot which we rented from a corrupt, absent landlord. My father was soon back to his old self, out on the short field from sundown to sunset, and our first harvest of carrots was a success. The money seemed well spent. Every morning I awoke in the rickety house before dawn and set to work until the night had drained all semblance of light from the earth, with only one goal: to earn enough to give to The Nobleman in order to reclaim my wife, or else to wait until he died when she would be free to return to me. I slaved and dug and tilled as hard as I could in order to stop my mind from wondering what she was doing at that moment, what she might have become.

Five years passed in this way, until one night we were woken by the sound of screaming and the thud of drums. I helped my father up and we rushed from the house to see the soldiers approaching the village. We were simple people, and knew little about politics, about the treaties and wars between the states. However, we had heard enough to know that we had to hide. My father and I ran until we reached a grubby ditch at the edge of the forest, and hid there until the sun came up and the sound of the marching army had receded into the distance. When we returned and saw that our house, just like all the others in the village, had been burnt to the ground, my father sank to the ground and fell into a sudden illness that, only a few days later, claimed his life.

Once more I was homeless, penniless and desperate. Only now I had neither the strength of my family nor the words of my wife to keep my heart warm. The lightning invasion plunged the state into chaos and famine and I took to wandering again, searching for work. I finally made it to a large town, where I worked as a rickshaw-carrier until my back began to bend and threatened to snap like a forest twig, and then I became a beggar on one of the many cobbled streets.

By the time I managed to find a half-decent job as a servant in the kitchen of a large house in the centre of the town I was close to the age my mother had been when she died.

I shared a cupboard-sized cellar room with seven other men, alternating our turns on the damp floor space depending on who had worked the longest without rest. All my waking hours were spent in and around the kitchen, breathing in the fumes of the exquisite dishes I would never get to taste while I chewed on a lump of stale bread. I washed the dishes, plucked feathers, cleaned up after the pigs, working for a whole year without seeing a member of the family I served, but that suited me fine — to see laughing children or beautiful women when I was the last of my line with no hopes for the future would only have forced out the envy and anger I kept buried inside.

The house was by far the biggest I had ever seen, newly built for a rich family fleeing the invasion. It so happened that after a year of service I was given the task of taking a receipt to the head of the east wing; everyone else was busy preparing for a feast that would be held that evening to welcome a posse of government officials from the new administration. Despite the simple directions, I soon found myself lost in the maze of endless corridors and the many doors that all led on to rooms and other corridors. All I knew was that I was surely far from where I was supposed to be. I felt overcome by vertigo, and I panicked, thinking I would be lost forever. Eventually I stopped at a random door, took a deep breath and knocked, hoping someone would take pity on me and send me back to where I belonged.

'Yes? Oh, what do you want?' A woman asked as she opened the door. She was dressed in a loose silk robe, and looked ghostly in her white make-up.

'I am terribly sorry to disturb you, madam, but I need to find my way back to the kitchen. I work here. I mean there. I —'

'Oh.' She cut me off with a wave of her hand. 'It's only a servant,' she called back over her shoulder, and I noticed that there were many other women behind her, each wearing the same loose robes and the same expensive make-up.

'I am afraid we cannot help you. This is the north wing, and we are some of the master's wives. Not very popular ones, though, I am afraid — *they* live in the west wing! Anyway, none of us has ever had any reason to leave our rooms. We have everything we need right here, you see, except perhaps attention.'

'Then I am sorry to bother you, madam. I will be on my way.' I bowed and began to retreat when I heard another of the women speak.

'Wait! Wait! Zao Jun . . . is that you?'

My wife ran to the doorway. She was plumper now, her face pinched, the uncoloured roots of her hair betraying her age; but it was her, as beautiful as ever. Tears filled my eyes as I reached out to embrace her, but the first woman pushed her arm out into the doorway between us.

'No men are allowed here,' she barked. 'If you are seen here, we will all be killed. Go on, get away!'

As I retreated into the corridor, my wife tilted her head and beamed at me. The door closed, but I was young again, if only for a brief moment, and as I made my way through the winding hallways I began to think about out how we could be reunited. Without noticing how I had got there, I finally found myself back in the east wing. This must be the work of some god, I assured myself, for how else could I have ended up a servant to the same man who had taken my wife as his?

Yet the more I thought about it, as I stood chopping and dicing in a little corner of the busy kitchen, the more it seemed the work of a god intent on punishing me. The more I learnt about our master, the man they called The Nobleman, the more I came to realise that he would never willingly let my wife return to me. Perhaps, I conjectured, the only reason I had been given this job was so that he could torment me with this terrible proximity. Just when I was close to giving up hope, however, I received a visit.

It was late at night, though I was still in the kitchen, helping to prepare dishes for the next morning's breakfast. My wife appeared in the doorway and beckoned. I made some silly excuse to the chef and quickly joined her in the deserted corridor.

'Take these,' she whispered, and thrust five cakes into my hands.

'Why?' I muttered, looking at them carefully.

'They will help us. Take them and perhaps things can soon change . . . I have not forgotten you,' my wife said.

'I cannot forget you either. I —'

'I know. But this is not the time — I must return to my room before anyone notices that I have left. We will meet again soon, I am sure.'

And with that she was gone, swishing down the corridor, leaving me with the five round cakes. Instead of returning to the kitchen, I paced up and down the corridor and thought for a while. Perhaps there was something magical in the cakes that could help me in some way. I took a bite from one. It was mediocre, a little stale, even. The others were the same. Then I hit upon it — I could sell them and earn a little money. With that money, I could join a local dice game and, with luck, double, triple or even quadruple my earnings. For the first time in close to a decade, I was pleased with myself.

The next morning I snuck out and sold the cakes. It was not as easy as I thought, competing as I was with noodle-stalls and housewives selling hot dumplings and steamed buns, but I still ended up with a handful of loose change. It was less than I had hoped for, but enough to kickstart my plan. I thought of returning to the kitchen before I was missed, but the temptation to join one of the back-alley gambling tables was too strong. I peered over the fighting crickets, the marbles and mahjong, until I found a dice table.

It took me less than an hour to lose all my money, less time than it had taken me to sell the cakes. I cannot remember how I got back to The Nobleman's mansion; my head was so filled with rage and bitterness. I hated myself, and what I had done. I slumped into my corner amid the woks and pans and tried to stop myself from crying. It was then that I heard the other workers gossiping with the deliveryman.

'Incredible!'

'I can't believe it!'

'It's true, I swear. He was walking along, chewing on his breakfast, when he felt something hard scraping his teeth. Well, he was just about to get angry when he reached in and found that it was a diamond. A real-life diamond! What's more, he soon found a couple more. One minute he's a street-cleaner, the next he's rich!'

'You're joking!'

Once again I felt dizzy, nauseous. It was now clear to me what my wife had done. Over the years she must have saved up all the trinkets and jewellery and other gifts The Nobleman had lavished upon her — as well as filching jewels from the other concubines, no doubt, when this last desperate opportunity presented itself — all of which she had hidden inside the cakes she gave to me. With those riches we could have afforded passage far from this county and The Nobleman's men; we could have bought a new life together. I had destroyed such hopes. I began to retch, but nothing but bile came up from my knotted stomach. Not only had I separated us forever, but I had put my wife in danger, for when The Nobleman found out what she had done, he would surely have her killed.

I screamed out so loud that everyone in the kitchen dropped their knives and pots to cover their ears. Then, before anyone could stop me, I rushed forward and threw myself onto the huge roaring fire at the edge of the room. I howled as the rasping flames began to blacken my flesh, as my skin blistered and bubbled and split at the seams while my clothes shrivelled and stuck to my bones. The last thing I remember was my tongue shrivelling to a charred stub and my eyeballs bursting, the bitter world disappearing.

For a time there was only darkness, and of what happened next I have only the testimony of others. It seems my wife, distraught at what I had done, came to weep in the kitchen and leave food there for my restless spirit. Every month she would come with offerings and private whispers, and in time she also placed a carefully drawn picture of the two of us above the fire. Our story spread through the town, then the county and the province, and within a hundred years people throughout the country had begun to do the same, setting our image beside their own stoves and hoping I would help them avoid the bad luck that had plagued my life.

And so it was that I awoke one morning up here, to find myself transformed into a god. My celestial body is similar in every way to my old earthly body, though the burns and scars have been washed away. I have everything I could want — great feasts, a wonderful house of my own, food from all the kitchens in the land, and the ability to go anywhere, watch anyone. Yet you who assume that my wife and I, depicted in together in all those kitchens, must both be gods are very much mistaken. My wife is an example of piety and love, and it is true that imagining one of us without the other would be like trying to picture the reverse of a coin that has no obverse. She has, however, been dead now for more than two thousand years, and is in a place which, because of my divine duties, I cannot yet enter. Perhaps at the end of time, if there is such a thing, we shall be reunited. Perhaps when we gods are completely forgotten, we too shall die, and I will meet her in the underworld. Or perhaps there can be no end, and the best I can hope for is that when this heavenly cycle draws to a close and time starts again I shall be able to relive those early days of my marriage, even if it also means reliving all my later mistakes.

My story may explain why the Jade Emperor made this bet with me — he knows well enough that I spend much of my time seeking out stories similar to my own, finding other loving hearts, if only to take a little comfort in the slight resemblances, in the smallest of secret details that bind us all together. That is why I picked Hou Jinyi and Bian Yuying. Like my own, their love story was caught up in the whirlwind of history.

Jinyi had not found her yet. That is why he kept walking.

One afternoon, just when Jinyi was beginning to think that he could no longer tell where his blisters ended and the rest of his feet began, he spotted a row of battered farmhouses held together with clumps of sun-hardened earth, each one leaning a little towards the next. The beginnings of a city.

Within a couple of weeks he had begged a job assisting an old man in a barber's shop. Zu Fu was almost blind, and rarely left the tiny shop for the wider world. The shop was dank and dirty, with cut hair and leaked water strewn across the stone floor. Its front room was filled by three stools, and a solitary mirror hung from the wall by a length of string. Jinyi swept the floor, washed hair, and learned the trade from watching the steady hands of his master. In return, he was allowed to sleep on the wooden floor in one of the backrooms, outside Zu Fu's own cramped bedroom, and share the little morsels gleaned from each week's narrow profits. He did not dare to ask for any more than that, and was careful to study the tics and flicks of the knife and scissors between the old man's fingers — if I can learn something of this, he started thinking, I could have my own shop, and a family in it to help me. Just as when next to the sugar vats, in the sewing rooms or at the home of the family he had served, he spent his work hours sifting through daydreams, as one might pan a river, hoping for a glint of gold.

He had come as far as Jinzhou, deep inside Manchuria, where the former Emperor Pu Yi served as a puppet figurehead for a Japanese-controlled state. Manchuria was flooded with the occupying troops, resilient and harsh since their arrival in 1931. They had been there for ten years, Jinyi calculated, not daring to predict what percentage of their stay this might represent. He occasionally overheard hushed talk of experiments on humans and forced labour camps a little further north. Like others, he knew too many ancient stories to dismiss these claims. Manchuria, or Liaoning, as it would later become, was like a well-worn robe, handed down from Manchu to Han to Japanese and — at the end of the war — to liberating Russian armies who stayed for the resources, then to the Kuomintang, and finally to the CCP. As it passed through each tight grip, Jinyi thought, it became weathered and stained, but retained something of the durable cloth that was woven before any of the occupiers arrived.

Jinzhou was huddled around a train station, which brimmed each morning with men whose faces were blistered black with soot. Where the lines of slim brick buildings finished, forests began, and these swarmed out into hidden villages and the endless nocturn of the forgotten and ignored. The city was a rung on a ladder, a stopgap between Beijing and Shenyang, and therefore, Jinyi reasoned, it was the perfect place for him.

'When I was a boy, in the mornings we'd sit in my aunt's room — there must have been about ten of us — learning some sums and some songs, and then we'd go down after lunch to watch our fathers and brothers laying the tracks. I've been here since I was four years old, when the city was almost all forest.'

Once Zu Fu started rambling, it was difficult to get him to stop until he ran out of breath. Jinyi did not bother to interrupt the sprawl of stuttered family history that spilt from him.

'My father was from the south. He couldn't speak a word of Mandarin, and he didn't have to neither. He hurt his legs when the tracks were almost finished, so we stayed here. No more scurrying after the black engines for us. Set up here, he did, and taught himself how to cut hair and give a good shave. This city was just beginning then, but look at it now. They all stop off here these days. You can't escape the trains. I've always known they were the future. The used to rattle us to sleep, those engines vibrating the huts set up beside the freshly laid tracks.'

'It must have been exciting to be part of something big.' Jinyi stopped mopping the floor to look across at the seated barber, trying to picture him young, trying to imagine living through the end of a century to see another sprout up. This country is too old, he thought. Too many tangled roots sapping all the goodness from the ground.

'Of course. My grandmother, though, she was superstitious. Like many of the folks from up in the hills round here. She thought that trains were dangerous, undermining the natural Tao. Didn't like my father working on the tracks, oh no. Said our family should stay on the land that they'd been on for centuries.'

'They were landowners. Were they rich? What was that like?' Jinyi pictured pot-bellied mandarins, hazy and sated with cups of glowing wine amid their giggling wives. He imagined a countryside estate where rich men might lose their memories of the outside world amid their endless hedge-grown mazes, while they drew up meditative poems as easily as tempting goldfish to the surface of glinting ponds.

Zu Fu nodded. 'Tenant farmers. No future, my father said. He was bluffing, of course, but maybe he was right. He used to say that his mother cursed him and the railways when he left. Said it as a joke, but I think it got to him, especially after the accident.'

'So you never wanted to travel, to leave here?'

The old man scratched his beard, then returned to sharpening the long blade. It was a slow day, as most were, and the shop was empty.

'We all wanted to travel. That's all my father ever talked about. He thought we'd settle here, save some money, and then either head on up the tracks to Shenyang, or down to Beijing, or even back home, though I think he had a bit too much pride for that. At the start he used to go over different plans every day. But look around you. How can you save

111

when there's no money? The only people getting paid in cash back then were the foreigners. Wasn't just the Japanese here in those days. There were Germans, Russians, English, Americans. But none of the locals had any money. They still don't. Cut the doctor's hair and you'll get some help when you're sick. Cut the troops' hair and you won't get any hassle. Cut a peasant's hair for a couple of eggs, or a fist of flour. You'll soon see what it's like. Not that I don't like it here, that's not what I'm saying. But you've got your ideas backwards, young man, if you think the world is as simple as clicking your fingers and making it change.'

'Do you really like it here?' Jinyi asked.

'It's my home. My family's buried here, beneath the stones on the hill. You didn't know that, did you?' He smiled, eager to share those titbits, as if they might vindicate his tired limbs, his quiet and unbending routine, his eyes that looked like the cream which floats on top of milk.

'My wife too; died only a year after we wed. She's out there, in the fields. Waiting for me. I couldn't leave now, even if I did have money — which, as you well know, I don't. There is no world beyond here for me anymore. Things shrink as you get old. Even the migrations of the birds, all that going and returning, seem like wasted journeys. Better to buckle down, keep yourself warm, save energy. That's survival. Believe me.' His lips parted once again to show his sand-brown teeth and zigzagging gaps. 'But what about you?'

'What about me?' Jinyi shrugged.

'Where are you from?'

'South of here.' He turned away from the barber, swishing out the mop. More work to be done.

'A lot of people from south of here,' Zu Fu said, with neither irony nor emotion. As Jinyi was considering his reply, the barber raised himself up and wandered to the backroom for his daily nap.

Jinyi went back to mopping and watching the shop. When the evening came he wandered out to meet with the street vendors, teahouse comics and overnighting railway workers who, unwilling to sit out in the lamp-lit street, gathered in backrooms to chat. Jinyi felt safe being near these strangers. Neither overnight traveller nor native, he was happy not to have to explain himself. When they were lucky they shared the dregs of re-brewed tea, and an occasional lip-wet rolled cigarette passed between grateful hands like a sacrament. Though the backroom crowd often changed shape, its unspoken rule remained the same — only the day that had just passed was talked of. Past and future, along with the patched-up hand-me-down coats and cheap fur hats, were left at the door. In this way the minutiae of everyday life took on a significance that, to Jinyi, seemed to redeem the smallness of their lives.

But when slumping down each night on the loose and uneven floor of the barber's storeroom, he found he remembered little of what had been said — the puns and jokes that kept the clock tumbling forward, the exaggerated arguments, over-earnest nods and murmurs of recognition. There is a hole somewhere through which my life is leaking — what I need, he told himself, is a wife, some children, someone to soak up the echoes of my own voice. I'm not that bitter little boy pulling my cousin's hair anymore, but I'm not yet one of these old men looking at today through an ancient prism that bends and splits the light like a magician's trick. I don't know who I am. Tomorrow I will wake up as someone else.

A war started on a distant continent. Now, let me tell you, I've seen enough of wars to know one thing — they all end the same way. But if I have to explain military history and blitzes and machine guns and the preference of fascist dictators for questionable haircuts and all that other stuff, as well as the workings of the human heart, then I'm never going to win this bet.

As Zu Fu became more uncertain of his failing eyes, Jinyi learnt how to carefully direct the blade, following the grain of weathered skin, how to move his fingers over a skull by gently pushing down with growing pressure, and how to taper, tie, clean and cut countless lengths of dark black hair.

A knock at the door one night hauled him up from the floating fantasies of half-sleep. Zu Fu was already dressed — he had been expecting this. Jinyi, rubbing his eyes as he sat up from his floorboard bed, was beckoned to rise. Behind the door was a stern-looking young man with rabbit's teeth, moving his fingers to and from his face as if brushing off invisible cobwebs.

'The time has come?' Zu Fu asked, but did not listen for an answer. The stern young man muttered something and then turned to walk briskly down the street, leaving Jinyi to lead his master into the night.

The barber seemed to know where they were going, although no more than two words were spoken between him and the visitor. They marched through the unlit streets until they came to stop at a small house without windows. Throughout the journey no one had spoken. The stern man put his hand to his mouth to cover it. The barber did the same. Jinyi was unsure whether they were forcing themselves to keep quiet or did not wish to breathe.

They tiptoed through to the main room, and Jinyi remained confused — the dead man lying across a line of three chairs would not be woken by their whispers, though the rest of the house might. For a moment he wondered whether they suspected that the dead man's soul might seep into their bodies through their mouths, or if they were unwilling to mix the breath of life with the groggy air of the stale room. Then, as they drew closer to the corpse, Jinyi noticed the bloodstains and the rip in the centre of the dirty shirt — a bullet to the chest, the preferred method of execution for the local Japanese troops. He had seen a hundred similar bodies piled up on the backs of trucks. They were usually taken to fields and hurriedly buried in shallow holes dug by prisoners of war. At least this family had managed to bring the body back to their house.

Zu Fu nodded in the direction of the body, and Jinyi led him to it. For a minute Zu Fu simply ran his hands over the stubbly face, feeling the matted strands of hair and the swollen plum-stone bulge midway down the neck.

A rich family would have called a professional man of the dead. This is their work, Jinyi thought, not the place for backstreet barbers. But nevertheless he did not move from his position, squatting beside his master. He was so close to the corpse that he could make out moles and goosebumps on the yellowing flesh. It was nothing like the wind-

116

eaten remains he had come across on the country trail, gun-metal grey and overrun with scabby, unpicked seams.

The body also bore no resemblance to his own parents, who had become small stones in a village to which neither they nor he dared to return. They lived now only among the other curios of his memory.

Jinyi knew nothing of the relationship between the two of them, but it was clear that, as the tools were washed, the face slowly shaved and the hair pulled back, Zu Fu must once have known the dead man. The work was done in silence.

'A friend, from my wife's family. I haven't seen them in years,' the barber whispered, and Jinyi nodded.

'We can't stay long.'

'Why?'

'We must leave them to their mourning. It is not a good time for strangers.' Again, Jinyi nodded, feeling tiredness rustling under his eyelids.

In a few small hours, when the light poured in under the door, the family would want to gather round the body, to look on it one last time before they bore it up the hill to be buried. This is the last of life, dressed up and disguised for us, Jinyi reflected as he took over from his master's shaking hands, his strokes discarding the rest of the dry stubble.

Jinyi had learnt to trust touch over sight;

our eyes, the barber had told him many times, change the world to fit their narrow illusions. Vision is limiting, made up of shadows and trickery that cannot be trusted. Touch makes the world solid, gives it depth. The dead man was probably a husband, a father, Jinyi thought. The bullet could have been for any number of tiny wrongs. Jinyi turned to the hair, winding the life back down across the knobble of shoulder. This, at least, would continue to grow.

After seven days the spirit would return for one night. Sand would be scattered outside the windows and door, and the next morning it would be studied for signs of the host animal the ghost had chosen. This man will return as a pig, snuffling and snorting around the smoke-tanned walls of his old home, Jinyi decided. If my Pa had returned like that a while after he died, then he wouldn't have liked what he saw. He would have pulled the room apart by his animal teeth and dragged my bastard uncle out of his bed and into the fields. But perhaps he was not a fiery countryman at all and more like me: quiet, uncertain, hiding his awkwardness with a play of boldness.

As they returned, dawn was already crackling about the distance like fat spat from a red-hot wok. In the shop they sat down to eat more of last week's gloopy millet.

'Do you ever think about death?'

'There is nothing to think about,' the older man replied. 'Eat up.'

Jinyi laughed, and, after a few seconds, the barber laughed with him.

Jinyi soon found he was smiling every day. The dead man had whispered to him while he was shaving the stubble from his rubbery jowls. Live, while you have the chance. Within a few weeks, with the Japanese soldiers taking free haircuts and Zu Fu growing increasingly unable to feed both of them, Jinyi would disappear once more. But at least now he knew what he was looking for. That strange, elusive magic he sought was slowly becoming clear to him. He wanted to live.

The Jade Emperor did nothing for a while, letting me suffer the long days imagining the many terrible things he might inflict on me. So when, some time later, I was summoned by a brigade of blackbirds, I was almost relieved.

Now, his palace is made of nothing. Not just the cheap, abundant nothing so common on earth, however, but real, thick reams of unending nothingness. Furthermore, it is impossible to speak of the palace, for it is not there; yet I can tell you that to become lost in those nonexistent corridors is the stuff of nightmares. After what seemed like days immersed in the deep recesses of this palace, searching for the Jade Emperor, I began to suspect that this was my punishment. The Jade Emperor is elusive, everywhere and nowhere, and changes shape and appearance so often that I am never sure what he will look like when I next see him. Therefore when I ventured upon a fountain of fireflies pretending to be a rogue constellation, or a rogue constellation pretending to be a fountain of fireflies, or even a simple stone, I addressed it with reverence in case it might reveal itself as the heavenly emperor.

Then suddenly I saw him, standing right beside me with the start of a smile on his face.

'Do you know how the Monkey King was punished for rebelling against me?' he asked.

I shook my head.

'He was imprisoned under a mountain for thousands of years if I remember correctly.'

'Oh,' was all I managed to say.

Seeing me standing there shaking with nerves, the Jade Emperor began to laugh, his portly belly jiggling as he giggled.

'Do you really think you could run the human world better than me? Do you know the amount of effort it takes solely to ensure that the earth continues to spin on its axis and the sun appears to rise every morning? I doubt you can even imagine it, let alone some of the finer details of my work. You can stop trembling now; I do not intend to punish you. In fact, I have something far more interesting in mind,' he said, stroking his silky black moustache.

'Heavenly Grandfather, you know I will do anything to serve you,' I quickly replied.

'Yes. Now, you think you know something of life on earth, having once been mortal yourself. But times have changed since then, my friend. I control the workings of a whole universe — I wager that you cannot even fathom the working of a single human heart,' the Jade Emperor said, clasping his hands together in front of him.

'That's it?' I stifled a laugh of my own. 'That's as easy as calling a hungry dog to eat. What do I win?'

The Jade Emperor's eyes met mine. 'Your freedom.'

3:
1944
THE YEAR OF THE MONKEY

The skin on the bottom of Bian Shi's feet was like the stale steamed bread left uneaten in the restaurant. She rocked forward on the balls at the base of her heel. Her broken toes were bent under the hook of her feet, the nails digging down into the ground like chicken claws. Three-inch golden lilies, her mother had told her. And she had overheard, amid the backroom belly-laughs of her horde of elder brothers, talk of the sublime ripples in the vaginal lips that are created by this tradition. Her mother had kissed her twice before pressing the loose brick down on her tightly noosed feet. She had been promised desserts for a week.

It was the smell that made her wretch, the sour smell of dead flesh and drunken men's breath. For this reason she never took her gold-hemmed slippers off in her husband's presence. Not even now, after fifteen years of marriage. She had forced herself to get used to his nocturnal journeys to the many women of the city's outskirts, to ignore the rumours of a regiment of hidden children. At least there was no other wife, no concubine, and Bian Shi thanked me and the household gods for this.

She had heard about the ghosts that haunted old houses even before she had been sent as a gift to Old Bian. She had therefore not been surprised to find that corners of the house were populated by the restless arguments, petty betrayals and hushed conversations of its past; that the voices of ancient relatives were caught like spiders' webs between the courtyard trees; and that the city moon forced its way through every tiny nook, turning the celebratory reds to war-like golds and reinvesting the damp bed furs with life. She had been used to sharing a bed with her elder, unmarried sister, their bodies knotted into its narrow frame. For the first few years in the new house she sank inside the large marital bed, never certain of which nights her husband would crawl in beside her and which nights she would spend alone, listening to the walls. These days, however, husband and wife slept on different sides of the mansion.

Despite her slow hobble, rocking on her heels as she made her way down the street, Bian Shi made it to her husband's restaurant just in time.

■ ■ ■ ■

The bulky, bald-headed chef had steam rising out of his nostrils. His right hand gripped the hair of a scrawny teenage boy.

'So. What is this about?' she asked wearily.

The head chef released his hold, allowing Hou Jinyi to spin around and catch sight of the small middle-aged woman who had just entered the cramped kitchen. Her pudgy stomach bore the leftover sag of a decade of pregnancies, but she seemed almost regal to Jinyi, with her blue dress swimming around her sides, her eyes narrow and dark. She in turn studied him. Despite his nineteen years, Jinyi was short, still waiting for an elusive growth spurt that must have run away from him when his back was turned. His hair had neither been washed nor cut in months. The residual grease and dirt allowed him to push it back behind his ears, revealing his oblong face and tightened cheeks.

The two of them were almost eye to eye. Jinyi dropped his gaze. It would only get him in more trouble if he did not accord her the respect an aristocratic lady deserved. So instead he looked down at his shadow, noticing how it had dribbled down around his feet like an embarrassing accident. His hunt for a new life was not going well — he was restless, uncertain, still wanting to put down

125

roots but never quite sure where the soil would be welcoming. Earlier that morning he had watched a Japanese truck filled with hollow-faced men driving through the city. He had recognised a couple of the desperate faces peering out from the back, each one avoiding the eyes of those down on the street.

'So.' Bian Shi had a habit of saying this, waiting for the gaps in her speech to be filled by someone else. 'You were caught stealing.' It was not a question, and yet he felt compelled to speak.

'Yes.'

Bian Shi nodded, something inside her bristling. Everything repeating itself, she thought; isn't that what always happens if you wait long enough? She had already decided that déjà vu was the gods' way of telling her something. (I can neither confirm nor deny the truthfulness of this, I am afraid, for even gods have gagging orders.) She did not consider that thefts kept happening because there were a thousand hungry mouths in the city and only a dozen households and restaurants with enough food.

'What did you take?'

Jinyi gulped.

'Mantou.' A small steamed bun. Flour and water. He had pinched a single bun from a plate returned at the end of a meal, piled by the kitchen's back entrance, waiting to be washed up. Though it was hard and stale, it

was the best thing he had tasted in weeks. 'I thought it was just part of the leftovers.'

Jinyi had been standing on the street, his hand creeping in through the door, his fingers crawling like spiders over the concertina of stacked plates, feeling for the discarded dough. Yet just as he had reached for another bun, a fist had clamped round his forearm and yanked him in. The kitchen was fast becoming a footnote in the history of theft, Bian Shi could not help thinking; a catalogue of hopeless journeys that somehow led to her. Yet she was incapable of ever turning anyone away.

'Could have been going for anything. There are expensive knives lying around,' the head chef said, standing with his heavy hands on Jinyi's shoulders. Behind the three of them the kitchen staff bustled about their tasks.

'We ought to call in the boss, give him a real beating. Or send him to the troops. They're always looking for workers. Get you sent to one of those Jap mines — how'd you like that?' the head chef leered. 'That would teach them all a lesson, that they can't mess with us.'

'Don't be ridiculous. He's just a hungry kid. And it looks like you've already started dealing out punishments,' Bian Shi said as she eyed the cut at the side of the boy's mouth, his left eye blinking up the beginnings of a bruise. 'Give him the stale *mantou.*'

The chef began to stutter, then folded his arms and walked back to his chopping board in the depth of the kitchen. 'Sure, why don't we take pity on all the petty criminals and undesirables in the city?' he muttered, frustrated, as usual, by Bian Shi's strange show of compassion.

The angry thwack of his cleaver on the wood rose above the noise of scuffling feet and relayed orders. You do not usually find a head chef lopping through the thin cuts of pork, but the restaurant was the emptiest it had been in years. This was thanks to the occupation: the only people who could now afford to eat there were the Japanese who were either stationed in the city or had recently followed the aeroplane trails to the new state of Manchuria. Among them there were many who chose not to pay, who put everything on a tab. And what, they seemed to ask, was the restaurant going to do about it?

'So. What's your name?'

'Hou Jinyi.'

'Not from here.' This was not a question. She looked him up and down.

'Not from anywhere. That's no excuse, I know. I'm sorry, but who was going to eat that? The chickens pecking through those baskets would have got to it a few seconds later if I hadn't.'

'So this is what you do,' she was still smiling, but the tone had changed, had sunk a little deeper.

'No!' He quickly looked round, happy to notice that the other staff were at least pretending to ignore the small scene. 'I'm not like that. Look at me,' he urged. 'I've either been working or trying to work every day of my life. And I can tell you which one is worse. I'd rather be sore with hernias and limps than edgy, always looking about for things to magically materialise.'

'What do you do?'

'Anything people want. Anything. I've worked fields twenty hours a raining day, tilled, ploughed, cooked, cleaned houses, looked after spoilt children, made candy, swept streets, counted coal shipments, cut hair, worked as a standby burial man, stitched up old shoes that have fallen apart and been fixed a hundred times before and are still being worn against their will, and,' he paused for breath and let his lips curl up toward his hedgerow eyebrows, 'more odd jobs than I can remember.'

Bian Shi leaned against the door. Lucky she had got there before her husband, she thought. She always did the accounts herself, despite not being able to read or write, totalling the figures in her head and dotting the boxes in the kitchens with numbers and doodles of birds, moons, dragons and lions, symbols that only she understood. When her children were not at school they were with

Peipei the nursemaid, while her husband spent his days in the parts of the city the settled troops did not bother to rake through.

'Show me your hands.'

Jinyi held his dirty hands away from his body, as if he was ashamed of them.

'You work with your hands?'

'Me and everyone else.'

'Can you cook?'

'Sure. Me and everyone else.'

'But can you cook well?'

Jinyi shrugged. 'Good enough to eat.' He let his hands fall to his sides, no longer knowing what to do with them; he reached for nonexistent pockets and, on not finding any, shoved his hands behind his back.

'Why not show us, then?' She nodded her head toward a workboard beside a battered pot of simmering water.

Jinyi did not dare look at her to check whether this was a joke. He walked to the workboard as casually as he could manage. The bruises drummed through his head, and his tongue flicked at the cut on his lip, his tastebuds fizzing with the metallic rush.

He studied the piles of ingredients, the pots, bowls, boards and knives.

'Do you want me to make dumplings?'

The head chef snorted behind him. 'Yeah, just saunter in and make dumplings. Ha!'

'Our dumplings are made from a secret recipe,' Bian Shi said, ignoring the chef. Jinyi

130

looked about him at the nearest bowl of minced pork. A secret? What? Spring onions? Garlic, certainly. Salt, pepper. Chillies? Doubtful. He caught sight of the dough, laid out in sheets and ready to be whipped into furrowed clouds around the marble-sized balls of mince. The secret must be the flour, he reasoned. A bowl of it sat next to him, heaped and ready for kneading.

'Why not make something more simple for us? *Wotou,* perhaps?'

Peasant food. For months Jinyi had eaten *wotou* for breakfast, lunch and, on the few days which stretched to three meals, dinner. These buns made of cornflour and water, perhaps some potato starch as a binder, are steamed for twenty minutes — or less, depending on the urgency of hunger. They are tasteless, but filling. I have seen whole lives lived on this bland snack.

'OK.' Jinyi reached for the bowl of cornflour and dipped his hand in, letting the grain slide out between his fingers. His eyes searched the worktop for things to add. What would impress them? He heard the chef's heavy breath somewhere behind him, and knew that Bian Shi was watching his hands. As quickly as he could, and not daring to look up, he stole a handful from the russet-coloured bowl of dumpling flour and mixed it in with his own. He sank a cup into a nearby pan and pulled out enough tepid water to begin combining the mixture into a gummy yellow glue.

With one hand he dribbled the liquid in, a bit at a time, while his other swirled the dough around the bowl, his thumb the pivot stopping it from sticking at the centre. This was the key: halting the flow of water before the dough was quite bound, still loose enough to break apart if stretched. The steam would do the rest, he hoped. Was this an audition, a test? Would school have been like this? Or was it simply a ruse to waste time until troops arrived to arrest him? He wondered whether he would be allowed to eat the food when he was done, and his stomach made a sound like the revving engine of a car that will not start. He suddenly felt guilty about the packed streets of people with whom he should be sharing these strange and wasted treasures. Unconsciously he shaped the dough into little yurt-like buns, pushing his thumb halfway up through the centre of each flat underside. His hands worked without him, as though he was still stirring sugar or massaging scalps, as though he was drawing back time. He finished quicker than he could believe, and he placed the eight *wotou* on the middle rung of a circular wicker-floored turret, ready to be steamed.

'Now we just wait?' he asked.

She nodded and then sat down on a flour-specked stool. 'We're Chinese, aren't we?

That's what we do.'

'That's what we do,' the head chef echoed, as if it was a motto or mantra.

'How many have we had today?'

'Loads. But paying? Eight maybe. But it's still early.'

They talked of the minutiae of dishes, stocks, orders, staff and profits, about which the chef tried to prise concrete information from Bian Shi's vague answers. They were occasionally interrupted by calls from the pair of waiters who wandered in and out, perpetually red-faced and sweating from darting between the different floors. Yaba, tall and thin now, with badly cropped hair, was hunched earnestly over the sink. Bian Shi began to scratch the surface next to her with chalk.

Have you ever dreamed of being invisible? It is easy, Jinyi thought. Turn your eyes to the ground while others are speaking. Be thin in a land of skeletons; be hungry around a man and his meal. Be hunched among the straight backs of men with medals and insignia; be dry among the drunk. Be a country boy in the crowded streets of the city. This is how servants and waiters do their work — it is the unseen masses who knot the country together, the busy atoms rushing unseen between slow bodies. Jinyi knew too how to be seen: have a coin in your pocket amongst the starving; speak out amongst the lip-stitched and silent; celebrate amongst the almost dead.

Who are you? People didn't even bother to ask Jinyi this anymore. Who, he wondered, were these sour-faced people who surrounded him each day? They were faces, graves, bricks, empty pagodas abandoned by malnourished priests. Jinyi had passed handfuls of these crumbling sites of rushed prayer on his journeys. One day they would be torn down, and smog-thick tower blocks driven in where they once stood.

The *wotou* were done, springy and glistening with condensation. Jinyi arranged them on a plate and handed them to Bian Shi. She took a bite and nodded, neither smiling nor scowling. The head chef was more picky, prodding the dough and watching it slowly billow back into shape before sniffing at it, doglike and unimpressed, and passing it to the nearest kitchen hand. Jinyi waited, holding the plate and feeling foolish. He flinched every time footsteps passed the door.

'You can start work tomorrow,' she said, breaking the silence. 'Get yourself cleaned up before then. And if you even think about stealing anything again you'll have more than the chef to worry about.'

Bian Shi had a thing for strays. Perhaps it was because she had been abandoned in a strange home with a strange new owner.

Perhaps it was because she had never been able to summon up the guts to run away herself. Or perhaps it was simply because she needed a hobby.

Hou Jinyi was not the only young thief she had taken under her wing. In fact, her first trip to the restaurant had gone much the same way.

Buddhists see repetition as something to overcome, but also something to learn from. People are born and born again, and each life offers the chance to see differently, to attain Buddhahood and escape the cycle. The same events may repeat themselves a thousand times, with only the slightest of differences. This is what history means. This is why Bian Shi could not turn away a single hungry mouth.

It had happened when she was still a young bride in awe of the size of her new home. In her first year in Fushun, she had only left the big house twice. She was unsure of how to speak to the servants, and suspected that their smiles hid designs against her — the first night her husband had left her she had lain awake listening to them laughing about the rustic country clothes she had packed beneath the wedding bounty.

All that fateful day, fourteen years before she met Hou Jinyi, the baby had gurgled and danced in her belly. It hung like a barrage balloon above her slim hips; she had already decided that it would be a boy. (This was what would please her husband, so that was what must be.) Despite the effort of the walk ahead, the sweat collecting on the dark hairs that laddered her belly, and her tight, child-like shoes, she had decided to venture out into the town.

'Go to the market, we need fresh fish for the dinner. You, yes you, go and find out who the best midwife is in this city. The rest of you: the master expects the room in the eastern corner to be fully furnished for the new child by the end of the week.'

This was the first time she had addressed the servants directly instead of sneaking past them. She sent off these sudden orders standing awkwardly in the doorway, and slowly began to relish the theatrical authority, even though the tone she modelled on her own ancient and regal aunts seemed strange escaping her lips. She was a teahouse opera caricature, and she was enjoying herself for the first time in months. As more lies came to her she raised her canary-like voice and set the house ticking. Afterwards she grinned to herself, her palms damp and the muscles at the back of her thighs trembling like piano strings.

As soon as the servants were distractedly busy, she slunk from the house, holding the only souvenir from her first home that she had not allowed herself to be parted from: a dark red hand-woven bag. She moved like a wooden toy, rocking herself purposefully forwards, out towards one of the dumpling restaurants where her husband might be. The Bian family owned three restaurants in the city, many-levelled wooden eateries in which the rich dipped the hand-crafted pastries and dumplings into shallow china dishes of soy, vinegar and oil swimming with lipstick-red chillis. He might not be at any of them, she thought. After all, it had taken her only two weeks of tearful evenings to see that he was not the kind of man she had been told she would marry.

She moved between unhurried horses leading men back from the market, past the squat traders, their sunburnt and scraggy skin dark beneath the slanting shadows of their straw hats. The slate roof sloped out above the restaurant ahead of her, the two dog-faced stone lions grinning or growling (she could not tell which) either side of the flight of steps leading to the door. A waiter loomed between the Fu Lions at the entrance; his scrawny limbs and stubborn movements reminded her of the well-fed mosquitoes that twitched sluggishly in her room. She turned down a side street, looking for the kitchen entrance. In the alley two naked toddlers were chasing each other, and a dog barked at the baskets of chickens whose necks had not yet been wrung. They squawked jittery hymns in time with the choppingboard rhythms spilling from the open windows.

It was then that she felt a hand at the string of her bag, loosing the lasso from her shoulders then suddenly tugging. Instinctively her fingers snapped out tight and pulled it back. The shocked boy, already poised to dart backwards with his prize, let go and stumbled into a crate of recently delivered vegetables.

'What do you think you are doing?' she shouted at him, grabbing his offending arm.

The would-be thief was prepubescent, his skin pulled tight over his turned-up shoulders and narrow, bird-like face. Bian Shi guessed that he was about eleven or twelve. His dark eyes were oil sloshing on water, and he blinked furiously at every small movement.

'Well?' she shouted again, the bag swinging from her hands. Then, remembering that she no longer had to play that role, she bent closer to where he was standing. Something about the pull of the baby, like the rudder of a lost ship turning instinctively to land, made her bring her face close to his. He squinted, scrunched up his nose. They were inches apart. He continued to blink rapidly, as if his eyelids were the shutter of an unstoppable panoramic camera.

'Open your mouth,' she whispered. He obliged.

She had seen those kinds of children before. The hollow floor of the mouth scabby and almost black; the thin stump where the tongue had been severed was the colour of an over-ripe pomegranate, the stub of a plucked flower set above the throat's turning. She tried not to retch, and, seeing this, the little boy closed his mouth. By the time his eyes next met hers, she had made her decision.

Xiao Yaba, she would call him, 'little mute'; and this name would catch on, for he had no way to tell anyone another name. There were many more like him — silent Chinese Oliver Twists, orphans taken and raised by networks of petty thieves, their tongues cut out at an early age by their captors so that they would not report them to the authorities or warlords, and, of course, so that they would be bound to the thieves. Having no other recourse, they would follow orders and enter a world of unlocked doors and tiptoes, of snatched bags and bruises. His flitting eyes attested to the tiny backrooms in every city, to the fact that everything has its reverse.

He did his best to meet her stare. 'So. What do you want to do now?' she asked forcefully, his wrist held tightly in her fist. She loosened the grip, but he did not move. Instead he tilted his head and his lips curled into what might once have been mistaken for a smile. It was instantly obvious to her that he had not practised this expression in years. A sudden thought came to her and she looked around.

Apart from the toddlers and the poultry, the alley was deserted. This is how lives intersect, where instinct subsumes sense.

'Do you want to come with me?' she asked, still not letting go of his wrist.

He said nothing. She took this as a yes. She smiled and, although her motives were not entirely selfless, felt a rush, not to her head but to her rounded stomach.

Yaba noticed the dampness of her small hands prickling up against his own skin. And in that drawn-out moment he compared them to the grip of his street 'uncles', the tightness that had pressed down his struggling arms and bucking head, the fat fingers that stank of raw garlic and stale piss that had pinched his nostrils together, the rough hands that had yanked open his jaw as he had gulped and gulped — his mouth filled first with a rush of air and then with the copper-coin tang of his own blood.

'You can stay with me now. We can help each other. Do you understand?' He nodded quickly, and she was reminded of ducks bobbing for food.

'My name is Bian Shi.' The wife of Bian — her maiden names were left under a floorboard in her father's house. 'I live over there.' She pointed down the alley, toward the wider streets he had never ventured near. He looked about him for his 'uncles', not believing what was happening. Was this a trick?

140

'First things first. What can we do?' She looked about her, and for a moment Yaba thought her tone might shift again, and that she might haul him to a judge. He flinched, an involuntary habit. 'Now listen, I can't take you home with no job, no purpose. He'll only get mad — at the both of us. No name, no family, that's bad enough,' she said, as if to herself, moving her hand to the small of his back and pushing him forward through the alley towards the side-door of the restaurant. She looked at him and winked, although her heart was beating faster than ever.

Together they strode purposefully between the clutter of boxes and deliveries into the kitchen. The floor was littered with the debris of offcuts, cigarette ends, potato eyes, spilt slops, the bad ends of discoloured vegetables and the overlapping footprints of the bare-footed chefs, assistants and young boys rushing about in the cramped and sticky heat. Dumplings floated to the top of vast pans of steaming water, woks fizzled and meat dripped from hooks on the wall. The man who might be assumed to be the head chef, stocky and unshaved, was cursing and shouting at the cowering staff, though his hands never strayed from the delicate curls of pastry he was wrapping around small nubs of mince. When he saw a well-dressed pregnant woman and a grubby street kid standing in the corner he stopped shouting. The deafening thread of

141

noise quickly trickled to an awkward silence. Then he spoke.

'I think you're in the wrong place.' His words were calm and measured, but had a sharp, urgent edge to them.

'No, I've come to talk to you. Are you the head chef?' There were a few titters of laughter. The thump of her heart filled her stomach. The chef went back to folding the pastry, his thickly accented words swilling from his wet lips.

'This is a restaurant. I've a job to do, so you'd better send your complaints somewhere else.'

The jostle of the kitchen began again, with more plates clattering in the overcrowded sink. The diversion was evidently over. But she did not move.

'Listen,' her voice quivered up to the next octave. 'I've come to ask you to give this boy a job. Something simple is fine, washing dishes or chopping vegetables. He'll give you no trouble, I can assure you of that. Just keep an eye on him, teach him what to do and he'll pick up the rest.'

The chef wiped his hands on his dirt-streaked shirt. His face was blotchy and red. 'There are no jobs. Where do you think you are? Now, I'll ask you again — *please*,' he exaggerated this word, mimicking a simpering civil servant, 'get out of my kitchen.'

'Just a simple job. I'm sure there's something that needs to be done in here. It's a mess, and you all look busy.' She tried to laugh lightly at the end of her speech, but instantly regretted it.

'If I came into your house begging for a job, I'd probably get the shit kicked out of me and end up in some stinking jail. What makes you think you can charge in here and order me about? Huh? I told you: There are no jobs! Why don't you —'

'Now look —'

'No! You look.' His voice was raised now, and the staff turned their heads down, closer to their work. 'You stuck-up bitches are all the same. Don't you know there are a hundred other starving families down the street, all begging for jobs? What do you want me to do, house a spastic, a lazy brat or a retard just so you can eat your fucking twelve-course meal in peace? Why don't you go back to your poor bastard of a husband, if you even have one, and take that runt with you? Go on, get out of my kitchen!'

He spat the last of these words, his cheeks glowing like coals. There were a few more titters, though most of the staff knew better than to stay in close proximity of the chef when the snake-like vein on his forehead began to throb.

'My "poor bastard of a husband" is the owner of this restaurant,' she said, her hands folded over her bump, her teeth pressed

143

tightly together. There were no more laughs.

'Your husband?' the chef stuttered, not sure whether to believe her.

'You look as though you're busy, and, as it's nearly time for lunch, it seems he had better start right away. I trust you will treat him properly.'

She nodded to the boy, and he took a step forward, borrowing from her strength. The chef finally bowed his head and gestured to a chopping board beside the strung-up birds.

'Yaba, I will come back for you at eight.' She turned and walked out of the door.

Outside she leaned her swollen frame against the alley wall and let her pulse shudder down to her shoes, the sounds of strained and muted swear words reaching her from the window. She clenched and unclenched her fists, bit her lips and, finally, smiled. When she returned to the house she instructed the servants to clear out a small bedroom in the north wing, and she then placed in it some of the toys and gifts that had been prepared for her own child. By the time her husband crossed the hall that evening, dead-eyed and clutching the wooden supporting pillars to correct his loose and sprawling steps, she had a carefully constructed story prepared and did not stop speaking, despite his slurred interruptions, until it was finished. The mute, she told her husband, showing a strong will that he had never imagined she possessed, had been treated badly by street-thieves and deserved a second chance, a childhood. If they helped him, she argued, then the god of children would be better inclined to show favour to their own baby. She then marched off to bed before her husband had time to formulate a response.

It was Yaba who, after Yuying was born five and a half weeks later, first weighed the screaming baby in his skinny arms and comforted her wails by humming mountain songs. And it was Yaba who later took Hou Jinyi under his wing when, more than a decade later, history got round to repeating itself.

Yaba's tongue was not the first of its kind, and it will not be the last. There is a fine thread that links the act of speech and the act of violence. It is with these threads that people wind the fragile fabric of their lives. Take it from me — I have witnessed my fair share of arguments. Dissent, disagreement, confession, free speech, talkback. These are all tinged words, words that are seared onto flesh. Words that people take too lightly.

Consider Sima Qian, working into the evening. The first century BC was sprawling to its sunset, though no one yet had comprehension of this way of measuring time. Even two thousand years later, the Gregorian calendar would be seen as something indeter-

145

minably foreign and, furthermore, unnecessary, as it was still possible to measure spans
of years in terms of the length of the current
emperor's reign. Sima Qian had followed his
father to become the royal historian of the
Han court. The book he was working on,
knotting the characters from the bottom to
the top of the page before sliding down to
the next column, was the *Shiji,* the first history to take in the dynastic characters, policies and economics of the previous two
thousand years.

Sima Qian traced out the ideograms until
the light was too dim to continue. He could
hear nothing but the night birds swooping
through the woods that sloped out from the
bottom of the garden, and the tinny creak of
the old timber. He wrote of the man who unified the vast country from disparate warring
kingdoms, the first emperor, Qin Shi Huang.

If you had told him that millennia later,
even when all dynasties were over, a leader of
China would unashamedly ape this first
emperor's policy of burning books and
strictly regulating information with the threat
of state-sanctioned violence, Sima Qian
would probably have simply nodded sagely,
not in the least surprised. The policies and
propaganda of the party that had promised
to liberate China, and the personality cult
built up around the chubby Communist
chairman, would be all too familiar to Sima

146

Qian. Chinese leaders, emperors, generals, warlords, presidents or politburos must be the unmovable anchor on which the state is moored. They must be gods to men; what else is there to stem the chaos? The themes of Sima Qian's history — the cyclical ups and downs, destructions and renewals, separations and unifications — suggest that little of the last dark century would shock him.

He could not sleep; he returned to the table and folded his legs under him as he tapered a tiny lamp. He rubbed his hands together, warming the skin. 'Though bitter, good medicine cures illness,' he wrote. 'Though it may hurt, loyal criticism will have beneficial effects.' His wrist slowed, the writing stopped.

The day had receded from the house like a tide that draws away from the shore only to build towards its eventual return. Even the birds were silent, yet still he could not sleep. It was then that the emperor's guards arrived to collect him. His wife and his children were asleep. He went with the guards peacefully, without a struggle. He had been expecting them for weeks now, ever since he had made the mistake of interceding to the emperor on behalf of an old friend, a general, who had surrendered to the enemy in a skirmish in the distant plains outside the capital. Sima Qian should have known, however, that loyal criticism (especially in the form of defending another who has dared to disobey the will of the living god) often had a cost.

'We will try and do this as quickly as possible. Bite down on this.'

He bit down. It was a thick ribbon of leather, tasting of night sweat and saliva. The surgeon was old and careful, with fat, steady hands. Sima Qian was naked, held down. He tried not to scream and shake, tried to control the functions of his bladder and bowels. He failed. This was a punishment designed to lead the guilty to commit ritual suicide in shame. Yet Sima Qian did not do this. After the operation, he continued working on his epic history, his newly high voice barely heard, bandages knotting his scabby, darkened lap. The thread between speech and violence overhangs everything, like a network of tapped telephone wires above a city.

In the same city where Sima Qian was castrated, with only mountain herbs for anaesthetic, where he was mutilated and carried home for the smallest of crimes, the bleeding stemmed by the expert stitches of the royal surgeon, this same cycle of speech and violence would continue. What is it about words — is it that they contain the threat of offsetting the delicate balance on which whole worlds depend? Or that they are so easy to give out, but impossible to ever take back? Words and fear, speech and violence. That which persists wins. Or, as the historian might have posited: no one wins, everything persists.

The day after he had tried to steal *mantou*, Jinyi arrived at the restaurant an hour before it opened and loitered outside till the back door was unlatched. Bian Shi was there again, swaying between the chopping boards, commenting and questioning. It was only after she left, half an hour before the lunch rush, that the kitchen became more lively and animated. The head chef, however, soon silenced the staff with a gruff shout.

'You. Thief. Yes, you. Come here.'

Jinyi turned and slowly approached the chef. The whole kitchen had stopped working to watch.

'Now, you can consider yourself safe when the boss's wife is here. But yesterday you tried to steal from my kitchen. I don't take kindly to thieves. I want you to know that. However, I'm prepared to let you stay and work here. I'm generous, see. I guess that's my biggest weakness.' He grinned, pleased with himself, and some of the staff sniggered.

'I pride myself on keeping a good kitchen. If there's a mistake, it's me who gets a kick in the balls. Understand? So, if you're going to work here, I need to know that I can trust you.'

'You can trust me,' Jinyi replied, perhaps too quickly.

'Ha. If your mouth is as fast as your nimble fingers, then I think your word isn't going to be quite enough, country boy.'

'So what do you want me to do?'

'Well, if you're as hungry as you said you were yesterday, when you stood there looking like you were going to cry or wet your pants, then I figure we ought to give you something to fill your stomach.'

The head chef smirked and reached behind him. When he turned back round, Jinyi's eyes moved to his bear-like hands. Gripped between his fingers was a jam-jar filled with warm pig fat, used to grease the woks and flavour stocks. Grey lumps floated like jelly in the thick, slimy liquid.

'I'm not drinking that.'

'It doesn't look like you've got a choice, boy.'

Jinyi looked around at the many expectant eyes. The chef was right.

'OK.'

'Wait a minute. You're eager, aren't you? I bet this is a delicacy where you come from. Ha! Now, I wouldn't want to hurt one of my workers by scalding their mouth. I want you to be able to drink it all down without spilling a drop. So we're going to do you the courtesy of cooling it down for you, aren't we?' He addressed the rest of the workers in the kitchen. They murmured their agreement.

The head chef pulled off the wad of newspaper stopping the top, and brought the jar close to his face. He hocked, a rattling sound coming from the back of his throat, and spat a ball of watery green mucous into the jar of fat. He then passed it to the worker beside him, who did the same. The jar was passed from hand to hand, with each person in the kitchen's spit dribbling into the sloppy oil. Only Yaba refused, with a shake of the head. They let it be — after all, the mute lived in the same house as the boss. The head chef finally took it back, and, after reinserting the wad of paper, shook it gently, mixing the froth. He handed it to Jinyi.

'Cheers.'

No one said a word. Jinyi held the jar, trying not to look at it. It was lukewarm, and more than half full. He closed his eyes and tilted it back, opening his throat and trying to ignore the sticky lumps. He swallowed and swallowed and, even when the jar had been drained, had to keep swallowing for fear of retching it all back up. He let out a loud belch and the head chef nodded, and, as though nothing had happened, everyone resumed their work.

The *Tao Te Ching,* those huddled characters mapped out millennia ago with strokes of black ink across sheafs of silk, reveal an ebb and flow of unstoppable process, the unwinding of all things according to the natural way, the Tao. The beliefs behind it survive in the minutiae of everyday rituals and actions. The metaphor at the heart of the Taoist work, namely the intricate balancing act of yin and yang, suffuses all aspects of life. Jinyi had heard this before, but only now did it become a working mantra. Inside the black, a ball of white, and inside the white a matching black marble: nothing is absolute. Black and white, night and day, electron and neutron, field and sky, feminine and masculine, all hovering on invisible scales. Yin and yang.

Take cookery, for example. In the kitchen they measured always the balance between the *fan* and the *cai* — the filler (rice, grains, dumplings and steamed buns) and the taste (meat, fish and poultry, various roots and greens floating in sauces) — making sure neither dominated a meal. Salty, sweet, sour, bitter, hot. Jinyi commited the five elements of taste to memory, as again and again he rubbed garlic into the minced pork and cabbage, as again and again he was told to bind the masculine and feminine, the grain and the flavour.

Each one of them, from the brick-shouldered head chef to Yaba with his twitches and signals that everyone in the kitchen interpreted in a different way, through to Jinyi himself, stood by the stoves from morning till midnight, stealing only five minutes somewhere in the middle of the day

152

for a meal of stale buns or the blandest of day-old pancakes.

The best days in the kitchen were those when the patrons ordered more than they could hope to finish — the expatriate Japanese bankers and businessmen often made a habit of over-ordering to impress their dining guests. After all, no one wanted to lose face. On those days, plates came back from the tables still bearing a dribble of sauce, a handful of dumplings or thin shreds of picked-at leftovers.

And so Jinyi learnt to join the sudden bustle of the kitchen staff when the waiters returned with a stack of plates, to plunge into the fight of splintered chopsticks and unwashed hands for the dregs of someone's unfinished dish. In this way he tasted things he had only ever heard talk of before, things that had once seemed as unrelated to his own life as dragons or unicorns. Yellow fish pulled up from between the coal barges on the river, shreds of sweet and sour pork, forest-picked mushrooms dark with soy. Each time he was lucky enough to get more than a mouthful he avoided sipping water for the next few hours in order to preserve his tongue's memory of the strange and melancholy tastes. Even the ever-glowing fire impressed Jinyi; at his aunt and uncle's they had clumped together dry grass and dung to feed a five-minute flame, braising food as quickly as they could before the fuel fizzled down to embers.

Yangchen, who Jinyi thought must have been around his own age, despite his receding hair, obsession with money and an awkward way of shaking his head from side to side while working, spent those first weeks pestering Jinyi with questions.

'You wanna know something?'

'Huh?'

'That man upstairs right now with a curled moustache — I saw him when I was hauling the buckets in — you know what they call him? The Butcher. Wouldn't know it from that Western suit and the furs slung round the shoulders of those giggling girls on his arms, would you? And you know why they call him that? Because he's —'

'Cut it out,' the head chef barked.

'He's right, Yangchen,' a passing waiter joined in. 'If Mr Bian heard you talking about the customers like that, we'd all be out of work, and you know it.'

Yangchen shrugged, then lowered his voice so that only Jinyi, standing beside him, could hear. 'I've never even seen the venerable Mr Bian. Not once, the whole time I've been here. Doesn't stop me hearing about him every day, though. I shouldn't be surprised if there aren't some people in here who even pray to him. We ought to have an altar or something.' He grinned at his own joke.

Jinyi realised he had made the mistake of

responding neutrally where everyone else either shouted or ignored. Yangchen had mistaken his casual nods for interest.

'Did you ever see a car before? Great big black things, like midnight lions. I almost pissed myself first time I saw one. Well, did you?'

Wearily Jinyi nodded his head. 'Of course. I've been in cities for nearly ten years.'

'Yeah, but you've still got that country look about you.'

'What look?' Jinyi asked.

'As if you don't quite believe anything you see.'

'The country isn't that bad. But I'm not a country boy, you can see that.'

The head chef barked again. 'He's right, you've got that look. It's the way you study everything as if you don't know whether to try talking to it or eating it. That's the look.' The kitchen bubbled with laughter.

'Better than bald and hen-pecked,' Jinyi retorted, and more laughter came. The clock ticked that little bit faster.

Jinyi soon felt at home in Fushun; it was a new feeling for him, a strange new sense of suddenly being relaxed in his own skin. It was not, however, the stone floor he shared with seven others in a cramped room at night, balled up on a mothy animal skin listening to newborns whine and be comforted with

155

hushed lullabies, that made him feel this way, but the sweaty kitchen where he stood for eighteen-odd hours of his day. I can understand this: kitchens speak to the body in a language of warmth and comfort. The more time he spent by the searing heat of the stoves, the more Jinyi was able to forget his humiliating introduction and that first beating he had received from the head chef. The more he did his job and garnered small praise and acceptance, the more he put to the back of his mind ideas about moving on again. Everything is paid and earned with time, he thought to himself, and he even tried to share this new idea with the others. No one listened; why should they, when you have to learn these things for yourself?

'We're lucky,' Jinyi would find himself saying. The other staff would mock him for this tirelessly, but he found he did not care.

A kitchen, he reasoned, could be any country. The smells conjured up provinces, towns, houses, people, treats. The hiss of cabbage curling in the pan reminded him of playing outside the window with the dogs and other kids from across the fields; a face full of steam from the towers of dumplings transported him to the crimson flush of early summer. Our olfactory senses bring back little memories that haunt us with our inability to locate them; smells taunt us with associations. Jinyi even imagined his uncle and aunt's pale faces appearing in the dust-clouds of ground flour rising from the fistfuls of dough, and he let them stay, watching him as he made dumplings.

'It's an art form. Anyone will tell you that.'

'Really?' Jinyi was not sure whether Yangchen was joking with him. 'Like calligraphy?'

'Exactly the same. Everyone has their own style, and that's just as important as what they create.'

'You can write?'

'No, course not. I can read, though. Well, some words. Enough to get by. And you?'

'No.'

'No, I heard that no one writes in the country. If they saw ink there, they'd think it was grape wine and drink it.' Yangchen grinned, pleased with himself.

'I'd like to. I've seen people doing it. Doing it properly I mean, with the right paper and the ink. Like painting the veins on a leaf. I'm going to learn one day.'

'Sure. You're going to learn after work. Petition the Japs to let you into a university maybe? Sure.'

Jinyi turned from Yangchen, engrossing himself in the task. He did not like to be mocked, especially when he was confiding in someone.

Was it an art? He was not sure. There are hundreds of types of dumplings, and those served in the three Bian restaurants were renowned as the best in the city. At moments like those, as Jinyi folded the seams of the thin sheets of dough tight around the stuffing, his fingers pinching ridges in the top before scooping them into baskets, he would not have been able to believe that this skill, the secret of the Bian restaurant dynasty, would die with him. He would have shaken his head and told you that people always need to eat.

'You know what you ought to do? Join the Communists. No joke — my brother has already joined up and gone down south, to help root out the Japanese,' Yangchen said.

'Don't be an idiot,' Jinyi replied, growing annoyed. 'How's that going to help? Running down south while we're stuck in the middle of Manchuria seems a bit cowardly to me.'

'Suit yourself. But at least I'm thinking of things to do, not just ignoring everything.'

Jinyi shook his head and laughed. Give too much space to silly dreams about the future, he thought to himself, and you lose the present.

'Tonight?' It was a giddy whisper, delivered in a tone usually reserved for lewd gossip. The question buzzed around the kitchen; even the gangly waiters looked more twitchy than usual.

The kitchen was blanched with summer;

steam foamed to the ceiling then spread into damp clouds, while busy, sticky bodies jostled together beneath. The fire crackled as the vegetables were fried.

'As soon as the shift finishes?'

Yangchen sidled up to Jinyi. 'You coming?'

The head chef, however, had overheard. 'Don't you even think about it! Not him. We've got enough already.'

Yangchen opened his mouth to speak, but could not think of any way to respond. Yaba, however, stooping near the solitary window, suddenly brought his fist down against the stained wooden worktop. Then he turned to face the rest of them, and brought his fist down a second time before looking at Jinyi and giving a curt nod. Everyone had paused to watch him by then, but he did nothing more except turn back round to carry on with his chopping. The head chef sighed.

'OK. But if he causes any trouble, we'll swear we don't know him. Right?'

Jinyi kept his head down and waited, as ever doing his best not to inadvertently hack off his fingers as his mind slipped somewhere above his body, like oil shifting on water. After the last customers had finished and the waiters had been fed, the workers threw the last of the scummy bowls, knives, boards and chopsticks into an oblong trough to wait for water to be drawn in the morning, and assembled beside the door. Yaba squatted to noose his dog's cumbersome body to a table leg. There were five of them left: the head chef, Yaba, Yangchen, a middle-aged kitchen porter with a limp, and Jinyi.

'OK, this is what we're going to do. I'm going first, along the river and up over the main bridge. Qingsheng, you and Yangchen go round by the covered market, over the walkway. Yaba, you take the country boy and go behind the houses and cross by the second restaurant. When you get there, today it's three knocks, wait, then two knocks. Understand?'

And then they were going their own ways, Jinyi striding alongside Yaba, waiting till the others' footsteps dropped out of range to speak.

'So where are we going? I mean, should I drop out now? I don't want any trouble, Yaba, you know that.'

Yaba turned and beamed, patting Jinyi on the shoulder before increasing his speed. They had passed the market-stalls and street vendors facing the restaurant, and were now approaching rows of single-storey terraces, their faces darkened by the coal dust heavy in the breeze. They skirted around the terraces to a mass of ramshackle buildings, the paving stones giving way to hardened mud and gravel. Then they were in the midst of scavenged shacks, with makeshift roofs of rusted corrugated iron shared across a couple of dwellings. Broken restaurant tabletops had been set up as sliding doors, and bricks were stacked precariously without cement to bind them, the summer wind whistling through the gaps. Yaba placed his finger on his lips, then pointed to a tiny alley running between the rows of houses.

They had to move like crabs, side-stepping as they squeezed themselves down the tight shortcut, their torsos pressed against the dark bricks on one side and their backs grazed by the junk-shop clutter on the other. Jinyi felt Yaba's hand steady at his shoulder again, stopping them just before the end of the tight path, listening for the sound of gravel crunching beneath scuffed boots, the unmistakeable sound of the night patrols. Jinyi could hear nothing but Yaba's steady breathing, thick and nasal, and was suddenly glad he had not simply headed back to the cramped stone floor where he slept off the hot days.

They were careful to walk slowly, casually, past Old Bian's second restaurant and over the horseshoe bridge.

'Is it true, that you live in their house? The Bians', I mean?'

Yaba nodded, neither turning towards Jinyi nor deviating from their measured pace.

'Isn't it a bit strange?'

Yaba shrugged, and Jinyi thought he understood. Of course it is strange, the mute seemed to say with his shrug, but then so is

161

everything else. How should life be? Jinyi thought of his uncle's house, of Dongming's family, of the elderly barber, and of the damp stone den he shared with starving families that spent their time looking for scraps of work, rifling through bins in the dark or just trying to keep out of sight of the occupying forces. How easy it is, he thought as they crossed the bridge over the slow river, to let the smallest changes turn you into someone else. And at this Jinyi found himself itching his scalp, wondering whether the part of the city this side of the river was a reflection of the other, whether his right hand would become his left, whether his crooked side parting would creep across his head.

They stopped outside a boarded-up restaurant and knocked three times, paused, then knocked twice again on the loosely nailed slats of wood. An old man appeared, peering out from between the boards, then vanished. A few seconds later he was at their side, leading them around the building to a cellar door. As they descended, they met none of the waves of arctic weather they had come to expect from such stone caverns, and it was soon obvious why. Once the thick door was pressed closed and bolted behind them, they ducked under a stained blanket hung from the ceiling and were confronted by a low rumble of muted cheers and curses. The cellar was filled with men, each one squatting or doubled over like graceless swans beneath the arched ceiling.

Unlike the modest cellar beneath their own workplace, there were no cabbages stored for winter or bottles of liquor kept chilled for the type of men they dreamed of spitting on. Every few steps they passed different games. Spotting the others on the far side of the sweaty stretch, they began to work their way past the small crowds to the back of the cellar.

They stalked past lotteries played out with thin strips of white paper of varying lengths, past dominoes thrown down as if they were offerings to some angry deity. They stepped around collections of small trinkets piled under a teacup, the participants betting on what remainder would be left when the pile was divided four ways, and moved between furious games of hands where sticks beat tigers which ate chickens which ate worms which gnawed through sticks, and numerous games played with splintering wood-cut dice. Gambling was not yet completely illegal (as it would become when the Communist Party took over, leaving casinos only on the Portuguese-leased island of Macau), but it was increasingly frowned upon during the fledgling republic. No one was sure how the Japanese would react to these nocturnal gatherings, though they agreed that they were unlikely to be supportive without their pockets being significantly weighed down.

Yangchen and the head chef were squatting around a highly animated circle. Jinyi had to push past to be able to see inside the tiny ring, where two dark crickets were dancing towards each other, being encouraged to fight. A set of gourds and clay pots, two with their lids discarded, lined the outer borders of the circle.

'I guess this isn't a singing competition.'

Yangchen looked round and grinned.

'There you are. You know, they're vicious little things when they want to be. I'm betting on the lighter one, see: he's scuttling around his enemy — yes, that's it, my boy — waiting to attack.'

Cricket-fighting had been a popular pastime since the early Ming dynasty and the reign of the Xuande Emperor, also known as the Cricket Emperor, who favoured the sport so much that every year thousands of crickets would be given as tribute to the imperial family, and state decisions were often based upon the ferocity of buzzing forearms. Singing crickets, with their hoarse and jittery hymns, had been kept as pets in the Middle Kingdom for thousands of years, in bamboo cages beside beds, or weaving their way through scores of autumnal poems, their wings ablaze.

'There used to be cocks here too, of course. But they all got eaten long before the invasion. Who's got poultry to spare now?'

'Then it was snakes. But they got eaten too,' the head chef added to the conversation, and got a laugh from some of the group, though Jinyi doubted that this was a joke. As the crickets moved in, the small audience grew quiet, expectant.

Throughout the cellar men were swigging from outsized jam-jars half full of wilting tea leaves swaying like murky swamp fronds in the candle light. It was then that Jinyi noticed what was being played for. There was not a single coin to be seen, though this was of little surprise. Instead, Jinyi counted a catalogue of lost objects: apples, knives, painted chopsticks, slippers with badly patched heels, a stained set of wooden teeth, buttons and other things he could not quite define, thrown down with each bet. He felt around in his trouser pockets. He had a length of string and a comb with half of its teeth broken. Where to begin?

Shouts spilled from the circle and were quickly hushed. Yangchen's cricket had won — the other was sprawled on its back, buzzing like a malevolent lightbulb. Yaba had moved to a mat where coins and chips were being divided into four piles, predicting numbers with awkward contortions of his fingers. Jinyi started moving to join him, but the head chef placed a large hand on his back.

'Better not. It's bad manners to sit beside a man when he's playing. If he loses, he'll think that you brought him bad luck, and if he wins he'll think you're angling for a share of his winnings.'

'What's more, who knows what he'll tell them back in the big house,' Yangchen added.

Jinyi shook his head. 'He won't tell them anything, Yangchen, he can't speak.'

'Ha ha. You know what I mean. It's got to be different, sleeping up there and even eating with them sometimes, then spending the day with us. It's not right. Gives me the creeps.'

'That's not what you were saying last month, Yangchen.' A short man looked up from where the wicker pots were being prepared and the wagers measured out for the next fight. 'I remember you saying you'd give your right hand to be sleeping up in the big house.'

'Well, sure. But that was before my brother told me about the Communists. Anyway, I don't give a shit about the money — though it might be nice to be able to have something more than stale bread to bring back to my folks. No, I was talking about the three daughters. Back me up here, Qingsheng! I know you saw them too, when they came with the boss for that banquet last year, when we cordoned off the whole second floor, remember? You know exactly what I'm talking about.'

The middle-aged kitchen porter shook his

head. 'One wife is more than enough for me. You're better off just dreaming about them, trust me.'

'That's all he does. Watch them and dream. I've seen his eyes glaze over,' grinned the head chef. 'Dirty bastard.'

'Yeah, pick on me, just because I'm on a winning streak. But you've seen those breath-taking girls, you know what I'm talking about. They look like they're made of porcelain. The eldest one especially, with that round face and huge eyes. Li, you said they were the most beautiful in the city, didn't you?'

Li shrugged, but Jinyi was already intrigued. Not by the tone of the talk, veering between the playful, the smutty and the subtly spite-ful, but by mention of the girls. Since he started working in Fushun, the only women he had seen apart from Bian Shi were the backs of heads leaving the restaurant, be-draggled prostitutes in the aubergine glow of badly lit side-streets, and the tight-faced mothers straining to feed their screaming infants in the room where he slept.

'Now, I only saw their feet at the beginning of the banquet, because I had to keep the fire stoked as it was snowing and all. But I remember them clearly. Golden slippers. I swear it, they were wearing golden slippers!' Yangchen was talking conspiratorially, whis-pering to his colleagues while the other men fiddled with their pockets as the next round of bets were placed.

'That much is true. I haven't seen such well-dressed Han in years. They were wearing silks too, and their hair was slinking down in shiny plaits. Graceful, they were — not like the type of women we usually get in there, hanging off the arms of soldiers or bankers,' Qingsheng conceded.

'It felt like hours, waiting for their meal to end so I could see the rest of their bodies, especially with all you lot going on about how they looked and what you'd heard. And just from seeing the movements of those gold scales shimmering across the floorboards, I knew all the rumours were going to be true! Oh man, they were —'

Yangchen stuttered to a stop as he saw Yaba approaching. The kitchen workers turned and sank down to watch the next match, the insects let loose from the gourds and driving at each other with a brittle whirring noise, like the sound of lone bombers approaching across an empty sky. Soon the restless flitting of the crickets seemed to infect the gamblers, and they became irritable and argumentative; Jinyi slipped from the cellar with a few others early on, careful to close the heavy door on the sounds of the raised voices. Most of the men would spill straight from the cellar toward the dawn shift, not bothering to stop for sleep.

The summer breeze hit Jinyi's face as he

drifted towards the stone room to sleep on his thoughts, moving instinctively and leisurely, as if lifted on the soles of golden slippers.

Lord George Macartney sailed back from China disappointed. Trade was still not forthcoming — British merchants in China were forbidden to speak to the locals and were even barred from learning the language. Within twenty years of Macartney's failed mission, the British, with their growing taste for warm drinks, were carrying millions of pounds of tea back from the Guangzhou port each year. Yet they had nothing to counterbalance this one-way trade, except their prized silver bullion. This was obviously unacceptable to a nation of shipbuilders and mid-morning tea-breakers.

In stretches of sun-lashed fields in rural India, the English East India Company hit upon a solution to reset the scales: poppies. From the unripened plants the resin was extracted and dried, and the chestnut-coloured mass tied into British trading bags. By the 1830s, despite the Chinese ban on importing or cultivating opium, British merchants had reversed the flow of trade. British silver, as well as silver from the quickly depleting Chinese stocks, began to trickle back across the ocean. To halt the illegal trade that was crippling the Chinese economy, in

1838 government representatives stopped ships and ordered the handover of opium. They then dumped nine million Mexican silver dollars' worth of it into the sea. For days the waves lapping at the harbour bubbled and foamed and frothed. The British viewed this as an act of war.

The Opium Wars succeeded in showing the military supremacy of the foreign forces. During the Second Opium War, British forces burnt down the summer palace in Beijing and forced humiliating treaties, including the perpetual lease of Hong Kong and an area around the Kowloon peninsula, on the defeated Chinese. Perhaps more importantly, the trade in opium was legalised.

This was one of the many reasons why Old Bian was reclining upon a cushioned opium bed, privately witnessing the swaying silk curtains melt into rain-like threads of light. Years drifted by for him like this, in the pull of gentle tides. His fingers clutched at the air, and he was handed the long bamboo pipe by a lithe waiter hovering nearby. He had come from a drawn-out lunch with one of his mistresses, and, eyeing up the skinny young waiter, wondered if he had enough energy to manage it again.

His mistress's room had been a mess, but she had at least prepared a few dishes for them to eat, though he left these untouched. The place needed a decent clean. Didn't he pay for the room, and its upkeep? Was she worth it — forced to listen to her whine about her brat for a couple of hours just for a maudlin, tearful fuck? He decided not. There were plenty of others he could rely on. Anyway, the outer contours of her face were beginning to pinch into crow's feet, and he couldn't abide that.

Before Bian got the hit, pain slipping away and bliss prickling up behind his eyelids, he was restless. Sleeplessness, itchy skin, constipation. He took another drag. His worries dissipated. Someone was talking. He raised his eyes, and felt his body floating, glowing; he could feel it tingling in his pores.

The establishment in which he was lying was built around a long, snaking corridor; the doors to each of the spacious rooms remained closed while there were people walking between them, so that for all one knew, one's son or neighbour could be in an adjoining room. Furthermore, no one ever seemed to leave by the same door that they entered, though Bian was not sure whether this was for the same reason or not.

The ball was black and firm in his hands, like a slab of dark honeycomb in the dull afternoon light. Of course, he had nodded to the waiter, just put it on my tab.

Old Bian's list of colleagues, backroom associates and rivals was changing almost too fast for him to keep track. Many had been closed down by the occupation, reported covertly to the new authorities for some offence or another — a word in the right ear after a long dinner was all it took. Others had been dragged down by the cost of free meals for the new first-class citizens, conspicuous in their camouflage. Meanwhile, those who had not headed south in self-imposed exile with the Nationalists were trying to buy their way out of trouble. This did not always work. Every week, where the river narrowed, fishermen hauled up pale, bloated bodies stopping the flow. After stripping them of clothes, rings and sometimes teeth, they were thrown back. So what? Bian thought. Serves them right. Bian was now used to the sight of old aquantainces shaking with withdrawal, grown men worn down to sandy-skinned ghosts, pinching pennies and wearing the same clothes day in day out, packing off their old girlfriends and concubines to whore-houses or different cities where they would not be recognised. So what? There would always be people to do business with: Chinese, Japanese, British, French, Germans, Americans or even the Russians, despite their crazy ideas. He chuckled. How does one talk business with people like that? He now ignored his former associates when he passed them on the streets.

It was his grandfather, bald and stooped from his early twenties to his premature death, who had expanded the first famous restaurant until there were three of them etched like birthmarks upon the resilient flesh of the city. And there he was now, raising a limp arm to the waiter to place a reclining chair beside Bian's sprawling pile of cushions. No, Bian thought to himself, that cannot be right, he has been dead for almost fifty years. He rubbed his eyes and saw that the man beside him was neither his grandfather nor completely bald — at the base of his shiny crown a slender black tail knotted down the back of his neck. He was talking.

'Ah, Bian. My blessings to your family. I trust they are healthy and happy?'

'They are. And yours?'

'They are wonderful. The Jade Emperor has watched over us both, has he not?' The two men acted as though the world was the same as it had always been, as though there was no invasion, no war, no famine, no poverty and no death. They both felt they must maintain that nothing had changed, or else they themselves would begin to disappear, to fade into the past.

'Business,' and here the pony-tailed man took a drag from his own pipe, letting the sentence hang in the air with the fine tendrils of smoke, 'is good? Well, I have no doubt of it. Xiang, I hear, is doing terribly. Pity.'

'It would be terribly vulgar to dwell on work —'

'Of course.'

'But the restaurants are in good hands.'

'Of course.'

'And I have no doubt that you are doing well. It is an auspicious year for expansion, or so they say.' Bian let his eyelids sink closer together as he spoke. He could not quite place who this man was.

'Of course, I quite agree, it would be vulgar to talk of it. Though, as you know . . .' But the words were already moving beyond Bian, merging with the buzzing of insects, the irritant rustling of wings rubbing together. He closed his eyes and let them carry him away. It was only when the room had sunk into silence that Bian realised he was expected to respond.

'Let the heavens be thanked for prosperity,' Bian said.

The man with the pony-tail nodded. He was pleased.

'Your daughters have nearly finished their schooling?' he asked with a hint of a grin.

Bian knew what was coming but could find no way to skirt around the required etiquette, the subtle sparring and dropping of hints. So this is what he wants, Bian thought. A match with my daughter. Bian reached for the pipe, trying to appear relaxed and congenial, though he was tempted to ignore the man and hope he got the hint and went away. He had emplyed this tactic many times, and it usually worked, with people eventually mov-

174

ing off as he stared unflinchingly toward the window. As long as the pipe was near. He calculated quickly and, though he still could not place the man's name, surmised that it would be foolish to risk offending him. He may yet, in some way, prove useful.

Bian sighed. 'They crave learning more than jewellery.'

'And why not? An educated woman makes for an enlightened mother, one who can bring up strong, intelligent sons.'

'If only it were that simple. She has plans for college.' They both knew who he was talking about — Yuying, the eldest daughter, fourteen and a half: marriagable age. It would have been disastrous to think of marrying another daughter before the eldest. That would be shameful. Bian saved the worst from his interrogator: that his daughter wished to continue to study Japanese.

'Ah, but when she is married, she will have more important things to focus her efforts on.'

'Of course, of course, she would not neglect her womanly duties.' Bian was anxious to end the conversation.

'My son, you know —'

'Will become a great man. I have no doubt of that. I have heard enough people praise him to know that he will equal his father.' Bian was used to making such false compliments; he had no memory of the young man he was talking of, but at least the pony-tailed man next to him was now smiling and bowing his head in false modesty.

'And I too have heard of the many suitors you have turned away from your daughter. Are we to be next?'

'No, of course not. However, she wishes to study in college.'

'But be sensible. These are the whims of women: they change every day. Today it is college, tomorrow it will be new shoes, a dress; the day after, a pet, a child. And so it goes.'

'If only.'

'I am beginning to believe that you do not want her to be married. You would rather keep your daughters close to you, your family within your home. It is not easy to give up a daughter. But she will get a new life. That is the way of the world. Think on it.'

The unknown man got up and moved wobblingly away from the bed of cushions, his pony-tail swishing behind him. Bian drew from his pipe and coughed up the harsh, scratchy smoke; it was run down, almost out. He finished it and closed his eyes. He hated these encounters, the false smiles and rules of mutual deception. Though perhaps the other man was right — of all the intermediaries that had come to argue the case of rich and renowned young men from the stateliest families in the city, none had impressed him enough to offer up a limb of his family. Once a girl leaves, she cannot return. Or if she does, it will be as a wife, as a mother, as someone else — not the daughter he had studied silently for over a decade. Grandchildren, well that would be fine, but what would they be — Lis, Xues, Wangs? What about Bian? Who will keep this name alive? Into his mind came the faces of the carved ancestors in the main hall of his home, their faces knotting and contorting with the flow of the auburn cedar's grain. (I have met each one in their time, and trust me, they were a hard bunch to please.)

The afternoon shadow conquered the chequers of the tiled floor, and Bian smoked and counted how many weeks it had been since he last slept with his wife.

He took another puff and let his thoughts roam to the brothel two streets down, and the girls there that he had catalogued according to their flaws: the buck-toothed adolescent, the pockmarked matron, the russet-haired twenty-something with the child-bearing paunch. He did not care about the pretty girls, the well-dressed madams who shyly slipped from silk to lie with the patrons on rustling cushions. He could find those types anywhere. What he wanted was the sight of veins, the smell of sour breath and the sound of grunting noises; the bristle of dark hairs on legs or underarms, maps of moles drawn across damp thighs, and all the other parts they no longer bothered to hide. There was an honesty in this that he denied himself in all other aspects of his life.

Why not take a concubine, like us, many of his associates had asked. Bian had nothing but contempt for them — groups of women sharing the master's secrets with each other and discussing him behind his back; what could be worse? It was safer this way, cheap rooms rented on different sides of the city, a jigsaw not quite pieced together. Creeping from bed to bed in your own home cannot be respectable, he thought to himself. And, despite the bad examples of his own urges (which, he told himself, it was too late to remedy), his daughters should learn that a woman need not disappear into the unfathomable depth of a man's shadow. It was often his daughters' faces that persisted between the dreams, and not those of the many sons — boys that, though they lacked his family name, had inherited his ravine jawline, chicken-thin legs and rice-bowl forehead — playing in the alleys he often sneaked past. How many secret children did he have? He was not sure. He kept pieces of fruit in his pockets to hand out when they ran up to him, so that he did not have to speak to them. He took another drag and tried to shake himself free of these thoughts.

In the eyes of his peers he was too reserved,

too unpredictable. All that money, but no concubines! And now daughters who showed no sign of leaving the family home! Bian knew all the things that were said about him. Furthermore, although he feigned ignorance, he knew that his wife now played a large part in his business empire (after all, someone must — and he had never had a head for figures, profit margins, stock-taking or staff issues). Shameful, people whispered. In an age when women were still treated like slaves in many rich households, and new wives were often known to commit suicide in the cold, harsh rooms of patriarchal houses, the sight of his only wife hobbling alone from the restaurant, rocking along on her dainty curled feet, was enough to get the last of the powerful families talking. Yet such was Bian's influence that few ever dared spread these simple truths in public.

Here are the things Bian had been offered (discreetly, of course, by the matchmakers sent scurrying to his house to sound him out) for his daughter:

Four donkeys and a mule (the latter past its best);
a diamond the size of a sucked-dry plum stone;
a pair of marble Fu Lions to guard his home;
a river of yellow Suzhou silk (the colour

previously reserved for emperors);

rice and wheat fields that stretched beyond the city's borders;

a Ming-dynasty carving of a demon, which he had eyed covetously in a rival's restaurant;

the several necklaces and rings that had previously belonged to the wife of a recently executed warlord and which had just happened to have found their way into a suitor's hands;

sprays of silver;

animal skins, tanned and beaten into clothes, rugs and wall-hangings;

a Qing-dynasty hand-carved dining table and stately chairs, replete with phoenix motifs;

storerooms full of different teas: fur-tip, melon-seed, oolong and jasmine.

It remains easy, even in the twenty-first century, to buy a wife. Everyone needs sons and heirs, especially when there is work to be done. And with the population snowballing in favour of men, there are distant villages, indeed whole rural towns, without enough women to go around. There is money to be made. And though they do not come willingly, they continue to arrive, these trafficked women forcibly migrated to places without even the most barren of broken roads to carry them back home.

Even the dead cannot begin their twilight journeys beyond the city's backstreets alone. Families in rural areas go to great lengths to secure the corpses of unwed girls to bury alongside the bodies of their sons; and if they cannot be bought, bodies are sometimes stolen. The unmarried, you see, only constitute half a life. If no corpse can be found, one made of straw will have to suffice. Perhaps in the streets of the dead these straw women will gaze upon their husbands and speak. What might they say? You can buy whole universes and hide them in places no one else will think to look. There are places you have not yet been that are more vivid in your memory than those you have left behind.

The coals were burning down to blackened embers in the grate, and the keening wind blew the window open. Bian listened to the far-off screech of truck tyres as the troops loaded and unloaded at designated outposts. He had decided what he would do. He distrusted the look of the matchmakers, all those sly, crooked smirks and winks and hints and pattings of pockets. Perhaps he thought of Pu Yi, installed as a puppet emperor in Manchuria to give an air of legitimacy to the Japanese rule, or perhaps he thought of his family name, the single arched character that had hung above the Bian restaurants for almost a hundred years. Perhaps he thought only of his daughter. But he now had a plan, and the heirs of the most important men in the city were unnecessary. He would find her a husband himself. Why give up a daughter when you can gain a son? All he needed to do was find a suitable candidate, someone who would follow orders, and it would be as simple as all his other subtle manipulations, the transactions he conducted daily with the most languorous of fixed smiles.

However, this was not the kind of magic trick he would have wanted me to reveal the workings of: his business deals, like his other more casual intimacies, were always conducted behind closed doors.

The next time I saw the Jade Emperor was when I was up in heaven, running errands petitioned for in backroom prayers. He was among the dragons and eight immortals, but as soon as he saw me he descended from his throne and beckoned me to a garden that sprouted out beneath our feet — within a few minutes I found myself beside a still stream, and I stood awkwardly as the emperor settled himself on a seat of humming stones.

'I thought I would see how it is going,' he said, smiling up at me. 'What have you learnt about the human heart so far, I wonder?'

'Well, Your Excellency, I know that the heart beats a hundred thousand times a day, that without it life stutters out and stops . . . that it is a four-roomed muscle which squeezes and contracts to pump blood through the body . . .'

'Yes, yes,' he said impatiently. 'It is the engine of a journey: life flows from heart to artery to capillary to vein and back to the heart. You will perhaps come to understand that everything is bound into this cycle. There is neither end nor beginning to this motion, though it may admit variation, or the eventual inevitable entropy of certain components. Take time itself, or the fiction humans refer to as history. There is only the circle. There is war, then peace, then new wars; the division of the country, then its unification, then the carving up of its borders; liberating heroes who become tyrants, then new heroes who rise up to topple them and establish new regimes; stagnation, then revolution, then conservatism; birth, then death, then rebirth.'

'Or perhaps it is that everything changes constantly, except the way we see it,' I ventured.

'No one sees the world but me,' the Jade Emperor declared emphatically. 'Everyone else simply interprets it. Alas, I regret that I have other business to attend to. Tell me, at least, how your research is progressing. A blackbird whispered to me that you had picked a man to follow purely by sticking a pin in a map.'

I shrugged. 'Your spy is correct. Well, how else could I pick from billions? At least I can now call it fate instead of preference. And my work is going very well, thank you — you ought to be getting nervous! For example, I have already found that no heart works alone: it take two hearts to make a story.'

'Yes, the yin and the yang knotted together, each incomprehensible without reference to the other. Not bad. You are beginning to understand something of the heart. But can you explain it?

After all, it is one thing to recognise something and quite another to explain how it works.' His dark moustache twitched into a grin. 'You will fail.'

'You underestimate me,' I replied. 'I do this every spring, and I have never yet failed to find you a story. I collect lives, the little secrets spilling out in kitchens and whispered about by drunken men or middle-aged women. You may hold infinity in your grasp, but I have at least learnt what makes people tick. Plus, I know where the heart lives: between thought and action.'

As I spoke, the stream before me dwindled to cobwebs, the humming rocks shrunk to swirling grains in dusty floorboards and I was back in a kitchen on earth; though somehow I sensed that the Jade Emperor was still grinning.

185

4:
1947
THE YEAR OF THE PIG

They had been travelling for two weeks, slowly trudging south as autumn drew down to its deepest earthen browns. Jinyi's battered, second-hand plimsolls were already falling apart and his oily black hair stuck to his forehead. Two bags of knotted cloth were suspended from either side of a slim rung of bamboo fed across his shoulders, and his slack arms were slung over the top. Yuying's stomach retained some of the extra padding from her recent pregnancy, and their six-month-old son, Wawa, occasionally wriggled and squirmed in the sling she wore across her chest. The baby babbled and his thick black eyebrows — his father's eyebrows, great dark caterpillars that were already bushy and fully formed when he was delivered — danced over his chubby face. Yuying hummed to him as they walked, and Wawa lay grinning, trying to clench his tiny fists around the folds of his blanket.

They had been married almost a year and a

half. Jinyi was twenty-two and finally going back to the place his ancestors were buried; Yuying was almost eighteen and had no choice but to follow her husband. Her red cloth slippers squelched through scatterings of leaves, mulch, murky water and, once every few days, stray bullet shells.

Even I was out of my element accompanying them into that immeasurable stretch of fields and thickets, without a kitchen in sight. Old Bian's trusty coachman had dropped them at the outskirts of the city, saying he could go no further, not while the civil war was still raging, unless he wanted to get shot or be forced to join up — he had not been sure which option was worse. So the young couple stayed close to dirt roads to keep their bearings, though they never walked directly on them for fear of passing soldiers. Neither did they dare wander too far into the woods and ranges that dipped and drove around them.

Towns and cities were not safe. Most villages' allegiances were to the Communists and, therefore, they were often happy to bed travelling strangers as long as they were neither Japanese, Kuomintang, Russians, feudalists, landlords nor traitors. At the start of the walk, Jinyi had tried to teach his wife how to act more like a peasant.

'It'll make things easier that way, just in case we meet any Communists who mistake you for an absconding landlord or something. Talk with your mouth closed. As if each word kind of got stuck in your throat. As if you've got a mouth full of broken teeth. And try your best not to use your nose when you talk.'

Yuying had pursed her lips together and mumbled incomprehensibly.

'Well, of course you have to open your lips a little, but that's a good start. And try not to walk so tall. Remember, you don't want to be looked at. So slouch a little. Good. There you go! And head looking at the floor, remember, as though your feet are the most fascinating things you have ever come across. That's right. And hug your body in a bit closer with your hands, like you're protecting it in case someone should try and steal it any second.'

He had stood back and observed her, standing awkwardly with her pale hands folded across the baby, her shoulders hunched up and her head thrust forward, peering down at the ground. She had looked like a myopic turtle. When Jinyi burst out laughing, Yuying's smile had vanished back into the neutral face she had been taught to use to hide her emotions. Wawa had no such reserve, however, and mirrored his father, giggling with his eyes squeezed shut and thumping his arms against his sides.

They walked on down a dirt track veering through patches of ragged trees, overgrown fields and slopes of slate and rubble, and though her common sense told her that they were moving forward, covering more and more ground, Yuying could not help but feel that they were only travelling in unending circles.

'Today go to Yue but arrive yesterday,' Yuying muttered to Wawa.

She was quoting a paradox written by Hui Shi, an early practioner of linguistic logic games. Don't get me started on those thinkers from the School of Names; they really tie my head in knots. But what Hui Shi's paradox seems to suggest is the fact that the world is only observable through the curved lens of the eye. Both time and space are subjective concepts, kept constant only by the observer. Any objective measuring of these is impossible, for who can step outside their position as viewer and see the world from another viewpoint? That is the work of the imagination, the work that makes people human. There are no differences between yesterday and today, now and then, except for the experience and cataloguing of them. All of which made Yuying and Jinyi's month-long journey more and more tedious.

Jinyi tried to stay good-humoured, though things had not gone as planned. However, he had given his word, and he would stick by it. All he had wanted was a family, and giving up his name seemed a small price to pay for getting everything he had ever longed for.

'How much further can it possibly be?' Yuying said.

'A couple of days. I think. Just try and relax, all right? I'm doing my best.'

'Shouldn't we find somewhere to sleep before it gets dark?' Yuying asked.

'We've got all afternoon yet. We could learn from Wawa here — he couldn't care less about where he falls asleep. Anyway, we'll come to a village soon. Don't you know any old folk tales? The heroes always find shelter and hope right at the last minute. Didn't I tell you I was going to look after us?' Jinyi said.

'Yes, I remember, I was just —'

'Well, trust me. This isn't the city any more. There are different ways of doing things out here. It's too late to turn back now, anyway.'

'I never said I wanted to turn back, Jinyi. I trust you. It's just Wawa is tired, and —'

'I know, I know. Look, don't worry, all right? I promised I'd look after you, and that's exactly what I'm going to do.'

There was a long silence. Neither of them was sure that he was being entirely honest. Yuying wanted to believe that he was just trying to save his family from the bombs and shootings that had filled the city, yet she couldn't help but wonder if he only wanted to take control — after all, despite the awkwardness of the first months of the arranged marriage, she had still been saddened to see this nervous young man hovering sulkily in undisturbed corners of the mansion. Jinyi wanted to believe that he was only trying to take his new family to the place where his ancestors' bones lay to bring a blessing on their new life together, yet he knew deep down that he had to escape the stuffiness of his new home before it suffocated him.

'It's funny,' he started again, to fill the quiet between them. 'Everything looks a little different when you come at it from another side. Did you know, there are trees that uproot at night and rearrange their positions so as to confuse travellers?'

'Really?' she asked sceptically.

'For sure. I came across some on my way up north. And ravenous birds which have stolen human voices and use them to call people from the tracks so that they can tear strips from your flesh for food. I didn't meet any of them though, thank the gods.'

'You must have been protected by something.'

'Maybe I was.'

'When you left home, did you think you'd come back?'

'No. Well, maybe — deep down. I always thought that I might return when I'd found what I was looking for.'

'And what was it you were looking for?' Yuying asked.

'A reason.'

'Is this the way you came when you were travelling up to us?' she asked.

'No.' Jinyi struggled forward. For most of the journey so far, he had not dared to look back because he was afraid of seeing his wife's face either pleading or worn-out. He worried that if he did so his heart would force him to give up and turn around. So he kept on until he found something to say. 'But I do know where we are. Roughly. So don't worry.'

'It's beautiful round here, isn't it? The light, I mean. And the quiet. Did you ever learn that poem, by Liu Zongyuan? We had to learn it at school. You know, the one about an empty village?'

Again he struggled on, and did not answer. He did not know the poem, and did not want to remind her that he never went to school. Was this place beautiful? It was barren and wet, with a mist descending from trailing peaks in the distance. Jinyi's fingers were numb, and all three of their stomachs were grumbling.

'It's called "Travelling through an Empty Village",' she said, and began to recite the words she had learned by rote years before:

The snaking dew smudges the grass with ice as the path slopes beneath my steps. I clear bridges over streams streaked with tawny leaves, and not a single person left living here. Flowers flare up between the weaving stream: my plans forgotten, the only thing I hear is the clatter and crunch of my restless stride scattering the startled, darting deer.

And as she spoke, Yuying was suddenly struck by the similarities between the travels of the Tang-dynasty poet she had learnt about in school and their own journey. She remembered the teacher telling them that Liu Zongyuan's career as a mandarin had been cut short, soon after the turn of the ninth century, when he was exiled from court after falling out of favour with the Xianzong Emperor (who, the teacher recounted with a certain relish, was allegedly later murdered by one of his own eunuchs inside the palace walls). The poet had travelled down from the imperial sheen of the north to the sparse and unyielding expanse of the southern provinces. As father, mother and baby made their way further from her hometown, Yuying felt a kinship with the classical poet who had been forced to leave his old life behind. But if the world seemed suddenly immeasurable, wild, and unpredictable to her, then it also seemed to shrink; save for each other, they were alone.

And the exiled poet too, thinking he was leaving his whole life behind when he gave up his well-loved routines and pursuits, had searched through the feral beauty of the endless country plots only to find himself once more, stripped down to bones, heart, tongue.

They had spent the first year of their marriage trying to work out what to say to each other, pinching themselves to make sure that this was really their life now. They had blushed and blustered. Yuying mistook Jinyi's uncertainty of how to behave in the mansion as dissatisfaction, and spent months trying to work out what it was that a wife was supposed to do to make a husband relax — both in the long silences when they sat together in the evening, listening to the sound of gunfire in distant streets, and when the lamps were put out and they drew close for warmth. In the first few months of their marriage they had been tentative, stealing touches beneath the blankets, holding each other and nervously waiting, neither one wanting to be the first to move. Aside from gossip and jokes, they knew little of what was expected. And in the damp heat of those last moments before sleep, lying intertwined after fumbled, awkward sex, Yuying would ask Jinyi who he was, and hug him close to check whether he was real. And he would hold her tighter back, in answer.

Life in the big house had not been as he had expected. The couple had been seconded in a crumbling corner of the building, left to listen to the mouse-like scurrying of the servants between the rooms. What's more, he had been blanked by his former friends in the restaurant. After work, he had found, for the first time in his life, that thanks to the servants he had nothing that needed doing — he had spent his time cracking his knuckles while his wife shared jokes with her sisters, who came knocking throughout the evening. Yet most of all it was the bustle and noise of the house that had seemed strange to him, so unlike the huddled field-houses where the days were punctuated only by the colic howls of the dogs, where people went weeks without speaking to each other. He and Yaba had met in the garden whenever possible, smoking the few cigarettes they had managed to club together, trying to ignore the servants who were also trying to ignore them.

Though the war with the Japanese had ended, the city had still been filled with soldiers. He remembered how, in the months straight after the troops disappeared, half of the city had been sick with constipation, heartburn or diarrhoea, their stomachs grown unaccustomed to the rice, meats and fish that they were suddenly allowed to eat again. First it had been the Russians, and then the Communists: scores of dirty-shirted peasant soldiers staking out the buildings the Japanese had deserted.

Yuying had grown despondent in Fushun. Her college had closed down because of the civil war: students were fighting in the halls, and the classrooms had been turned into makeshift barracks for the ragged army of craggy-faced fieldmen and teenagers who had not yet started shaving. Those same troops had stolen her books and burnt them to stay warm: studying Japanese didn't seem like such a good idea anymore. At least the Japanese had brought order; after they had left, life only seemed to become more dangerous, with cars being overturned in the street, the sound of gunfire slipping through blocked-out windows and the bodies of deserters (identified by a single swirl of mangled red where the right eye should be) found lying in side-streets and alleys. She had spent most of her time in her room, knitting things for the baby.

And then the baby came. Hours of sweating and moaning and cursing everyone in sight, and suddenly a slimy wrinkled pink thing handed to her as she lay back in the bed. As she took her crying son in her arms she also began to cry. The two of them were still crying when Jinyi was allowed in and, despite the speech he had spent weeks preparing he too began to cry. And so it was that the small creature with his mother's round face and his father's dark eyes and wild eyebrows bound them together; suddenly they had something in common that transcended the big house and the differences in their backgrounds, and they celebrated each gurgle, each laugh and each burp as though they were little miracles which only the two of them fully understood.

The baby's horoscope had been drawn up by an elderly man, as fat as the Buddha, with as many chins as he had fingers. He wrote painstakingly slowly, as if drawing a line too quickly might invite disaster upon the infant's entire life. After every pristine brush-stroke he would stare up into the distance, shaking his formidable jowls before he let the brush once more travel from the ink pot to the scroll. Perhaps this was a professional trick, perhaps an unconscious tic or eccentricity. From the dates and stars he culled for them a life. He had asked for the exact minute of the birth as noted from Old Bian's antique grandfather clock, then named the child's zodiac animals. Wawa would be quick-tempered, honest, and with great strength and resolve, his anxious parents were told. The new parents nodded eagerly and before the elderly astrologer had even finished speaking they were finding proof of his words in the way Wawa gurgled and blinked at them and flailed his podgy arms up and down against his sides.

Not even the sleepless nights could stop their proud smiles and endless amazement at the chubby child who had appeared, as if by magic, in the middle of their lives — that is, until the day the roofs fell through the three houses at the other end of the street. And then Jinyi was home, the restaurant closed and taken over as a temporary barracks and canteen, and all that was left were the rumours of what would happen to the people living in big houses if the peasant army won. The civil war was fought bitterly in the north, the Kuomintang forever launching counter-offensives against the Communists who, buoyed by a rural army trained in guerilla tactics, had no trouble taking over the whole region, and, once installed, did not plan to leave.

The look on Old Bian's face had been unreadable when Jinyi had told him he was taking Yuying and Wawa back to his uncle and aunt's, but it was clear that it was a development neither of them had been expecting.

Yuying caught sight of a thin curl of smoke rising above the trees and nudged her husband, desperate to be seen to be of some use. They made towards it and passed through the sloping line of firs, skidding and gripping each others' wrists for support as they wound down between the knotted trunks, a dense tangle of branches blotting out all but a few lithe slivers of light. It took them an hour to descend little more than half a *li,* clutching the wailing baby tight. When they cleared the mass of trees, they saw the house. Backed up by a couple of vegetable fields, it was made of earth and stone, padded together with dry straw, the roof a cross-stitch of thatch. A small fire was burning in front of the porch, slowly heating a battered pail of water. Squatting beside the fire and feeding it twigs and leaves was a small girl, who Yuying guessed was about nine years old. The ash blew onto her bare legs so they looked like stone.

'Hey there. You need a hand?' Jinyi asked, his wife quickly slipping behind him. The girl looked up to take them in, then went back to teasing the fire.

They stood awkwardly in front of her until an old man appeared from behind the building, wandering toward the fire. He too stared at the strangers.

'Long journey?'

They nodded.

'Of course. We see a lot passing through. Have you eaten?' They shook their heads and he turned toward the house.

'We were wondering if we might be able to stay for the night. Just one night. In your stable, say. Anything would be fine. We've got a little money, not much, but —'

The old man turned back. 'Put it away. I don't need your money! You can stay a night — we've got some space in the storeroom where you and your young one can rest. You're not the first. Come on then.'

The girl whispered to them as they passed.

199

'Granny's a witch.' Her voice was deep for her age, a slow, wispy burr.

The old man laughed as they walked away. 'Don't pay too much attention to that. She's not a witch, my aunt. But she can see the future. Here we are. Well, after you.'

They wandered into the darkness and shed their bags in the stockpiled straw.

'Thank you for your kindness and hospitality, noble uncle —' Jinyi began.

'Forget it,' the old man broke in. 'You can help me find firewood.'

'And me?' Yuying was not eager to keep the baby too long in the stuffy storeroom, which smelt of straw and of the manure used to patch up parts of the crumbling walls. The old man looked her over.

'Kitchen. My son's wife will be needing some help.'

And with that he strode out again with Jinyi following close behind him, heading back toward the small clump of firs from which Yuying thought they had come — it was hard to be sure, as trees crowded the house on all sides, stalking ever closer.

It was not difficult to find the kitchen. A wicker cradle was suspended from a ceiling rafter, and in it gently swung a red-faced baby, curling its fists into balls as it slept. Another child, perhaps two or three, skirted round a young woman's knee, pulling at her long, grubby dress. The mother was, Yuying quickly calculated, at least three or four years younger than herself. She smiled a toothy smile and approached Yuying and Wawa, ignoring the boy clinging to her calf.

'He's a handsome one, isn't he?' she said.

'You think? He looks like his father, though don't tell him I said that,' Yuying smiled.

'Put him in with mine, they can rest together.'

Yuying reluctantly passed her tightly swaddled bundle to the woman, who laid Wawa alongside her own sleeping baby. It woke and gurgled at the intruder, but with the other child swinging the wicker bed, both babies soon closed their eyes.

'Can you skin the rabbit?'

'Er, I . . . I'm . . . well . . . how?'

'I'll show you.' She beckoned Yuying to the table, where a rabbit was splayed out, a sack of bones pressed into furry flesh, ears pulled back above its frozen-open eyes. Yuying stared at the faint gash stretched beneath its plump neck.

'You're from the city, right?' The girl grinned.

'I suppose so, yes,' Yuying said.

'Hmm. Never been, myself.'

'Well, it's just like here but with more people, really,' Yuying lied.

'Oh. I see. I always thought city people would be taller. So how old is your little boy?'

Yuying opened her mouth, and then closed

it again. Of all the things she thought the young mother might comment upon — the damp and mud-stained bottom of her navy blue dress, her loose bun of nest-like hair or her once perfectly maintained fingernails, now shabby from two weeks' growth and dirt — it was only the child that interested her: the rest was not worth speaking of.

'Nearly thirty weeks. His name is Bian Fanxing, but we call him Wawa. He's a cheeky little monkey already. I can't bear to think about how naughty he's going to be by the time he starts walking.'

'Ha! Enjoy it while you can still keep track of him. One minute they're all giggles and cuddles, and the next they're running rings round you.'

'You've got two children?'

'For now. Look, first you've got to make a cut, down here by the feet.'

'Of course. How did they catch it?'

The young mother looked at Yuying as if this was the most ridiculous question she had ever heard. 'I'm sure I don't know. Best to hold it by the ankles, like this, then drag it down. I'll start, and then you can take over. Just watch.'

Yuying watched the rabbit's bloody skin slowly slip from its tangle of muscle. The young mother finished it herself, then passed an old, wooden-handled knife to Yuying to chop it for the stew. Between their tasks they each tried to chat, haltingly, about how they falsely imagined the other's life to be. Yuying was unsure how much time had passed since she and Jinyi had arrived: she desperately wanted to be able to wash and change her clothes, but she did not dare to ask. She did not want her host to think her spoilt or unprepared to work. In this way the afternoon faded down to darkness, and Jinyi and the old man reappeared with armfuls of freshly chopped tinder.

They soon gathered around a small table in the next room. A woman so lined with wrinkles her skin resembled the bark of an ancient oak soon entered and felt her way to her seat at the table. She was completely blind, but the rest of the family sat waiting silently for her, not daring to ask if she needed help. Her nephew, the old man, sat beside her. Then there was his son, Wei (whose young wife remained in the kitchen, nursing both her own child and their guests' while eating her meal straight from the pot), and finally the ash-sprinkled nine-year-old. Jinyi found himself sitting next to the old woman whose skin, on closer inspection, seemed to have been folded from reels of the starchy crepe paper used to wrap around cheap holiday lanterns.

'So you two are the travellers?' The old woman turned in the general direction of Jinyi and Yuying.

'Hopefully not for long. We're going to my family home, not far from here,' Jinyi answered.

'You should never forget your family young man.' She reached out and touched his arm. 'Or else you too might be forgotten.'

'Of course, you are very wise, old auntie,' Jinyi said through gritted teeth.

She grinned. 'Oh, don't take me too seriously! I'm just an old blind woman. I'm sure you're a good son.'

There was an awkward silence, which Yuying nervously filled with the only thing she could think of. 'If you're blind, auntie, then how do you see the future?'

The old woman laughed. 'Young lady, you don't know anything if you don't know that you should never ask that! I bet this young imp here told you I was a witch, didn't she? Ha! Pass me some more *mantou*.' She trailed the dough through the soup before stuffing it into her mouth. The juices spilling down her chin, she talked as she chewed.

'I listen to the calls in the forest, the shudder of the walls at night. I'm sure you've noticed them too. Seasons, patterns; I feel them. Just listen to the world, and it will tell you what's coming. What are you two, a tiger and a dog? I can tell from the sound of your voices. Not been married long, am I right? You're young, but you're not children anymore. Anyone can see the future, if they just look.' And here she laughed again, a deep squawk that rattled the chopsticks set beside the wonky clay bowls.

'Tomorrow,' the old woman added, 'has already happened. There is nothing new, just the wind murmuring to the trees at night, the sun and storms and draughts and harvests, all gnawing through to your bones.'

'All right, old auntie,' Jinyi said. 'What is next for us, then?'

'You'll go back where you came from, of course. Everyone always does . . . Time for bed, I think.' With that the old woman pushed herself up from the table and, despite the fact that everyone else was barely halfway through their meal, walked away, her hands trailing against the walls as she guided herself towards her bed in the next room.

After eating, the young mother came in and collected the empty bowls. The pair of candles were blown out, and Yuying retrieved Wawa from the kitchen where he was giggling at the older baby kicking its feet in the crib beside him. She carried him back to the storeroom in the peculiarly dense rural darkness to which both their eyes were slowly becoming accustomed.

They set Wawa in the wicker crib they had carried from Fushun, and once they had sung enough lullabies to let his eyelids begin to flutter heavily, Jinyi and Yuying huddled together beneath the sheet that tied their

205

belongings, still dressed and too tired to talk, although neither of them could sleep. The sound of animals scuttling over wet leaves carried miles in the vast pastoral quiet, creeping through the rafters, across the loft, and into their faltering dreams.

Before she had left the city with her husband and baby, Yuying had sat cross-legged together with her sisters on the marriage bed in her room, the baby set in the middle of the straw mattress, where it always slept, indented between jittery bodies.

'Is this a joke? Does he want you to wear trousers and learn to walk swinging your huge bottom from side to side like a bumpkin?' Chunlan had asked her elder sister.

'I think it's romantic. He's just trying to look after you, isn't he? Like a prince taking you to some distant castle. Not that he has a castle, but it will be a change. Who wouldn't want to be rescued?'

'Oh, shut up Chunxiang!' Chunlan had said. 'It's not romantic. It's ridiculous. What's the point of studying for all these years just to become a washerwoman, with loose flesh jiggling from your arms as you mop a stinky floor! All I can say is, it's lucky Ma didn't have our feet bound — you wouldn't be able to walk a hundred *li* like that!'

'Come on Chunlan, don't be like this,'

Yuying had admonished her. 'What would you do? It's not safe here, especially for a baby. Look at him. His eyes scrunch up and he kicks his feet every time there's an explosion or a gun-shot. We've already lost one servant in the rubble out there. I think it's brave of Jinyi. It's noble. He's only doing it for us. And when the civil war is finished, we'll come home and everything will be back to normal.'

'He's doing it because he's scared of Daddy. I've never seen the two of them stay long in the same room together. You don't think that's odd?'

'But what about the wedding, wasn't that Pa's idea?' Chunxiang had asked.

'It doesn't matter whose idea it was: we're married now, and nothing is going to change that. So you'll just have to get used to me being gone. Come on Chunlan, what's the matter? You'll be getting married after the Spring Festival, and things are bound to change anyway. So give us a chance.'

Chunlan had not smiled. She had yet to find out where she would be sent for the wedding and which family she would join, perhaps a journey of several days away from her home and her childhood. For once, she had held her tongue — not daring to voice her opinion that everything was different for Yuying, the favourite, and that she was throwing everything away just to please her husband. Ladies do not say these types of things, she had thought to herself. They are silent, stoic, supportive.

'At least you don't have to study at home!' Chunxiang had whined. 'I swear, I know more than mad old widow Zhang. It should be me getting paid to teach her! I have to sit through her ramblings four times a week. And some of Peipei's interruptions — I can't make head nor tail of them. Between the two of them they'd have me believe that a woman lived in the moon, that the Chinese invented everything and that all the things they didn't invent should be ignored!'

They giggled. Life had been different since the schools closed. Going somewhere new had to be better than sitting at home all day in the ever more crowded house.

'You can come and visit anyway. The baby will miss you both,' Yuying had said, and they had hugged, each sister aware that this would not happen.

Outside, as a flaky cigarette was passed between callused fingers, a similar conversation had taken place.

'What else can I do? I can hardly run to somewhere new. And now the restaurant has been closed down, I don't know what to do with myself. I need to be useful. It's either stay here and hope we don't get caught in crossfire, or go back and hang my head. I'd rather be humble than have my family shot full of holes.'

Yaba had nodded sagely, and passed him back the cigarette. Jinyi had spoken slowly and hesitantly, unsure of himself and unaccustomed to being the main contributor to a conversation.

'Thanks. I have a history back there: my parent's house, their land. I'm losing all that here, shedding it like snake skin. I've already been forced to give up my name and my dignity. But I can still pass some of it on to my son. I can show him his ancestor stones, and teach him how to survive on his own skills, to live with the land. All he'll learn here is how to dodge men with guns and juggle ideologies. That's not what anyone wants.'

Yaba had nodded again, rubbing his hands together for warmth.

'Yeah, all right, so maybe I'm thinking about myself a little bit too.' Jinyi had said, leaning closer. 'Sometimes I feel like I'm standing in really big shoes, or like my features are blotted out by the huge shadows cast here. I want Yuying to see my — no, our — family as it should be. Not borrowed from anyone. Just us and the baby. I want to be the head of my own family. Surely that's not too much to ask?'

Jinyi had paused, still clutching the cigarette he had yet to bring to his lips.

'I know, I'm being stupid. But look at us. You know what people say. "Country boys, hired hands." "They've sold their souls." People in this house might not think it, but you know others do. "They don't belong there, up at the big house." You've heard it too, though you might have pretended not to. Especially since Yangchen joined the Commies. And if you can't change other people's minds, how are you going to change your own? That kind of work takes years — rituals, every day, like prayer or piety or anything else you have to do in the gaze of gods — you force yourself to do it until you really believe it, until you don't have to force yourself anymore.'

Yaba had shaken his head, putting a hand on Jinyi's shoulder.

'You know, when I was young, when I was travelling or sleeping on dirty floors and stealing food if I could, all I could think about was having a family. Not to look after me. But so that I'd have something to care about, something that made me feel I belonged. Now I've got Yuying, and we've got Wawa to think about. The only thing that matters now is the three of us, and I don't care if I have to take them to the other end of the earth to keep them safe, I'd still do it. This might be my only chance.'

Yuying had taken days deciding what to bring with her on the trip; she must impress her in-laws. She had settled on two pairs of shoes

— one bright red, the other deep blue — four
long silk dresses slit up to the thigh at the
side, a pair of thick cotton longjohns, a lambs-
wool scarf and two hand-embroidered shawls.
Then there were the gifts she had to take.
Jinyi had tried to stay out of the room while
the packing took place. He waited in the hall,
where Old Bian and Bian Shi took turns
pressing banknotes into his reluctant hands,
telling him that they were for the child. How
could he say no? After all, they all knew what
he earned. Dressed in the same warm patched
jacket he had worn for five years, Jinyi found
his body bulked up by the tightly balled wads
of cash bulging from his four front pockets.

Yaba had shaken Jinyi's hand for almost a
minute, and bowed low before Yuying. He
then kissed Wawa just above the baby's bushy
eyebrows, just as he had kissed the child's
mother seventeen years before. The hair in
the mole on Yaba's neck stretched out between them, a solitary shrivelled whisker link-
ing the child to the past.

This was the image Jinyi and Yuying carried
away with them of the world they left behind:
a tall, silent man almost in tears while the
rest of the household stood emotionlessly at
the door, seeing them off. Her father had
been inside somewhere; her mother had her
hands on her hips, her eyes half closed; her
two sisters yawned through what seemed to
them the longest of drawn-out farewells; and

Peipei, the nurse, waved earnestly as she pushed to the front of the gathering group of servants eager to steal a five-minute break.

However, after this the couple's thoughts diverged: at night, lying together with the little crib between them, there were other images that poured into their minds. Jinyi's were of food, of hands slapping dough and tugging out noodles from sheets of flour. Yuying's were of dragons on silk jackets, silk dresses and Japanese textbooks, of the last minutes of light and the baby's face squeezed up into a smile or a yawn. And in those seconds, before wakefulness trailed out like the last lines of smoke from a snuffed-out candle, their legs twitched, kicked, then slumped.

The next morning Wawa woke them with coughs and cried, and Jinyi scooped him from the crib and held him tight against his chest as the first light of dawn spilled between the slats in the rickety old barn.

'Brave little thing, aren't you?'

'Maybe he wants to go home,' Yuying said as the baby looked between the two faces staring down at him and began to gurgle and grin.

'He is going home. He's just eager to get going, isn't that right?'

As if in answer to his father, Wawa thumped his arms up and down, as though everything was decided.

They splashed water onto their faces from the rain-filled trough behind the house, thanked the family, and started off again, their bags padded down with steamed corn bread that they felt guilty for accepting. They continued steadily, quietly counting off scores of two-house villages as if they were lost hands of a card game played solely to kill time.

The great river followed them through the counties, past hills, forests, fields, paddies, forests, valleys, hills and fields; at times they could not work out which part was reflection and which was real. It was possible to believe that each was simply a reflection of the other, and that even they themselves existed only in their mirror image; that for all their blistered feet and cramps and stitches, somehow, parted from their usual surroundings, they were no longer real. The dirt tracks they followed were scars mapped across the flesh of the province, while the shrubs and hunchback cedars, the gingko trees and the litter of needles, the dead grass clumped across the path, all were scabs grown over the uneven ground.

Following Jinyi and Yuying on their travels, I was reminded of another journey made by pimple-speckled young men and women over a decade earlier. After brief periods of coexistence, the Kuomintang, led by Chang Kai-shek, had begun a series of purges in an attempt to destroy the Communists. By 1933, around half a million Kuomintang surrounded the city of Jiangxi, one of the last strongholds of the Communists, aiming to stop the vital flow of trade and force them to surrender in a war of attrition. At the end of the next year, the weakened and starving Communist forces, sick of the humiliating failure of their attempts to attack the surrounding army, had little choice but to mount a full-scale retreat towards Hunan, leaving Jiangxi to the sieges of the Kuomintang. That was the beginning of what became known as the Long March.

And because they could not take bodies with them, instead of leaving them lying in fields, they slid their friends beneath the water, then waded through themselves, as the corpses bobbed downstream. The water stopped at the tops of their stomachs, their chests, and they were thankful for that. Time to pick up pace. They too avoided the roads, ploughing instead through forgotten villages where there was no difference between electricity and magic, for both were the stuff of legends. Coughing fits, gangrene, exhaustion, trench-foot, babies abandoned in fields (their cries would give the troops away), landmines, dodgy amputations carried out by people with little to no medical training, shrapnel, barbed-wire gashes, traitors turning in the soldiers for a pocketful of change, flu, measles, heart attacks, heatstroke, leeches, fleas, worms, pneumonia, malaria, frostbite, diarrhoea, dehydration and too many other dangers to mention. This was the red army: bloody, battered and unrepentant.

From October 1934 to October 1935 they retreated across the country, always moving west and north. They were walking backwards into the future: a few ragged mules, single-file on mountain tracks, and men with type-writers and bone-bending munitions balanced on their backs.

That is where knowledge receded into the plains. They might have been tempted to believe that history had ended, that each day was a repetition of the one before, with one crucial difference: each day fewer and fewer of them made it to the camps, barns, caves, forests or safe havens before darkness distorted their line of vision and drew in their borders. Trees transformed into soldiers at night, their branches machetes, guns, the glinting edge of a bayonet. They avoided lighting fires, and instead lined themselves close for warmth, lain out top-to-toe like the dead, limb pressed close to clammy limb, shivering through the sleepless nights.

Against all odds, they picked up more peas-ants as they went — these men would later say that they joined because of firm belief in the Communist ideal, though historians have argued over how many were actually kidnapped, blackmailed or lured by female officers with offers of sex that never materialised. They bit their tongues through nettle patches. Some of them did not even know why they were fleeing. It was not only the Kuomintang, but the Communists themselves, under Mao's direction, who carried out purges of their number. Who, they must have wondered, could they trust? Their throats were raw just from breathing in. Tens of thousands deserted, and disappeared from history.

Then, in 1935, they changed tactics. They broke up into smaller units which were harder to find, and moved in twisting, unpredictable patterns, like the flick of a dragon's tail. Towards Shaanxi, to regroup with other troops and begin the war afresh.

Fourteen years later, at the end of the civil war, their fortunes had swung full circle, and it was then the Kuomintang who were forced to beat a lightning retreat to Taiwan, laying fields of mines and setting fire to prison camps with prisoners still inside as they went (incidentally, taking all of China's gold reserves with them).

And if it does not seem possible to see between the myths, the heroes, the propaganda, the hindsight and the tall tales, then do not panic: this is the way the house of history is built, and you are already locked inside. The door has no key, and what you thought windows are simply finely drawn pictures, blurred from the touch of too many fingers.

'So what are we going to do?' Yuying tried not to let her voice betray her tiredness.

They had stopped, as high as the trail took them around a series of hills that rubbed together like hunched shoulders in a crowded train carriage. Above them, cranes soared towards the distance. The last village, where they had spent a night amid hooded ploughs and ox tethers in a barnyard loft, was almost eight hours behind them. She will know it, Jinyi thought to himself; even if I only think of giving up, she will know it. She will be able to sense my confusion. Ahead they could see nothing but the thinning of the mountain range and perhaps, if they squinted, the glint of the river they had been using to locate themselves.

Jinyi thought for a moment as the two of them leaned together, catching their breath. 'We'll have to find somewhere to camp down for the night.'

She looked at him. 'There's no other choice?'

'Don't worry. We'll find somewhere sheltered, soon, before it gets dark, then find some wood and start a fire. Should be fine. We've still got enough food in the bags for a picnic. We'll get a bit of water from one of

217

these mountain streams, and boil it up on the fire. It'll be good for us.'

Wawa coughed up a mouthful of sick, thought about wailing but decided against it, and instead nuzzled into his mother's damp clothes.

As the trail started down again the grass was darker, stunted and foot-worn where it wound between the chalk and stone. Yuying walked behind Jinyi, one hand on his shoulder, the other clutching the baby knotted in a sash against her chest. The sun hung above them like a vulture on the watch for carrion.

When she was a girl, Yuying had occasionally been allowed to accompany her father on little business trips. It was brief phase and could not have lasted more than a year, and yet it seemed to swell and fill the memory of her childhood. She had spent afternoons sitting at restaurant tables, waiters competing to entertain her with small magic tricks and flattering fortune-telling while her father discussed things she did not care about with other middle-aged men. Each time they left a restaurant, her father would set her before one of the twin Fu Lions which guarded the entrances, stopping her each time she tried to reach for the rattling stone globe trapped between the beast's stone teeth. 'Listen,' he would whisper conspiratorially, 'I share the lion's eyes'. And she would look between them and note the similarity of the huge dark irises. 'So, even if you can't see me, I will always be able to see you,' her father would continue. 'If you can see a Fu Lion, then I am never far away, so you will never need to feel scared.' Yet there were no Fu Lions on the hilly passes or within the forests, Yuying thought as they continued walking; only wailing wolves and jittery bats.

'We'll be there soon,' Jinyi said, trying to sound upbeat. He made a point never to ask how she was feeling, and never to tell how he really was. In this way he hoped to save up their strength, to harden them. Though really it made no difference: when she was tense or exhausted he felt it throughout his whole body.

'What is it we're looking for? A cave?'

'Could be,' he said.

'Are you teasing me, Jinyi? Don't you know?'

'Not yet.' He had said it. Though since neither had the energy left to argue, they laughed — what began as a self-conscious giggle grew into a shared belly laugh, unstoppable and absurd.

'You have no idea where we're going!'

'The baby knows. Ask him, he'll tell you.' Jinyi turned around and grinned, and though she tried her best to keep her expression fixed and serious, Yuying soon started smiling too.

They found a ring of well-dressed trees overhanging a dip in the rocks and, below a rig of wiry bramble, a stretch of grass. They squeezed themselves down into the covered patch, and became invisible from any soldiers or bandits passing on the trail, protected by the bulky shade of the sinewy firs and the fencing of the sharp brambles. Jinyi set down the bags along with twigs and branches he had collected along the way. He spilt these into a ragged circle, and prepared to rub them into fire. Yuying pulled out blankets and some spare clothes, to arrange as bedding and padding for the three of them. Wawa lay on his stomach, chirping as he bunched the folds of the clothes around him.

They drew as close to the flames as they could without getting mouthfuls of smoke and ash. The twigs began to burn down quickly, and Jinyi aimed a longer stick to hook out the bubbling tin of water set in the little fire's hollow centre, as though he were luring a twitching fish up from a line. They had stale corn bread and what was left of a string of dried mushrooms, long-stalked and squat-topped, shriveled and rubbery, wrapped in blotted newspaper from a village supper two days back. They tore these up and shared them. Yuying heated up a jar of thick, pale rice stock, which she slopped into a thimble-sized cup for the baby, as she was no longer strong enough to produce any milk for him. He feeds on mountains instead, they told each other, and sucks moisture from the clouds.

'It will make him strong enough to fight demons, to wrestle meteors. Nothing wrong with rice stock. More than I had,' Jinyi said, tearing a long mushroom from the string. Yuying nodded pensively.

He sighed. 'Women worry too much.'

'And men not enough.'

He laughed. 'You're right. I'm not worried. Don't you remember what I told you on our wedding night? I will look after us.'

'I remember that when you said it your knees and feet were shaking beneath your clothes, despite the warmth.'

'That doesn't mean it wasn't true.'

'Nor did it mean that I didn't believe you.'

'Oh.' He considered another hardened chunk before stuffing it into his mouth. 'And now?'

'I don't have to believe you anymore, I'm beside you.'

'But believe me anyway. He will be our little emperor.'

'Because his father is a dragon?'

'Because his father is here.' It is nearness, Jinyi thought, that binds lives. Not words, nor touch, nor money — just knowing someone is near.

As the fire started to flitter down and the baby settled noisily in the covered crib, they curled up, resisting everything but each other.

Their sex was sweaty, silent, quick. In the half-light of red embers in which they drifted to sleep, they did not notice that the baby was unusually quiet. But when stray comets of dew began to blink across the grass, he coughed and howled, and they woke, their lungs aching as though birds were trying to fly free of their chests.

By noon the river was in sight again. It was ugly and wide, and unavoidable.

It grew as they got closer, the scuffed path stopping at the slippery banks. The water was silty, as thick as coffee, and almost as dark. 'It looks like the type of lumpy noodle that apprentices always make on their first attempt,' Jinyi said to his tired wife.

A dirt road started up again on the other side, thirty-odd metres away. A group of men loitered on the opposite bank, sitting on the arms of a scruffy seat like unwashed, ragged kings.

'Is this the way to Pig Snout Village?' Jinyi hollered across.

'Of course,' they shouted back.

'Then where's the bridge?'

At this they moved, getting up and feigning a bewildered search. There were five of them, clasping hands over foreheads, looking up and down the river in shock and searching frantically beneath the seat. Before long, this small pantomime descended into giggles.

'It must have been blown apart by the armies passing through,' Jinyi said to Yuying. He had no idea which army, nor which 'tactical' retreat, would have taken apart this bridge, though they both knew that the practice was common enough.

'So what do we do?' she said.

'Well, it doesn't look too deep, so . . .'

'No! No way. There has to be another bridge somewhere, or . . . or a thin stretch with stepping stones, or, or something.'

Jinyi shook his head. The men on the other side had stopped play-acting, and started waving instead.

'Hey! Hey! You really want to go over?'

'Sure,' Jinyi called back.

'You're in luck. It's pretty cheap.'

'How much?'

They haggled about the price in raw shouts over the flow, the numbers bouncing off the bare rocks on either side. Yuying looked at her husband, knowing full well that he had no idea what they were agreeing a price for. But they still had some money left from her parents, and she wanted to find a bed instead of a bundle of crunching leaves to lie on that night. She hugged Wawa tighter, and the men agreed upon a figure.

At this the five men started arguing amongst themselves, until four of them picked up their seat by its four corner-poles. It turned out to be a hastily constructed sedan chair, with a poorly knitted cover. They hoisted it over their shoulders then unceremoniously scrambled down the bank. In the centre of the river the heaving water darkened the top pockets of their ragged jackets, but they strode forward regardless. The empty chair, held as if it bore an invisible emperor, appeared to glide above their heads. They gradually began to rise, their wind-licked hair bobbing like upturned ducks' tails, their rust-coloured teeth sharpening into focus.

When they had finally hauled themselves up the other side of the bank, they dropped the chair at Yuying's feet, and stood panting, their ribs billowing in and out beneath their soaking clothes. She sank down into it, Wawa still clutched to her chest, blinking in the cold. Jinyi held out a bag. She raised her eyebrows but didn't protest when he set it on her lap. He thought better of trying to give her the other one as well, and lugged it back up over his shoulders. Then she was hoisted up above their heads, and the grubby group descended to the water.

The river slinked towards the distance, a coiling tail with flinty scales shimmering in the loose shifts of light. Rivers are controlled by the spirit dragon, which also has power over the rain. When the dragon is angry, rivers flood. Jinyi stumbled, sinking deeper, and his knees quickened. He walked as if gravity had been forgotten and the world was suddenly heavier. The dragon-god purred, its currents driving faster past the fields. The water sloshed up to Jinyi's chest, pulling to his left, and he held on tightly to his bag to stop it being tugged away by the tow.

Yuying juddered above his head, in the hard square of straining shoulders. Her round face peered out, somewhere between nervous and stubborn. Jinyi silently dared her to look down at him as they slowly crossed, but her eyes remained fixed on the steep and muddy tracks of the banks at the other side. The chair overtook him, and he struggled to find his footing, to push on with the bag held ever higher against the flow.

It was as the four men were rising on the bank that Jinyi slipped completely, and ducked under. His head rose quickly, spitting out sour water as the heavy bag trawled behind him. He gripped it with both hands, and his eyes opened to a burning blur; he could just about make out a furious, shoving movement on the banks. The one idle man had already dived into the water, and the other four turned and dropped the sedan chair, letting it thump and slip back toward the water. Yuying screamed and called out for help, echoed by the baby's shriller imitations, as the chair slid backwards, skidding down the wet soil, tilting back until a pole caught and suspended them in the mud. The water licked at her ankles and pulled at the trails of her skirts as she felt the pole begin to shudder; it would only be seconds before the river claimed them both from the almost-overturned chair and swept them away. Yet the five men had forgotten her, and were already sloshing through the water towards Jinyi, elbowing and punching each other out of the way.

Jinyi tried to shout — Don't be idiots, forget me, help my wife and my son! — but then he looked around. It was not him they were coming for.

The pockets on the front of his waterlogged jacket had burst open, and paper money was swimming out from him in all directions, as hard to grasp as handfuls of oil. The last bits of cash that Old Bian had given to Jinyi were now bobbing off with the current. Their were so many banknotes floating out on the surface of the river that if I had still been mortal, you can bet that I'd have been scrabbling around in the water too. The five men were pushing back through the flow, and suddenly Jinyi was surrounded.

He pushed his head up higher as the splashes of the men whipped up around him, trying to keep his wife in sight. While keeping the wailing baby held close to her chest, Yuying was attempting to struggle up from the abandoned sedan chair as it slipped backwards. She couldn't manage it. Each time she put out a foot she skidded in the streams of mud building up around her. He had to get to her.

Yet for a second something stopped him. He reached out a single arm, not daring to let go of the bag. Heaving himself forward he grabbed one, two, three banknotes, but soon there were twelve scrabbling hands sifting angrily through the water and clawing for the cash. He flung out his elbow, smacking one of them in the back of the head and sending him reeling backwards into the water. His grabbing hands latched onto another note, then another. Jinyi tried to think of what some of his friends had said in support of the Communists — that they would do away with money altogether, that money would become meaningless, unnecessary, because if everyone worked together then everyone would have everything they needed. They were fools, he decided, as he thrust his hand out once again.

Then her scream caught him. It snapped him back and he realised it was he who was the fool. Though the men were still splashing around for the last of the cash, Jinyi made a choice; he bit his tongue, grunted, and pushed past them, towards his family. There was nothing else he could do.

Jinyi put his arms around her and hauled her up to the top of the bank, where the pair of them slumped onto the waterlogged bag. Wawa stopped crying, kicked his feet, and stared up at the two soaked adults peering down at him. He smiled. They could still hear the men in the river fighting over the last of the banknotes.

'I know!' was all Jinyi said. There were a few seconds before the inevitable.

'What are we going to do now? What about the money?'

In place of an answer Jinyi picked up the two bags and started along the track, resisting the urge to turn back and kick the abandoned sedan chair into the river. Yuying had no choice but to follow, her cheeks welling up red as their feet sloshed through the colourless patches of grass and over the stone. In the river behind them, limbs still flailed and splashed.

They squelched away along the track, damp and angry. Wawa began to cry again. Yuying had to summon every last reserve of will power to prevent herself demanding to be taken back home, right now. The sun began to simmer down lower in the sky, and her temper bubbled and hissed like a pan of oil left unattended on a hot stove.

'I can't believe —' she began.

'Don't, Yuying. Just don't. All right?'

'But how are we going to —'

'Don't do this, I'm begging you.'

'I mean, what on earth —'

'Stop!' Jinyi dropped the soggy bags at his feet and spun around to face his wife. His face was red and blotchy, his clothes dripping. 'What do you want me to do? Go back and wrestle every bloody note from their hands? I'm sorry. Is that what you want? Does that make it all better?'

No, it did not. They both seethed in silence. She wanted to stamp her feet and summon a carriage to go back home. But there were no carriages. There weren't even any donkeys. Just the dull grey track and her wet husband and her bawling baby.

'Look, the money's gone, so let's try and leave it in the past. We'll be at a village soon, I'm sure of it. Let's just keep walking.'

Yuying nodded, and her husband picked up the bags. She wanted to ask why it was she who had to leave her hopes behind while they went in search of the past. Yet, even though they had only been walking a few weeks, she was beginning to understand the pull that home has on the soul, and the infuriating way that the things you promised to escape from snag in your mind.

They walked on without words, and eventually Wawa slipped into a grumbling half-sleep at his mother's chest.

Don't you know I'm only doing this for you, Yuying wanted to say. Because I was told that love blossoms only in the fertile earth of sacrifice. Because I know you want to protect me. Because I want you to protect me. But she did not say it — instead she bit her lip until it bled.

Jinyi listened to her shoes slopping against the stone and gravel, the bitter coda of their day. Don't you know that I'm only doing this for you, he wanted to say, but did not.

The money had been worth less and less anyway. In the weeks they had been travelling the value had halved, and then halved again, until they did not know whether anything could still be bought with a whole wad of grubby cash. With the inflation caused by the re-ignition of the civil war spilling through the cities, people had to fill baskets with crumpled notes for the simplest of shopping trips. Even in large cities, markets and reputable shops had backtracked to allow bartering — a couple of eggs for half a cup of cornflour — while cobblers exchanged their work for home-made envelopes pressed full of tea leaves or sunflower seeds. Throughout the country, everyone was saying the same thing: these notes are only good for one thing. And what that thing was, well, that is best left to your imagination.

In the next few hours they saw two other families heading in different directions, each choosing the stony mule-track rather than the road a couple of *li* to the west. Their faces were masks of exile, their sagging clothes maps of the places they has passed through and the people they had left behind. There was no communication between the scattered travellers as they passed each other — each journey was made up of private regrets and hardships which could not be shared. The flow of people indicated one thing, however: that up ahead there must be a village large enough to be able to provide the straggle of broken stories with beds for the night.

Jinyi and Yuying walked with their heads down, ignoring the hills dipping and reaching into fog beside them, the river rushing further behind. Instead they watched the track scuff and narrow under their feet. Was the landscape still beautiful? No, it had changed. Nothing is beautiful without being seen; which is to say that only by looking at something does it become real. The surroundings faded to the colour of rust, to ruined canvases forgotten in attics. Jinyi wondered again whether this was all a mistake, trying to prove who he was by dragging the three of them back into the heartland he had abandoned as a teenager. He pushed to the back of his mind his fear about what they would find of each other when their journey reached its close. Yuying kept her mouth shut, stroking Wawa's hair and ignoring the sighs and rasping coughs of her husband.

What was it Peipei used to say? That the perfect wife had no tongue, but six hands. A pair to cook and clean, a pair to nurse and raise, and a pair to hold and caress. The image of the Guanyin, a bodhisattva in the

Chinese Buddhist pantheon, with eyes burning through each of her hundred outstretched palms, passed briefly through Yuying's mind. And perhaps it should not surprise us that this goddess of mercy was first depicted as male, before going through a sex change around a thousand years ago. Compassionate, many-armed, merciful, and with the strength of men, Guanyin gave up the blissful nothingness of nirvana in order to help others, to guide people through the dizzy cycle of reincarnations. Her name means paying attention to sounds, hearing prayers. She listens, but does not speak. A lovely lady, take it from me.

The inhabitants of Putuoshan, an island off the east coast, have their own story about the origins of this Bodhisattva, who they say was incarnated in China around two and a half thousand years ago. Where the rustling baritones of the wheat-thick plains in the cool northeast met the shrill whispers of paddy fields in the humid south, there lived an old king. Of his three daughters, only the youngest was still unwed, and so the king was busy examining the extravagant gifts and proposals received from the various princes of neighbouring states, having forgotten which of these he was presently at war with. Yet when his daughter, Guanyin, announced that she intended to become an initiate in a distant temple, he said nothing. For days he paced the endless corridors of his home, clenching and unclenching his fists, grinding his teeth until his servants had nightmares of chain gangs grinding rocks.

In the end he relented. Go to the temple, he told her, but you must work there cleaning the latrines everyday. She went. Weeks later, when she had not appeared back in front of him with her resolve broken, his calculated smile began to slip into a scowl. This had not happened before. As always seems to happen, the king was faced with two choices: let her remain in the temple and lose face with the warring kingdoms bordering his own, or have her executed for disobeying him?

Late that night, two soldiers were sent to the temple, disguised as pilgrims, with swords hidden under their saffron robes. After a show of exaggerated prostration and prayer, they crept between the buildings until they found the dormitory floor on which the princess slept, and, luckily for them, found her curled closest to the corridor, the more ample floorspace taken up by an array of snoring nuns. Yet when the first soldier swung the sword down to the girl's neck, it shattered into a thousand pieces. They looked down to see the shards of metal fallen from the sword were nothing more than drops of water reflecting the pink-tinged moonlight around her head. With this they flew from the temple and returned blabbering and incoherent to the king, only to find out the hard way that the second soldier's sword did, indeed, cut through flesh.

The following night the king sent a general to the temple, with no pretence of disguise. He tiptoed barefoot across the sooty roof slates trailing towards the back courtyard, then hung by his fingernails from the jutting eaves, before letting himself drop, feline and four-legged, at the entrance to the dormitory. He gripped Guanyin's neck and did not let go until a full twenty minutes after her last rasping burst of breath had stuttered to a stop. He then returned to the king to collect his pay and titles.

Guanyin awoke in hell, her throat dry and throbbing. She looked about her as the writhing blackness slowly found form. Her larynx bulged, stretched. Something flittered behind her, then at her side. She opened her mouth to scream, but instead of sound there emerged a rabble of white butterflies, sparking colour into the caverns. She stepped forward and, in the light thrown out from the beating wings, saw flowers stretching up from the reddened clay wherever her feet fell. (For, when your line of vision reaches only as far as the border of your own field, what else can mercy mean but a forgiving soil?) It did not lake long for the king of hell, restless and hungover, to notice that something was wrong. The blossoming of bright flowers through the cracks in the earthen walls bothered his conjunctivitis, and he rubbed his eyes and shouted, bringing forth a colossal wail from the pit of his churning stomach. With that, the walls closed in on Guanyin. The whole earth knotted itself together around her body and slowly pushed her upwards, squeezing her through the strata until, with a gurgling belch, she ripped through the earth's surface and found herself, breathless and exhausted, freed from the country of the dead.

She had been pushed up to the island of Putoushan, a short stretch of sea away from her father's kingdom. And it was here that Guanyin decided to stay, having found that in the course of her strange journey she had acquired the power to heal the sick with the lightest touch of her fingertips, and call lost fishermen away from shipwrecks with the simplest of melodies carried on the island breeze. For nine years she worked to cure the crippled, the tired, the diseased, the broken and the exhausted brought before her, sleeping only the few minutes between patients and tides. Though she did her best to ignore the chatter of the crowds that passed through her room as they bickered over battles, princes and taxes, after nearly a decade away from her first home she found it harder and harder to block out the increasingly frequent conversations she overheard about the king's ailing health. He was dying, his bones slowly rotting from the inside out.

Having searched through the mysterious texts she found she could decipher in the cliff-faces and falling leaves on the island's central mountain, Guanyin discovered a recipe for an elixir that would cure her father. However, the recipe relied on the inclusion of human flesh. Giving in to her boundless compassion, she ordered a monk to pluck out her eyes and slice off her arms to complete the potion and then sent it to her father. In the crystalline light of her blindness, she wandered into the forests at the top of the mountain, and disappeared. Across the sea her father recovered and, overcome with gratitude and regret, summoned the greatest sculptor in the kingdom. Make me a statue of her, the king ordered, with arms and eyes so impressive that everyone will marvel at the extent of her sacrifice. The result of the sculptor's work, a thousand-armed goddess with eyes staring out from each of her open palms, outlived even the second youth of the rejuvenated king. But then, our actions always outlive us.

By the time they got to the village, Yuying had forgotten the goddess. She struggled along, clasping the tearful, snotty baby to her chest while holding a hand to her own mouth as she sneezed and coughed, her feet still sloshing as they walked. Her husband made no such pretences; he simply turned his head to one side, pressed a finger tight against a single nostril, and showered the ground with stringy puddles of gelatinous green.

Stalls selling a few shrivelled white cabbages lined the streets between the squat houses of packed earth and warped timber. This was the type of village, Jinyi thought, that a single stray match could level in one evening. They passed a shared well where two streets met, with scrawny old men queuing up to draw water, muttering to each other about the daughters they had lost to places they could no longer pinpoint on a map.

Two wooden tables were set outside an open-fronted kitchen, their rickety legs shaking whenever people sat, stood, or reached for the small clay pots of vinegar or chilli oil. Jinyi and Yuying joined the slightly less crowded table and sat Wawa in the damp crib atop the soft bundle of bags. They ordered bowls of noodle soup, the only thing for sale, and, like all the locals jammed in around them, hunched themselves protectively over the broth, scared of letting even the thinnest wisp of warm, thick steam escape them. Wawa stared wide-eyed at the world wandering by, his sooty eyebrows darting up and down as he noisily slurped the warm noodles his father fed him.

'Excuse me, aunties,' Jinyi said to a pair of old women sitting nearby who were eyeing Wawa. 'Is there somewhere round here a family could stay for the night?'

'There are many places,' the first, balding old woman replied. 'Most friendly village in the county, this.'

'She's right,' the second, lightly moustached old woman said. 'I've never left, but my sister here, she's been all over the country. She's been to three, maybe four different villages. It's true. None as nice as here. People passing through have been known to say so too.'

'I don't doubt it,' Jinyi said. 'So where would you recommend?'

'Recommend? Well, I don't know about that. Nice young couple like yourselves, well, you could easily get cheated.'

'She's right, there are people would do that without blinking an eye,' the second old woman added.

'Don't want to be taken for a fool, do you? I've seen it happen to these city types what come through here.'

Jinyi picked up his bowl and drained the last of the oily broth along with the few short noodle stubs that had sunk to the bottom. He was getting tired, and, as his wife's head began to bob with the onset of sleep, Wawa started to whine for attention.

'We're not city types. We'll be fine. Thank

you for your help.' He began to get up.

'Steady on now — if you're looking for a nice warm bed, nothing fancy, there's an empty room in our brother's house. His son's gone to the forest, hunting. Won't be back for a few days.'

Jinyi sat back down. 'That's very generous of —'

'Well, of course,' interrupted the balding woman, 'He'd have to clean the room out first, and get a fire going, and that would mean losing half a day of work. But I'm sure you wouldn't be so rude as to not compensate him, just to make up what he'd lose, you see.'

Jinyi nodded. He had been waiting for this part. 'Certainly, we wouldn't want to cause any trouble, gracious aunties.' He looked to Yuying, shaken from her grogginess by the crabby baby beside her. He nudged her arm.

'Yes. That will be fine,' she said, not turning to face them as she dipped her little finger into the broth before presenting it to Wawa's open lips.

Jinyi noticed the faces peering at him, unashamedly waiting to see how he would deal with his wife. He blushed, bit his tongue, and shrugged.

'Thank you for helping us, gracious aunties. It has been a long trip.'

The two old women set off together, arm in arm and stooping in short steps across the road, to ready the vacant room for the travellers who, they would find the next morning to their disappointment, were not as rich as they appeared.

'Wawa's sick,' Yuying said, not caring how many people were listening.

'He's just woken up. Bit of a cold, the same as us. Nothing some food and a warm bed won't cure.' Jinyi said.

'No. He's sick, look at him.'

Jinyi looked at the baby. Wawa's eyes were a little puffy, but this was surely just tiredness. Jinyi then looked at the dark spoonfuls of skin under his wife's eyes, and rubbed his own.

'We need warmer clothes. And more money. I'm not sleeping outdoors again, and neither is your son,' she said.

'Listen Yuying.' Jinyi leaned closer to whisper, his breath full of steam and a hint of the garlicky broth. 'I'm trying. Just trust me a little. I'm doing everything I can. We'll be there soon, so relax. Don't fret and please, don't embarrass yourself here. Remember it's not the city any more, all right?'

'No,' she said through bared teeth. 'It's not all right. Look after Wawa, and don't leave here!'

Yuying set the baby on Jinyi's lap, and, before he had time to stutter a surprised reply, she strode across the street and round the corner, one of the bags clutched in her hands. Jinyi pulled up his shoulders and tried to ignore the people staring at him as he rocked Wawa in his arms, weighing up his lumpy bulk. Wawa gurgled lazily, nuzzling into the crook of his father's elbow. Jinyi's cheeks burnt red; he had lost face. To distract them both he began humming, reedy and low enough that only Wawa could hear, the song he always sang to his chubby little son, a tune that came naturally from some out-of-reach corner of his memory.

Once she turned the corner, Yuying leaned against a dirt wall to catch her breath. She did not want to cry. Her mother had told her that love had to be earned. She pushed herself forward and reached out for a middle-aged man lolloping down the street, gripping him by the shoulder.

'The pawnshop?' she whispered. Her eyes were frantic, like water suddenly stirred up by the wild movements of hidden fish. The middle-aged man sniffed, a loud juddering drawing in of oxygen and mucous, and looked her up and down.

'The pawnshop?' she spoke louder this time, clutching tighter at his dirty shirt.

He raised his hand and pointed, then turned and started walking, shaking his head and muttering to himself about city types. Unlike her husband, Yuying no longer cared how people looked at her. She smoothed the folds of her mud-speckled red jacket and pulled her scarf tighter around her.

The door opened only halfway, since it was

blocked by piles of cluttered wooden boxes. Yuying squeezed her way in and saw a long-bearded man sitting on top of what appeared to be a circular dining table. The shopkeeper's outfit was testament to his profession — a medley of mismatched colours, including a red skullcap, flowing blue pantaloons, and a Qing-style green jacket, a contrast to the waterlogged greys of the streets and people outside. He was building a house of cards.

'Clothes. Am I right? Silk? Is it real? Don't answer that, I know it is terribly impolite of me to ask that question of a lady.' His voice was a high-pitched whine.

This must have been one of the only pawn-shops that lacked a display window — the shopkeeper preferred to let the needy, the broken and the bargain-hunters come to him. In a place where everybody knows everybody else's business, a little discretion goes a long way. Yuying looked around at the strange collection of objects filling the small room. In the silence before he spoke again she was sure she heard the flutter of wings from near one of the chests of drawers. Behind the shopkeeper was a large wardrobe with one door open, as if to flaunt the hint of the long robes hanging inside. A solitary marble Fu Lion sat on the floor, looking for its mate. Beside the wardrobe was a large empty cage, and three clocks, each displaying a different time. Their ticking echoed around the cramped room, bouncing off the odd cooking pots, the bottles of herbal medicine, the abandoned heirlooms and the uncatalogued paraphernalia of the desperate.

'The foxes are louder this year. Have you heard them? They must have been building up their courage, because I swear now they're padding right through the night. Paw prints everywhere, my dear. By morning they've all disappeared, of course. My grandfather became a fox, you know. One morning, he just wasn't in his bed. We never saw him again, but a fox began to howl for kitchen scraps soon after that. He left the house to the squabbling of an aged wife and four bitchy concubines. Can you imagine!'

He talked without expecting a reply in order to put his customer at ease, as though setting foot inside the shop was itself shameful. His eyes never left his tapering pyramid of cards.

'Fathers can be like that. I never met my grandfathers, but some days my father becomes a ghost,' she said as she opened the bag and began to pull out some of her dresses, still damp and reeking of the river.

'Yes, I quite understand. Your clothes are beautiful,' he drawled.

'Everything has its beauty, but not everyone can see it. Isn't that what they say?'

'Ah, Confucius. I'm not as uneducated as you might think,' he replied. 'Inside this shop it is a different country, not shown on any globe mind you, and about as far from the village outside as you can imagine. You might have noticed that things are different in here. You can trust me.'

'So, how much will you give me?'

He stretched out his hands in front of him.

'You have two options. I'll give you five for each piece if you sell them to me straight. But if you want them back, you'll need to pay the going price at the time, whatever that may be. Or, and this is the more popular option, I'll give you two a piece and you can buy them back for the same amount any time within a year.'

'And how many people come back?'

He said nothing. The house collapsed with the penultimate card, the last one still flexed out between his upheld fingers.

'I'll come back. Soon. So I'll take the second option, thank you. It's just for a few days, you see. A week perhaps,' Yuying said.

'Of course. Then I will see you again soon.'

They both spoke without thinking, as though they were reading from a familiar script. Yuying handed over every one of her dresses, trying not to cry. The owner then discreetly pointed to a space beside the wardrobe, where she could remove the dress and jacket she was wearing.

Jinyi's eyes rose to meet her as she strolled back to the table with the empty bag. She tried to read them for acceptance, apology, love, but could make out none of those. Despite the tender moments, his lopsided smile and his gentle way of rubbing the backs of her hands, as he was now doing with their snoozing child, Yuying was never quite sure what Jinyi was thinking. She knew from her secret hand-sign conversations with Yaba that he was like that in the kitchen too: quiet, defensive and thoughtful. Next to the bustle and shouts of her family and the other girls she knew from school, his measured thoughtfulness seemed strange, almost frightening. She remembered the way he had hovered in the doorway for his first week in the house, waiting each time for permission to cross the threshold, the way he had tentatively asked her if she could teach him to read and the way his eyebrows had twisted into knots when she had then laughed, thinking that he was pulling her leg — surely you can read! But once the house was left behind, neither of them were certain whether those roles still held. If he could, he might have told her that he was only trying to look after the first family he had ever known. If he could, he might have mentioned love, the strange butterfly feeling in his stomach that he could not understand. But he could not, and he would not, which was why they usually walked in silence.

Is this more like the way he expected a wife

to look? Yuying wondered. She was now dressed in the drab woollens worn by everyone in almost every village they had passed through. Manly, waist-pinching trousers, layers of itchy woollen undershirts and a bulky black zhongshan jacket, all second-hand and dirt-cheap from the pawnshop. Her glittering slippers had been replaced with warm, furlined boots. Am I still myself without things from back home, she wondered as she stood before her husband. How many little parts have to change before I stop being my mother's daughter and start being someone I have never met? She had picked up some furlined blankets for Wawa, but nothing for Jinyi. He at least seemed happy in his old, dirty clothes. They two of them now looked almost identical. Jinyi's lips rose up into a grin as his eyes roamed over her.

'Are you laughing at me?' she asked.

'No, no, of course not! Don't be so silly. I was just thinking about what your parents might say if they could see you now.'

She smiled too. 'They'd think that you'd corrupted me.'

'And that I'd undone all their hard work. It's lucky we've given them a grandson, or they would really be mad with me. Come on, he's exhausted. He didn't even giggle when I tickled him. Let's wrap him up and get to the room — I can see those old spinsters coming back.'

246

This was how their truces usually worked, each one pretending nothing out of the ordinary had happened, each one pretending to forget. It was easier than saying sorry. In the small room they shared a single stone *kang,* the bricks beneath them heated by a small fire. Though it was only afternoon, they collapsed with Wawa between them, kicking his little feet against them. In the other room, the owners shuffled about, boiling pot after pot of river water, and the little family slowed towards a drifting, fitful sleep.

Yuying woke with the mêlée of animal noises that always attended sunrise. Straight away she felt confused — Wawa hadn't woken her once, and had last eaten at the same time as them. Her heart thumped so loudly she could hear nothing else. She lifted the baby's sleeping form closer to her. He was heavy, a limp sack of pebbles. She opened her mouth to scream, but instead of sound came a dry rasp.

They buried him half a *li* away from the village, where a hillside flexed up into mist and wild grass. Jinyi did not argue with his wife when she placed the new blankets, the warm sets of clothes she had knitted and the small double-tiger pillow into the shallow stretch he had dug, handful by handful, gripping the crumbling earth between his fingers. Wawa would need them to take with him, beyond their reach. They did not only bury his wattles of puppy fat, his cheeky smiles, his duckling frizz of black hair and his jet-black eyebrows that had been forever dancing above his curious eyes, but also his sobs, his tugs of his mother's hair, his first tooth and first teething bites, his tiny pyjamas, and all his possible futures.

They lost each other to the silent undertow of grief, the wordless tug pulling them as they struggled through the depths of thought. Its waters had a strange clarity, as though the layers of stained glass through which they usually saw the world had suddenly been shattered and the sky was burning through, its vast spectrum scarring their retinas.

'He has my family now,' Jinyi said, though not loud enough to be heard.

The suddenness of it shocked them. They stood in silence, tormenting themselves by cataloguing the coughs they had ignored, the midnight whimpers they might have slept through, the reddening cheeks, the colour of his soiled swaddling cloths, the lack of breast-milk, the cleanliness of the water and the tiny cup carried at the bottom of the damp bag, and most of all the tiring journey they still had to see through to its conclusion. There were words and hopes and sobs stopped inside them

'I'm sorry,' Jinyi whispered, shoulder to shoulder with her, so close that his breath seemed ghostly, almost unable to believe that the universe had collapsed without pulling them down with it.

Yuying said nothing, her mouth full of salt, full of tears. He said nothing back.

It was hard to tell whether they stayed beside the tiny mound of earth for minutes or for days. Finally, they began to walk again. And because death is terrible, there is nothing that can be done but to give it the quiet it deserves; for nothing so demeans our feelings of grief as to have them set down or spoken. Even us gods are powerless here.

They pushed their sobs down to the bottom of their guts, and kept walking. Somehow it was easier now to hate each other than to think of the last year. Even the day before suddenly seemed unbelievably distant, perfect in its innocence.

There are two countrysides. One people carry with them, carved from the words of books read in the safety of well-lit houses; the other exists beyond people, and its words are indecipherable howls, its language that of barks and bracken and vine. It is the second people face, if they face the world at all. And in this way there are two futures — the one that people conjure up to make the present seem easier to stomach, and the second, a caged bear which will not be tamed, and which will not dance. It is his rough and clammy paws people feel on their skin at night.

They saw the house from the distance, marked out as a hunched silhouette against the swelling horizon, near the bottom of a squat valley. They would make it before night fell. It looked like all the other dwellings they had passed over the last few days: a narrow russet-coloured main building with a mill stone and trough on the left, and on the right a roofed frame under which clustered tools or animals. A knee-high rough stone wall ran around the courtyard, with a single thin break as an entrance. Yuying was only alerted to the uniqueness of this latest house by the change in her husband. His pace slowed, and Yuying could hear his jaws begin to grind, though she was tactful enough not to mention it.

'You can put your bags in your old room — your cousin isn't here anymore,' the fifty-something woman said, striding out into the courtyard to get a look at the approaching travellers. She towered above both Yuying and Jinyi. The skin around her pug nose was pinched and pockmarked, her hair inexpertly cropped. Her voice was neither welcoming nor cold; she simply sounded exhausted.

'Thank you. You are looking well, Auntie Hou. This is my wife, Bian Yuying.'

'Then you must be Bian Jinyi. Though I'm not sure why you are calling me auntie, as you left this family when you took another name. What, no children yet? Are you sure you're really married?'

Yuying tried, but did not manage to suppress a sob. Auntie Hou looked at her with a mixture of contempt and confusion.

'Well, I expect you need a rest after your journey. We've eaten, but there's some broth left. I'll heat it up,' she sighed.

'It's nice to meet you, Auntie Hou,' Yuying stuttered through her tears.

'I'm sure. Nice to meet you too, Bian Yuying. I guess you're both staying? Then I hope you will be comfortable here.' Even before she had finished speaking she was moving away, sinking into the last half hour of dusty sunlight.

The broth was lukewarm water in which an unripened vegetable might once have sat for a couple of hours. They gulped it down, not daring to look at each other. Across the fields a heron darted, still slick from the water it had grazed. On a hill somewhere behind them, a hill indistinguishable from the many they had passed and would not be able to find again, a sapling began to ready itself beneath the earth, waiting for spring to come, to push out roots.

I am ashamed to say that I found it impossible to forget the Jade Emperor's words, and I gradually let doubt gnaw at my fingers and toes until my whole body felt sore. Maybe he was right. After spending weeks worrying over my abilities, I decided to take action. I would ask a real writer for advice. And who better, I surmised, than Li Bai? After all, everyone was always saying he was probably the greatest poet our country had ever produced. So I set about finding him.

I took a couple of bottles of cheap, sour liquor, and sat on the bank of the Yellow River, swigging and singing old songs about the trees and the beasts as I waited for night to fall from the sky. When I was so drunk that I was seeing two of every star puckering in the dark fabric above me, I took off my shoes and jogged down into the river. I waded through the murky waters until I found the spot where the full moon was reflecting in the sway; and that was where I dived under, immersing myself in the silver light.

My head came up almost instantly in the middle of a small pond. I clambered out and shook the tangled weeds and small Koi carp from my robes, then looked around. It was night on this side as well, though the moon seemed closer, filling half the sky between the mountains to the east and the mountains to the west. Before me was a small wooden cottage with chipped eaves, the only building in the vast, dark valley. I banged the fat brass knuckle of a door-knocker and went in.

'You are perhaps a traveller,' said a short man who was seated on the floor with his legs folded beneath him. He was surrounded by half-empty bottles of rice wine and piles of paper; on the wall were ink portraits of women of unimaginable beauty.

'You are perhaps a traveller,' he repeated, 'forever searching in vain for a way to return to your hometown.'

'Well . . . not really,' I replied. 'I have come to ask your advice, honourable poet of the Way. I must find a way to describe the working of the human heart.'

He nodded slowly. A sharp slither of black beard jutted down from his round chin.

He finally spoke. 'The long journey carries us through a river of stars.'

It was my turn to nod, though I was not sure this was helpful. Had he heard me properly?

'Do you mean that the heart is like a river, sir?' I asked.

'No,' he said, sounding irritated. 'I mean that life is a journey, and we are carried along like uprooted waterweeds. You can either keep trying to work out where it will take you, and ignore the things that pass you by, or you can enjoy the stars reflected in the river and not worry about where you will finally end up.'

'I see,' I said. And I thought I almost did.

'Of course, many would disagree. If you are serious about studying the vicissitudes of the heart, perhaps you should talk to my friend, the great poet Du Fu. He is sure to have a different view.'

'Thank you, sir,' I said, retreating towards the door. 'And where might I find him?'

'You must cross a bridge that curls over ravines as though it were a rainbow,' Li Bai said, before returning to his rice wine.

5:
1949
THE YEAR OF THE OX

If you have never lived in the fields, taking part in the sowing and tending and trading and planting and weeding and knitting and weaving and milling and kneading and chopping and baking and tilling and ploughing, all before the sun sizzles down like a broken egg yolk over the hills; if you have never felt that the only solace in life was the hope of a few hours' rest, children, grandchildren, and a painless death; if you have never measured the borders of your world with a stretch of river, the shadows of a forest or a few sun-furrowed faces from the only village you have ever visited, then you would not understand. But wait — whenever I try to tell a story like this to the Jade Emperor, he stamps his feet, on the verge of one of his tantrums. Which you do *not* want to see — trust me. Anyway, he always tells me that we can imagine anything, and that everything is connected. So I'd better suspend my scepticism and start this bit again.

It seems to me that many of our greatest poets, such as Bai Juyi, Du Fu and Qu Yuan (not that I like to name-drop, but I do know most of them pretty well), seemed to share a knack for falling out of favour. Now, when driven across the continent on an emperor's whim, in exile or in some humiliatingly distant official posting, these ancient poets would slowly disappear into their verses, their bodies fading until all that remained were their words, loose couplets marking their paths in place of footsteps.

Those were the verses that Yuying had learnt by heart and recited to herself back when she was still her father's favourite, back when she was still a student and being offered the privileged position of translator for one of the units of the then resplendent Japanese army. Now, once again, she muttered the rhymes under her breath as she squatted in the turned earth, her muddy hands gripping a rusty trowel. And where once the poems had seemed surreal, strange and giddily romantic to her, they now seemed hard, crisp, unyielding. The scrunch of leaves underfoot; lone, soaring birds; abandoned temples, empty villages; moonlight seeping under doors and through the cracks in walls or reflected in the swell of a river — all of these images had become entwined with her new home, with the endless stretch of empty land on either side. Yuying clung to the old verses to make her new life seem more bearable, to try and slough off her loneliness and regret. She told herself she was not the only one. In the most minute of details, the poets seemed to have found the truth about the whole world; inside the slightest of prized-open atoms, there are whole universes.

Yuying searched for a similar clarity, a way of taming her strange surroundings by making them surrender to her scrutiny. As she worked, she guessed the names of the weeds and flowers, pulled up alike, for both were of little use if they could not be eaten. She felt the second baby kick in her stomach and fought off a smile, moving to the next row of the short field. Jinyi was searching for firewood, his aunt boiling up ancient stock in the kitchen, his uncle out of sight on the other side of the house.

The walls were scuffed wooden slats over a pounded earth foundation. Across the windows were wind-thwacked sheets of paper. The first thing Yuying had looked for after they arrived was the tiny niche in the front wall, which held a small clay bowl. She was happy to have found it, but also surprised at herself. You were not so superstitious as a child, she told herself, though she was not sure whether that was true or not. A little rice wine — the kind with a warm, shivery bite — floated in the bowl, a thin layer of recent dust and ash settled on the top. It was an offering for the God of Heaven and Hell, for appeasement or atonement, a prayer for constancy in times of irreversible change. Even the garden birds stayed away from it, though this may have had more to do with the acidic punch of the liquor than their fear of a spiteful and unpredictable deity.

The house was divided into three rooms, the smallest of which Yuying and Jinyi slept in, huddled together on stone slabs covered with mangy furs. It used to belong to Jinyi's cousin, but they found it was best not to mention him to the elderly couple; he had been conscripted by the Communists during the war against the Japanese, and had not been heard from since. The room was sticky and prickly in the summer and draughty and damp the rest of the year. Despite the fact that the floors were swept at least five times a day, they were always dusty from the thick desert winds that swept in from the west. The winds also carried curses, but everyone was so busy preparing for the approaching birth that they did not pay them much attention.

The nearest house took almost half an hour to walk to. The midwife, whose visits were getting ever more frequent, travelled almost twice that to reach them. She was hare-lipped and stocky, her head broad and doughy, and the pushy manner in which she took to her vocation suggested that she had entered it only in penance for the accident of her own birth. She poked and prodded Yuying with her wrinkled fingers, clucked and tutted as if she had never seen a poorer excuse for a would-be mother. Her advice rang in Yuying's ears, and as she worked she heard her hectoring tone again and again:

'You stay this thin and the child will be a scrawny little wretch. Remember what I said? More carrots and tofu if you want a boy, which I'm sure you do, because only a fool would pray for a girl. For heaven's sake, don't rub your belly like that, or you'll end up with a spoilt little brat! Don't they teach you anything in the city?'

Yuying ran a hand over the stretched flesh of her blossoming stomach, then set back to work.

The days began to merge into one for Yuying as summer approached; yet they also managed to be both monotonous and to introduce new petty humiliations.

'You've got bags under your eyes, both of you,' Auntie Hou would say, without a trace of emotion in her voice.

'The sun's coming up early now, so you'd better be ready in the morning. Can't be frittering away your time, or all our work will go to waste,' Old Hou would add. This was the usual extent of the conversation at dinner, a few undercooked vegetables and pancakes made from sweet-potato flour.

As she watched Yuying grind the flour with the dirty and misshapen millstone, Auntie Hou moaned, shaking her head, 'Been here more than a year, and don't know what you're doing! I'll only show you this one last time, all right? Better be careful with that baby in you too, or the hungry ghosts will get you both,'

'Yes, I'll just —'

'You're sagging round the sides, girl. What are you, eighteen or eight, eh? Push into it, there you go, and turn. My gods!'

This is how we measure ourselves, Yuying thought, her haunches tense and pressed against the wind — by finding out what we cannot do, by finding out who we are not. She looked at Auntie Hou, still shaking her head as she walked back towards the kitchen, and studied the bruises on the old woman's face and neck. Some nights she and Jinyi would lie silent on their stone bed while Old Hou shouted in the next room, his voice loud and raw, making no effort to hide his half-cut rage. Then would come the sound of his fist or belt meeting her flesh, though they never once heard her cry out. This is the difference between here and home, Yuying thought. Bruises here were worn like birthmarks, the simplest bare facts of flesh. People were proud of their calluses and blisters, and took their beatings as if they had earnt them. Yuying stopped turning the wheel for the briefest of moments, to send her prayers on the frayed winds that the war would soon finish and they could both go home.

When neighbours passed to barter and discuss the crops, Yuying would slow her work, tilt her head and listen to the voices.

'The hardest in years, I'd say . . .'

'. . . devils in the fields, messing with the soil . . .'

'. . . a dry one again . . . longest in memory . . .'

'. . . one hundred days of mourning . . .'

'. . . well, we got through the others, we'll get through this one . . .'

'. . . so what about your son, any grandchildren yet? And if not, why not, not that I mean to pry of course . . .'

In all these voices she registered a throaty rattle like the crackling of logs on a fire, the dry throb of the oesophagus, and the way every sentence seemed to end with an assertion. They have learnt the land, she thought, so that they know it as well as they know the touch of their wives or the nails on their fingers. They will never know books or teahouses, mooncakes or servants. Where has he brought me?

As the season stilled into warmth, a herd of oxen was driven past the bottom of their field, and Yuying could not believe that she was not dreaming them up from a distant art class,

261

from a trail of black ink dipping through misty mountain passes. She wanted to run and point them out to her husband; she wanted to feel as she had felt as a child, awed by the smallest details that everyone else took for granted. She wanted to take Jinyi's hand and watch them together, the slow and cumbersome sweaty creatures, swatting at fleas with their stubbed and effete tails, their heads swaying as they lolloped onward. She could imagine the feel of their breath, warm and musty and cloying, but did not dare move any closer, instead letting them haphazardly drift away, wet muzzles pressed against the furry side of the animal in front.

Jinyi heard a soft, guttural low from the other side of the house, and turned for a second to watch them. They were probably work animals, he thought, prices dropped because of the war and half of them riddled with disease, being hurried to market; or else the crafty oxman was looking to let them nibble from someone else's land. Jinyi shook his head, thinking about the things he could do with a couple of oxen and a bit of land. He heard his wife's footsteps, and set back to work.

'I can feel him turning, trying to get comfortable. He's shifting his bulk, as if he's not quite sure of his body,' Yuying said to Jinyi that night.

'What does that mean? If you have a body, you're sure of it. If not, then you must be some kind of ghost. If you feel aches or pain, that just tells you you're alive, and you should be thankful for that. It's when you don't feel anything that you ought to worry,' Jinyi said, rolling over on the ancient animal skins that smelt of many generations of sweat.

'You know that's not what I meant. I'm just worried. After last time, I —'

'I know, I know. I meant that these are signs that give us hope. Movement, that's a good sign. A beating heart, a curious body. We should take comfort in these. He'll be fine.'

'Why are we both so sure it will be a boy?' Yuying said, a smile forming in the dark.

'Because it must be a boy.'

'And when he is born? What will we do then?' She was angling, hoping to hear Jinyi tell her that they could go home.

'Then we'll look after him. We won't start walking somewhere else again, I promise. We've got a warm bed here, a safe house, and enough food.'

'As long as he likes sweet potatoes,' she muttered.

That was all they seemed to eat. The fields surrounding the house were planted and ploughed only for that tuberous root that could be pulled up snug in a single tug, the size of a clenched fist. They ate boiled sweet potatoes, mashed sweet potatoes mixed with salt, fried sweet potatoes with onion if any could be traded, and, for celebrations and festivals, caramelised sweet potatoes, the orange lumps glowing with strands of hot dark sugar. The flour they milled was also ground down from sweet potatoes, mixed with the off-white of wheat only on the rare occasions when trade went well. A few of those clay-red sacks of fleshy mulch were stacked beside the bed, the tubers shaved off as the vegetables were stored for winter. Just thinking of sweet potatoes made Yuying want to be sick.

'There's nothing wrong with sweet potatoes. My family have been farming them for centuries. There was once a passing warlord who decided to stop fighting and settle here because he swore they were the best sweet potatoes he had tasted in all his expeditions. Well, that's what Uncle Hou says anyway,' Jinyi said.

'I know. That's the only story he ever tells.'

'Come on, it's not that bad. This is where my ancestors live. They're still out there; we just can't see them. When you hear the wind chimes, or calls from birds you don't quite recognise, or distant drums, that's them. That's what I used to think about my parents, to stop myself from going crazy here when I was young.'

Yuying imagined their children growing up there, and felt suffocated. Their days would be filled the same way as hers, with mud and ache and hunger. The house sat on the side of a valley, linked up with a few others higher up to form a spindly, set-apart village. There was a market day at the closest small town once a month, and a small abandoned school-house on the other side of the hill. Each of the families on the hillside lived like spiders in the centre of a tatty web of prayers, curses, hopes and the ever-present dead ancestors who watched over their shoulders, their faint breath almost noticeable on the downy hairs of their necks.

Yuying noticed that Jinyi's leg was twitching. He was half asleep, yet she did not want to give up yet.

'I heard some of the traders talking the other day. They said that the civil war is nearly over.'

'Hmm.'

'It could be finished by next year.'

'That's good news. Who's winning?' Jinyi mumbled.

'You mean you don't know?'

'Of course I do. I'm just joking. Let's get some sleep.' Jinyi yanked the hairy blanket tighter about his ears; moonlight peeked in through the tears in the paper across the square window.

'It'll be good news for my family. The city will be safe again.' As soon as she said this she was unsure of what she meant. As safe as when the Japanese were there, guarding anything that fell within the sphere of their interests and herding everything else into shadow? Or as safe as before the invasion, a time known to her only through the foggy nostalgia of her mother's occasional reminiscences?

'That's good,' Jinyi said.

'Though they might need help rebuilding the house and getting all the restaurants running again.'

'It won't be easy, but they'll manage.'

'Is that all you've got to say?' she asked, turning and pressing her head up onto his turned shoulder.

'Yes. Goodnight.'

She let him sleep, and surrendered herself to the small aches and jabs of the baby pushing against her sides, tiny hiccups juddering across her abdomen.

What is it that drives people so far from themselves? Is it to see how much they can give up while remaining the same? Or to witness what is left when everything is stripped away? And why do they do this? For love? A few years ago, Yuying would not have hesitated to say, 'Yes, for love', but now she was not so sure. This thought made her blush with guilt as she lay beside her snoring husband. She wondered whether her mother too had had to make and unmake herself. And this was simply another version of the question she asked herself every day: What will happen to me if I never return?

Yuying lay awake, rubbing her fingers into her bulge, trying to stir the baby into kicking, into sharing her sleeplessness. What will happen to me if I never return? Jinyi snuffled and snored beside her. Might it be that we find ourselves only in how we are perceived, she wondered, and if this changes, then do we change too? She did not like this thought, so she turned instead to imagining her husband suddenly having a change of heart, and she smiled to herself as she thought of Jinyi taking her hands and announcing that they must return home.

Pain suddenly arched through her, as though she was a spark plug or an old tractor engine being started, and she roared loud enough to wake not just her husband but the whole house. It gripped and squeezed her, pulsing and tensing and piercing her muscles. Her husband sat straight up, roughly rubbing his eyes while his knees pushed off the blanket, and she bucked into the spasms of pain, and in that second she knew.

And again it came, the pain starting at the base of her spine and suddenly filling her; a clenching, tongue-biting lurch of pain mangling her inside out.

'Get help,' she whimpered at Jinyi, who was already up and pulling on his trousers.

'Are you all right? What's the ma—'

'Get help,' Yuying cried. She opened her mouth, and closed it again, the pain replaced with an ooziness, the sloppy flop of her stomach turning over. She pressed her fingers to the tops of her thighs and brought them up, sticky and smelling of rusted copper and the acrid tang of old soup stock. And though it would be hours before the room would have even a scrap of light, she knew that they were covered in blood.

In the next few hours the local midwife arrived, her hare-lip visibly twitching and her short rings of hair stuck to her oversized brow, and Yuying began the bitter push of delivering the stillborn baby, tinged blue and bloody. There was no comfort in knowing that they had been right, that it was a boy. The little twisted mess of clammy skin and wrinkles was passed quickly from the room, hidden from Yuying's sight as she lay back, stoic and sweaty and silent on her elbows, speaking to no one, and no one daring to speak to her. She stared steadily at a point on the ceiling while her lips knotted into a tiny oval, a half-formed expression that she could not bring herself to utter. If I speak it, she thought, it will become real. People moved in slow-motion around her, leaving her to the depths of blood and grief; the haggard midwife had other women to see, aunt and uncle were already out at the work that needed to be done no matter what. Eventually only her husband was left, nervously watching her chest slowly rise and fall.

As the sun came up, she asked to see her son. Jinyi moved to the child tentatively, almost afraid to touch it. It was clammy and small and tied in a bed sheet on the kitchen table, waiting to be taken by the men to be buried at the end of the field. It was only to the child that she would speak, worn-out whispers given to his peeled red stub of an ear. She moved her mouth close to his wrinkled head and closed eyelids as though her warm breath might suddenly make him move, speaking to him so softly that her husband had to leave the room, unable to bear the muttered hum of her gentle words, her tone that was warmer and more delicate than anything he had heard from her before.

Once outside Jinyi tried to catch his breath, stunned by the suddenness of this second ending; six and a half hours since he woke and he could only remember a few moments, ones he would try his best to put from his mind. He felt as though his heart had been crushed, mangled; and yet he suddenly wanted to relive it all, both of the babies' brief half-lives, to see all the moments he had missed, to treasure every single second, even if that meant reliving all of this again. A scream curdled in his throat and tears scratched at the corners of his vision; he picked up the trowel and descended through the rows, because what else could he do?

Somewhere along a mountain pass, or in some private forest, Jinyi and Yuying must have caught the attention of some hungry demon, whispered Auntie Hou to herself. Snake-headed, all black teeth and charred tongue, he must have crept behind them all the way to the Hou's house. Already he had claimed two of their children. Had they been girls, it might have been all right, but these were males, the blood of a family, its strength and its name. With every rustle of wind-gathered leaves, or the creak of the warped timber in the walls, Auntie Hou grew more and more convinced that the demon that had taken both the children was still out there, waiting. When not working, she collected dried grass to burn in place of incense before the grubby altar that squatted behind the kitchen table. She tried to remember all her sins and urged the grieving husband and wife to do the same. You are cursed, she assured them.

Jinyi was the first to begin believing Auntie's words, and drew chalk lines over their door to stop the demon returning. The claw-filled nightmares that left him matted with sweat were at least preferable to torturing himself over whether it was somehow his fault. It was almost harvest, the sticky warmth slowly being blown south, and Jinyi spent all his spare time praying to the handful of deities whose names he could remember, asking that the next baby would be healthy and strong. Yuying spent the same weeks vowing to herself that she would never let her husband close to her body again.

'There is a doctor — don't worry, not one of those new-fangled ones fiddling about with Western medicine! Oh no, I mean a *real* doctor — who may be able to make sure the demon never finds you,' Auntie Hou told Jinyi.

She had heard of him from a neighbouring family whose sick child had been brought back to life by the doctor decades ago. Jinyi consented without asking Yuying, suspecting she might be uncooperative. She does not have to know, he thought. However, despite their best efforts, sending messages with everyone passing by and even sounding out the crowds at the market, the famous doctor could not be found. He had not been seen, apparently, since the civil war began.

Yuying was soon up and wandering through the rows again; yet she would often stop and spend hours studying the points where the rayed corners of the fields dipped into the haze and smudge of the horizon, her mind elsewhere. She felt closer to ninety than nearly nineteen, her body a catalogue of

271

aches, her mind awash with what could have been. She followed the others in when the sun crept down unexpectedly about her, and sat with them in the tiny kitchen jammed between the two bedrooms, chewing her food halfheartedly.

'It hasn't been a bad year overall for sweet potatoes, has it?' Jinyi said, awkwardly trying to fill the silence. In response his uncle finished his unhealthily rushed spat of spooning and gulping and left the table, without a word, to begin whittling a thin stick with a dirty blade in the next room.

'Why don't we take them to the market together, next week? You could help me out this time. I think we ought to be able to get a bit of tofu, and maybe a few eggs, in return. What do you think, Yuying?' he continued.

'If you need me to, I will come,' she sighed.

He nodded, and it was settled. Yuying put aside her chopsticks and followed Auntie Hou to the storeroom at the back of the house, where the few candles were kept.

Jinyi was left eating on his own, wondering how much he could bargain for the sweet potatoes and how much better they might do next year. He stopped himself, and thought of a little plan to cheer up Yuying — with a little wheat from the market, ground down to flour, he could make a few dumplings for her. He left the table for the bedroom, and was asleep within ten minutes. He slept in his clothes, letting them soak up the autumn sweat. The women would wash the dishes with murky water from the rain trough at dawn.

In the storeroom the candles had been lit and Yuying and Auntie Hou had set the groaning loom into life, clanking the wooden frame to wind through the thick tease of cotton, picked from a spot not half a day away. In this way they ruined their eyes long into the night, stretching out and unpicking the fine string until it was ready to be knitted into winter underwear, socks, scarves and vests. With every turn of the mechanism the loom croaked and muttered to itself.

'Pay attention, or else we'll have to start from scratch. Come on, girl,' Auntie Hou chided, though in a lowered voice so as not to disturb the men sleeping on the other side of the wall.

'You don't think much about death, Auntie?'

Auntie Hou sighed, feeling her patience tested.

'Death is everywhere, young lady. Life just gets in the way. That's why we work, to do everything we can to keep death at bay, but it still creeps in somehow. There are even ghosts in the water trough, giving me frights when I dip to fill a bucket. But you get used to them. That's just the way it is.'

Auntie Hou paused, looked across at Yuying

273

and shook her head. 'At least they are to-gether; they have each other. But down here, nothing changes. You'd do well to remember that.'

Yuying nodded, not taking her eyes from the loom. 'Yes, Auntie.'

'Don't lose concentration now! My heavens! There, come on now, carefully.'

Even after Auntie Hou had shuffled through to bed, Yuying continued to tug at the frame, pulling and shuffling the fine strands. She had a plan.

Later that night Jinyi woke and, feeling Yuying fidgeting beside him, tried to comfort her.

'It's going to be all right, you know.'

'Hmm.'

'I've got an idea, to make sure the demon doesn't find us again.'

'Not the demon again, Jinyi. Please, just forget all that nonsense. We failed them, and it won't do any good trying to find anyone else to pin the blame on.'

'Don't say that. Just listen, all right. I've been thinking, if we saved up a little, maybe got a bit of a loan from your father, then we could get our own plot of land not too far from here.'

She shuffled in the bed. 'Why?'

'What do you mean, *why?* So we could grow crops, have a real home for our children, build a house with a little altar to my ancestors to make sure any demons won't dare come near. What else could you possibly want?'

She didn't reply. Eventually Jinyi decided that she must be mulling over his suggestion, and he fell asleep. Yet Yuying still lay awake next to him, hoping that in her dreams the children might crawl back across the fields to be comforted, to be held once more.

The walk to the market necessitated leaving the house in the dark. It was a relief to see the breaking sunlight swimming over a different set of fields, the dirt track between them swaying in the honey light, and Yuying imagined it washing over her, making everything new. They were soon marching as fast as they could and overtook a shepherd with a dwindling flock, undoubtedly heading the same way.

'What's in that bag?' Jinyi asked, looking at his young wife more closely now that it was light. Hauled over both their backs were dirty sheets knotted to hold as many sweet potatoes as possible, but Yuying also had a smaller, brighter pouch, a remnant of their journey from Fushun, tied across a shoulder.

'Things I've made.'

'What things?'

'Hats, bibs, nappies, socks, vests. You know. Embroidered. You've seen them.'

'No, we packed the ones you and Auntie

made last night. They're at the top of my bag, with the *mantou* for lunch. Wait!'

He stopped, forcing her to do so too.

'What did you say they were?'

'Hats, socks, vests, nappies —'

'— and bibs, yes. Yuying, are those the baby's clothes?'

She started walking again, using up all her energy in forcing herself not to shout.

'Yuying?'

'No!' was all she said, not slowing down, and her tone was enough to stop Jinyi from speaking again, though he could not help wondering whether she had kept the baby's clothes for the next child, or whether they had been buried with the stillborn boy. He did not doubt, however, that she was telling the truth. It was another *li* before she opened her mouth again, still facing forwards.

'They're things I've made. After your aunt went to bed. We already have some to trade for food, which I helped to make. I just wanted to make a few more, to see if anyone wanted them today.'

'Why?'

'I wanted to try and get a little money.'

'You don't have to do that, Yu. We have enough, don't we? I'm doing my best, and if there is something else you want, you should just say.'

'It's not for us. I want to write a letter to my family.'

'Come on Yu, your family is here now.'

'Do you want me to forget them? Honour your elders: that's what you said; that's what my father said; that's what Confucius said. That's why we're here, isn't it? The memory of your family. Anyway, I just want to find out if they are all right, what with the war and everything.'

'I'm sorry. Write your letter.' Jinyi was stung — is this really why she thinks we are here? he asked himself.

As he could not read or write, he had a fear of the power of letters, as though they were an act of magic. All the news and gossip in the fields was carried by voices alone, taking on the low cadences of the local accent, the sense of a rumour wholly dependent on who was recalling it.

'There is a post office in Baoding, half a day or so from here. I've never been, but I'm sure they could help. Or we could try and find some people heading north, and ask them to take it with them. There must be some migrant workers going up to the coal plains soon. There are usually lots of them in the winter, especially after the harvest.'

'I'll go to the post office,' Yuying said.

'Wait, I have a better idea. We should save the money and spend it on medicine. You know, for your womb. At the last market there was a young man selling ground tiger bone. If we could save enough to buy a little, just a little, then everything would be all right.'

'And the demon?'

'Even demons are no match for that kind of strength. The strength of tigers.'

'I'll think about it,' Yuying said, if only to stop the conversation.

At the market they squeezed between the crowds into the pulsing centre. It was simply an open stretch of flat dusty land between a few clumsily built brick buildings, and it seemed as though there was no order, no stalls — only relentless groups of people trying to barter one thing for another. Most people kept moving, eyeing up someone's goods as someone else eyed up theirs, then eyeing up each other, wondering how good a deal they would get. The market was stuffed full of people with broad-brimmed wicker hats speaking in shouts, careful not to waste a single syllable. Yuying flashed the small embroidered bibs and vests in front of passing faces, hoping for a response. Jinyi made time amid the bartering to approach the young man who furtively opened a sack containing pale bone, but left him after only a few curt words. Tiger parts are expensive — after all, poaching takes time and energy. And trust me, the demons I know, the ones with frothing lips and reptile eyes, are not so easily put off. Once they set their minds on something, they will rip the world apart to get it.

It seemed that no one ever got as much as they hoped for; the voices that drifted steadily from the muddy square in the late afternoon were indistinguishable in their little laments and sighs, the bodies uniform in their slouching shrugs and shuffling feet, everyone swinging their hard-bargained wares across their backs.

'It could have been worse,' Jinyi said as they started their walk back home, picking up the pace as the sun became tangled in the wiry branches of the trees lining the western rises.

'I know.'

'At least we got some flour. Not much, but if we ration it, easily enough for a couple of months. Eggs too. How much did you get for your letter?'

'Not enough. Half a *jiao* maybe. A stamp will cost four.'

'You'll have to make a lot more bibs then,' he said.

'I'm not going to give up.'

'I believe you. They looked nice, by the way.'

'Really?'

'Of course. Especially the one with the cranes on.'

Jinyi paused, then picked up the pace again, looking directly forward as he spoke.

'I used to watch for cranes, you know. Every autumn staring up as they went, every spring waiting for them to return. There aren't many round here of course, but there are still some up by the lakes, and they used to fly past. It wasn't just cranes, of course, but geese too. All of the big ones.'

'I used to do that too, and we would celebrate spring when the birds came back.'

'Oh, but it was the leaving I was interested in. Whole flocks jutting out with the same strange purpose, something they didn't even have to remember: they just did it. I liked that idea. And as soon as someone told us kids that the world was round, well, I thought that must be what they were doing. Going all the way around, never touching down, just flying over the whole of the earth. I thought they were mapping it, taking it all in, and never stopping until they came home.'

'Even though they came back from the same direction they left in?'

'I know. I can't have been too clever, can I?' Jinyi's voice lilted.

'No, that's not what I meant,' she added quickly. 'We were both watching them, though. That's a nice thought.'

Yuying did not mention that the birds' journey, exploring then returning, mimicked her private longing. It was too soon for that. She needed to sound out her family first, once she had saved up for a stamp with half a dozen more trips to the market. And so, as soon as they got back to the house, she set up the loom again, and squinted her way through the nights until the wicks were burnt down to waxy stubble. And once she had the twine, she could start to knit, and send the frail outlines of tigers, dragons and cranes dancing across the little sets of clothes.

Confucianism stresses routine as a key virtue. Life is a set of actions, and the proper performance of these actions, whether in relation to respecting one's elders or performing one's job, however menial they might seem, is central to living a good life. Routines and rituals enable us to locate our position in the world. Yuying respected her husband, because she was his wife, and she knew that's what wives should do. She worked because she was alive. Yet this repetition scared her, because there was only one way out from the endless routine, and even Confucius himself was famously silent on the issue of the afterlife.

It took three more trips to the market to get four *jiao* for the stamp, though Yuying had lost track of what day of the week it was, what date of what month, and she realised that she had become the same as the rest of the household, measuring out trips to the market depending on the contents of the cupboard, the number of sweet potatoes still stored up and the size of the moon.

'I'm going to go to the post office tomorrow. Is that all right?'

'I guess. We can manage without you for a

day, if we have to. Have you written your letter?'

'Yes.'

'Did you mention the demon?'

'No, of course not.'

'Good. Writing things can make them more real you know.' Jinyi paused. 'So what does it say?'

'You know what it says.'

'I have no idea. And you know I can't read it.'

'It doesn't say anything bad. Why would it? My parents care about us, remember. Both of us. It just asks how they are, and tells them how we're getting on. I just want to talk to them.'

'You can talk to me, you know. I'm still here.'

'I know.'

But they had nothing else to say to each other, and she had to get up in a couple of hours to start the long walk.

The letter was written on a corner of wind-hardened poster paper torn from a brick wall that bordered the market. She had traced the characters in meticulously small handwriting, using an old painting brush and rainwater mixed with soot.

It read:

Ma. How are you? Please tell me of Fushun. Life here in Stone Monk Village is difficult, but I feel it is good for me to learn of hardships. My husband is taking care of me. Your darling grandson did not survive the journey. Those are the hardest words to write. I hope to hear from you soon. Your daughter.

Yuying held it tight in her hands as she walked, not daring to fold it or press it into a pocket.

In the house nearest to theirs lived a grumpy couple and their five sons. Yuying had passed the house a number of times on the way to the market, and Jinyi had told her the reason why she only ever saw one of the children at a time. They only had one pair of trousers between them, he explained, and so only the kid who left the house, to work, to fetch water from the well or to run an errand, got to wear them, knotted tightly or not so tightly with string, depending on their size. She had laughed when he had told her, thinking it was a joke, but the upward slice of his furrowed eyebrows showed her instantly that he was serious. Jinyi and his cousin had shared a single pair of plimsolls between them until he had left, and he would never forget that sticky feeling of pushing bare feet into the damp warmth of a recently worn shoe. As she passed the house, she wondered what they did all day, the four children left behind, the fire burnt down in the single room they shared, and nothing but their imaginations to make the hours pass.

Yuying arrived at the post office in the early afternoon. It was staffed by two men, both of whom wore their faded uniforms as if they were second skins, saggy with age and hopelessly uncared for. They stood close together in the smoky warmth of the dim light trailing in from the window, tipping their cigarette ash away from the bags of unsorted letters surrounding them. The stamp was, as she had been told, four *jiao*.

'But an envelope is going to cost another two, because we can't deliver anything that isn't properly sealed in an envelope.'

She put the letter down on the wooden table that doubled as a counter, dizziness suddenly fluttering through her. The two men stood waiting, and though Yuying quickly pulled a hand to her face, she could not stop herself from crying. She coughed and half choked on her tears, but they only increased until she was letting out stuttered and snotty sobs, and she tried to speak in the midst of her hot and vinegary tears. Neither of the two men, still standing awkward and embarrassed in their official poses on the other side of the desk, could understand a word.

'I haven't, I haven't got it. I haven't got any more.'

They were nervous, touching their lapels and rubbing their chins.

'It's the official policy —'

'We're both very sorry —'

'Otherwise, of course —'

'We wouldn't hesitate —'

'But, well —'

'We're both very sorry.'

She nodded and tried to smile, rubbing her nose with her pulled-up sleeves. One of the men started rummaging between the bags to extricate a child-sized wooden stool, which he offered her. She sat and stared at the door.

It took a full ten minutes of them pretending to be busy at work before one of them thought of a solution.

'It doesn't need to be one of our envelopes though! Look, you could fold up your letter —'

'Yes, with your writing on the one side —'

'And turn the corner over —'

'And seal it with a little glue, of course —'

'We have some here you can use —'

'Then write the address on the other side, put the stamp on, and —'

'And there you go.'

Yuying sobbed her thanks until both men were blushing, and then delicately crafted the letter into its own envelope, remembering the delicate paper swans her classmates used to construct whenever they got a spare scrap of paper.

The sun was already sinking when she left, so she steered away from the main track, looping closer to the scattered villages so that the only people she met would be women taking in the washing and tethering up the animals. If she barely saw any of the ragged men, deserters, beggars, migrants and wanderers she passed, it was only because she kept her eyes trained on the distance, watching for a horseman heading north with a saddle bag full of letters.

Jinyi noticed his wife become calmer, her shoulders held a little higher as she worked, shrugging off the last two years, the time between the glowing and hardening of the first pregnancy and the second child's burial. Her long black hair was pulled tight across her scalp and bunned up, whereas before it had bounced about her eyes. Only three years since the wedding, and Jinyi already found it hard to level the stoic grace of the crouching woman with the nervous giggles and forthright blushes of the sixteen-year-old who had guided him round her father's home. Time must be on the upswing again, Jinyi convinced himself, like a waterwheel hauled up by the same sway that lugged it down. Everything will turn out right. If we both work just a bit harder everything will be fine. He did not think about the horseman with his bag of messages slipping north, nor did he imagine that the postman would almost give up his search through the ruined, shrapnel-ridden city where street signs had become meaning-less, and that only in stopping hungry and exhausted at a restaurant would he recognise the name and press the letter into the hands of one of the waiters — no, Jinyi just moved on along the rows dragging a spindly rake behind him.

No letter came in reply. Instead, a month and a half after Yuying's visit to the post of-fice, they were woken, sometime past mid-night, by the scuffle of hooves on the gravelly track near the house. Auntie Hou was the first up, meeting the driver outside before he even had time to bang at the door.

'We don't want anything, so you can turn around now if you think —'

But her voice trailed off as she spotted the coach to which the horses were harnessed. It was a covered wagon, wooden but solid, and the driver in front of her, Auntie now real-ised, was wearing a sombre black jacket and, much more importantly in her eyes, sturdy dark plimsolls. You can always tell a man from the state of his shoes, she thought.

'I've come from Fushun. This is the Bian residence, is it not?'

'It most certainly is not! My name is Hou Shi, and this is my husband's home! Wait here. Jinyi!' she shouted toward the house.

She needn't have bothered. Both Jinyi and Yuying were already in the doorway, watch-ing the restless swagger of the horses.

287

'Unless I'm much mistaken, this has something to do with you two, doesn't it?' Auntie Hou said wearily. 'I'm going back to bed, but you'll be wanting to tie up those horses before you wake Old Hou up, understand?'

Jinyi stepped closer to the confused coachman.

'Who sent you?'

'Mrs Bian. I've come to take you back to Fushun, on her orders.'

'On her orders? What does that mean?'

The driver looked at the two of them nervously. 'She said to tell you both that it is safe now. The war is over . . . but, of course, I'm sure you know that. She said to hurry back, because Old Bian is sick. And, well, she sent this.'

He held out a small wooden box. Jinyi reached forward, but the driver cleared his throat and retracted his arm.

'For her daughter.'

Jinyi reached out and snatched it from the driver anyway, before passing it to his wife. The two men watched Yuying, but she simply held it close to her chest, making no attempt to open it.

'Well, no one is going anywhere,' Jinyi said shaking his head. 'Of course, you'd better come inside and get some rest from your journey. There's no point going straight back. My wife will make a bed up. Come on, I'll help you lead the horses round the back.'

Once the driver and horses were settled, Jinyi and Yuying collapsed back in their room.

'Aren't you going to open it?'

'What did you mean, "No one is going anywhere"?'

'I meant we've just got settled. We've made a start of a new life together, and we can't give up now. Anyway, don't you want to know what's in it?'

'I think I can guess,' she said under her breath as she pulled off the tight square lid.

Inside was a pile of twenty fat silver coins, chipped and bitten but drawing the light nonetheless, like a magnifying glass tilted to fry an upturned insect.

'Oh fuck,' Jinyi exclaimed, his mouth caught in a perfect O.

Yuying quickly put the lid back on, and placed the box above their heads at the end of the bed.

'There's no need for that kind of language, Hou Jinyi. Now, let's get some sleep. We can talk about it more in the morning.'

However, neither of them could sleep, and so they lay exhausted and still, back to back, till morning, each one worrying about what the other would do next. By the time they had stretched up and slouched off towards a breakfast of leftover grains in a gloopy stock shared with the nervous coach driver, they were both resolute.

'Jinyi,' she half whispered it, her head leaning low across the kitchen table. He gurgled in response as he drained the last of the liquid from his bowl. 'I want to go back.'

Jinyi had to force himself to swallow to stop from spluttering the food back out from his mouth, his Adam's apple hitching quickly up his neck.

'Listen, Yuying, we've been through this before. You're just homesick. We're just getting set up here. Listen, if you still feel the same in a year, two years, then we'll go back, I promise. But we've got responsibilities here. We can't leave our children's graves. They need to be tended, their spirits need our protection.'

'Jinyi, that's just supersition and —'

'No! I'm sick of other people telling me what to believe or how to behave. My parents are here, my children are here, even if you can't see any of them. This place is a part of me. This is my history, my past, my future. It's the only place I really belong, even though it took me fifteen years to see it. With that money we could buy our own farm near here. We can start our life together properly, just the two of us, and our family.'

'But the war is over. Isn't that why we left?'

'No. We left so that we could make a new start. So that we could find somewhere where we could be equals. This is the only place I understand. We can't just give up and go running back.'

'Why not? My family's there. Your old job will still be waiting. And it is safe now, Jinyi, I'm sure of it. I hear your cough here, it's cold and full of frost and it sounds like it's tearing a hole in your throat. We'll feel better in the city. We can be comfortable again. We can be happy.'

'Aren't you happy here with me? Tell me you're not happy.'

'You know that's not what I mean. I'm glad we came here, I'm grateful. But this isn't us. Look around: this isn't our life, Jinyi. I've tried, I've really tried, but I'm tired and I want to go home!' She was shouting now. 'I don't fit here, surely even you can see that!'

'Listen, we don't own this land, Yuying, but it owns us. My parents, me, even our children now. All of their spirits are bound to the soil. If we go back, the demon will only follow us there. We have to face him on our own turf.'

'Jinyi,' she reached out to him, pleading, drawing out the second syllable, but he pulled his hand away.

'My father is sick,' her eyes were already red and blotchy.

'Come on,' he sighed. 'Let's talk about this later. There's work to do.'

'No, Jinyi listen. I'm going back with the driver. Today. There won't be another chance. Please, I won't ask you anything again, I'll be the perfect wife from now on, I promise! I swear it to the Kitchen God right here,' she said, pointing to my effigy in the corner of the room. 'Just take me back to my home!'

He looked at her, staring out her puffy eyes, her shaking cheeks.

'I'm not leaving, Yuying. I can't leave our children here alone.'

'They're not here, Jinyi. They're dead,' she was sobbing.

'I can't do it. Not again. I'm sorry, but that is the end of it.'

It was a bluff, but he did not let it show. He wanted to say, I would be lost without you. Stay with me. I love you. He couldn't. He pushed out his chair and got up from the table, heading out towards the field, his heart thumping out percussion in his chest.

Yuying turned to the embarrassed driver.

'How long?'

She moved quickly through the bedroom, searching for the things she had brought with her. There was nothing from the first journey that hadn't been traded or pawned for more practical clothes and blankets. She took her two warm jackets, both mud-stained and patchy, and the child's jacket she had been decorating, a half-finished tiger crawling towards the pocket, and left the rest. From beneath the furs on her side of her bed, she retrieved Wawa's blanket, moth-holes dotted across the hem. It was the only thing of his saved from the burial; the only thing she had left to remember him. 'There can be no loss,'

Chuang Tzu had written thousands of years before. Everything must continue. Embarrassed at the lack of possessions bundled up in her arms, Yuying followed the driver from the house.

While he yoked the horses, she strode across the plots to her husband, who was resolutely facing the other way.

'Jinyi,' she whispered so that no one would overhear. 'Come with me. Please.'

'I can't.' His voice was cracked. 'Yuying. I can't leave them.' He was pleading.

'We have to leave them. We have to choose. The past or the future. And I know our future is together, Jinyi, if we want it. Look, I know this is fast, it's difficult. We will start again, just like you said. As equals. But not here. Let's leave all the bad bits here, all the bad luck and the ghosts and the angry little gods that govern this place.'

Jinyi shook his head. She did not seem to understand that it was not that simple.

'Jinyi. I love you,' her mouth was so close to his face that he could feel her breath tickle across his neck. She felt awkward saying this: it was not the type of thing people should have to say in real life.

He nodded, still not turning to face her. I love you too, he wanted to say. But the words got stuck in his throat. He ran a hand under his nose and sniffed, a slobbery canine sniff, before nodding again.

'Jinyi, I'm going. I can't live here. You must have known that, even if we didn't talk about it. I'm going now, and I'm not coming back. Please.'

'I can't leave them.' That was all he could say. And he knew, even then, that he would regret that day for the rest of his life. But still he could not say it.

'We've still got the rest of our lives. I can't spend another fifty years here. I'm sorry. This is the only chance to go back. Please.' There was silence.

'All right. Take these, please,' she sniffled, and pressed ten of the silver coins, exactly half, into his palm. 'They are yours now. If you change your mind, you can use them to come and find me. You know where I'll be. I'm not giving up, Jinyi. I'll be waiting for you.' She was crying now, unashamed of her tears. 'I'm still your wife, and I'm not going to stop being your wife. I'll be waiting for you . . .'

She wiped her face. 'Be careful, Jinyi.'

Yuying turned and strode, as calmly as she could, to the coach.

'I love you, Yuying. Please, stay.'

She was too busy climbing into the carriage to hear him. By the time the eager horses had strutted off and she could bring herself to look back at the fields, he was already slinking away in the other direction.

■ ■ ■ ■

Jinyi stayed because he wanted more than anything to hold on to the memories buried there; Yuying left because she could not forget.

She spent the return journey half asleep, her head lightly buzzing against the coach's frame, her legs tucked underneath her on the wooden seat. They stopped a couple of times for bowls of wontons bobbing in broth, then ploughed onward, covering a greater distance at night than by day. They took the main road, a straight line untangled from the swoop of hills and forests, the land patted flat from the retreats of many different armies. They passed small road-side villages that had been left abandoned, scores of deserted hideouts, and shadows quickly disappearing behind the side of buildings. The journey back took only two days. How much easier it was to undo than to do, Yuying thought, knowing that the opposite was really true, that even the clumsiest of knots are easier to loop than to loosen.

The money she had left him ought to be enough to bring him home, when he came to his senses. Forgetting was, after all, an expensive commodity, one that few could afford. Yuying could not quite believe that he had taken the money and not called her back, though she did not once consider asking the driver to turn the horses around. She chewed her lip and prayed to the warring gods of the fields. Suddenly she realised how much she would miss him. If Jinyi did not return, then there would be no future for her except to grow old among her childhood toys, for no man would want a hand-me-down with the whiff of shame.

The river wind, scraped off the paddies and pens, whispered through the cracks in the carriage, toying with her skirt. Was that the demon's breath, panting behind her? She shook her head; demons do not enter cities.

'Nearly there,' the driver shouted back to her.

As if she would not recognise her hometown. And yet it was different; the buildings wore their spray of bullet scars like medals. Tatty banners, hastily scribbled in smudged ink, hung from the bank, the post office and the sprawling mansions of those associates of her father that she thought would have had better taste. She did not yet know that those houses were no longer filled with the family friends she once saw at lavish parties. The red flags told her that the war was over, and though she had already heard this, it was a shock to think of a city still working without it, as if its clockwork mechanism had depended on the music of gunfire and fear to keep it turning. Fu Lions grinned from the restaurants and rickshaws were heaved through the streets, dodging the afternoon drinkers and the old couples leaning on each other for support as they walked towards the reopened park.

When the coach drew up on the paving stones outside the family home, Yuying looked down to see Yaba smiling up at her, just as he had when she was young. As she stepped down, Yaba brought a hand to his face in mock surprise, and mimed clutching armfuls of the air around him. What, no bags for me to carry?

'No bags this time, you'll be pleased to know. Only me. I bet you're thinking I'm looking old, no?'

Yaba shook his head. Then, as he saw her walking into the house, he ran to stop her. He was too late.

As Yuying entered the house, a sour, dry scent enveloped her. She turned to Yaba with a sob bobbing up through her throat as he pulled two fluttering hands across his face like curtains, miming death.

Her father had died the day before, on 1 October 1949. It was only months later that Yuying realised the significance of the date, and in later years, with the rest of the country (though for different reasons), she made a habit of dividing life into two separate eras: those of before and after the establishment of the People's Republic of China.

Old Bian had died in the morning, bed-ridden and silent, choking on his own breath. And at that same time, as he had slipped from the room towards the bottom of the world, a slight, crinkly fog had begun to clear from Tiananmen Square, which brought a sense of relief to the official artists and cameramen and photographers eagerly gathered there. The recorded footage would not be seen, of course, for only a few millionaires had even heard about the strange magic known as television, and anyway, those foreign electric boxes were signs of bourgeois corruption, so people would not want them even if they were being given away.

Standing on a rostrum raised above the crowd, surrounded by high-ranking officials, was a short man wearing a blue jacket, knotted up to the neck with looping cotton toggles. He was a little portly, though as yet lacking the sagging gut that would mark him out in later years while half the population starved, and his pasted-back black hair was already beginning to recede at the edges of his forehead. A dark mole stood out from on the round chin of his full-moon face. He was standing in front of the Gate of Heavenly Peace, at the entrance to what was once the emperor's private celestial city, ready to proclaim peace and revolution to the nation. He gripped his notes in his hands, and leaned toward the bulky black microphone.

'The Chinese people have stood up!' Mao Zedong began. His voice buzzed and echoed from the bulky loudspeakers, and the men flanking him nodded, some stern and patriarchal, others showing their crooked teeth in wide grins.

As he announced the establishment of the new state, of the 'democratic dictatorship' led by the people, the thousands crammed into the square feverishly shouted and clapped, and the whole centre of the city seemed to become a foamy sea of fluttering red flags. People were shoving, shoulder to shoulder, up on tiptoe for a better view — and why shouldn't they have been happy? This was the end of war and feudalism and repression and injustice and poverty. This was their country now. This was the beginning of the future. Some even slapped each other on the back, unable to keep still. When the speech finished, the crackly feedback from the speakers gave way to gunshot salutes, spasmodic drumming and the bangs of a thousand reels of firecrackers, leaving trails of red paper littering the streets like the first crinkly gifts of autumn.

A few days later Yuying sat in her childhood room in the east wing, a white robe wrapped around her shoulders. Death clothes are snow made thick, her mother had said; they are possibilities made hard and real. But the white was not the white of winter fields, mountain peaks or expensive panda fur. It was the symbol of an absence, like the scorched landscape of nuclear fallout, the fuzzy albumen of slow-growing cataracts.

Leaving the room, Yuying had to navigate around stacks of boxes and bags. The house was emptying itself out, preparing for grief: her younger sisters now tended to their new husbands' needs, and the servants were quitting in hope of fresh lives in the newly socialist state. Yuying's mother would be left alone with Yaba, each in separate wings. Between them, all the things that the inhabitants could never say rattled around the dozen abandoned rooms, jostling for space with the dust and mildew.

The wake had been going on for days, the body lying in the silent main hall. Yuying almost expected her father to rise up at any second, and stroll from the house, shaking his head. At the foot of the coffin was a portrait of Bian, younger than any of the gathered friends and relatives could remember him ever having looked in real life. The household gods had been packed away, all the mirrors covered. Yuying moved beside her father and took his cold hand, remembering how he had gripped hers whenever he had taken her to a showy banquet as a child: a small girl facing the upturned noses of the eldest sons of other businessmen, the only female in the room. If her father had possessed countless flaws, then he had also had strengths. Either he had never cared what anyone thought of him, or he had been canny enough to know that few would risk his wrath by bad-mouthing him.

The hired mourners that sat behind the regular guests provided a great spectacle of grief. They wept and howled and tore at their clothes, all for a very reasonable price. The dead nibble on these showy sobs, still trying to save face, even in the underworld. And it is there, incidentally, that the more hearty meals of the gods are provided: screams and guttural wails, tears lashed from flayed skin. I've never been down there myself, of course, but word gets around.

The final chanted prayers faded into silence, and the mourners turned their backs as the coffin was closed and sealed. Yuying's eyes sought out her mother among the hung heads — she had unusually let her greying hair fall freely, covering the craggy lines of her furrowed brow. She had not yet asked Yuying anything about the last two years. This is what all families are best at, Yuying thought: pretending to forget.

The coffin was hoisted up from the table above the small altar and carried from the house. The slim procession, with its white memorial banners, meandered around the city, and each of the sisters wondered why more of Old Bian's associates had not joined them. The streets were busy, though the milling crowds parted, and stopped to stare and appraise, as they let the mourners through. This was not simply out of respect for the dead — most of the watchers were silently calculating the cost, working out how much had been spent on the funeral. Yuying looked around, ignoring the staring faces. Everyone around her seemed distant — her mother confused and slow, Yaba leading her carefully by the elbow, her sisters trying to outdo each other with the amount of tears they could shed — and she found her mind wandering to where her husband might be.

The mourners stopped in the courtyard of the biggest of Old Bian's restaurants, to offer the final prayers before the coffin could be carried to the hillside and laid in the ground. They burnt huge bouquets of paper flowers, dense wads of fake banknotes, and even a horse created from finely bunched coloured paper, to send to Bian to help him in the next world. After tears, there is nothing better than a meal of smoke for a god or a loose soul. The billowy cirrus from incense, the thick slobbery char from paper and card, thin delicate rings wobbling from pious lips, or the luscious mist rising from the burnt offering of sacrificial sows; each and every wisp is delicious. I am no connoisseur — the Buddha and his posse of bodhisattvas, even old Lao Tzu and the Taoists, get their fill in temples every day. I get candy once a year at the Spring Festival. Not that I feel bitter.

They found the streets on the way back home even more crowded than before. On every corner, square or crossroads there were men standing on chairs, surrounded by throngs of onlookers. Each man's raised voice veered between agitation and excitement, and some went as far as to raise their fists into the air to punctuate their declarations. Yuying was the only one of the quiet group not yet used to this sight.

'This is the beginning of a new life for us, my comrades. No more tyranny from land-lords! No more suffering at the hands of greedy employers! No more poverty! No more foreigners telling us what to do! Chairman Mao has proclaimed —'

She turned a corner, beginning to lag behind the rest of the mourners, only to spot another speaker, the crowd around him nodding exaggeratingly in agreement.

'— everything split equally. A dictatorship of the people! A great country once again! But it will not be easy, my friends! Oh no! There is much work to be done, land to be redistributed, traitors and landlords and tyrants still to be hunted down —'

If you ask me (and why not, because I've gathered my fair share of opinions over the millenia), then this is how ideas travel best, borne by hungry mouths and clenched fists. It doesn't really matter how ridiculous they are — anger and indignation are infectious. And everyone wants a better world, don't they?

Yuying walked on, not wanting to be left behind. A few posters had been plastered to the walls of abandoned buildings, and the air was like electricity. What does all of this mean, she wondered as they reached their own street. And, will it mean Jinyi will return?

'We've been saved from the Japanese! Saved from the Nationalist devils, from persecution and injustice! Throw out the old broken gods, throw out the old ways. We are free! The Party promises complete economic and social reform, complete equality. Soon —'

Another one was crowing to a smaller gathering near their house, but Yuying was no longer listening. There was no need to listen, for the words oozed between cracks in walls, blew in through open windows, crept under warped doorframes and down through skylights, and were soaked up in soggy bread. The words would be there every time Yuying went out, repeated in every teahouse, restaurant or family dining room until they stuck to her clothes like the smell of smoke, and finally seeped through into her pores.

Yuying and her mother returned to keep vigil in their rooms, waiting, as custom dictated, for the soul to return seven days later. They scattered flour in the doorways to try to catch the telltale footprints of Bian's spirit transformed into its zodiac animal for one last trip back before the greater journey. They would not consider the possibility that his spirit might have chosen to wander to one of his other women instead, or that it had become lost in a city whose shape was changing daily.

I followed his directions and soon came to the bridge the poet had described. Though from a distance I might indeed have mistaken it for the sublime swoop of an arching rainbow, when I got closer I found to my dismay that it seemed to be constructed entirely from bones, which a hundred winters had trampled down to juts and footfalls. Furthermore, much of the pathway had crumbled to dust and grit, leaving huge holes opening on a bloom of mist that disguised the inevitable fall. It took me many days to scramble across, half of the time on my hands and knees, my hail-rapped fingers grabbing for the next gnarled knot of bone to pull my body a little further forward.

When I eventually clambered down on the other side my feet were blistered and bloody and my head was spinning. In front of me, at the highest point of the gorge, was a small thatched cottage. As I approached, I noticed that the cottage was surrounded by a swarm of noisily buzzing fireflies; they were nosing around the flowers in the garden, setting the stone walls and the straw roof agleam, and could even be seen inside the windows, flitting around the study. I pushed past them and entered through the half-open door.

'Honourable Du Fu,' I said, addressing a seated old man with a light beard that turned out to be, on closer inspection, a muzzle of fireflies. 'I have been given your address by your friend, Li Bai. I have come to ask your advice, poet of history. I must find a way to describe the working of the human heart.'

'Ah ha,' he nodded. 'The heart is a traveller who never arrives. I suppose old Li Bai told you that the heart lives in the tiniest details that it takes in?'

'He did indeed, in a manner of speaking. Do you agree, then?'

'I have lived through much suffering: poverty, arrest, exile, being snubbed by the court, war, disease and the death of my child, among other hardships. I tell you this not out of pity, for in these I am not alone. There will always be great mansions where the wealthy hold lavish feasts, and outside the gates of these mansions there will always be beggars shivering with hunger. There is perhaps no limit to the winds that can blow through the heart, and turn it cold. You must find what makes it survive.'

'You mean, if I find out what makes the heart keep going, despite everything, then I will have found out how it works?' I asked.

'Precisely. Remember, though, that just as hearts are slaves to love, so men are slaves to history. All you can really hope to do is catch a moment, a feeling, a glance, before it is gone.'

I thanked him profusely, and left him to the sonorous murmurs of the fireflies that filled his home.

6:
1951
THE YEAR OF THE RABBIT

To celebrate the Mid-Autumn Festival, Bian Shi bought mooncakes, those octagonal pastries full of sweet red-bean paste, fruits and jams, sometimes with a plump golden egg yolk hidden in the centre. She could think of no other way to cheer Yuying up. It surely cannot be healthy to sulk for more than a year — it takes a while for life to catch up again, she told her daughter. Yuying took half a bite of one the cakes, then left it, with a crescent of teeth marks, on the antique kitchen table.

When she was a little girl, Yuying had looked forward to the Mid-Autumn Festival, to the sweet mooncakes and the stories her mother used to tell about Chang E, the woman on the moon, who had lived out her early life in the Palace of the Immortals. She was one of those divine beings whose beds are the silky underside of summer clouds, back in the days when the names of us gods and goddesses hadn't yet been dragged through the mud. She was tall and slender, her charcoal mane sloping down to her pale toes, and, let me tell you, the rumours were true: she was the most beautiful woman who ever drew breath. Her eyes looked as though they had been formed from shards of arctic ice. Pouting and cold, she possessed that singular kind of heart-stopping, double-take beauty that allows its owner to get away with almost anything.

Chang E's husband Hou Yi, meanwhile, was an average man, renowned only for his skills at archery. He woke up beside his wife one morning and found that he could barely open his eyes because of the stark rays of red light blistering the sky. Shielding his face, he stumbled from his room and looked down to see the face of the earth beneath slowly blackening and bubbling in the heat. Ten burning suns were spinning through the sky like a freshly broken pack of pool balls. Hou Yi quickly reached for his longbow and quiver and, without a moment to lose, shot down nine of the suns, leaving a single burning star hanging in the heavens.

'What's all that ruckus?' Hou Yi heard his sleepy wife simper from back inside.

'Nothing, dear,' he called. He then mopped his brow and went back to bed.

Husband and wife were woken several hours later by the furious shouting of the Jade Emperor; when he is angry, the whole universe knows about it. The enraged emperor wanted to know why Hou Yi had killed nine of his sons. Hou Yi stammered, muttered a little, blushed and hung his head.

'You are no longer welcome in my kingdom. You are both banished to earth, where you will live out the remainder of your life as mortals,' the Jade Emperor announced.

Chang E sulked and moaned for the next month, sitting around and fanning herself while her husband built a small house for them in the crumpled mountains to which they had been exiled. For a year they lived alone, Hou Yi chopping wood, growing vegetables, hunting hares and cooking meals while Chang E brooded and threw tantrums. Then one night, Chang E suddenly sat up in bed and woke her husband with her laughter.

'It's so simple, yet I never thought of it before! Didn't you ever hear about the Mother of the West? Everyone used to say that she knows the secret of eternal life.'

'Yes,' he replied, rubbing his eyes and yawning. 'I think I heard that one. But isn't it just a story?'

'Of course not! What a strange thing to say! You must find her and learn the secret, and then we won't be condemned to become ghosts in this horrid place.'

'For you I would do anything,' he said. 'I will leave as soon as the sun rises.'

Tears began to blossom in the corners of

her eyes. 'But how can we possible sleep now, just knowing that we don't have to die in this dirty, smelly —'

'Yes, you are right, my darling. I will set forth immediately!' he told her, already pulling on his clothes.

Hou Yi saddled his horse and set off in the direction that the sun had gone down in only hours earlier. I could tell you about the red-hot mountain peaks he ascended, the endless rivers he swam across, the meals he was forced to make of barbecued horsemeat, and the thousands of *li* he marched through parched desert plains and dense whispering forests, but that would take more time than we have. Perhaps you would be more interested to know how Chang E survived on her own, having to cook and provide for herself for the two years in which her husband journeyed west? That is much simpler — for even in the most remote reaches of the earth, there are always men willing to help out a poor, beautiful woman fluttering her dazzling eyelashes and pouting her cherry-red lips.

The Mother of the West was a wide-hipped matron with a permanent grin set amidst her basset-hound jowls. She took pity on the thin, bedraggled man who hobbled into her palace and kowtowed before her.

'I have heard of your unfair treatment, and I know you have travelled far to reach me. Therefore, I am prepared to give you this medicine.'

She summoned a dog-headed lion, which carried a small box in its mouth. Hou Yi stepped closer as she opened it to reveal a small silver pill, the size of a shelled cashew.

'No doubt you have heard that there are now emperors down here on earth, as well as in heaven. What you may not know is that Shen Nung, the second emperor of this country, was fathered by the great imperial dragon himself. While giving birth to Shen Nung, his mother's screams caused earthquakes and avalanches. This pill is made from the tears she shed as the dragon's child emerged from her breaking body.'

She placed the pill in his hand and grinned.

'Break it in half — half of this pill is enough for anyone to become immortal. It will therefore enable both you and your wife to live forever. Again. Good luck, Hou Yi.'

Hou Yi thanked her for her generosity, and kowtowed until his knees and palms ached, then hurried from the palace. It took him another year to make the return journey, by which time his wife was growing impatient.

'What took you so long? Don't you know what I've had to put up with while you've been away? Oh, that any woman should have to suffer as much as me!' Chang E said, sitting outside their house and looking in disdain at the mud-caked, emaciated man walking towards her.

'I am so sorry, my darling. But I have done it! I have a pill from the Mother of the West. Here, let me show you,' he panted, handing her the box.

She raised her eyebrows as she peered down at the silver pill. 'Is that it?'

'Oh yes — this is the key to eternal life. Half of this pill will make us immortal again!'

Hou Yi leaned down to kiss his wife. She wrinkled her nose and raised a finely manicured hand.

'What do you think you are doing? You're filthy and you smell worse than a rotting dog! Don't even think about touching me until you've had a thorough wash. Ugh!'

As her husband traipsed inside to wash, exhausted but content, Chang E studied the pill once more. Half a pill — would that really be enough, she wondered. If half could make them immortal here on earth, then surely the whole thing would be enough to return her to the Palace of the Immortals. And what's more, she considered, it was all Hou Yi's fault that they had been banished down here in the first place. He was dirty and thoughtless, and clearly didn't deserve her, so why should she share it with him? And with that thought, she popped the whole pill into her mouth and swallowed.

Suddenly she was overcome with dizziness, and something began to splutter and gurgle in her stomach. Pins and needles numbed her fingers and toes, before spreading through the rest of her body. She felt tipsy and light-headed, and only then did she realise that she had begun to float into the air. She gripped frantically at the eaves of the house as she ascended, but she could not hold on, and began drifting higher.

'Hou Yi! Get out here now!' she wailed as she began to rise over the tops of the tallest trees.

Her husband rushed from the house, half-undressed, and gasped as he saw Chang E disappearing into the clouds.

'Help me! Hou Yi, do something!'

He fumbled for his quiver and, without a moment to lose, fed an arrow into his long-bow and took aim.

'What do you think you're doing, you idiot? You'll kill me with that! Think of something else, quickly!' she hollered.

However, by the time he had put down the bow, it was too late. He had to squint to see the tiny speck that was his wife, continuing to rise steadily through the sky. She shook her arms and kicked her legs furiously, trying to stop the ascent, drawing curious looks from the high-flying birds soaring around her. Soon they too were beneath her, and she felt a sudden squelching pop as she burst free of the earth's atmosphere, and yet she still could not stop. It was only when she tilted her head backwards that she spotted her destination, craggy and yellow and swelling larger and larger as she approached.

It was with an unladylike thwump that Chang E tumbled to the ground on the surface of the moon. After dusting herself down, she looked around. There was nothing but murky craters and rocky ridges. She spent the first couple of hours on her new home jumping up and down, frantically flapping her arms and trying to take off, but to no avail. She was stuck. It was only then, as Yuying's mother used to emphasise with a raised hand pointing to the sky, that Chang E began to miss her husband and thought about all the things she had now lost because of her rash decision. For what is the use of being immortal if you have to spend eternity on your own?

Seeing the stream of bitter tears blotching Chang E's once beautiful face, the rabbit that lived on the moon took pity on her and bounded up to Chang E to sit beside her, twitching his ears to try to make her smile. They are there to this day. Look up at the face of the moon on a clear night, and you will see them — a lonely young woman stroking a white rabbit.

Yuying could not take her mind from this childhood story, lying once again in her old room, where the moon stared down through the curtainless windows. Bian Shi was too tactful to mention Jinyi in her daughter's presence, but this did not stop Yuying tormenting herself with blame for what had happened. Despite the enduring grief — something she suspected was, like the colour of her eyes or the mole under her left shoulder blade, simply a part of her now — she now saw the death of the two babies as something binding them together, not separating them. No one else understands but us, she told herself. No one else knows how this feels, this splinter lodged in the arteries, these ghosts in my stomach.

There is a huge list of people who, throughout history, have offended the gods in one way or another, but, aside from Chang E, only one was banished to the moon. He was a lumberjack named Wu Gang, and he was sent there for trying to become divine. His punishment was simply to ply his trade — once he has chopped down the solitary tree that grows on the dark side of the moon, he will be free to leave. However, every time he heaves and fells the trunk, the stump grows a new one in its place, until, within minutes, it has sprouted branches and reached the same height as the freshly cleaved timber left rolling on the ground. For every tree he chops down, a new one grows in its place. Yuying's hopes were like this, dismissed as irrational and silly each day, only to somehow grow again inside her by the next.

■ ■ ■ ■

At eight every morning Yuying stood in line, along with the rest of the staff, outside the factory. It was a huge brick building shoddily erected along with the new barracks in what was once a private park. The whole area smelt of sewage and rotting vegetables, but the new workers did not let this put them off. They would stand to attention, their appearances and posture carefully appraised by the new boss. Both the men and the women there had been assigned that workplace by the local authorities. Every morning they listened to the young buzz-cut Party member, his fifteen-minute speech always punctuated with wild arm movements as though he were address-ing a pack of dim primary school children; only after he finished, and they shouted their allegiance to the new republic, could work begin.

Soon after the new decade had started, Yuying and her mother had been visited at home by a pair of uniformed officials. This was not unexpected, as gossip had spread quickly amidst the city's restaurateurs and businessmen.

'The state now owns the three dumpling restaurants,' one of the officials had told them.

'We understand. We will do anything we

can to help our country become great again, to help our comrades,' Yuying had eagerly replied.

'You will be allowed to remain a partner in the business, Ms Bian. A silent partner, of course.'

'And the staff? They'll still have their jobs?' Bian Shi had been quick to ask.

'Certainly. Everything we do is for the people. However, as representatives of the people, these decisions will rest with the Party official for Fushun. We can't have any bad elements sabotaging everything we've worked so hard for now, can we?'

'No, of course not,' Bian Shi had agreed, not quite knowing what they meant.

Since her family had been working with food for centuries, Yuying was allocated a job in a bread factory. For once she had been proud of the dry skin on her hands, the frayed cuticles, broken nails and the hardened circles marking the start of calluses; when the officials had made a quick study of her hands they had nodded their heads approvingly — despite the ostentatious surroundings, she was obviously not the spoilt bourgeois element they had predicted.

Yuying felt strangely satisfied by this allocation, and not just because some of her old schoolmates had been told that they would now be fruit pickers in the glaring sun or dish washers in the public canteens. She felt proud to be part of the new way of doing things, excited by change, especially since she was aware that previously the only option for a young husbandless woman was social ostracism, becoming a nursemaid or nanny to her siblings' children, or slowly fading into the background, given up to bitterness and talking to shadows. This is the way it should be, she thought, being chosen especially for something rather than slipping effortlessly into it because your father is a friend of a friend of the boss.

Bian Shi took a few of the surviving jewels and silver coins she now kept hidden in an old chamberpot under her bed, and traded them secretly (for if her riches were found, they would be requisitioned by the state to be redistributed) for a bicycle for Yuying to travel to work on. Yuying was so embarrassed by the brand-new bicycle that she deliberately left it out in the rain so it could collect a veneer of rust to match the others lined up outside the factory. While Yuying worked, her mother pottered about the big house, waiting for letters from her other daughters, now living in distant cities, or for Yaba to finish his kitchen shift and come and sit in silence beside her. When she became bored, Bian Shi took to sitting in the courtyard, listening for the sounds of the local regiment marching past, or else for the muffled voices of other well-off families packing up and discreetly leaving their unsubtle houses.

Yuying's job was to lift the trays of steaming sweet bread out of the ovens and carry them to the work station, to be prodded, packaged and stamped with an allocation for a particular food hall, where they would later be exchanged for vouchers and the newly pressed notes of the People's Bank. Everyone got the same. She had been doing the job for two months, and now her hands began the task before her mind even considered it. As Yuying knotted the flimsy paper around a springy loaf, Mrs Li nudged her shoulder, and whispered from the side of her mouth.

'Look out, he's coming.'

She did not have to look up to know that her colleague was talking about Comrade Wang, the young boss with a buzz-cut and a sombre and sincere passion for two things: the Party and Yuying. His voice was high-pitched and he had a habit of unconsciously letting his tongue rest on his lower lip when he was not speaking.

'Ah, Comrade Bian, I trust that we are well ahead of schedule.'

'Yes, Comrade,' she answered. Comrade Wang had repeatedly told the workers not to call him boss. Behind his back, Yuying's colleagues explained his earnestness: his father had worked for the Japanese as an 'administrative assistant'; the son had joined the Party at the end of the war, and was keen to escape

321

the shame of the family name.

'We are expecting a visit from the central office any day now, and I know you are as keen as I am to impress them with the fact that we have exceeded this month's quota.'

'Of course, Comrade.'

'We shall show them that all of you are examples of the promise with which this country now glistens. Oh yes, oh yes, the work is not just being done in the countryside and in parliament, but also in our hearts.'

'Yes, Comrade.'

'Remember that you each play a vital role in rebuilding the country.'

'We will, Comrade.'

And with this he walked off, nodding purposefully. The women exchanged glances, then carried on wrapping the paper around the warm bread. The visit from the central office would, of course, never come. Instead, representatives of representatives carried out repeated spot-checks, during which they always assured the workers of the certainty of an impending inspection.

Another month, another spot-check. Comrade Wang was salivating and almost skipping as he led the bored grey-haired representative beneath the echoing tin roof-slats and between the fire-burping ovens.

'And this, sir, is Bian Yuying, another of our new additions. As you can see, only twenty years old and yet fully embracing the collective spirit which we —'

'Quite. Bian, hmm. I recognise that name. From the dumpling restaurants?'

Comrade Wang cut in before Yuying herself had time to reply.

'Oh yes, they were bourgeois restaurant owners to the core, which makes her transition and re-education here all the more wonderful as an example of —'

'Yes,' the representative carried on wearily. 'Your husband is in the same work unit I assume.'

'No, sir. He is currently doing some important work in the countryside.' She had to work to stop herself blushing as she spoke. Truth is always malleable.

'I understand. A lot of important work is being carried out there.'

'Yes, sir.'

'Many of our best men are giving their lives for the revolution. That is how it should be. We cannot all be having it so easy in warm factories. Isn't that right, Comrade Wang?' The representative briefly raised an eyebrow, causing Wang to shuffle his feet and lick his lower lip even more than usual as they moved away.

Wang did not speak directly to Yuying again. It was in this way, with the subtlest of euphemisms, with discreet words or movements whose meaning may forever remain unclear, that lives were rearranged. It was because of a moment as subtle as this that Wang had joined the Party in the first place. He remembered tottering between rooms as a child, when his father had his bosses — bureaucrats and town-planners in the Japanese army — to dinner. Standing a metre tall and sleepy in the doorway, Wang had watched a Japanese colonel, with slicked-back hair and new spectacles, slip his hand under the table and onto Wang's mother's thigh, as she did her best to pretend to giggle and keep smiling. He had soon been shooed away as the door was closed. This was his way of making things better.

Wang's family history, however, would come back to haunt him. After a public denouncement a decade and a half later, he would be attacked by students on his way home. And when they pushed him over, called him a traitor and a conspirator and pressed the heels of their muddy plimsolls down onto his face and told him he was the scum that was ruining the country and kicked his ribs and flabby stomach until a kidney ruptured and he began to bleed internally, he would think of his wife putting their two daughters to bed, his wife who, in the half-light, if you really squinted, might be mistaken for a young woman who worked in the factory where he had once been the boss.

■ ■ ■ ■

At home after work, Yuying pushed the bland and rubbery cabbage around the bowl, trying not to look at her mother sitting across from her. The two of them were in the dining room, which had once been used only for special occasions, but was now so packed with spiders' webs that it resembled a river through which translucent nets were carelessly trawled. Her mother was still not used to surviving without a cook, and was trying to reclaim some simple recipes from memory. It was a doomed endeavor, especially now that I, the god of kitchens, had disappeared, with the last of the servants, from their home. Will people never learn?

'I met old Zhao at the market this afternoon. He was getting himself in a bother trying to figure out the new system, and not doing too well. I had to tell him to keep his gold coins better hidden if he didn't want to lose them,' Bian Shi said.

'That's not the way things work anymore, Ma. Everything should be shared equally now. Old Zhao ought to feel guilty about having them in the first place. He only has them because of the suffering of others.'

'Oh, I know. It was a shame, that's all, to see him looking like that. He used to be such a handsome, confident man. You remember

325

— he used to come to the restaurant to speak with your father.'

'I remember. He used to carry a walking stick topped with the wooden head of a dragon, and told us that it would peck our eyes out us if we stared at it too long.'

'Yes, that's right. Ha. Anyway, his youngest son has just returned from his posting and is now stationed at the new barracks built near your factory. You know, the handsome one, with big eyes. A real gentleman. He's bound to have good prospects now, what with having been with the Communists since before the Japs came. If only we'd known what was going to happen. Yuying?'

'Yes, Ma.'

'Are you listening to me?'

'Of course.'

'All right then. I don't care for talking to myself. Wait, where was I? Oh yes, I invited them both for dinner next week.'

'They won't come. We're not important anymore, Ma. We've had our time, and now we have to make up for it. Things are different now. Old Zhao will probably forget having bumped into you today anyway.'

Bian Shi pressed her palms flat against the table to push herself up. 'You should remember that your father would not have tolerated your new way of speaking. Don't think he can't hear you. I just want you to be happy, and the Zhao boy really is —'

'I'm sorry Ma,' Yuying hung her head, 'But I still have a husband.'

'I know that. But a lot of people are going missing. I hear my friends whispering about it everyday. If he doesn't come back, no one would have to know that you're still married. It's been a year now, Yuying. You'd still make a good wife to a good man, you know.'

It was true — people had been going missing, though no one was supposed to talk about it. The redistribution of land and resources throughout the country was not voluntary. Many peasants, encouraged by the new government, organised trials to bring their own brand of justice against landlords; within a couple of years around a million landlords had been executed, and many more sent to be re-educated in provinces far from their own. Everyone knew someone who was missing; no one knew anyone who had returned.

'A good wife would wait,' Yuying called after her mother, who had left the room.

'A good wife does whatever she has to,' her mother muttered as she tottered slowly down the deserted corridor.

Yuying could think of nothing else to do but return to her bedroom and bury herself beneath her sheets, the smell of burnt rice wafting in with the warm summer air through her open window. She lay and listened to the evening marches of the young men being trained for a war across the border, their panted call-and-answer mingling with lazy birdsong and the hacking coughs of workers heading out for the night shift. She hated herself for wanting him to come crawling back to her, but she no longer felt she knew who she was without him.

The spring of 1951 quickly settled in, hurried by the latest accounts of the army pushing hard south on the peninsula, helping out the neighbours in Korea. Yuying found she slept better when she knew there was a war happening. It was not the symphonic noise of breaking glass, men scuffling frantically through rubble or jamming rifles being cursed and thumped that calmed her — for, after all, the latest war was hundreds of miles away — but the feeling that her problems were small again, dwarfed by the scale of the chaos that existed outside her bedroom. She was comforted by the reminder that life was fragile, precious and threatened. Lives shrink, and so do troubles. Yuying stood in queues and markets and canteens straining to overhear snippets of conversations about local boys who had gone to Korea, about stealthy advances and unexpected counter-attacks. Soon she had memorised the names of the northern cities that their armies had taken, the foreign syllables muttered under her breath as she tried to get to sleep. This was how time passed.

The collection of ancient Chinese ideas on waging war, attributed to Sun Tzu, depicts war as a delicate art form. And just as art forces people to confront the borders and peripheries of their knowledge of themselves, so war provides them with the endpoint against which the rest of their desires and experiences can be measured. And to escape the horror of mass slaughter, mutilation, torture, pain and death, whole systems of belief are slowly pieced together. Sun Tzu stressed the stupidity of seeking rules that would explain or dictate any outcome, and yet this is what people have always done to survive. The paradox is this: people need war, because without it they do not know who they are, they do not know what it is to be human. The world is made up of close and faraway, wrote Sun Tzu, of danger and safety, of open plains and hidden paths, the possibilities of life and death.

Rain was slinking across the tops of the old mansions that had recently been converted into Party headquarters and hospitals, and Yuying's bicycle was thudding through puddles, splashing the wet and dour faces queueing outside a food hall. She joined the hundred other bicycles wobbling from the factories and work stations towards the bridge, back over the river to the crammed tenements and new apartment buildings. She steered with a single hand, zigzagging with the rest of the storm-lashed commuters, using her other hand to push her matted hair from her eyes.

Her clothes were sodden, sticking to her skin, by the time she got home and dismounted to haul her bicycle through the gate and into the courtyard.

'Yuying.'

She turned, instinctively into the storm. He was standing, umbrella-less and barefoot, the short collar of his dark jacket clutched high around his neck, on the other side of the street. Behind him the line of trees bent double in the wind. For a minute, perhaps longer, she simply stood staring at him, before she collected herself and beckoned, then turned to pull her bicycle up into the entrance hall.

Bian Shi was eating from a pile of sunflower seeds on her lap when her daughter entered, followed sheepishly by her soaked husband. As Yuying hunted through the nearby rooms for a dry towel, or at least a clean sheet, Bian Shi cracked the seeds between the teeth she still had left, pulling the salty kernel back with her tongue, and watched her son-in-law as he bit his nails. She was not going anywhere.

'Have you eaten?' Yuying asked.

'Yes, don't worry.' They both knew he was

lying to be polite.

'Are you staying?' Yuying surprised even herself with her forthright second question.

'Yes. I mean, if you, well, I mean, yes. Yes,' Jinyi said.

'Good.' They stood face to face, awkward and unsure whether to move closer. Yuying rubbed her hair with a damp towel, the only one she could find that the moths had not shredded, and then handed it to him. The sound of her mother crunching seeds echoed off the stone walls.

'How are you?'

'I can't complain. I see not much has changed round here,' he replied, obviously ignoring the bombed-out shops down the street, the flags and banners on every building and the air of disappointment and neglect seeping through the musty old house.

'Not too much. Well, I'd better make a start on dinner.'

And that was all that was said about his absence. Yuying moved to the kitchen, and added another hunk of wood to the little fire beneath the stove. She did not ask how he had travelled back, how he had survived the eighteen months, though something in her calculated that it might have taken that much time simply to cross provinces now that borders were controlled and communes strictly regulated. It shamed her to think that while she had sat here doubting him he might well have been trying to get to her, forced to avoid every big city and to stop and work in tiny village farms for a month or two every so often to earn enough to keep going. Indeed, with so many sent to the countryside and plans for the issue of urban-residency cards to curb the large exodus of people to the cities, it was exceptional that Jinyi had been able to move so freely. He would never mention how he had managed it.

'Do you want to go back to the restaurant, Bian Jinyi? Yaba is still there. He'll be back in a couple of hours and he'll be delighted to see you, I'm sure. He would be glad to have the company in the kitchen, now that so many of the old faces are gone,' Bian Shi said, following them into the dining room as Jinyi settled at the table.

He shrugged, and Bian Shi nodded as if she understood.

Yuying did not ask about the money from the box. She did not ask if he had missed her — the blisters on his feet, the scars on his hands and the tired smile he wore for her were proof enough. He had returned; that was all that mattered — returned with only a pair of trousers and a frayed jacket to his name. They both resolved never to talk of the separation, the seventeen months, one week, two days and five hours that she had counted out while her hands carried red-hot trays of bread from the oven.

■ ■ ■ ■

'I dreamt that my bicycle could fly,' she said, as if to herself, as they lay squeezed in her childhood bed. They had not dared to return to the honeymoon room, for fear of both bad luck and any nasty surprises the departing servants might have left. They were pressed tight against the wall, but not quite touching, not quite ready yet. The rain slid xylophonic across the roof and rasped at the cardboard now pasted over the window.

'Maybe you knew, deep down, that I was on my way,' Jinyi replied. 'The truth wears such strange disguises.'

They remained like that, lying on their backs with only an inch of warm air between them, until they fell asleep. They woke up in the morning with their hands entwined.

Within a couple of months they were allocated a little house near the factory — where Jinyi had been given a job manning an oven by Comrade Wang, who had remembered the words of the inspector. They left Bian Shi and Yaba to the big house, to a past they were happier to erase. Their new home was two square rooms with bare brick walls, the smoke from the wood-burning stove caught by a flue and sent around the house, warming the clay *kang* bed on which they often sat and talked. It was a good allocation, they were told by their new neighbours: space for lots of cots in the bedroom, a water pump round the corner, and only a short walk to the recently built toilet shack, though admittedly this was nothing more than a hut containing wooden slats criss-crossing over a river of sewage, where local men came to chat and share cigarettes as they squatted above the filth. When the northeast wind blew, they could smell it from their new home.

This was where they would begin again, three *li* from the house where Yuying was born, in the city that Jinyi joked was a city of a thousand winters — each time one appeared to finish, another, colder and harsher than before, suddenly began. Jinyi felt childlike again, amazed by the snow now it no longer affected his livelihood, amazed by the cold northern city hazed in white. Together they learnt to look at the world around them anew, to draw from the thousand winters a thousand possibilities. They pointed out to each other the thousand forms of snow: the crystal flecks that inflicted tiny grazes on those braving the streets; the Catherine-wheel fingerprints of thin ice; the haze of dragon's breath swelling the morning; the thick frosts that claimed the whole horizon; the tangy, tongue-tasted snowflakes; the crunchy duvets of snow that slurped up army boots; the snowmen wandering lost and bemused between parks and communal gardens; and the dry-ice puffs of pale fog with aimless snow-balls flitting by. This was to be their thaw.

Bian Shi visited when the black ice had been swept away and the streets were safe for her tiny feet, in order to tut at the cramped flat and the scrawny sofa they had set between the table and the stove. She brought round a grandfather clock as a gift, to catch their time, and an old ink painting of a pair of cranes to hang on one of the bare stone walls. The three of them sat at the table, discussing Yuying's sisters and their errant husbands, one hen-pecked and flustered, the other large, stoic and silent, and passed between them a zealous leaflet handed out at the factory.

'Will you teach me to read?' Jinyi plucked up the courage to ask her again.

This time Yuying did not even think of laughing.

'I would be delighted to.'

'I mean, if I can't read, how am I going to know what's happening? Everyone is talking about the things in the papers, like what we should be doing or the new rules or how we should be helping the country. I'm part of this too — I've lived in the countryside, I know what it means to know injustice. If anyone knows about righting old wrongs, it's me. If everyone is equal now, well, I should be equal too. But without words I'll be lost in this city soon,' he explained.

'Don't worry. Within a year you'll be flying through the newspapers. We can start after dinner.'

'I always wanted to read,' Bian Shi chirped, though husband and wife paid her little attention. 'There were a hundred books in my father's house, but not one that we were allowed to touch. Books that could bring people back from the dead, dictionaries that had the names of all the animals that lived in this country thousands of years ago, and huge tomes that would slurp the marrow out of winter, he used to boast. But I never even saw a page.'

'Well, you can listen too,' Yuying sighed.

'Oh no! I'm far too old, and anyhow, some things are better left as wishes. Oh, look, it's snowing again.'

Winter seemed to last for years, with its long underwear and the sight of small children swamped in their father's coats, with its hibernation and huddled nights. Winter is a bet, a challenge, a test of strength. Winter says endure or else give in, for there is no other choice. Winter says give way to death and be born again, that every story must begin with an ending. And if the noise they heard as they drifted to sleep on those long winter nights was not the sound of a hungry demon hitching a ride on the thick clouds, then it must just have been the braying wind easing the hinges a little.

After work, with their hair still dusted grey with traces of flour, Yuying and Jinyi settled at their fold-out table and the lesson began. Yuying took the stick of ink and rubbed it carefully into a sliver of water on the small porcelain plate. She then let the brush hover for a moment, considering where to begin.

'This one,' Yuying said, swishing the brush downwards with a flick to the right, then another to the left and a final horizontal strike through the centre, to create what looked to Jinyi like a headless stickman with out-stretched arms. 'Means *big*. It —'

'Yes, yes, even I know that one!'

'All right. But look, draw another line, a flat roof across the top, and it becomes *heaven, sky, day.* That's how you can remember them: this top line is the limit of vastness, the border of *big* — for nothing is higher than heaven, and sometimes it can seem like there is no time longer than the span of a day.'

In this way they worked through the ideo-grams, piling them together until they had a vocabulary in common, until the intricate brush-strokes had become bridges which they could wander over together. And in the very year they started, a process of simplifying the language was begun in the capital: pruning the overgrown branches into a slimmer script, tidying up the ancient forest so that light could shine between the thick pines. Over a thousand and a half characters in everyday use were simplified. After all, the old words, people agreed, were tainted with the blood of peasants forced to make ink for greedy emperors. The new language would be completely democratic — though, of course, everyone would have to speak the Beijing form of Mandarin, the Party officials agreed — for if people spoke in tongues they could not understand, how would they know what was being said about them?

As winter huddles turned into summer yawns and the table was edged closer to the stopped-open door, Jinyi graduated to newspapers and leaflets, and they made a game of testing each other. 'Communism' — that meant the end of poverty and injustice. 'Imperial' — that meant unfair and repressive. 'Bourgeois' — that meant anyone who had enslaved the people and made money from their misery. 'People's' — there was People's Park near where the river curved and pulled its belly in, People's Square where the flag was flown and where statues were being built, People's Government, People's School, People's Money printed by the People's Bank in the People's Republic of China — well, that meant it belonged to them, didn't it, at last receiving what they deserved.

Yaba accompanied Bian Shi for dinner more often in the summer. The large-muscled mute helping the hobbling old woman was the only person from the restaurant not ashamed to be seen with his former employers. With his delicate hand movements, he told Yuying about the changes in the layout, the service, the customers and even the menu in the restaurant, and Yuying translated to her husband, while her mother buried her face in her hands in exasperation after every other sentence.

'You still make money from it, Ma, and it's only changing to make the country a better place for everyone, not just a few of us.'

'Well, it's just lucky your father isn't here to see this. He would have gone mad with some of these changes. Those are the oldest dumpling restaurants in this city, remember, and they've been in your family . . .'

And so the embellished history was rattled out, the one Yuying learnt as a child and could repeat word for word along with her mother. The truth was a little different — perhaps Old Bian was lucky to be gone, but only because otherwise he might have ended up like his friends, the portly businessmen with whom he gambled and smoked, who were now wheezing and straining as they shouldered ploughs through endless brown fields in provinces they had previously never even heard of.

Jinyi soon joined in, his curiosity getting the better of him.

'The grumpy old head chef, is he still there?'

Yaba shook his head.

'What about Liu, the waiter?'

Yaba shook his head.

'Yangchen?'

Yaba shook his head, his hands swooping up into a salute.

'He's a boss? Of what? A factory? Huh, seems like he hasn't done badly out of his brother joining up in the war — it always helps to be on the winning side. Are any more of the old guys still in Fushun?'

Yaba sucked on a cigarette, and shrugged his shoulders. New times, new faces. He had different expressions for every kind of resignation to the inevitable.

'Oh, well. There must be a word for this kind of sudden change, but I don't know what it is,' Jinyi joked, and he and his wife giggled. Yaba threw up his hands, as if to say, 'Well, words are no business of mine!'

The language has always been like a South Chinese Tiger — it has no desire to be tamed. Near the beginning of the Qing dynasty, the Kangxi Emperor, keen to ingratiate himself with Han mandarins still faithful to the defeated Ming and suspicious of the Manchus in the palace, set them to work on the compilation of a giant dictionary. On completion, it contained around 47,000 different characters. Just like Chairman Mao, the emperor knew that the way to get people behind him was to give them tasks that kept them occupied while the world around them was irrevocably altered. He must have known that to wield power over language is to wield power over people's thoughts. He was the longest-reigning emperor in China's history.

With dipping brushes clashing like chopsticks and the ink stick mixed and stirred with water, Jinyi and Yuying set about rewriting their history. They drew lines beneath the long months of mourning, of guilt and blame and recriminations and doubt that separated them, and began again. They blotted out the talk of demons or spirits, and started to scribble in the present tense. Each word they wrote was a promise, a vow.

That's the funny thing about humans. I mean, don't get me wrong, I was mortal too once, but you remember how well that turned out, don't you? Now I'm a god I have a different perspective. Humans seem to think they can control their own lives. They think that, somehow, if they act a little differently, they can make everything turn out right. It's never that simple. You can call it fate, if you like. Or karma, or destiny, or whatever. But something always gets in the way. Isn't that what history means?

Even as the summer began to bubble up through the paving stones, they huddled close, thinking that if they were separated even by a couple of inches then everything might fall apart again.

'Promise me,' Yuying whispered into the dark at night, listening to him breathing beside her.

'I promise.'

'We will never leave each other's side again.'

'I promise. You?'

'Of course.'

'Go on then.'

'Jinyi, I promise.'

And then their hands met, and their faces drewer closer, and they would briefly fool themselves into believing that these promises, which would prove impossible to keep, were enough to keep them safe.

The days stretched out into russet and burnt amber, so sticky that when Jinyi finally emerged from loading trays into the belching ovens and fetching others out all day long, he found his hair turned itchy and damp, and his face transformed into a puffy pink sigh. The factory stayed open another hour with the sunlight. This extra hour of work was greeted by the workers not with annoyance, however, but with celebration. Everywhere people seemed to be excited, awash with energy, saying they would work for free if the

Party asked them to and competing to see who could show the most loyalty to the new state, 'a China finally run by the people'. They stayed in the factory, in the reallocated fields, the food halls and the building sites until all traces of sunlight had disappeared, until their tense muscles had begun to sob, until they were sent home smiling.

As Yuying and Jinyi soared back through the crowded streets on their shared bicycle, dodging marching soldiers and market officials shepherding crowds back to the greener outskirts, slipping past the last few rickshaw men unsure what to do with themselves now they had been forced to give up their feudal trade, Jinyi had to remind himself to keep pedalling. He was distracted by his satisfaction, by the twenty-one-year-old perched on the handlebars, and by the hopes he had squeezed to fit her life. If he forgot, they would topple into the pavement, where, if they lingered too long, they would be removed from sight. The streets had to be kept clean — appearance was everything. It was only when they turned the corner onto Bian Shi's street, with the older stone mansions poking out from between the hastily assembled brick huts, that they heard the commotion.

'Aiii! Old woman, you are making no sense! Just give us back our chicken and we won't report you to the authorities, how about that?'

Bian Shi was standing in the courtyard of the old house, doing her best to make her small frame fill the large gate. In front of her stood a man and a woman — each with dark faces, red noses and knotted, dirty hair — who could keep neither still nor quiet. From behind her, in the house, the leisurely clucks of a chicken could clearly be heard.

Bian Shi puffed out her chest. 'This is my chicken. How dare you accuse me of stealing! I've never seen you before in my life!'

'Look!' They tried agitated reasoning. 'We were working at the market when we noticed that one of our chickens had escaped, one with white feathers and a black plume. We looked everywhere, and someone on this street said they had seen you pick up a chicken, one with a black plume and white feathers, earlier today.'

'Who? Who told you that? Tell me!'

'It doesn't matter. Look, we know you've got a chicken in there. We can hear it! Don't think you can cheat us, just 'cos you're hungry! You've got it easy here, old woman, in your big house — we're supposed to be equal now!'

'Now, listen to me. I don't care for your insinuations. It's my chicken. I've had it months. And I certainly don't intend to eat it. It's a pet.'

They poor couple stared at each other with shocked, open mouths. They did not understand. Animals fell into two categories: work or food. Horses, donkeys, oxen and mules comprised the former. Pigs, cows, sheep, goats, horses, donkeys, mules, dogs, snakes, rabbits, mice, any kind of bird, cats, squirrels, monkeys and many others made up the latter. To keep a plump, juicy animal and not eat it seemed the very embodiment of the crazy bourgeois they had been warned about.

'You're crazy! We can't go back without our chicken — we've got quotas to fill, and we've already made offerings to the god of heaven and hell to keep our brood safe.'

'Well, you're not supposed to be following those feudal superstitions anymore, so it serves you right!'

'And you're not supposed to boss us around anymore. We may be peasants, but we're also citizens now. We know the cadre in our village — he had supper at our house last year. Ha! Wait till he hears about this!'

Bian Shi sighed and reached up, her hands pushing through her lank grey hair. She unhooked her earrings and drew them both into a closed fist, which she slowly extended in front of her. For the briefest of seconds she let her hand open a little, letting them see the slick glint of tiny gemstones, like bright scales shimmering through a clear river. The peasant couple nodded, and the man shook hands with her. They wandered off with their shoulders held high, without anything more being said.

That was not how deals were supposed to be done. In fact, it would soon be difficult to buy anything officially with money or jewels. At work, everyone was given coupons, two-inch coloured paper stubs, that could be exchanged for twenty *jin* of rice, say, for ten *jin* of potatoes or a small bag of salt. Money was supplementary — it could help you get a little more (for us Chinese cannot resist haggling and bartering in search of a good deal), but on its own it was almost useless. Behind closed doors, however, rules always take on different meanings. Even though Bian Shi would continue to be given more than enough coupons from her silent partnership with the state in her husband's former restaurant empire, she would store them all up in a jewellery box in her room, for her family had worked hard for their money, and she would not surrender her pride, despite her daughter's protestations.

'Ma,' Yuying began when they were sat around the ancient dining-room table, food cooking in the kitchen and the hen trotting proudly round their ankles, 'where did the chicken come from?'

'It came here of its own free will, young lady — and keep your voice down, will you?'

She then leaned closer to the table to whisper through the side of her mouth. 'It's your father.'

Yuying and Jinyi looked at each other. Neither was sure how to respond.

'Isn't it too late for his spirit to return?' Yuying found that she too was whispering, so that the nonchalant bird would not hear. 'I mean, after seven days it returns for one last look, then continues on its journey. But Father died nearly two years ago.'

'I know. Poor thing, he must have been looking for us all that time. I knew I should have listened to my heart. Whenever I wanted to peer at my Pa's library, my mother would tell me that there's more in our hearts than in books. And she was right.'

'Ma, those ideas are just stories. Haven't you read the news at all? They were just superstitions, designed to control people and keep them from wanting more from their lives. We don't have to fall back on them anymore. We have science, and hope.'

'I have hope too, and it's finally been repaid. You said it yourself — year of repression and invasion and poverty and finally we're getting what we deserve, if we just wish for it and work a bit harder then we'll have a country we can be proud of. Those were your words.'

'They're not *my* words! We're all supposed to be working together now, for the motherland. Not stealing poultry off the street and pretending it's the spirit of a dead man!'

'I won't listen to any more of this! How

347

dare you.'

Bian Shi gathered the squirming pile of feathers up in her arms, and marched to the doorway, only to turn before she left the room.

'I thought we'd brought you up better. All those lessons, everything you desired, and in the end you'll throw away the old for the new without even blinking. I pity you.'

With that she closed the door, the chicken clucking from behind the thick walls. Yuying sighed, and Jinyi put a hand on her shoulder.

'Let her be. Think about the war, or think about *us.* believing is better than giving up on everything.'

'Even if what you believe is wrong?'

He nodded. 'Especially if it's wrong.'

They finished eating and left the house without saying goodbye. Over the next weeks mother and daughter avoided each other, Yuying biting her lip and growing restless and uneasy, while on the other side of the city Bian Shi cleaned the hen's speckled smoky feathers with her own toothbrush, made a bed for it from an old suitcase filled with torn-up newspaper, and carried it with her whenever she left the house. She fanned the small piles of black droppings from her room, and patted its head before she went to sleep. The old house began to reek, and Yuying and Jinyi made excuses for not visiting.

By love we are transfigured. Loneliness is

just as strong. That is certainly my experience. We accept that we are powerless in relation to love, its symptoms and the way it splays the blank pages of our heart's book, etching in storms and battles. The strangest capacity of humans, it seems to me, is that they can invest anything with love. A toddler with a dog-eared blanket, an old man nursing a gangly plant in a small plot of garden, a widow doting on a ring or a trinket or a dog or a cat or a chicken.

Jinyi gently shook Yuying by the shoulder, and she mumbled as she rubbed her eyes. It was not yet dawn, though there was a dim light spilling from night fires in the courtyards and chimneys of nearby houses and all-hour work stations. Outside rang a giddy symphony of bicycle bells, the hollers of lost postmen and the dragged-out steps of the late-shifters finally shuffling home. Yuying took out the chamberpots and returned with a pail of washing water while Jinyi tended to breakfast in the dark — dough sticks deep-fried by candlelight, to be dipped in soya milk or eaten with last night's leftovers. Even before the last mouthful had been swallowed, they were swinging their legs over the bike.

Since the officials prided themselves that every day in the factory was exactly the same, there is little that can be said about the daily actions of their hands while their minds wandered.

'We need the next batch before lunch if you can fit it in, as we're a couple short,' Yuying relayed the message to her husband and the other workers around the ovens, trying her best not to look just at Jinyi. She shifted on her feet, working to stop her lips from curling into a smile. There were other couples in the factory, but each of them pretended, after arriving together, that they were merely acquaintances; each keen to prove that work — the work they did for a new China — came first.

'Of course, no problem . . . Comrade,' Jinyi replied, as neutrally as possible.

Yuying leaned forward and whispered self-consciously. 'I have invited Mrs Li to come to dinner with her husband on Friday. Don't let me forget.'

He nodded, knowing that she had timed the announcement so that he could not argue, and they both hurriedly returned to their work.

They did not eat lunch together; in spite of the attempts by Comrade Wang to integrate the workforce, people were wary of discarding their old habits, and different teams sat together at their different tables, women on one side of the room and men on the other.

After Yuying and Jinyi finished another twelve-hour shift at the factory ('We need to catch up with the Western economies!' the newspapers and street-speakers announced daily), they tested a shortcut home. They manoeuvered the bicycle through narrow alleys filled with people: old women ignoring the recent anti-spitting campaign, old men in their underwear washing their spindly bodies beside rusty taps, a street cobbler fixing an official's shoes while another taped up a commuter's puncture, small girls knotting dirty string around each others' fingers while their big sisters hung out their patched-up second-hand clothes. Entering their small house they found Bian Shi sitting in their kitchen, crying.

'Ma? What are you doing here? What's happened?'

'Oh nothing,' she cleared her throat. 'I was walking home from the restaurant — I just stopped by to have a look and a chat with the Fu Lions, as I sometimes do, so don't give me that look, young lady, I just wanted to see what was happening, that's all — anyway, I was walking back, when I heard a man making a speech. You know, one of the street-corner soap-box speakers. Well, I wasn't in a hurry, though everyone else seems in such a hurry these days, so I listened to him for a while. I thought I might hear some news. Peipei, your old nurse, she said it's the best way to get the news now, and did you know she's got a little room of her own and a job as a cleaner at the new school, can you believe it?'

'That's great, Ma. But I asked you why you're upset.'

'I was just getting to that! Now, I thought the man might say something about the weather or give some useful advice from the Chairman, but instead he told a story about a peasant girl. Only eight years old, never gone to school, and has to look after two younger brothers. Her father died from over-work and malnutrition because of a greedy landlord, her mother was taken away by the Japanese, and her older brother was shot by the Nationalists. But she never gave up, she kept working every day in their little field to feed her little brothers. Now she is part of a commune, she gets to go to school and so do her brothers.'

'Well, that's good, Ma, isn't it? Why are you crying?'

'It just made me a bit tearful, that's all.'

Yuying nodded, and said nothing, but she did not believe her mother. However, she decided not to push the issue and invited Bian Shi to stay to share their dinner.

Later in their room, Yuying interrupted Jinyi's attempts to recognise the words on an old single sheet of newspaper that he had taken to reading and rereading.

'What did you think about what my mother said?'

He did not stop running his dirty finger along the line. 'Not much. I've heard a hundred stories like that. So have you.'

'But that's my point. Don't get me wrong, I find those stories sad too, and sometimes they stick in my mind and then maybe I work a bit harder and I feel a bit better knowing that everything has changed. But they don't make me cry. And you know my mother, she doesn't think in that way. She's tougher than that.'

'Maybe she's finally realised that everything has changed.'

'Ha! I don't think so. She's still waiting for the restaurants to be handed back to her. You've seen the way her nose twitches when I talk about the factory. She thinks it's a phase people are going through. No, it must be something else. Well, we'll just have to make sure she's not still moping around here when the Lis come to dinner.'

Jinyi looked up. 'What? Who are the Lis?'

'I did tell you at lunchtime,' she blushed as she said this and turned away, aware that he was now raising his eyebrows. 'Mrs Li has been in my work group since I started. Anyway, she only lives in the next street down, and it seems a shame not to have a little company. All our other friends have dispersed, and my sisters are in different cities. I just thought it might be nice. Plus, her husband is a Party official.'

'I see.'

'Don't say that, I know exactly what you're thinking when you say that. As if you have everything worked out.' They both laughed.

'I'll put on my best jacket,' Jinyi joked — he only had two teal jackets, which he alternated between, identical except for a scuff on the elbow of one.

'And that reminds me, we have to go through the things we can't talk about.'

'I don't think I understand.'

'Things we shouldn't mention when they're here. Of course, we mustn't talk about the arrangement of our marriage . . .' She trailed off and looked to him for support.

'I see.'

'. . . and the entrance exam I took to be a translator in the Japanese army should be avoided; best not to mention much about my father or you changing your name; and don't say too much about where you were before when I first started at the factory. Then we should be all right.'

Jinyi nodded wearily and put aside his sheaf of newspaper, his fingers now an inky purple. He tried not to argue with her anymore; since returning he had wanted to be a different man, to remake their lives — if the country could start again, then why couldn't they? They fell asleep quickly, too tired to find comfort in each other's bodies, while out in the streets around the old mansion, an old woman was searching for a missing chicken.

The first thing they noticed about Comrade Li, as he implored them to call him, was his resemblance to a stick insect: he was bony and tall, his long arms held out like spindly pincers.

'I do not usually eat in the evenings,' he announced, while his petite, moon-faced wife stood silently beside him. 'So many official lunches, you see. And also, I wouldn't want to be taking more than my fair share.'

Yet at dinner he ate as quickly as he could, swiping at each dish with his outstretched chopsticks — fried white cabbage, spicy oblongs of jade cucumber and a small mound of tofu floating in a watery brown sauce.

'You know, I think this is wonderful,' he said with his mouth full. 'Peasant food. This is what we should all be having. Very democratic.'

Yuying and Jinyi quickly exchanged glances, unsure whether they had been praised or insulted. They felt like schoolchildren awaiting the results of an unexpected test.

'How are your children?' Yuying asked.

'Good.' Li did not smile. The Lis had three buck-toothed boys. 'They are with their grandparents. Chairman Mao has told us that large families are glorious. Our children are the future of this country, you know. How are yours?'

'We don't have any. At the moment,' Yuying said.

'Oh,' Li let his hand sweep out, remembering that his wife may have mentioned this. 'Well, remember the words of our wise Chairman. You have it in your power to make our country burn brighter.'

'So, Li Shi, my wife tells me you are from Jinzhou,' Jinyi said, trying to shift the focus of the conversation. 'I stayed there for a year once, working in a barber's shop.'

'Yes, she's from there,' her husband replied. 'Poky little town. We met when I was passing through on the way home from the Long March.'

Yuying was amazed that her friend, bubbly and giggly and always the first to pass on snippets of gossip and rumour at work, was so nervous and quiet next to her husband.

'You must have seen a lot, Comrade Li.'

Comrade Li remembered the first time he had killed a man; he had been amazed at how easy it was, how little it had bothered him. Not even a Nationalist, simply a peasant preparing to rat Li's regiment out from the man's barn that they were hiding in, overheard bragging to his son about how the Kuomintang might reward them. Li had crept up behind him and slung down a loose brick, twack, cracking the skull as though it were an egg. He remembered the body stumbling forward, slowly going slack. He had watched the peasant slump, knees giddily bent up, while a comrade with a rusty blade had chased after the son. There's really nothing to it, he had told himself.

'The whole country. How else could we know the needs of our countrymen so intimately? Revolution is action, after all, not imagination.'

'Yes, I know what you mean,' Jinyi nodded, looking over Li's shoulder. 'You can't really know a place till you get there, until it shows you its hidden life, its invisible alleyways, its people and their stories, their souls.'

Comrade Li half choked on the cabbage, and to wash it down grabbed a thimble of the stale rice wine they had saved for the dinner. 'Soul? Soul?!'

He paused with his long arms in mid-air, and then relaxed — these are simple people, his smirk seemed to announce, who need the world explained to them before they can understand it. 'No such thing. The "soul" is a child's plaything, a noose knotted by landlords and bureaucrats. You will find that these ideas will soon fall away, though of course we do not expect it to happen overnight.' He laughed.

'Ah. Of course. Well . . . a toast,' Jinyi suggested, though only he and Comrade Li were drinking from the three-inch bottle. 'To a prosperous future.' Then, as the thimbles were close to their lips, he added, 'Not for us, of course; for the country and the people.'

They emptied their thimbles and sat in silence.

'You know, my husband doesn't like to boast, but it isn't all laws and speeches.' They were all a little taken aback to hear Mrs Li finally speak. 'Just the other day, for example, we made a dinner for a poor family my husband had met on his way back from work. A pregnant woman, with five young children, and her husband dead from TB. Each of them as slight as snakes — I swear you couldn't even see them from side on. My husband heard them hawking up blood outside a food hall. All six of them had been sleeping on the damp floor of a derelict park shed.'

Comrade Li nodded and beamed, trying his best to muster a modesty that he did not possess.

'Anyway, call it luck or fate if you want, but that same day a chicken had just wandered into our house. We tried to chase it out, but it just wouldn't go. It was an unusual one too, with a proud black plume and fine white feathers. It must have been a sign. So we gathered some potatoes and onions and cooked up a dark chicken soup and took it to them. You should have seen the looks on those children's faces — they thought it was the Spring Festival come early!'

Comrade Li grinned and puffed his chest.

'It seems even the poultry are becoming socialist!' He laughed at his own joke, while Jinyi and Yuying stared at their feet.

After they were gone, Yuying turned from the dirty plates bubbling in the wash bucket. 'I think I'm going to be sick.'

'Don't tell her. Disappearances are better than facts, everyone knows that.'

'I mean it.' She pushed through the door and hunched into the night; Jinyi could see the rippling of her back as she tensed and began to vomit.

She nudged the door back with her body, taking in a wheezy breath.

'You're right. We shouldn't mention the chicken in front of Ma — she'll probably just think Father had finally worked up the courage for the journey.'

'Or been snapped up by the god of heaven and hell for trespassing. Yu, how are you feeling?'

'Tired. I'm sorry about tonight. I just thought it would be nice to find some more people to talk to.'

'That's what we have work and family for.'

'I know, but —'

'I'm just joking. But seriously, you've got me. We've got each other. And whenever you want to talk, please just talk to me. I mean, I might not understand all the long fancy words you use, but still —'

She hit his arm playfully, and he turned

and caught her wrist in his hand.

They drifted to the bedroom and slumped into each other's arms, both wondering whether there was anything to the fact that she had vomited three nights in a row. However, to speak of something means to mould it from the malleable substance of hope and longing into something concrete. So instead they nestled into each other, both their imaginations silently conjuring up rushed horoscopes for the next child, lying close beneath a pale moon that was netted in the flaky reels of fishbone clouds.

It only occurred to me after leaving the poet's thatched cottage that I had no idea how to return home. Now, on earth and in heaven the procedure is pretty simple for gods: we merely need to think of the place we wish to end up and we arrive there — it is, unfortunately, only the Jade Emperor who is omnipresent. Yet I was now in neither heaven nor earth, but somewhere between the two. Not only that, but I was also stranded at the top of a perilous cliff, and I did not fancy climbing back over the slippery bone bridge. I walked to the edge and stared down into the mist. There was only one thing for it. I closed my eyes and jumped.

As I had expected to flail through clouds and fog for hours or even days before reaching the ground, I was surprised to find my feet suddenly touching down, as if I had fallen no more than a few steps.

'Hey you! What do you think you are doing? Get out of there!'

I opened my eyes and turned around to see a

stocky, red-faced man running out of a barn and shaking his fist at me. I seemed to be standing in the middle of a small pen. Curled up in the straw in one corner was a sleeping phoenix, its fiery feathers quivering as it breathed. I quickly hopped over the waist-high wooden fence and approached the angry man.

'I'm sorry. I just sort of fell here. I don't mean any trouble. But . . . erm, could you tell me where I am?' I said.

'Ah, I see! Well, this is the Jade Emperor's private zoo. Actually, you're the first visitor since we started, which must have been about ten thousand years ago now. We're pretty well hidden away. Would you like to have a look around?'

I murmured apprehensively and he began the guided tour. I was not surprised to see the four guardians of the compass perched on raised platforms at opposite corners of the park — the black tortoise watching the north, the blue dragon staring out into the rising sun, another red phoenix raising its plume toward the south, and, looking west, the pale qilin. It was the first time I had seen that ferocious unicorn, a strange cross between a tiger and a dragon, though I had heard stories about it. It is said that when the great fifteenth-century mariner Zheng He returned to China after his voyages to Africa with a giraffe, the courtiers all prostrated themselves before the long-necked beast, believing it to be the heavenly qilin.

I was more intrigued, however, to see a vast enclosure containing a bale of fat, waddling *bixi* — giant turtles which fly down from heaven at the behest of Confucius, carrying stone tablets of his lessons on their backs. Beside it was a cage teeming with ravenous *tao tie,* grubby little gargoyles tearing flesh from each other in their insatiable hunger.

'This is just the first section,' The red-faced man beamed at me. 'We've got a lake full of giant devil fish and dancing cranes; a skulk of fox spirits and nine-headed blackbirds and rain-birds in our little forest; and even a couple of demons in shackled boxes out the back.'

'That's impressive,' I replied. 'But I've got to return to my post before anyone notices that I'm gone. Do you have any idea how I can get back to earth?'

'Not a problem. You can ride down on one of the qilin — they'll be out tonight anyway, and they never have any trouble finding their way back,' he said.

'Thank you, that would be wonderful. But what do you mean by "they'll be out tonight"? Surely you don't let them loose on earth?'

'Oh, they don't run loose. They move through people's dreams. They need the exercise, you see — we can't keep them locked up in here all the time,' he replied.

'If they move through dreams, do you think they have anything to do with the human heart? You see, I'm trying to find out how it works.'

'Hmm.' He rubbed his chin. 'Maybe. The way they get into people's dreams is through the stories they know. After all, no one dreams about things they've never heard of. And I'll tell you what, if you want to know about people's hearts, learn what stories they listen to, what stories they tell their children. If you ask me, that's the only way to know what people really believe, to see how they really view the world. Now, let me find a saddle for you.'

He left me and entered the barn, to be greeted by a sudden flurry of squawks and jibbers; I did not even dare hazard a guess as to the kinds of creatures kept inside.

7:
1960
THE YEAR OF THE RAT

Despite the fact that her brother was a year and a half older than her, Hou Manxin took his hand and led him past the lolling hollyhock to the stone outhouse that served as a classroom. Hou Dali liked the hollyhock: the leathery pig ears surrounding stubby antennae, the damp purple incongruous amid the untrimmed bushes and troddenin footpath. The sound of children playing and arguing reached their ears and he flinched. Unlike his sister, he did not enjoy school. It was not so much Teacher Lu — although the stinging ruler slicing across knuckles when he could not recall the words to Chairman Mao's poems seemed brutally unfair — as the other students, the playground games which he tripped and sniffled through and the taunts he tried his best to ignore. All in all, he had decided, it was not easy being seven. He could not wait to be eight.

'We'll meet back here when the bell rings and we'll walk home together, like Mama said,' Hou Manxin told her brother patiently. She did not like it when Dali wandered off.

'I know!' He wrestled his hand from hers and strode toward the classroom, making a show of the confidence he lacked. He had his father's wild scrawl of dark hair and lack of height, his mother's round face.

Dali joined the forty others cross-legged on the concrete, peering over rows of prickly heads that had either been shaved for summer or knotted into plaits. In front of them was a dirty chalkboard, which still displayed the ghosts of words written ten years before. Dali was happy that it was not his turn to attempt to clean it. Above it was pinned a black-and-white picture of Chairman Mao, smiling and looking out of the single window, perhaps, Dali imagined, to see which children dared turn up late.

'Let's begin by going back over what we learnt yesterday. The words of our great leader. Deng Liu, begin!' Teacher Lu paced up and down in front of the students, his wide nose twitching along with his salt-and-pepper eyebrows. His cap almost matched the one shown in the picture behind him. Dali wished he too had a cap with a star on it. Then he would never get teased.

Deng Liu leapt to his feet and clasped his grubby hands behind his back. 'Our leader has taught us that it is possible to accomplish anything. The glorious motherland . . .'

Teacher Lu nodded along, waiting for a slip-up. They learnt by rote. After all, the great leader himself had said that it was harmful to read too many books. If they did well they would be rewarded by being allowed to sing a song about a little lost fish. Teacher Lu watched the children's faces, ready to punish any hint of a yawn or a sideways glance. He had once been a renowned calligrapher, but he now found that he could not stop his hands from trembling whenever he picked up one of the delicate reed brushes, at least not till he had sunk a glass of rice wine, which was harder and harder to come by. He scowled and picked up a piece of chalk. A little maths, then a few characters mapped out on the dirty board. That ought to be enough for today.

Lunchtime was a throng of little bodies pressed on wooden benches in the cramped canteen, slurping tiny bowls of millet soup. Dali found ways to lose the pieces of fruit his mother always left out for him to take — he did not want to be picked on for being bourgeois again. He had no idea what bourgeois meant, and neither did the other pupils, but they had heard a teacher say it and spit, so it must be really bad. And after lunch, a nap, the best bit of the day, sprawling on the fur-covered floors and the dull warmth of sleep half taking hold. When they woke the school day was done, and they were free to play in the field and around the crumbly buildings all afternoon until the teachers waved them home. Dali hung back around the classroom door, hoping that the boys would let him join in their games — they were soldiers liberating the overgrown corners of the field from the evil Nationalists, the casual shouts of war spilling over into scrums and bruises.

'Hou Dali! There you are. Mama said to meet me when the bell rings.' Manxin stared down, bewildered at her elder brother crouching timidly behind a bush, mud dried onto one side of his face. Her chin-length pigtails bobbed as she spoke.

'I know!' He looked about, then straightened up and pushed a stray strand of hair from his eyes.

'The bell already rang, Dali. Didn't you hear the bell?'

'I know. I heard. I was playing a game. You wouldn't understand.' He wiped his muddy hands on his new Zhongshan jacket. 'Come on then, let's go,' he said impatiently, and started walking.

They passed worn small houses that backed onto rising fields of tawny blonde stubble, and even closer to home the busy streets were heaped with stockpiled husks of corn, while strings of tanned and speckled cobs hung down from roofs and doorways. Each single cob was closely guarded by suspicious eyes — everyone had heard the rumours about the famine in the countryside, and no one wanted to take any chances.

'I like corn. Yellow corn. Shaoqui told us that ghosts eat corn. That's why people put it near doors, to feed the ghosts. They must be very hungry. That's why we don't get much, even though we can see it everywhere. Is that right?' Manxin asked.

'No. Ghosts only eat people's hearts, and only when people want something — really really want something — that they can't have.'

'Oh.' Manxin did not understand, but she did not say anything else. She wanted dumplings for dinner, but she did not think they would get them. Was that what he meant?

The little girl occupied herself with counting the number of bellowing backyard furnaces burping out smoke behind buildings, and when she grew bored with this she played at spotting pictures of that jolly man with a dimpled chin who peered out at her from most of the houses they passed. The pring of bicycles brought both of the children back from their wandering thoughts, and Manxin's head swivelled to steal a glimpse of the open market — this was surely the most magical place in the city, for Ma only had to mention that she had been to the market for there to be something new to eat. Manxin remembered the last Spring Festival and the sizzling pork, which she wolfed down until her tummy had ached and moaned.

'How was school?' Granny Dumpling, as they called Bian Shi, asked as the two children pushed through the door.

Granny Dumpling had found that she preferred to spend time at her daughter's house, where husband, wife and three children were crammed into one sweaty bedroom, than stuck in the expansive empty sprawl of her own. The echoes scared her; the loneliness scared her. Her long white hair was fighting loose from her fuzzy plait — it turned white, she had told the children, because I told a lie and my ancestors came alive at night and stole the colour: don't let the same thing happen to you! She was cradling the baby girl in her arms and mixing yellowy water and the ration of state-produced formula together with her little finger. Manxin squeezed her baby sister's dark arm.

'Look what I learned at school today, little Liqui. I'll show you.' Manxin swayed from side to side, holding out her baby sister's chubby hands, lisping the words from the school song. Dali slunk to the table to look at the blurry pictures of aeroplanes which he had torn and saved from second-hand newspapers found discarded in the streets or retrieved from scrapheaps.

'Your Ma will be back soon, so why don't

you go fetch some water for your old grandma?' Granny Dumpling said to Manxin.

She had given up asking Dali, since he always came back sulking, and often took twice as long as his sister. Other boys often pushed in front of him in the queue, and he did not have Manxin's bug-eyed glares or un-selfconscious loudness to stop them. Anyway, Granny Dumpling reasoned, he was the only boy, and for that reason alone he should be allowed to do as he wished.

'Come on, chop chop, before a dragon swings its tail and brings us rain.'

As Manxin took the wooden bucket and meandered out of the door, Granny Dumpling turned back to her grandson, who was absorbed in the pictures of planes. She watched him trace his fingers across the pages, then turned towards the stove.

Back when Dali was still fluttering in her stomach, Yuying had turned to Jinyi and told him they were going to do things differently. Firstly, despite the prohibitions, they would take an offering to the nearest temple. (Jinyi would end up going by night, telling those he passed that he was visiting a sick relative. He found the rotund pagoda a few miles outside the city boarded up, and the monks vanished, but he managed to limber over a crumbling wall and leave the offering of two apples near where he vaguely remembered the fat Buddha had once been.) Secondly, Yuying had continued, when the child was born she planned to stay inside for the first few months, just as her mother had done before her, not letting even the slightest breath of the wind lick at their skin. Jinyi had agreed and even had an idea of his own.

'We need to change our name.'

Yuying had looked at him sceptically, unsure where he was going. She liked her name; it was the only part of her father she had left.

'Listen, I'm serious. It's not just because I'd like our children to carry on my family name — Hou is a fine name, though — but because it will save them. Bian is cursed. Everything has been strange since I took your name. And most importantly, if they have a different name, the demon won't be able to find them.'

So they decided to give the children Jinyi's old name, and let the family line flow through his side to stop the stream of dark fortune from her own. The only problem seemed to be telling her mother, who in the end took the news so philosophically that Yuying had worried that she had not understood.

'The world is filling up with new names for things,' her mother had replied. 'Everything seems to have a new name now. We used to be honourable, and now we're bourgeois. Sometimes I don't even know what these new words mean. But just as long as the things themselves stay the same, I say you can call them whatever you want.'

Yuying took the opposite view — that even the subtlest alteration of a name could exponentially alter the thing it referred to: things only existed in how you saw them. Names fixed things in the world, defined their boundaries. But she had held her tongue, and that had settled it; the children would take Hou as their surname. Jinyi was wrong, however, about the demon — it would find them, but it would just take a little more time.

There are not many family names to choose from. In the tenth century the *Book of One Hundred Surnames* was compiled, and it instantly became immensely popular. Beside the lists of names were lavish illustrations of important historical figures bearing the corresponding family name — it is not difficult to surmise that at least some of its popularity derived from people's love of making the past correspond to their own lives, to have their view of themselves heightened by a relationship to someone more illustrious.

I gave up my own name when I became a god, though I cannot say I miss it as much as I miss the people who used to call me by it. By the time Jinyi and Yuying's children were born in the 1950s, however, when people did dare mention me at all it was in a tone of disgust. I was just another symbol of feudalism and the tyranny of belief, apparently. A few people still prayed to me, and filled my mouth with strands of syrupy toffee when the new year rolled around, but they did it guiltily, with one eye on the door. That hurt.

Where do gods go when they are given up, proscribed, forgotten? Nowhere. We're still here, just biding our time — you'll find we're pretty good at that. In cupboards, attics, cellars; in keepsakes, cobwebs, books; lodged in the back of a mind and itching to be taken out and polished. I was one of the lucky ones: easy for kids to remember and hard to shake from memories of the taste of candy and sugar. Furthermore, as famine slowly began to spread across the country, a god dedicated to the kitchen stopped seeming like such a bad idea.

Hou Manxin waited diligently in the line for the tap, stuck between a stocky man in his twenties and a lanky teenage girl whose home-decorated plimsolls, dotted with poorly embroidered rose blooms, betrayed a hint of personality beneath the familiar uniform of dark blue tunic and slack black trousers.

A voice from the back of the line cut through the dull quiet. 'At least the tap's still running, so even if we starve we won't be thirsty, eh?'

Heads turned cautiously. The speaker was unshaven and unsteady, as if one of his legs was having trouble keeping the other in line. He must have been around forty, his cropped hair specked with grey.

'I mean,' he continued, a little louder than before, 'it's gonna be us soon too, you know, we aren't going to have anything to eat, and it wouldn't surprise me if someone makes off with the bloody tap to melt it down to meet a quota.'

By now heads had snapped back towards the tap, the people in line willing the old adage to be true, that if you ignore something it might disappear. However, that did not seem to put him off.

'You all know what I mean, don't you?' His tone was somewhere between pleading and petulant. 'My cousin, he lives in the country, not far from here — couple of hours, that's all, couple of hours north. And he's at the furnace every day, and so are his boys, and even his wife. No surprise there, that's what the rest of us are doing too. *For the good of the country.*'

Here he paused and grinned, almost oblivious to the fact that the small group was trying to inch away from him. Manxin and her bucket were slowly being edged closer to the hiccupy flow of yellowy water. His words were drifting over her head; it was the clearing of throats and rigid shoulders around her that alerted her to the possibility that something was not right. There were three more people in front of her — soon she could go back home. She willed them faster.

'So, what I want to ask all you is, while they are working at the furnace all day and all night to meet their commune's quota, who do you think is in the fields, who do you think is growing the rice?"

The group shifted as the stocky twenty-something in front of Manxin turned and slipped from his place in the line, clenching his teeth.

'You're drunk, and you're making a scene. Pull yourself together! You ought to be ashamed of yourself, talking like this in front of women and children.'

'I'm not ashamed of the truth, boy,' the man muttered back. 'You're not blind. What do you think is going to happen?'

'That's enough! Now, we're going to go back to waiting in line, and you're not going to say another word. There's police and soldiers all around who might be interested in your opinion, but we're not. So why don't we all forget you said anything, understand?'

The man opened his mouth to reply, but instead mumbled under his breath before turning and stumbling away. They caught a few words left over as he walked off — 'trying to be helpful . . . you'll see . . . nothing pretty about the truth . . . idiots . . .'

The whole line seemed to shake itself off, but remained quiet, pensive, though Manxin had forgotten all about the strange conversation by the time she had finished her turn at the tap and hauled the slopping bucket back to her impatient grandmother.

Yuying returned soon after, and bent straight to the small stove without bothering to remove her jacket. Her hair was tightly bunned, and thin furrows of skin twitched at her smile as she swept through the ragtag clutter of the busy room. She was henlike, happy to be busy, to not have too much time to stop and think, getting lost in the little corners of her own life. She looked at her son and thought of her husband. Her hands tipped the pan to heat the last slither of oil above the fire. She shouldn't feel this way. This was not what she had wanted for her future: all of them walking all days with hunger churning their bellies; barely seeing her husband or her children because of her shifts at the factory and then at the communal furnace, where they were just as set upon building a new country as she and Jinyi had been of building a new marriage. But, despite it all, she was happy. They were together, still, and coming home late at night to the sound of three children snoring in the dark of her room was all she could ask for.

While Yuying fried the last of the cornflour batter into pancakes, Manxin pondered why it was that her father, who was the best cook in the house, was also the person who cooked the least. The best things must be stored away or else they will lose their powers, she concluded. To become too good at something can be dangerous. She vowed not to practice too much at anything that mattered.

'Eat up,' Yuying told her two eldest. 'This is going to be our last meal at home for a while.'

They looked at her as if she was joking.

'Is that because there's no food left?' Manxin asked.

'No,' Yuying laughed. 'Of course there's food! We'll still eat, only you and your brother are going to have to eat all your meals at school, and your Pa and I will eat at the factory.'

'But I hate the school food. It's not fair! Why must we eat it, Ma?' Dali asked.

'Because we need to take our cooking pots to the furnace. Oh, don't pull that face, Hou Dali. The sooner we make more steel, the sooner our country will became powerful again. You want to help, don't you?' Yuying said.

Dali nodded sheepishly, but he was not convinced.

When you have lived as long as I have — which is to say, longer than anyone should be asked to remember — it becomes easier and easier to spot similarities in the smallest actions. The push towards dining halls and communal eating, for example, reminds me of something that happened under the first emperor, Qin Shi Huang. Now, you cannot unify a huge country by being diplomatic: Qin Shi Huang was ruthless, bloodthirsty and merciless, but he got the job done. Naturally fearing reprisals and rebellions, as soon as he had defeated the last of the resisting kingdoms he sent an edict out around the country: all weapons were to be handed over to his army. This included kitchen knives, garden tools and any other sharp implements that could be misused. Without kitchen knives, communal eating, with meals shared between large groups, soon became a necessity. However, the edict ignored one important point: when deprived, the first thing people do is improvise.

Both Yuying and Granny Dumpling picked at the edges of the dishes, pushing them towards the two children, who nevertheless complained of unquenched hunger once everything was finished. Yuying noted that her mother had been eating less and less since they had received the news about her middle daughter, Chunlan. She and her husband had died in a local struggle at the beginning of the year. The starving locals in the rural village had broken down the door to their house when they heard that the well-off family had been stockpiling food for themselves during the famine, and, in the ensuing fight for the few measly supplies in the backroom, the villagers had bludgeoned to death husband, wife and their two toddlers.

Yuying wrapped a single soggy pancake in a sheet of smudged newspaper for Jinyi. She kissed the baby and then searched through the cupboard, to see if there were any knives, nails, keys, spoons or anything else made of metal which she might have missed during the last search.

'Now, you be good for your Granny Dumpling and go to bed when she tells you. If you're good, I'll be back to tell you a story,' Yuying said, hovering by the door.

'Ma, why do we have to burn things?' Dali asked as she turned to go.

'Why? Well, fire makes things pure, and it helps us,' his mother replied.

'How?'

'We use fire to change metal, to make new things that help people. But we must be very careful, because fire can become angry and jealous.'

'Why?'

'Because it is so hot. Think how uncomfortable you would be if you were boiling hot and sweaty all day.'

'Oh,' Dali paused. 'But why do *we* have to burn things?'

'Because we want to be good Chinese. Don't you want to be good too?' Yuying said, before turning and leaving.

'Why don't you go too, Granny Dumpling?'

'I'm not strong enough. The ancestors stole my strength when they stole the colour from my hair. But I'm sure you will be strong enough soon. Not long now and you'll be able to go and help them. Would you like that?'

Dali did not answer, but looked back down at his collection of aeroplane pictures, his eyes skirting over the smeared whirl of propellers, the slick tilt of lazy wings and, somewhere amidst the blur, the squinting, grinning pilots. After a while, he looked back up.

'Would I have to melt bits of planes?'

'Oh no, I shouldn't think so,' she reassured him, but the truth was that the people manning the obligatory furnaces seemed to be melting anything they could get their hands on.

Fire is not only furious and possessive — it is also the condition of existence. All is burning, the Buddha began the Fire Sermon; our longing for the world is aflame. For where we think fire to be the reckless abandon and impulse of unchecked passion, we are wrong; it is the sober work of the senses, and because of this it is even more dangerous. Longing, greed, suffering, hatred, sorrow — these are fires afflicting every pore of the body, spreading through every crevice of the mind. These are fires that cannot be quenched, that are fed by every attempt to extinguish them. Only by becoming dispassionate, the Buddha noted, by giving up the fiction of the self, the idea of being in the world, can these fires be tamed, managed.

The tumbling gushes of smoke shaded the shrinking moon, and Yuying instinctively covered her mouth as the air became thick and dry. The whole of their block had been organised to man one furnace, and each of the households brought their own possessions, along with an unspoken sense of uncertainty, to feed to the fire. She entered the compound, loosely marked out by a straggly wire fence, and Jinyi waved to her, a lopsided smile spreading across his face. He was sweaty and red beside the puffing brick hulk that the group had hastily assembled in imitation of the one the young army recruits had built near the factory. When Jinyi had begun asking questions about the process, a young soldier had pushed a lump of rough ore into his hands and said, 'Here's the science part: keep it fucking hot!'

'You look tired,' he said, concerned. He dropped the glowing tongs and pulling off a singed glove to wipe the sweat from his face.

'Everyone looks tired. That's how you know how hard people are working.'

He laughed. 'How are the children?'

'They're good. The baby —'

'We don't have time for your bourgeois

chats!' A potbellied man with receding hair interrupted. It was Yangchen, the head of the commune now, the friendly manner that he had shown in the restaurant kitchen turned into a semi-permanent sneer. 'I know you must be finding it difficult, Bian Yuying, following my orders when once your family treated me like a slave. But times have changed, and you will have to accept that. You know the rules. The commune is your family now, so don't try and pretend you're any better than the rest of us.'

Yuying blushed and bit her lip.

'We'll make the quota,' Jinyi said. 'So please forgive me, Comrade Yangchen. It was my fault, and I must have caught my wife off guard. She has had a busy day at the factory and —'

'We're all busy,' Yangchen replied. 'We all must work for the good of the commune, the good of the country, the good of the people. You two are no exception. You may think you are special, Hou Jinyi, but we all know what you really are. Have your little chat; do what you wish, but do not think it will not be noted.'

Yangchen rolled up his sleeves and huffed along with the furnace, and Jinyi and Yuying muttered to each other in lowered voices, drowned out by the busy movements of the small crowd around the insatiable brick beast.

'They're good. The baby is eating a lot,

which is good.'

'What about Dali? Has he been in a fight again?' Jinyi asked.

'No. He's fine. They're all fine,' Yuying replied, impatient to be seen to be joining in with the work.

'OK, OK. But how can I know? I'm never there. I'm always either here or at the factory. You know, this isn't what I expected family life to be like.'

'Don't say that. You'll only get us into more trouble. You know you have a family, and that every single one of them looks up to you. You know it all in your heart, even if not with your eyes. Now come on, we'll talk later, I promise.'

Yuying strode away towards where the ladders and pipes crossed beside the roaring furnace, and Jinyi tried not to lose his temper. He had spent his youth longing to have a family of his own; now he had a wife and three children, only to be told by the state that the commune was to be his new family.

The quota would be made, but only if they were to do the same thing they did last month: lie. It's no big deal — everyone does it, they all assured each other; we are bound to make up the difference next month, oh, without a doubt. What they did not know, though some were beginning to suspect, was that the lumpy pig iron they made was useless — the quality of their finished product was, predictably, poor. The Great Leap Forward, designed to enable China to overtake Britain in steel production within a decade, was in fact driving the country backwards into a squalor of waste and shortage. However, not everyone can share this god's eye view, and the men and women panting through the long hours in that little compound were usually happy enough to confuse busyness and increased fervour with progress.

As midnight drew closer, Yuying sidled close to Jinyi, who was standing near where the extracted ooze was cooling. 'You're thinking about him again.'

He shrugged. 'How do you know?'

'I can usually guess what you're thinking. Isn't that what marriage means? You're still worrying.'

'No, of course not. I was the same at his age, fantasies and little bits of dream spilling out of my ears. It's just boy stuff. I'm sure he can take care of himself.'

She knew he was lying, lying to give her hope, so she thought better of giving her doubts strength by voicing them. Instead she said, 'So you don't think he's —'

'No. Whatever you are going to say, no, I don't. Worrying about things just makes them more likely, you should know that. Come on, I've only got an hour left, and I'll check on them all when I get back.'

'What about Yangchen?' she whispered.

'I'll find a way of calming him down. We used to be friends: it shouldn't be too hard.'

The muddled group of workers all wore identical outfits, dark trousers and jackets in various stages of decay, though not all had the luxury of shoes. The exhausted faces looked crab-pink in the moonlight, and they scuttled around the furnace as if they were indeed crustaceans, worshipping what could have been a giant husk of shiny shipwreck washed to shore.

There was something about their son that both Jinyi and Yuying could not place. Perhaps it was the furrowed brow that was often the start of a tantrum, or the sentences he came out with that only made sense to them days after he had spoken. Perhaps it was the unhappiness he never owned up to.

Jinyi set down the last pile of the night's freshly chopped logs, and wandered over to where Yangchen was standing watching the other men and women scrabble round the heat.

'Cigarette?' Jinyi offered his last scuffed half-stub to his old colleague.

Yangchen took it and lit up without replying.

'Comrade, you remember that night during the civil war when the restaurant's roof came crashing down, and we were all off work for weeks? Bian Shi kept paying us, and brought

386

food to those of us with families, she —'

'I know where you're going, Jinyi. That's your problem, clinging to the old ways. All of that is gone now, wiped clean. We're remaking the world from a blank slate.'

'I just wanted to apologise, Comrade. You can see we've been working hard here; there's no one come near this furnace who would deny it. Neither my wife nor I will talk out of line again, I swear. Perhaps, if you could spare an hour or two of your time, you might honour us with your presence for dinner some time, and let us prove how devoted we are to the cause.'

Yangchen weighed it up. 'Tomorrow,' he said.

'Tomorrow? Well, of course, we would be delighted, but —'

'Then tomorrow it is. Don't worry, I know where you live.'

Yangchen threw down the butt, then strode off to shout at a pair of gloved women bickering over the fragile apparatus. Jinyi sighed and set off home, while the rest of the compound families drew closer to the furnace, as if to prove their hearts by enduring its heat.

It was only a few hours later, after two night feeds and one nightmare, that Jinyi and Yuying awoke entwined, a mess of limbs and tousled hair, with the baby crying and light beginning to haze shyly through the windows. As Jinyi kissed his wife, he whispered of his conversation with Yangchen.

'Dinner? On the only night of the week we don't have to be at the furnace? Without a wok, without any food? Do you want us to lose face?'

'We'll take a few bits back from the canteen and make a few cold dishes — cucumbers in chilli oil, a few tea eggs — and the rice wine will make it go down fine.'

Yuying considered mentioning the children and their endless appetites, the dwindling supply of liquor left from her father's cellar, or the rumoured shortages sweeping from city to city, but decided against it. She didn't want to risk the children overhearing and getting scared.

Jinyi looked at her and smiled, knowing how to change her mind. 'I know you, Yu, even if we were starving you wouldn't turn away a guest.'

Yuying raised her eyebrows. 'We couldn't starve, Jinyi. That's a thing of the past. The Party will look after us now, as long as we work hard.'

Jinyi left the bedroom and the waking children to his wife and mother-in-law — this was their part of the day — and picked up the pail to refill it at the nearby tap. Yet as soon as he had pulled open the stiff, unlocked front door, he was confronted with the green shirt and cap of a grumpy postal worker, who shoved a dirty piece of paper into his hand. On one side were a few barely legible characters, and on the other was written 'Bian Jinyi'.

'Wait. Where's the envelope?' he asked the postal worker.

The grumpy man sighed. 'Strange thing, actually. This bit of paper was found inside a package sent to the official at the market. It must have been shoved in secretly by someone who couldn't afford the postage. You're lucky you only live round the corner, and that there aren't too many Bians round here anymore.'

'My name isn't Bian,' Jinyi said. 'I mean, it used to be, for a while, but —'

'I don't really care,' the grumpy man said. 'I've done my bit.'

With that he strode down the street, leaving Jinyi holding the dirty sheath in his hands. He finally flipped it over and read through the short note:

Bian Jinyi. Old Hou wants to let you know your aunt has been shot. Burial on Friday. He is in field hospital here. Farmhouse taken by commune, everything gone. Come as soon as you can. A friend.

Jinyi drew in breath, and put down the pail. A friend? He didn't know that either he or his old family still had such things. Auntie

389

Hou, gone at last. Old Hou in trouble. Good. He screwed up the dirty sheet of paper and threw it out into the alley.

For the next hour, he pushed through the morning rituals of tantrums and hair-pulling, of bicycle bells and dodging dark puddles, telling himself throughout that he should not care. Throw out the old ways, he told himself; that is what the great Chairman has told us. They are better off in the past, where they belong. Yet Yuying had forgiven him his mistakes, his faltering heart. His thoughts slipped down through his body; he spent the day beside the bread oven scalding his hands, until they were red and blotchy with the scars of his guilt.

'Are you all right? You seemed a bit quiet this morning. I didn't want to say anything in front of the kids, though,' Yuying said, catching him in the queue in the factory canteen.

'Oh. I'm fine. Just stuck in a dream. You know how it is,' Jinyi replied.

'Well, don't dream too much. You know dreams only cause trouble.'

Sometimes we tell lies so that we ourselves will believe them. Even gods lie, you know, but only because some things are too difficult to be told, or so I have heard the others say. There were plenty of men, some that Jinyi even ate and shared bad jokes with at work, who had knotted fake pasts from the loose coils and frayed strings of their wants and needs. There were whole scores of Nationalist soldiers who had deserted once the end had become inevitable, hiding out until the noise died down. They were everywhere, dressed in the ill-fitting disguises of commitment and modesty. Sometimes we wear our lies in our eyes, in our hands, and sometimes they wear us, weave us chrysalis-like with words, until we emerge, lithe and changed.

These are the things Jinyi had lied about:

The Spring Festival noodles left to cool outside while Auntie answered a call of nature, that he swore the dogs had taken;
Where he came from;
Who he might have been before;
Being happy;
What he could and could not remember.

Other things were glossed over in silence. These are the things that Yuying had lied about:

The doll she stole from her sister and buried in the garden late one night;
How much she had yearned to pass the exams and become an interpreter for the Japanese army;
Her feelings.

The latter had changed with the years, with

391

the fast-forward of life, with the little acts of tenderness that replaced passion, with the gradual wobble of her body and the scars and stretch marks, the fierce pride of motherhood and the fear of losing everything in a second to something unexpected and unexplained. She risked attention and nuzzled closer to her husband in the queue, letting his quiet calm engulf her.

Lies are like demons padding at your heels — take this from me. They are always just a couple of steps behind you, slipping quickly out of sight whenever you turn. Their panting and salivating, their smacking of lips that dribble in perpetual anticipation, are mistaken for a leak in the roof, for creaking doors or other miscellaneous city noises. They bide their time, waiting to catch up with you.

Jinyi came home with a new burn swelling across his palm, and pockets crammed with the stale bread destined for the factory bins. There must be interesting things that can be done with hardened crusts, he told himself. Dali and Manxin, as if drawn by some extra sense that would be lost in adolescence, left Granny Dumpling and the paper lanterns they were crafting in the bedroom to line up beside the table in a mock military formation. And just like new recruits they were both expectant and naively eager.

'Where's the guest, Pa? Is he invisible?'

Manxin asked a quarter of an hour later.

'Invisible? Of course not, all the invisible guests are already here. Why don't you and your brother take a little food and go and entertain them in your bedroom with Granny Dumpling, eh?'

Yuying, sweeping through the room while repeatedly unknotting and retying her hair, amazed at the recurring dust that no one else seemed to notice, nudged her seated husband, knocking his elbows out from where they were propping up his cheeks.

'If we're lucky, he'll just have been winding us up. I'm not sure he'd really have the nerve to come round here.'

'Well, if he's not coming, then he's not coming. Give the food to the kids, they need it.'

'It's bad luck,' Granny Dumpling called from the bedroom. 'A guest who does not arrive is as bad as a hungry ghost, a wind stuck in a room and swirling a whole house towards disaster, or things crawling out from children's nightmares to take shape —'

'Yes, yes, I understand,' Jinyi huffed. 'It's bad luck. But it would also be bad luck for him to catch sight of you again — it might remind him too much of the old days. Yaba will be waiting for you.'

It was only a few minutes after Jinyi had led his hobbling mother-in-law out of the door that it swung open to reveal Yangchen and another taller man with a dark moustache, both dressed in crisp navy blues.

'Ah, Comrade, please come in, we —' Yuying said, rising from the table.

'Good evening, Comrades,' Yangchen interrupted. 'This is my brother, whom I am sure you have all heard about.'

The tall man nodded curtly, his moustache bristling.

'General, we are honoured that you have joined us,' Jinyi said, frantically trying to remember the general's name — after all, he had probably been told it a hundred times. 'May I introduce my children: this is Dali, my son, and these —'

'Yes, yes. I'm sure we'll have a chance for that later. We don't have much time; my brother is a very busy man. I am sure you can imagine,' Yangchen said with a wave of his hand, and seated himself at the table. His brother followed suit.

'Why don't you go and look after the baby in the bedroom?' Yuying whispered to Manxin and Dali. They grimaced, but did as she said, pulling the door closed behind them.

'So, General, you must have lots of important local matters to deal with,' Yuying said as she placed the lukewarm dishes onto the wooden table.

'Yes,' the general grunted. 'And all of them confidential. Is this it?'

'I'm afraid so. Please forgive us, if we had

known you were coming . . .' Jinyi said, seating himself next to the general, leaving his wife to settle, uncomfortably, next to Yangchen.

'It will suffice. Now I recognise you. Used to work in the kitchen with my young brother here, didn't you?' the general said.

'Yes, that's right.' Yangchen said. 'Hou Jinyi. Or is it Bian Jinyi? I can never keep up with all the changes. Yes, Jinyi has always been a dedicated worker — he even went as far as to marry the boss's daughter.'

Both Yuying and Jinyi began to blush, waiting for their guests to pick at the dishes before they themselves could begin. A nervous silence descended like a layer of mould over the plates and wobbling piles of lotus roots, stale buns and chilli-dressed cucumbers.

'A toast,' Yangchen said with a leer. 'To the Great Chairman, who has helped us to be rid of the cruelty of landlords and the bourgeois.'

The three men drank in silence, the general coughing on the liquor to make clear his disapproval of its quality.

They ate quickly, Jinyi and Yuying pushing around the dishes and topping up the thimbles with rice wine. Jinyi tried to think of a way to make a joke about the old days in the kitchen, to find a fond shared memory, something to bridge the years between them. The chopsticks clicked and snapped in double-time; if even the officials are this hungry for our poor scraps, Jinyi thought, then perhaps those rumours of countryside famines are not so far from the mark.

'Passable,' the general commented, to no one in particular, following a loud belch.

'So, Jinyi, whatever happened when you left the restaurant? One day you were there, the next you'd left town. Everyone knows what happened to me, especially after the revolution rewarded my loyalty and faith. But I heard at one point that your wife had arrived back in Fushun alone. Surely that must just be a horrible rumour, for who could leave such a beautiful, well-bred woman, hmm?' Yangchen said.

Jinyi looked at his wife, noticing the colour welling up on her cheeks again. So this is why he agreed to come here, Jinyi thought; not to make up with us, but to humiliate us for some ancient slight.

'I stayed to help my family. They were suffering from a poor harvest and other troubles. Luckily, the revolution soon came and solved all their problems, so I could then return.'

'Interesting. Very interesting,' Yangchen replied.

'So, General, do you have any children?' Yuying asked, trying to change the course of the conversation.

'No. My brother and I have found that we devote too much time to the motherland to have any to spare for other trivialities,' Yangchen replied for his elder sibling. 'Perhaps you might care to come and see my office some time, Comrade Yuying, to learn more about the important work we are carrying out. I think I could teach you quite a lot.'

'Perhaps . . . sometime . . . of course that would be very generous of you,' Yuying replied, her head lowered. 'But, maybe it would be best to wait, as we are so busy at the moment, with the factory and the furnace and sending things to my sister's village to help her out during the food shortage there —'

'There is no shortage!' the general snapped. 'That is just defeatist talk, rightist propaganda. Everything is fine. Read the newspapers, listen to the radio, look around you. The country is in a better shape than it has ever been.'

He thrust himself up from the table. 'We have other business to attend to. Good night!'

The general marched out of the door, with Yangchen behind him, followed by Jinyi and Yuying as they garbled their thanks for the honour of his presence.

Yuying turned to her husband. 'We can't let them just go like that.'

'They're officials. They've probably got somewhere else to be. They only came here to get some free food and drink and make fun of us.'

'Don't be ridiculous. We'll lose face. At least find Yangchen and apologise for the poor dishes. We can't afford to upset him,' she pleaded.

Outside the last threads of light were already nuzzling the rooftops. Jinyi sighed his way through the smoke from the local furnaces, dodging the packed-up stalls and marching cadets. Pasted on almost every wall, colourful posters showed rosy-cheeked peasant girls pouting among a bumper crop, or strong hands holding out a platter of glowing corn-cobs, barley, glistening apples. Despite having just eaten the meagre dinner, Jinyi tried to stop himself from licking his lips.

He hated having to apologise. And now he would have to think of excuses to stop Yangchen spending time alone with his wife. He jogged through the streets, looking for anyone plump among the stickmen still outside. After twenty minutes of looping circles around the furnace, Jinyi gave up. They have obviously decided to disappear into our worries instead, he thought.

The few men he saw on his way back avoided his gaze, suspecting that he too, being out at that hour and not beside a furnace or a family or on a night shift, must be up to something not approved by state legislature. He kept his eyes trained on the distance, on the next street up from his where buildings and fields took turns overrunning each other as the dirt road eventually trickled into shanty huts and empty pig-pens.

Yuying sent the children to bed without letting them eat the leftovers; for even if they would be stale tomorrow, even if they would taste like shreds of hardened newspaper, well, that was still better than getting used to being completely full, because then the children would come to expect that feeling of a satisfied stomach and measure every other miserable meal against it. She then took the black soap and washed her face in the night bucket before joining Jinyi in the wooden bed, both of them too tired and embarrassed by the evening to risk talking about it. Jinyi kept his eyes open, seeing the leaping red of furnace flames in the movements of the lazy moths and the window's shadows, thrown from a world which, in its race ahead into the future, would not allow itself to rest for even a second.

'Of course, China has always been ahead of the rest of the world; it is just that the rest of the world has not always known it,' Teacher Lu was fond of saying. He made all his students memorise the four great inventions of the ancient Chinese and made sure they remembered the way they were claimed by foreign powers centuries later.

The compass: a floating lodestone first used

to divine iron in mountainous Taoist temples, then later used to draw the world along its axis. Gunpowder: Qin Shi Huang's search for an elixir of immortality had inadvertently led to the creation of fireworks, a source of beauty and enjoyment until foreigners took the stuff and used it to create modern warfare. Printing: wooden blocks arranged to stamp down characters over a thousand years ago. (Movable clay type was also created, and then quickly abandoned — it would never catch on, the printers agreed.) And paper: the eunuch Cai Lun's experiments with hemp and bamboo, with silk and mulberry bark, led to the first crisp sheaths. This careful art was later taken abroad after the kidnap of Chinese papermakers by Arabs, spreading that most dangerous invention of all (and if you still think that gunpowder is more powerful, then you have not been paying attention).

Teacher Lu paced in front of the class, peering down at the rows of bowed heads, many freshly shaved for the lice season. He was worried that the swift whip of his ruler, the trusted slap when the back of a head met the back of his hand, and even the corkscrew twisting of an ear between thumb and finger, were losing their effect. What was more, there was no one he could complain to, despite knowing the cause of his class's recent concentration problems. Teacher Lu knew that dissent was a dirty word, and these days, so was hunger. Keep your head up, and keep quiet, and you'll do well in life, Headteacher Han often said to both his staff and his pupils. Teacher Lu heard muffled voices from somewhere in the back row, but tried to ignore them. After all, with his stomach mewing and his mouth slathering, he was also having trouble keeping his mind on the question in hand: If Farmer Wang brings ten *jin* of rice to the collective, and Farmer Bai brings fifteen, then . . .

Hearing the rush of students from other rooms, the sound of doors being battered back, the whooping from the first off the mark and the cries and whines of those knocked over or trapped at the back of the pushing crowd, he let his class go.

'Ah, lunchtime. Now, please, stand in formation and —'

He did not get to finish his sentence as the children rushed out around him, and he felt dizzy and confused as to how they still had energy left. The logic of the world was slipping away from him, and it was all he could do to keep the times tables from running themselves backwards toward zero.

If the mad scramble to the canteen showed the optimism untethered from memory possible only in the very young or very old, then the subsequent retreat to the classrooms showed the bitterness of experience. Water and potato flour made into a flat pancake and blackened in an oil-less pan, or cups of soapy broth in which bobbed a few hardened flecks of millet, or rubbery boiled potatoes that had been waiting in cellars from back when there were still good harvests: even the teachers wondered if it wouldn't have been better to eat nothing at all than to share so little that the stomach was tempted and awakened without being sated.

'At least we haven't got it as bad as in the south,' a colleague whispered to Teacher Lu. 'My uncle lives a few provinces down, and last time I saw him he looked like a dog's bark could bowl him over. Thin as a willow. He told me about a woman in his village with three children, how the eldest had died and they hid the body, so as to keep getting the dead boy's rice allowance, and by the time the authorities checked on them they found the corpse missing an arm, both legs and parts of the chest. Now *that's* hunger. We should be glad.'

'Silly rumours. The papers say it is not that bad. With everyone working so hard now, how can it be?' Teacher Lu replied, failing even to convince himself. He did not approve of this loose talk: that is what does for us all, he thought, but he did not have the energy to properly castigate his colleague.

When the last bell rang at the end of the school day, Manxin found her older brother dabbing at a freshly black eye behind the giant oak the children called Old Bearded Master, and led him home.

'Who hit you this time?' Manxin asked.

'Nobody.'

'You look like a panda,' she giggled.

'No such thing,' he replied grumpily, still rubbing the bruised flesh around his eye.

'What? Of course there are, everyone says so. They eat bamboo.'

'Have you ever seen one?' he said.

'I've seen pictures.'

'Ha. There you go then.'

'Just because you can't see something, doesn't mean it's not real. Like the wind.'

She had trumped him, so he sneered and laughed to hide the failure of his teasing. They passed tiny worn houses that backed onto fields of swirling dust. Even closer to home the deserted streets were blessed with flakes of ash and soot.

It is a common misconception that hard times make brothers of us all. This was not the case. Ration tickets dropped on the street were always gone by the time the owner bent down to retrieve them. Families clung jealously onto the little they had, and suspicions grew in the dark of every hungry stomach. A few gaunt men were salivating at a poster that showed a bumper yield of crops, the bright colours smudged by the strange artistry of the dust clouds.

'It's just boy stuff, nothing to worry about.

A few scraps and scrapes will make him stronger,' Jinyi whispered to his wife when they returned from the furnace that evening. 'Don't make a fuss about it, all right?'

'It's not the first time, though,' she said.

'Best to keep your eyes open.' Granny Dumpling said, inviting herself into their private conversation. 'When I was his age, kids in our village were being kidnapped and sold as slaves to the local warlords. Well, I know there aren't warlords anymore, but people don't change that quickly. Old ways, new ways, bad ways, better ways, old problems, new problems.'

'So what do we do?' Yuying asked Jinyi, ignoring her mother.

'There's nothing for us to do. They're just kids, they'll grow out of picking on him. It's part of growing up — trust me, it will make a man of him.'

Did it make a man of you? Yuying wanted to ask, but knew better than to be disrespectful, at least when others could hear.

'Well, we'll wait for now, but if it happens again . . .' Yuying said, her resolve weakened by her inability to think of something she could do to change the situation.

While the rest of the family slept into the one weekend day off the next morning, Granny Dumpling was already doddering along the streets. Wobbling determinedly on her small feet, which, despite the changes in the law, she had not dared to unbind for fear of the embarrassing sight and smell, it took her almost an hour to reach the other side of the river. She noticed that the snaking alleys behind the riverside restaurants, usually filled with strays scavenging and fighting over scraps, were conspicuously quiet. Where the town used to come alive at night to the noise of howled love songs, revving snarls and cracking teeth, there was now only the rhythmic slop of the restaurants tossing out their dirty water. As she walked, Bian Shi recalled a recipe for dog-leg stew, brimming and bubbling with cabbage and chillies and tofu, the chewy russet meat bobbing to the surface.

The old street was a curved arc, an unusual antidote to the right angles and measured parallels of the more recent additions to the city, and she had to duck to avoid the fluttering washing hung out on wooden poles at varying heights. In between two cobblers' front-room workshops, she spotted a tiny wooden shack with the single window boarded over, the marker she had been told to look for, and she checked the faces about her before sidling in through the small wooden door.

'Doctor Ma?' She sent her query into the gloom of clay pots and glass jars fighting for space on slanted shelves and stacked on the floor amid parchments and string-bound scrolls.

'I'm sorry, this all belongs to my uncle. I'm just visiting him.' A short man with tiny paper-cuts for eyes and tufts of grey hair said, waving his hands apologetically as he emerged from the backroom.

'I was sent here by a woman at the hospital — Comrade Lin — who told me that Doctor Ma could be of some help for my grand-son's . . . erm . . . ailments.'

'Ah, I see. I am Dr Ma. You'll have to forgive me for that little fib just now, but you can never be too careful. Though you may find it hard to believe, there are some who would like me to stop offering help to the sick and the needy. The revolution is truly wonderful, do not get me wrong, but I remain a little sceptical about the use of so much Western medicine in the hospitals. After all, my family has been healing people for over a thousand years. Please sit down, and tell me more about your grandson.'

He cleared some papers from a stool and, as she spoke, began to unfold a large chart, punctuating her sentences with exaggerated murmurs of interest.

'He does not seem to be doing very well at school — trouble with other boys, I think. He says that because his stomach is always rumbling he cannot concentrate.'

Dr Ma cleared his throat and posited a

theory — an imbalance in the stomach.

'The stomach, what we doctors call the sea of water and cereal, is a *fu* organ, and is bound with the *zang* organ of the spleen. They are both elementally tied to the earth. However, it seems that the balance has been upset. Not doing well at school, now that is because the spleen dominates the intellect. Cold palms? Lack of concentration? Yes? I see, well there we have it.'

'You don't think he's just hungry then?'

'Oh my, no, no, no. Our body and mind are bound together, and if one is upset then the other will suffer. Luckily, there is a remedy. Of course, these are unusual times, and we are all doing all we can to help the country, so . . .' Dr Ma mumbled, waiting for her to interrupt.

'Ah, yes, you are very kind to help us in this way. Please accept this in return.'

She reached into her pocket, and pulled out a red jewel. Dr Ma examined it uncertainly, trying to decide whether jewellery, whatever its worth, might be of any use when the only trade those days was carried out with ration books or secret handshakes.

'Oh, I couldn't possibly . . .' he said, almost hoping she would replace it with a *jin* of rice or flour, something his senses could more easily measure.

'Please, I would not want to take something from you without giving something in return.'

And so the bargaining, disguised as courtesy, reached it climax; he thrust the jewel into his pocket, and she left cradling a small clay pot, stuffed with rank-smelling dark grasses and what looked like jellied fungus.

If everything is intertwined and the world is fluid, in flux between motion and invisibility, as the doctor asserted, then the blur between the heat of the community furnaces and the burning certainty of belief, the balance between expectation and reality, had become tangled, inseparable. Granny Dumpling wondered whether a cure for this fervour that seemed to have overtaken the city might also be found in a mixture of herbs and prayers. Her stunted feet throbbed and she squatted down to rest on her heels as a donkey, its scabby fur stretched over vast ribs and spindly legs, whimpered at the jaundiced man beating it down the street. The body, she had learnt from experience, is a trap.

She entered her daughter's small house to find Jinyi raging about a tuft of hair that Dali had pulled from Manxin's head. Yuying was trying to rock the baby to sleep. They never knew what to do with the few scraps of time they found alone with their family.

The fumes from the medicine frothing the pot Granny Dumpling set on the under-used stove quickly filled both the rooms.

'Oh, Granny Dumpling, go and cook that stuff in the public toilets and scare away the other bad smells,' Manxin pleaded, pinching her nostrils.

'What kind of evil things live in that pot?' Dali asked nervously.

'Never you mind what's in it; it is the effect that counts. Just one sip will give you special powers, magical powers. What, you didn't think magic potions would taste like honey, did you? Nothing good ever happens without some kind of sacrifice.'

Granny Dumpling then proceeded to force the thick liquid down Dali's throat, cupful by acrid cupful, unheedful of his gags and splutters and gurgles while Manxin stared, unsure whether to laugh or applaud. A small trickle of the brown syrupy goo dribbled from the corner of his mouth. The last cup contained only the soggy dregs of floating leaf mulch and lumpy twig bits, but she shrugged and told him to hold his nose while he swallowed. He coughed and choked.

'Come on, I'll take you two to the dining hall and get that taste from your mouth. It's almost time,' Jinyi said quickly, before Dali had time to start crying.

An hour later Jinyi ushered his two children — their disappointed stomachs still pleading for more than just the measly portion of stewed turnips they had been allocated — back to the house, where Yuying was waiting with the baby. He then jogged to the furnace, where he stood with Yaba and a few others in front of the cage of spluttering flames, debating by how much they should report that they had exceeded the monthly quota. When he returned again, plucking children from beside his wife and slipping into the warm space himself, he was at least halfway content. He suddenly thought of his dead aunt, but quickly pushed her from his mind. There is still time left for love, he thought to himself, for the rekindled hope — learnt and unlearnt and learnt again — of knowing someone else's life besides your own. His hands strayed across his wife's arms.

She smelt the smoky, sour smell of his greasy hair with her eyes closed. 'Is this what they mean?'

'What?'

'The proverbs, the stories? Is this what they are talking about?'

Silence. The moonlight shuffled, the shadows cleared their throats.

'I think it is.' He smiled into the dark.

Outside the window, in the western expanse of the sky, in the provinces of the White Tiger, near Turtle Beak and across from the Hairy Head, was the constellation of the Stomach Mansion, known to some as Aries, the three brightest stars shedding their light from lifetimes of the distant past.

And next to the well-used crib, on the warm *kang,* top-to-tail with his sister, Dali tossed

410

and turned in the starlight, his stomach rumbling. He was quietly dreading another day at school, another round of teasing and nicknames and taunting, another chance for humiliation. All in all, he had decided, it was not easy being eight. He could not wait to be nine.

We sifted through the sky as though we were autumn leaves slipping downstream, leisurely surfing on the sway. I gripped the huffing beast behind its pricked ears, holding on until its hooves brushed against the cobbled stone. We had touched down in the courtyard of a temple — the only place qilins are allowed to appear. Yet the whole place seemed to be in ruins, and the parts of the old walls that were not crumbling were covered in creepers and vines. Weeds poked up among the cracks. Scratches in the stone showed where the iron incense trough had been upturned and dragged away to be melted for scrap.

'Where will you go now?' I asked as I clambered from the animal's bristly back.

'There is a hairline crack between thoughts and dreams. I will go there, and wait for it to open.' the qilin snorted, before reeling up and cantering away.

Its reply seemed plausible enough to me — I have spent enough time skimming through human thoughts to know that many strange and inexplicable things happen there. I decided to take a look around. The courtyard led on to a small rectangular building. Fire had devastated the inside, and the roof tiles had all been stolen. Once my eyes adjusted to the shadows, I saw that birds had nested beside the charred remains of an idol of Lao Tzu, and a snake was leisurely making its way towards the antechamber at the back where the young novices would once have slept. I rubbed a layer of dust and ash from the centre of the main wall to reveal the huge round *taijitu*.

'I hear you have been getting some help,' the Jade Emperor said, and I spun around to see him standing casually behind me.

'That's not against the rules. You never said I couldn't,' I stammered in surprise.

'You may get as much help as you wish,' he replied. 'But you might wish to remember that all hearts work a little differently — the hearts of Li Bai and Du Fu might not teach you anything about the hearts of Bian Yuying and Hou Jinyi.'

'Oh, I'm not sure I can agree with you, sir. To know a heart you must learn at least a little about everything it is connected to.'

A smile darted across his thin lips. 'Then you are doing better that I had expected. Tell me, what were you looking at?'

I pointed at the grubby *taijitu*. 'You mean this?' I asked. How could he possibly not know what it was?

As if reading my thoughts, he let out a little laugh. 'Humour me. Explain to me what it is, if you would.'

'All right. It's a circle in which are represented the yin and the yang.'

'Tell me, do the yin and yang exist?'

'Of course. Everything is made up of them: day and night, man and woman, light and darkness.'

'So, do circles exist?'

'I'm sorry, I don't understand.'

'Have you ever seen a circle in the natural world?'

'Well, I've seen things that are a circular shape. But never a perfect circle, no. I mean, there are only three-dimensional shapes in the natural world, like spheres and oblongs. Nothing exists without depth. But I have seen people move in circles.'

'Ah, there we have it. Not only the light and dark of the yin and yang in this picture, but also the circle that encloses them, are symbols. Yin and yang are the very fabric of the universe; time is the endless unbroken circle that encloses them.'

'Yes, I see. But what has this got to do with the heart?' I asked, and once again the Jade Emperor's unnerving grin spread across his face.

8:
1967
THE YEAR OF THE SHEEP

Jinyi heard the slap of the front door suddenly snapping back against its hinges, then the muffled voices and whispered orders: the checklist of little signs he had been expecting. He had not slept in weeks, anticipating the event, playing out the possible accusations and outcomes in his head, rehearsing the lines he had committed to memory. By the time they called out, he was already up and at the bedroom door, having lain fully clothed in the dark. On the lukewarm *kang* were his three daughters: Manxin, almost fourteen; Liqui, nine, and the newest, Xiaojing, four. His son was not home, for which Jinyi counted his blessings before slipping through to the main room. He was sweating already, damp in the early summer humidity, and if someone were to tell him that on the other side of this tangled planet they were calling this the summer of love, he would not know whether to weep or die laughing.

The truth was that Jinyi had not slept properly for close to eight months. He felt dwarfed by the wooden bed with no one beside him. When he was not troubled by the indecipherable auguries of bad dreams, he would lie and watch the children sleeping, trying not to think about where their mother was. It had all happened so quickly. Of course, they had read the banners and newspaper reports and proclamations, and Jinyi had whole-heartedly agreed with everyone else that something more drastic needed to be done about the imperialists and bourgeois who had caused the famine and were trying to undo the work of the revolution. But he hadn't thought they were referring to people like his wife.

Following the Criticism Meeting in the local food hall, she had been told to 'have a rest, take a break' from work, and their friends had slowly stopped talking to them. After even the traders in the covered market had started either spitting at her or pretending she was invisible when she went to buy vegetables, Yuying had taken to sitting at home all day. Until the truck had arrived one morning and taken her away.

'Close that door. We don't want to wake your children, uncle. Please, sit down.'

The politeness confused Jinyi; this was not how he had imagined it, being offered a seat at his own kitchen table. He hesitated, then sat.

There were four of them, teenagers in identical dark green jackets, somewhere between forest fern and dank emerald seaweed, collars folded carefully down away from faces wearing false smiles. Each had a green flat cap with the five sharp points of a tawny-yellow metal star studded at the front, and red cotton armbands sewn on below their shoulders. They had spent hours in the half-light of shared bedrooms patiently embroidering these with the yellow lettering that announced their status: 'Red Guard'. Two boys and two girls, and three of the four, Jinyi quickly noted, were taller than him.

The speaker was a stocky boy with an oily fringe and his two front teeth missing — the other three hovered around him, twitchy and impatient, watching for signals that would allow them to leap in.

'I must say, uncle, this is a fine little house you have, though you seem to have misplaced your picture of our great Chairman, which I would have thought you would have hanging in pride of place instead of these . . . these funny birds,' the leader said, motioning to the scroll hanging on the wall.

Jinyi patted his top breast pocket, from which the frayed corner of a palm-sized book peaked out, thin and greasy sheaths stuffed between a waxy red cover. 'His words are always with me, close to my heart. It is his ideas, after all, that are of importance. Not that he himself is not important, I mean; we would all still be slaves of the Japanese and landlords were it not for his great strength. But where are my manners — can I get you some tea?'

'Anyone can profess respect for our great Chairman: it is only action that counts,' the oily-haired leader sneered, and the others allowed themselves to grin with satisfaction. 'Yes, a fine little house. But I can't help but wonder, if you and your family have been living here, what you have done with all your riches? I don't imagine you've just given them away. Come now, no need to be coy. We have heard all about you from Comrade Yangchen. He really is a fountain of knowledge.'

Jinyi tried to keep smiling. He was not surprised to hear Yangchen's name again — it was he who had complained about Yuying.

'We don't have any riches.' Jinyi resisted the urge to add: if you know so much about us, you ought to know that already.

He forced a small smile, then regretted it, knowing he must have looked as pathetic as he felt. But he knew there was no other choice.

Only last week he had bumped into Teacher Dong, a physics expert from his children's high school, limping back from the hospital. It was shameful to see a man still in his thirties without any teeth. He was using a knobbly branch as a crutch, his face a murky pool of purples and reds. Teacher Dong had not managed to see anyone at the hospital: too full, too busy. He would go back to the abandoned schoolhouse and rest: perhaps when things calmed down some children might return for lessons, he had said. He had then stumbled at the crossroads, and whispered, blushing, to Jinyi to point him in the right direction towards the schoolhouse, because they had smashed his glasses. That was what had marked him out as bourgeois: a twenty-year-old wire-rimmed pair of scratched spectacles. Jinyi had led him for the first few steps, then fallen back in case anyone was watching, anxious to rid his mind of the coincidence that some of his children had been out until after twelve with their own factions the night before.

'If you're not going to be honest, uncle, then how can we help you?' The leader leaned closer. He cracked his knuckles and waited for an answer, while a few of the others began to search through the cupboards, in the flues of the fireplace and in the old pots and boxes stacked in one corner.

The leader prided himself on his strict adherence to the words of the Chairman. His group believed in justice, in punishing crimes that could no longer be ignored. Many of the other groups that visited households or dormitories late at night acted differently: bursting down doors to start the beating as soon as possible, or else letting the public declarations of guilt slip into retribution far too quickly. This was foolish, the gap-toothed leader considered, though he admired their spirit and the zeal with which they took to the task. He preferred to weigh up evidence, as the Chairman might, before deciding the level of punishment. Was it fitting to break the ribs of both a rightist and a traitor, an intellectual and a critic, a nationalist and a collaborator? He thought not. His group picked the parts of the body they would work over according to the particulars of the crime they sniffed out.

'I swear, I am being honest. There are no riches: my wife's father was wealthy, I admit, but he squandered his money just like the rest of those filthy bourgeois, without a care for anyone else. But that was before I joined the family,' Jinyi said.

'And I bet that annoyed you, didn't it? Because you did all that work, sucking up to the rich, kissing arse — yes sir, no sir, of course sir — to wheedle your way into a bourgeois family, only to find that you weren't going to be as rich as you thought you were going to be. Yes, Comrade Yangchen told us everything. You must have craved wealth pretty badly, to give up your home, your family, your noble peasant's way of life, even your name, all to get your hands on a little gold. What kind of man are you?'

'It wasn't like that. Before the Chairman and the great revolution, life was difficult, it was unfair. I had to leave the countryside because of the landlords and the corruption, so —'

'That is no excuse. Members of the Party were risking their lives at that time, for all of us. Why didn't you join up if life was so hard for you?'

'I, well, I wasn't sure how to. Who could I ask? If I went up to someone on the street and said, "Are you a Communist?" they might have attacked me, or else suspected me of being a Nationalist spy.'

Jinyi's mind was rushing forward, trying to stay a few steps ahead of his mouth. Yet he was painfully aware that his words sounded less believable out loud than when he had practised them in his head.

'There's nothing in any of these.' This time one of the girls spoke, turning to the leader from the pile of boxes and cupboards in the corner. As she turned, a single plait whipped across her shoulder, hanging limply from her cap. Two beady, blinking eyes stared out from her equine face, searching for further instructions.

Jinyi knew what they were looking for. Only last year Mao had announced that although the bourgeois had been defeated in the

421

revolution, their ideas had not. Books, antiques, portraits, poetry; anything that looked suspiciously like the culture of imperial China was not to be trusted. Like most families in the neighbourhood, Jinyi had, at that time, gathered together all their books, old paper banknotes, photos and relics from the restaurant era, vaguely colourful clothes and whole generations of school notebooks. He had stuffed these down his trousers and tucked them under his jacket and had then walked with a false, play-acted calm through the busy alleyways until he had reached the bonfire outside the university where two teachers had been killed and twelve others hospitalised the week before.

The leader seemed to have read his mind. 'Of course there isn't. They may be bourgeois, but they aren't completely stupid. They probably destroyed anything they shouldn't have. They're sneaky, crafty, liars, the lot of them. You should know that, Comrade Weiwei.'

'Yes, Comrade.' Weiwei returned to the group which now encircled the table where Jinyi was sitting, his hands folded in front of him.

'Listen, Comrade.' Jinyi knew this was a dangerous tactic, speaking directly to them, but he was worried that their contempt for his wrinkles and grey tufts, his forty-something years lived without revolutionary activity, would soon brim over, and he felt he had to do anything he could to try and placate them.

'When I was born, there was nothing but struggle. We didn't call it class struggle then, but we did everything we could to survive. Struggled to eat, struggled to live. Struggled not to get shot by the Japanese. I didn't have my own pair of shoes until I was almost thirty, and a married man.

'Listen, I even stole, only ever from the rich though, you understand: a bit of bread in a mansion's window or swiped from the kitchen of a posh restaurant. Life was bought and sold, and so was my marriage. It wasn't done for my benefit, let me tell you — Old Bian already controlled an empire of restaurants, and I was just someone he could boss around. It was as simple as that: he gave an order, and you did something. There was no other choice back then: he was one of the most powerful people in the city, and if I wanted to work or eat or even take a shit in this city again then I had to do as he said.

'Comrade, I am grateful for the revolution. It's made this country fair, and I thank Chairman Mao every day that things are different for my children, for my brothers in the fields, for my comrades in the countryside. But I am an honourable man, and I got married, and there's no turning back from that.'

The leader shook his head. Jinyi felt his

mouth fill with saliva, the sour taste of jittery nerves.

'Honour, uncle, is serving your country, is helping your comrades, is fighting for the revolution. You're just a typical rightist.'

Jinyi became aware of a drop of sweat snaking into his eyebrow, and resisted the urge to wipe it away. A rightist. There, it had been said, and it could not be taken back. They had labelled him, and with one stroke repainted his skin, resculpted his life into something he could not quite recognise.

The other boy, bug-eyed and pudgy, then took a turn to speak. 'Why is it that you turned your back on your country, on your comrades? Your generation had the chance to change the world, and you failed.' He spat, a large gob of yellowy jelly.

Jinyi was unsure whether they were really trying to fathom his life or were simply toying with him, enjoying the build-up before the real action began. He let his eyes run over each of them in turn.

And in a flash Jinyi began to understand the enraged hunger in their eyes: he had been the same when he was young, wanting to redraw the boundaries between knowledge and possibility. Yet they truly believed they possessed the ability to split the world into black and white, to take this bulging, rippling, monstrously overgrown country and hold it in the palms of their hands, to strip down millennia of formalities and rituals into a list of rules that could be flexed by a fist.

'Well, what's your answer, *Comrade?*' the leader leaned forward and hissed through the gap where his front teeth should have been.

'Why did you neglect the Party, turn your cowardly back on revolution and class struggle when others like you were on the front line? Tell us,' and here he allowed himself a smile, 'what you really think of the Chairman.'

Jinyi tried to remember when the whole mess had started. Was it on the day the furnaces were shut down amid the famine, the day mistakes were first admitted? Was it in the middle of the previous summer, in 1966, when the newspapers announced that all rightists, intellectuals, nationalists and imperialists (among others) had to be purged? Was it when the Cultural Revolution Group of the national government had decreed, 'The proletariat must continue the struggle, must change the very minds of society, must criticise and crush and destroy those following the capitalist road, those teachers, artists, bureaucrats, intellectuals and all others weakening the foundations of the revolution'? Or was it the day Jinyi's stomach gave in to the new climate of fear and left him sprinting urgently to the fetid public toilet six or seven times a day?

No. It had begun earlier than that. Jinyi remembered the day when the plague of locusts and flies and mosquitoes descended from the mountains and took over the fields on the outskirts of the city. A huge black whirring buzz had swept over the houses, a fog of flitting insects storming in through every crack or gap in the walls. That must have been a message from the gods, he thought, a warning of dark times coming.

Jinyi's skin itched just remembering the days when he could not open his mouth to speak without insects diving in. The government had previously declared that sparrows were to be considered an enemy of the people, since they were responsible for the great famine. Everyone was encouraged to drive them away with sticks and spades, to beat pots and woks to keep them in perpetual flight so that they would die of exhaustion. It was only a few months after the order that the cloud of insects had covered the country with their colossal shadow.

As the leader lunged and shoved Jinyi's chair to the floor, Jinyi listened out for sounds of movement in the bedroom; even as his knee hammered into the bare floor and his hands scraped out to support his fall, half his attention was trained on making out his daughters' voices through the thin walls. His leg sung with a throbbing pain, and he pushed up onto his hands and knees, hoping they were still asleep or, even if they heard the sudden thump, that they had the sense to keep quiet.

'You've had your last chance, so why don't you just admit what you've done? Hand over the money and it can go where it belongs, to the people whose backs were broken while the family you were sucking up to were getting rich off their misery.'

'If they still had some,' Jinyi said, trying to pick up both the chair and himself in a manner that would not offend the uniformed teenagers, 'then they never told me.'

'Bullshit. You've been married for what, nearly twenty years? Even if we are to believe your flimsy excuses about being made to marry — which I must admit, uncle, don't impress me — then you can't also expect us to believe that you didn't get your hands on anything you could. Rightists are always thinking about themselves.' The leader pronounced the last sentence to the others as if it were a profound truth that he was deigning to share with them.

Jinyi felt the sting spreading through his cheek. It was nothing compared to the pain that squeezed his chest every time he thought about where his wife might be. Yuying, he muttered under his breath, as though her name was a prayer.

'He's lying. Comrade Yangchen told us he would. It must be hidden somewhere,' the tall girl added.

'Perhaps his wife took it all,' the chubby boy said. 'She was a traitor after all.'

The leader nodded.

Jinyi weighed the idea up. What would she do, if she were here? Anything to protect her children, he thought. 'Yes, my wife —'

'Your wife! Your wife is a dog, a fucking whore. That's right: a whore. A traitor.' The leader was now really beginning to enjoy himself, and his curled lip suddenly reminded Jinyi of the dumpy-legged pure-breeds that guarded the mansions before the revolution, letting loose low rumbling growls if you even so much as thought of walking on the same side of the street as their masters' lavish homes.

'Yes. She learnt Japanese, that's true, and stowed away money, but I thought she would change, what with a new husband, and a new China to believe in. All the rest, though, the stuff that came out in the public denunciation, I knew nothing about it, I swear.'

As soon as the words left his mouth, Jinyi felt sick. He imagined her standing beside him, asking in sobs why he had buried her name in lies.

'A good husband would have kept his wife in line. Chairman Mao has told us to protect the interests of women and children — but sometimes people need to be protected from themselves. Sometimes people need to be taught right from wrong.'

The leader stretched his hand above Jinyi's face, holding out his pristine fingers, free from the burns, blisters and calluses of Jinyi's own. 'You do know how to use one of these, don't you, uncle?'

Jinyi nodded tentatively, trying his best not to cower. 'But I —'

'Perhaps you need some help. Let me remind you.'

The leader swung it suddenly down, the smack of knuckles sending Jinyi's head reeling back.

The chubby boy looked at the shorter of the two girls, whose nervous hands were worrying her plait. 'Remember,' he whispered across to her, quoting from the book, 'to be rid of the gun, it is necessary to first take up the gun.'

Jinyi forced himself to speak through the smarting pain spreading below his eye. 'You're right, of course, you're right. But listen, I've always been treated like a servant here — people would stop talking when I entered the room, they'd whisper about me behind my back. I'm just a peasant trying to look after his family in the city, that's all.' Jinyi was starting to stutter. 'The revolution saved my life, made me equal, and I will be grateful forever. And, and, I am a . . . er . . . a good citizen: I help others at the factory . . . I always eat less at the food halls . . . I have never once doubted the wisdom of the Party. That's the truth.'

'After all the chances we've given you to confess, uncle, why do you have to lie to us? You've had a hundred chances to help your country, and you turned your nose up at all of them, just like you are turning your nose up now. All you had to do was admit your failings — admit you've let the country down, let the revolution down, let your comrades down.' The leader's voice was straining, reaching towards a pitch that the stars of Beijing opera, in the days before all the theatres were burnt down, would have been proud of.

'Is it that you hate your country or just the people in it? You're no peasant — you're a traitor!'

The leader gripped the edge of the wooden table, and shoved it over. It hit the floor with the noise of a phonograph needle ripping across a record, jumping scratchily from a familiar tune to yelps of fuzzy feedback and violins played with teeth: the sound of the future. As the teapot and unwashed dinner bowls and tea cups smashed, as chaos was unloosed and Jinyi lost all sense of time amidst the boots and — he thanked his luck — battered plimsolls that thudded into him until he was nothing but a jangling bag of joggled bruises and broken bones, as the leader shouted, 'The Chairman is the burning sun in our hearts!' and those of the group not spitting at, kicking, stamping on or throwing things at Comrade Hou Jinyi began tearing down the shelves and crushing everything on them under their feet, amidst all of that, Jinyi closed his eyes and tried to conjure up his wife.

Stepping back from the fury of their companions' feet, the two girls pulled open the cupboards and drawers before smashing these too to the floor.

Yuying's reading glasses were stomped on; ornamental chopsticks emblazoned with a pair of cranes, a wedding gift, were snapped in two; letters were torn up; bowls smashed; the chunky radio (a gift from Granny Dumpling) thrown against the wall; photos flung from albums; ink sticks broken.

Jinyi sank under the welts, bruises, cuts, breaks, blows; his mind slipped in and out of the room.

The sun slunk under the door, shyly nudging up to the bloody body curled amidst the broken wood and shards of china.

'Manxin?' Jinyi called hoarsely. Yet he found his voice was a low groan that would not reach the bedroom. With one eye half open, one swollen shut, he looked about the mess of the room. The Red Guards were gone. He had a mouth full of loose teeth, the copper taste of blood buzzing about his tongue.

'Liqui?' When he drew breath, his chest rattled, the curved bones wringing out his lungs. This must be why they call it a cage, he thought. He pulled his legs up beside him, lying where they had left him beside the broken tabletop, and waited.

His daughters were awake on the other side of the door, their hands clutched together under the sweaty bedsheet, though their eyes remained squeezed shut in the topsy-turvy logic of fear that convinced them that anyone searching the room would then quickly retrace their steps for fear of waking three sleeping girls. They had stayed that way until dawn, blotting out their father's groans, just audible despite the girls' combined heavy breathing, not daring to leave the room even though the yelps and scuffles and clattering smashes had stopped some time ago.

While he lay curled on the concrete floor, Jinyi counted the times in the last months when he had heard his son in the night, lying face down and muffling the quiet wheezy sobs with his sheet, thinking everyone else was asleep. More than his wounds or bruises, Jinyi thought of where Dali might be, and when he would return home.

'Aiya! Pa! Are you all right?' Manxin had ventured out of the bedroom with the buttery sunrise. She did not wait for him to respond before continuing, 'Let's get you up, then. Here we go.'

Manxin and Liqui, her long plait bobbing around her red eyes, managed to pull Jinyi's slouching body to the next room and help him up onto the still-warm *kang*.

'Thank you.' Jinyi reached an arm out for his skinny middle daughter. 'That was quite a fall I had,' he said, and tried a smile. It came out as a mess of burgundy gums, and was met with silence.

The two older girls began cleaning the main room, neither of them daring to refer to the night's events. Instead they would clean and mend and sweep and bin and hope until the room had been rearranged to exclude the past. Little Xiaojing moved towards the bottom of the bed and, despite her fear and confusion, was soon asleep.

Jinyi lay there, letting the room swim around him, until he could no longer bear it.

'Girls,' he called weakly. The two of them gathered round the bed, handing their father warm water but not looking him in the eye. Manxin was stocky and almost assured, Liqui lithe and fidgety. 'I think I should go to the hospital. I know you're busy, but can one of you help me?'

They exchanged glances. 'Perhaps if you get some rest you'll feel better later, Pa,' Manxin said.

Had they heard him talking about their mother? Did they think he had betrayed them? He wanted to say that he did it for them, so that he could stay and keep them safe — their mother had already been sent away, but there was still a chance for the rest of them. Two parents with bad names, two adults sent to the countryside, where would that get them? But he did not say any of that.

'Are you hungry? A good meal and you'll soon be feeling all right,' Manxin continued.

'No, no, you're right, I just need a good rest.' Jinyi turned away onto his side, suppressing a groan as the pain coiled and juddered like broken springs in his chest. His daughters were too afraid to take him out, to admit the truth of what had happened. They were ashamed of him. He could not blame them. He was ashamed of himself.

As he curled up on the bed, waiting for his daughters to disappear, Jinyi found himself wishing that the factory had not been temporarily boarded up following a Red Guard demonstration against the manager last month, so that he would have somewhere to go, someone to be.

His daughters left the house to spend the day marching through the city and combining violent denunciations with earnest community volunteer work in their own groups of Red Guards and the Red Guard Youth Movement, to which Liqui took her bewildered little sister.

Jinyi waited a little after their departure before heaving himself out of bed and hobbling out into the street. Every step sent erratic shocks through his body, and it took him an hour to walk a few hundred metres, people crossing as he neared them, looking away from his blood-stained jacket, his lumpy pomegranate face. Even the crooked street-lamps, which were installed at every corner two years before and had worked for three weeks before the power shut down, shook heads at him. You should be ashamed of yourself, the bicycle bells pringed and the washing lines sang. I know, he answered. I know.

A quick glance in the hospital waiting room gave Jinyi the suspicion that most of the patients had arrived far too late and were already dead. Only the vivacity of the wounds, the ruddy baked-clay redness of fresh gashes and the plush Martian purples where flesh had been mangled, bruised or crushed, convinced him that the people crowded into the small waiting room were still hanging on. Jinyi surmised that even if life was evidenced by the barely stifled groans escaping from the bodies — as each patient attempted to balance the stoicism expected of good citizens with a desire to make it known that their ailments were in need of more urgent attention than the people around them — the smell of the room was of death. There were three wooden stools and close to thirty people, slumped at the base of walls, leaning, lying or folding themselves into the smallest of free spaces nearest the door to the main hall. Jinyi squeezed in and nudged his way to a corner of wall, to lean and pant with the rest of them. He fished in his pocket — he knew the order of admittance: first those who knew a doctor in some way (a distant relative, a business contact or an old classmate); next, those trading in a favour; then those with a significant-enough gift for the hospital, and finally those like Jinyi who had scrambled together a few mangy grease-stained bank-notes to spread across a couple of palms. The walls bore testament to whole days spent waiting and swatting the greedy legions of mosquitoes that swamped the summer.

The queue of patients looped into the closet-sized exam room, and the harassed and chain-smoking doctors made no attempts to lower their voices. Mould blotted one of the windowless walls, fat blotches and abstract shapes in pre-school green.

In the afternoon, Jinyi did a quick head-count of those before him in the makeshift line. The man at the front, limping on a mangled leg, settled onto a stool, coughed into his hand and then said, 'I had a nasty fall, Doc, must be getting old. Is there anything you can give me for it?'

The women were being sent to the only other spare room; half of the nurses had disappeared and the recent glut of power cuts had left the operating surgery a risky last resort. Jinyi clutched his sides, trying not to groan. He was now second in line, watching the battered man ahead of him lean in close to a young doctor and say, 'Sorry to trouble you, doctor, but I had a bad fall.'

Jinyi's turn came with a doctor about his own age, clean-shaven and swapping pen and lit cigarette between his lips as he nodded and scribbled on a pad of cheap lined paper.

'Good afternoon, doctor. Well, I fell over last night and I'm in a little pain,' Jinyi said, as quietly as possible.

'Where?' the doctor replied wearily, making it clear that he had little interest in the answer.

'Oh, here. My chest. And my head, a little.'

'The head is just bruises, perhaps a little concussion. Both are trivial. Now let me see your chest.' The doctor rose and, tucking his cigarette behind his ear, prodded at Jinyi's upper body.

'This hurt? I see. This? Right. You've got a couple of rib fractures. Nothing serious. From the sound of your breathing, the jagged edges of the breaks have not punctured your lungs. Count yourself lucky.'

The doctor sat back down and began writing. Jinyi was unsure whether or not this was the end of the consultation, whether or not he should say any more. He wondered what

437

Yuying would do.

'Is there a cure?'

The doctor stopped writing, and his eyes met Jinyi's for the first time. 'Rest, and take plenty of deep breaths.' He beckoned the next patient. 'Be thankful that your injuries are so slight: that is the cure.'

Jinyi's quiet thanks were lost under the inventory of the next man's symptoms. As he limped through the waiting room, forcing back a cough and all the stabbing tremors that would accompany it, he overheard two men discussing a box that could photograph the inside of a man's body.

'They have one here, I swear, hidden away in the basement.'

Jinyi shook his head. People will believe anything. Didn't they know that this type of talk was dangerous, especially now?

How can one man turn the tides of history? The first emperor, Qin Shi Huang, spent the last decades of his life searching for a way to become immortal. As well as building an immortal terracotta army to replace his soldiers made from less durable flesh, he sent his chief alchemist, along with five hundred boys and five hundred girls, to the seas off the eastern coast to find the Isle of the Immortals. Instead of returning with news of their discovery, the alchemist and his charges are said to have found and populated the islands of Japan. The emperor himself is reported to have died, just like a Ming emperor some thousand years later, from an overdose of mercury, which he drank daily in the belief that its ingestion would stop his body from ageing.

Chairman Mao, however, had found a better way of achieving immortality: through books, badges, banners, posters, newspapers and threats. For a few years after the failure of the Great Leap Forward he had been forced by critics to take a backseat, but soon the need to renew the revolution, to mould the country according to his vision, became overwhelming. He hit upon a plan: he would manipulate the will of the people to purge the Party. After all, he still had his myth — he was the father figure who symbolised a nation's struggle, the figurehead of revolution istelf.

It had started with a swim in the river. The sexagenarian stripped to his underwear and let his pale stomach sag out as he pottered into the Yangtze River on a spring afternoon in 1966. He managed a light backstroke and a lazy bobbing crawl, later rewritten as a vigorous aqua marathon. A camera crew had been invited, as had reporters for the state-controlled broadsheets. He fought the current, then let it drag him easily back to where he started. After close to five years behind the scenes, allowing others to attempt an economic overhaul to fix his previous spate of bad planning, he had had enough. Enough of the government's veering to the centre and diluting his policies; enough of the new generation of leaders letting things slip; enough of local bureaucrats using Party membership as a stepping-stone to power and notoriety; but most importantly, enough of hiding in the wings. He nodded to the cameras as he trod water, but did not smile. This swim was to prove that he was still alive and well, was still fighting fit and filled with fire. Within months of his dip the newspapers were crammed with Mao's speeches and proclamations calling for young people to form groups of Red Guards, to criticise the failings of the old ways, to rise up and fight to make the socialist utopia a reality.

After the schools had closed, Manxin and her siblings had joined various Red Guard groups. This is real education, they were told, not something silly from stuffy old textbooks. Dali held out as long as he could when the groups were being established, but the sheer sway of the phrase 'You are either with us or against us!' and the mathematics behind it soon convinced him of the necessity to manufacture an outward veneer of commitment to the new cause.

'Unite and arise! Unite and arise! Forever forward with the revolution!'

440

Manxin and her friend Liuliu added their voices to the chant, its volume ebbing and rising as the marchers crossed the bridge and rounded a corner toward the long street that used to house the foreign department store. Shoes slapped urgently against the uneven paving stones as the pace picked up, fists pumping the air in time with the shouts.

'Dare to struggle! Dare to win!'

There were around thirty teenagers in lines of four or five, thirty peaked caps bobbing as they pushed forward, thirty medals glinting with the silver visage of the Chairman.

'Smash the counter-revolutionaries!'

'Rise up and join the class struggle!'

'Destroy the old to create the new!'

At the front was a middle-aged woman, with frazzled grey hairs escaping from her tight bun as she was pushed forward by a straggle of competing hands. She had a sandwich board of neatly written criticisms strapped over her shoulders, and was doing her best to keep her eyes to the floor. Her mouth was a muddle of blood and burning holes where her teeth had been wrenched out. It had turned her face into a leer. She was a shopkeeper known for taking bribes and saving the best wares for special customers. That day's parade was in her honour. She was shoved forward, and tripped, the sandwich board knocking against her chest and sweat squelching in her armpits, dribbling

441

down the inside of her jacket.

'If we do not speak, who will speak? If we do not act, who will act? The People must rebel. Find the traitors and rip their skin off, smash their skulls!'

Their group was called the Scarlet Guards, while Dali belonged to the Young Red Soldiers. Each rival faction sewed their names onto their armbands, and avoided contact with others, believing that theirs was the better way to uphold revolution.

Manxin caught her friend stealing a glance at a lanky boy with the first faint wisps of a moustache under his bulbous nose, and nudged her arm.

'Come on, Liuliu!' she whispered from the corner of her mouth. 'Don't you remember what happened to Chunhua?'

Liuliu nodded and turned back to face the front, adding her voice to the call and response of the catechisms from the Little Red Book.

Yet the truth was that neither of them was sure of what had actually happened to their classmate, Chunhua. The rumours were constant and contradictory, though they agreed on the following points: too many late night-strategy meetings between herself and the leader of the local group she had joined (the Red Youth); an envious cousin who alerted her family to a stick of red lipstick hidden among Chunhua's books; the subsequent shame of the family and the disappearance of the girl herself. Muttered speculation suggested that she was now wading through back-breaking paddies in a province so far south that, in the summer, a thousand flies flitted under your clothes, seeking respite from the merciless sun.

As they marched through the residential areas, the families doing their washing in metal tubs on the pavement and the old men discussing imaginary pasts slipped into their houses. Doors were pulled to as subtly as possible, and crumpled wet sheets were left clumped in cooling water. Even half a year ago the procession would have expected to be confronted by an irate citizen, a local cadre worried about things getting out of hand or a begging apologist for the person being humiliated. However, having learnt that this only made them next on the list of capitalists, traitors and rightists to be denounced, people had begun accepting these marches as everyday occurrences.

Most people had few friends now anyway; with petty rivalries quickly spilling into official criticisms, it was difficult to find anyone to trust. Even the toothless shopkeeper's family had stayed away, shunning her and the dishonour that contact with her might have brought. The world was finally beginning to see sense, the Red Guards told each other with slaps on backs.

■ ■ ■ ■

Jinyi woke with aches knotting his body. He forced himself up, to find that his daughters had prepared shivering piles of tofu for him. It tasted of the first times they had called him Pa. He remembered when they were just gurgling and giggling and he had first announced his new name — 'Pa's home' or 'It's all right, Pa's here' — savouring the short plump syllable, the glow of his new role at the centre of a little universe. He tried his best to nurture the memory, to make it last, before the present forced its way in.

He thought of the promise he and Yuying had made, that they would never be apart again. Jinyi had been counting the days since her disappearance. He would keep counting. He flinched as the door swung open.

'I heard a great speech today, Pa,' Liqui said to break the silence as the four of them sat around the clay *kang,* which now doubled as their dining table. 'It won't be long till everything is turned over, and everything will be fair. Isn't that great? By the time Ma comes home everything will be better.'

Jinyi nodded pensively. 'She'll be happy to see our dreams come to life.'

'Not just dreams, Pa,' Manxin said. 'Liqui is right. We've got a real chance now, with all the local leaders getting active, and no

444

imperialists like Liu Shaoqi left in the government to stop us. The whole world is going to be looking at us, and following our example.'

'I know. I only meant that it is important to be patient,' he mumbled.

'The time has run out for patience. Your generation sat around waiting for the world to be changed for them, and people Granny Dumpling's age still remember being waited on hand and foot and deferring to corrupt emperors and relatives. It's up to us now.'

Manxin was addressing her sisters, who followed her words carefully, while their father picked awkwardly at the dish. Her short pigtails swung out around her cheeks as she spoke, her cap set down in front of her. 'Look at our dinner for a start. Only five years ago we would have had nothing but broth and stale husks, if we were lucky, and would have felt too guilty to eat them with all the news about hard-working peasants starving only a few communes away. But now we've got enough — now everyone is beginning to get their fair share.'

Jinyi nodded. His left ear was ringing, a dial-tone buzz. It is strange how children remember things, he thought. They didn't feel guilty back then: oh no, they ate till there was nothing left and then whinged and moaned and cried and sulked and stamped their feet. But then, he surmised, the past is even easier to change than the present. He thought of all

445

the little treats: the sugar-coated crab apples and trips to the People's Zoo, the homemade kite and the handcrafted holiday dumplings, the help with homework and comfort through countless nightmares, and the only thing they seem to remember from those early years was the time he had got angry and cuffed them round the head with the back of his hand. Jinyi shook his head. He could not even remember why he had got so upset.

'What about you, Xiaojing?' he said, trying to change the subject. 'What did you learn today?'

Xiaojing waited a second before she spoke, and puffed out her chest, her short hair rowdy and electrified. She had taken to telling everyone she met that she was five, as if she had already raced through the next four months in her head and arrived there early. 'Me and Weiwei and Shuxi learnt about the hardships of peasant life from some sheep people.'

Jinyi smiled. She had obviously spent a long time carefully memorising that phrase. 'I see. Sheep people, yes, let me remember, they're the ones with human heads and furry bodies and little hooves, right?'

Xiaojing was not impressed. 'No, Pa. They're dirty men with sheep. They smell funny.'

Jinyi and Liqui laughed, but Manxin scowled. 'They're called shepherds. And they

446

are not dirty, they just don't have the op-portunities for hygiene that you are so lucky to have. They are noble, honest, warm-spirited people, just like all peasants.'

'So what did you learn about their hardships?' Jinyi asked his youngest daughter.

Xiaojing ruffled her nose. 'Sheep are dirty!'

Before Manxin could step in again to cor-rect her sister, the main door creaked open, and they all turned to see Dali slinking in. His eyes were trained on the ground in front of him, and his short, scrawny body was caked in mud — it had dried in streaks across his dark jacket, clumps of dusty earth drop-ping from his cap as he squeezed it in his hands. Though at first he simply picked his way between the debris and mess that had been carefully brushed into neat piles by his sisters, he soon stopped and looked around at the main room, noticing the absence of the table and chairs as well as the shelves and everything on them, the scrolls and all the usual knick-knacks, and he tilted his head as a dog might when confronted with a punish-ment it cannot comprehend.

Jinyi did everything he could to resist the urge to ask his son where he had been for the last twenty-four hours. Finally he said what he thought his wife, had she been there, might have said. 'Why don't you sit down and have something to eat, Dali? You must be hungry.'

Dali shrugged, but crossed into the bedroom and sat down beside them on the wooden bed anyway. For ten minutes they ate in silence, mouths slurping and chopsticks snipping at the dwindling dish, padded out with small clumps of overcooked rice.

'You look like a shepherd!' Xiaojing said, keen to try out the new word.

'Thanks. This is how we're all supposed to look now, isn't it?' Dali replied, brushing dirt from his shoulder onto the sheets.

'Don't be ridiculous, you'll confuse her,' Manxin said.

'No, I'm serious.' He set down his chopsticks and looked at the rest of them. He was still shy and awkward, but with a gangly kind of grace that both surprised and unnerved his family. His lack of height was intensified by the way he hugged his shoulders into his chest, while even his prickly eyebrows skulked so close together that the gravity of his face seemed to shift downwards.

'How do you think peasants really live? They live in pigshit, sleeping in blankets made of coal, coughing up black phlegm and blood.' He lowered his voice until it was little more that a whisper. 'I mean, that's the way things have always been. Why do we suddenly want to be like them now?'

Manxin opened her mouth to argue, but before she could Jinyi reached out and put a hand on his son's shoulder, risking the pain that the movement sent lumbering through his ribs. 'Best to keep ideas like this to yourself.'

'I know Pa, but —'

'Your mother would say the same.' In the last few months Jinyi had learnt that this was an effective way of shutting down any argument. It seemed that Yuying was like a ghost-like presence hanging over every word, somehow more fully with them now than she had been before her denouncement and exile. That they were unsure of where she was only served to reinforce the idea that she was somehow keeping them all bound together.

'But I mean, well, don't you ever wonder what it's like in other countries?' Dali continued. 'Imagine: your hair might be gold instead of black, your eyes might be emerald instead of black, you might —'

'That's enough!' Jinyi rasped, and his son's eyes darted up to meet his. 'This is crazy talk. I don't know what you've been doing today, and I don't want to know, but this has to stop, or else you'll end up in serious trouble. Go wash yourself — you're filthy. And wash those ideas out of your head while you're at it. If I ever hear you talking like that, you'll get a worse beating than you can imagine.' Jinyi was aware how hollow his threats sounded, coming in between coughs and wheezes. He clutched his chest and looked at his daughters. 'The same goes for all of you.'

As Dali rose from the *kang,* clutching the empty metal bowls which his sister had borrowed that afternoon from the only neighbours that still acknowledged them, he muttered a slight apology.

'Just try and be like everyone else, OK?' Jinyi sighed. 'Now get out of here, you lot, I need to get some rest.'

'You can't Pa. Not tonight. There's that performance in the food hall. We're all going to go,' Manxin said.

Jinyi made to lie down, but the girls would not leave. He gestured to the bruises spilt across his face. 'It wouldn't be right for people to see me like this.'

'But if you don't go, everyone will think you prefer the decadent old operas and don't enjoy the new revolutionary plays,' Manxin said. 'Or they might think that you have something to be ashamed of, something to hide.'

'Do we have something to hide?' Xiaojing asked, curiosity bubbling up in her eyes.

'No!' All three of them said as one, the force of their answer shaking the wooden bed beside them.

'Pa,' Xiaojing sidled up to him, 'when is Mummy coming home?'

'Soon,' he replied.

'Promise?'

The whole family stopped to see how their father would answer. Jinyi clutched his ribs

450

and moved toward the bedroom to get ready for their outing.

'I promise.' Jinyi's lie hurt as much as his broken ribs.

As his father disappeared into the bedroom to get ready, Dali pulled up slopping handfuls of water from the bucket in the kitchen, slapping it onto his grubby face and cursing to himself. He hated his days with the petty boys of his Red Guard faction, with the orders and the taunts and the humiliations.

'Aren't you proud of this country, the work we're doing?' Manxin asked as he washed.

'Of course I am,' Dali snapped. 'It's just there's still so much wrong, I wonder how anything is ever going to change.'

'Things are changing. Things get better every day, and we have Chairman Mao to guide us.' She touched her brother's shoulder. 'If you believe in it, it will happen.'

Jinyi did not sleep that night. Each breath he drew stung him. Each thought of his wife burned him. He could not stop wondering where she was, wondering if she knew that he was thinking of her, wondering if she too was holding tight to their promise.

What distances can love travel? Let me tell you. Take Yue, for example, a large mackerel who lived back before people started bothering too much about dates. She was born in a bean-shaped bay on the east coast, flanked

451

by overgrown hills and by a slanted pagoda and fishing village. Both her mother and father were also fish. She lived a contented life — as contented as a fish can be, I would imagine — arching like a bronze dart through the ashy waters, nibbling on smaller fish and insects and watching the strange world that sloshed giddily along on the other side of the surface.

She had learnt to avoid the spindly nets and bow shadows of fishing boats pushed out from the shore, but grew more adventurous in swimming closer, watching the wavy shapes of families seeing off husbands and sons with gifts of rice wrapped in bamboo leaves and fluttering prayers. It was on one of these occasions that she first caught site of Shen, staying behind on the bank while his father drifted toward the distant stretches of the sea. Tatty book in hand, he was short and dark-skinned, with a pointed chin and pointed eyes and a melon slice for a mouth. She found him fascinating. Every day he would sit at the pagoda, his skinny legs dangling over the edge and his grubby toes occasionally stirring the surface of the water while he read from his book. As Yue grew bolder and swam closer, she was able to hear him reciting the old poems to himself, closing his eyes and fumbling over the verses he was trying to memorise. She heard him swear and then mutter, 'Only a month until the imperial examinations! Why am I kidding myself? I'll never make it as a mandarin; I'm just a bumpkin doomed to be stuck trawling for fish for the rest of my life.'

It was only when he left the village, driven to the capital by an ox trader to take the imperial examinations, that Yue realised she was in love. Perhaps, she thought, I could use part of my magic to help him achieve his ambitions. For, you see, all animals are closer to gods than humans, who every day drive themselves further from the divine, and all have a little magic — fish in the flick of their tails, deer in the nod and twitch of antlers, birds in the tips of their outstretched wings. However, before Yue could make up her mind, Shen had returned to the village.

For the next month he was sulky and pre-occupied, skimming stones across the bay while awaiting the exam results. One night, after getting drunk on the rice wine that his father brewed in the backroom, Shen wandered tearfully to the pagoda and was suddenly startled by sounds behind him: a series of sloshy splashes, the crunch of wet leaves, rustling bracken. He spun round, his eyes darting, making himself dizzy, only to dismiss the sounds as the usual noises of the wild. He was used to these: the calls of egrets and herons, the roar of wolves and chatter of monkeys high up the rocky hills. Then he heard something closer: footsteps padding toward him. He spun again and rubbed his eyes: how much had he drunk? In front of him was a girl so beautiful he firmly believed that it was his imagination that had conjured her up, for how could something so exquisite possibly be real? But she was real, and her round face broke into a big-dimpled smile. He opened his mouth to speak, but instead she leaned forward, letting her lips gently graze his, and he lost his hands in the cascade of her waist-length ebony hair.

'My life is full of secrets. If you promise not to ask me yet, I promise I will tell you in the future,' she told him later, after weeks of meeting every evening after his chores.

'I promise. If I pass the exams we'll go and live in the city and be married, and our pasts won't matter at all because we will have each other,' Shen replied.

When he left her just before dawn each day, Yue slipped back into the water and into her original form. It was not long before a messenger rode out to the village, to deliver a banner to Shen's house. He had passed the exams. His father tied the banner across their door, and fried a giant pike with garlic and ginger, to be washed down with the last reserves of the home-brewed liquor. The old man also renamed his house and added a stone step over the courtyard threshold to signify the family's new status. Aunts and cousins and second cousins and half-heard-of great-uncles arrived for the celebratory dinner, at which, while mouths were still crammed full of flaky white fish, Shen announced that they had another thing to celebrate, for he would soon be married.

His short speech was met with stony silence. His father turned red, his guests embarrassed for him.

'What about the matchmaker, the role of the parents, the bargaining, the dowry, the arrangements, the traditions?' his father stuttered, aware that he was losing face in front of almost everyone he knew.

'I thought you would be pleased,' Shen replied.

'What about her family? Tell me, she is from a good family at least?'

'I have no idea. There's no need for all that. We've fallen in love,' Shen said.

'Love? Love! I've never heard anything like this in my life. That rotten poetry has gone to your head! Love! You have brought shame on your family. Forget this wedding at once. If anyone finds you a suitable bride, it will be me!'

Shen stormed from the house, and, finding Yue waiting at the pagoda, began the journey to the capital, whilst his father tore down the celebratory banner and changed the name of the house from 'Scholar's Residence' back to 'Ten Generations of Fishermen'. Yue and Shen were married the day before his new post in the outer palace began, and they honeymooned in the room they had started renting in an old woman's rundown house.

It was here, however, that the Jade Emperor became interested. For it was one thing assuming human form and having some fun — everyone has urges, after all — but it was altogether another getting married to a human when you were still, beneath the suit of pink skin, a fish. Everything has its place, and this, the Jade Emperor announced to the guards in his celestial palace among the clouds, was too much.

The next morning, after her new husband had left for work, Yue was washing clothes in the river that bisected the capital when she felt the light wind begin to tremble and hiss like a candle being blown out. Before she had time to turn around, a swarm of blackbirds had swooshed down and grabbed hold of every small square of her clothes with their arched beaks. She tried to tug herself free, manically flailing her limbs against their tight grip, but her hair and clothes tangled in their grasp. Suddenly they began to beat their wings, dark feathers flapping as they uprooted her, and she screamed as they tugged her higher above the dark red rooftops.

Shen returned home to find that not only had his clothes not been washed and laid out, but also his dinner had not been cooked. For a second, he let doubts about her love for him enter his mind. Had his father been right — is this what happens when you marry someone whose family you do not know? While he cursed himself and wondered whether anyone at work would notice if he wore the same clothes two days straight, Yue was sitting on a cloud, surrounded by the posse of blackbirds who flapped and bustled and squawked whenever she tried to move. After only an hour, she began to cry, her tears startling and scaring her rowdy guards. Before long, a shrill call was heard, which the birds took as the cue to change formation, and they danced nimbly behind her, nudging her firmly in the direction from which the call came. She had no choice but to begin walking.

Yue was led to the palace of the Jade Emperor, who was sitting, as usual, on the back of his mighty yellow dragon, twirling his fingers in its wispy moustache.

'I know why I am here. I apologise, Your Grace, I know I shouldn't have got married. But I beg you, do not imprison me simply because of my heart.'

'We are all,' the Jade Emperor replied, 'prisoners of the forms we are given. And,' he nodded indulgently, 'we are each a prisoner of our longings. I do not intend to keep you here: your life is below, in the sea.'

'But I cannot return there now! I cannot abandon my husband. We are in love.'

He sighed. 'There are rules, rules that even I cannot break. The universe depends on balance. You must know that to become human takes centuries. It has been done: with prayer, with meditation, with hope and with effort, you can use your magic to become human. Fully human, not just transforming your scales into skin every morning. But you must prove yourself. And that will take a thousand years. I wish you luck.'

'But I do not have a thousand years! By the time I become human, my husband will be dead.'

'I am sorry.'

The dragon yawned, puffy clouds of air spilling from its purple tongue, and the blackbirds were already bustling her towards the door when she spoke again.

'There must be another way! Is there not anything I can do to be with him?'

The Jade Emperor grinned. 'Of course. There are always choices to be made, or else everything would be simple. When you return to the bay, you could shed your scales. It would be excruciatingly painful, but you would become human very quickly. However, if you lost your scales in this way, you would also lose your magic. No more powers and, more importantly, no more immortality. I think you will find that patience is much more attractive. It may even do you good. Farewell.'

And with that Yue was falling through the sky, the birds nowhere to be seen, and her pristine white fingers were retreating to slippery fins. With a thunderous splash she was back, flapping her tail through those home waters, her gills pulsing as she slinked through the sunlit blue. And somewhere between the seaweed and the smaller schools of shrimp and the colder, darker deep, she thought of Shen, alone in the capital, and she realised that she could not wait, that she would trade magic for loss, for what good was eternal life if it was to be lived alone? With that, she began to shake the length of her body, squirming from pursed lips to thrashing tail.

At first nothing happened. However, Yue did not stop, but threw herself harder into the movement, smaller fish and eels clearing away from where she was stirring up the waters. Then there was the sound of something ripping, the whistle of a seam splitting, and the first scale flicked from her body like a button bursting from a tight pair of trousers. She screamed in pain, but continued to contort herself, the scabby silver flecks peeling from her and the water turning grapefruit pink. As her body ripped and blistered, her shrieks pierced the surface of the water and sent the diving gulls fleeing in panic.

Yue's wails reached the sky, and the clouds shook as they shared her anguish. To this day, if you see fishbone clouds, the altocumulus sprawling loosely over a blue canvas in mimicry of a fish losing its scales, know that this is the sky's way of showing its sympathy for the fact that, somewhere, someone is giving up something of themselves for love.

Shen watched the mackerel sky from a slot-window in their new home, and felt his heart leap, twist. The next morning, an hour before dawn and the cherry specks of cloud still low across the horizon, Yue limped through the door, sweaty and panting and her whole trembling body painted with cuts and bruises. And that is how the story ends — both of them growing old in their little rented room, which grew to a house of their own with children messing around in the garden, which shrunk to twin graves, thin shallows of earth set side by side on a hill overlooking a bay.

My point is this: love is a matter of wilful disbelief, of contortions and ultimatums. Love fights in us, and makes us fight. It is what drives us on. And yet there is something about this tale that bothers me. For it is the kind of story the Jade Emperor himself enjoys hearing from me, one where the focus, indeed the whole point of the tale, is the grand heroic choice, the cinematic action. He is always telling me to hurry up, to cut out the needless detail, to do some editing and present him with the stripped-down version. But life is not like that. The fight to ensure the survival of love is more likely to find its toughest battles amid small snarls about changing nappies or midnight feedings or plain old boredom; it is more likely to focus on little betrayals or hurtful slips of the tongue, to feature the day-to-day heroism of pretending not to be aware of a thousand little annoying habits. In short, love is hard work, and the fairytale ending of our story is only the beginning of the real work of keeping love alive. That is why it bothers me; and yet who can deny the fact that we are always in need of love stories?

The performance at the food hall had been long and excruciating. The family had worked hard to keep smiles of enjoyment fixed upon their faces as the revolutionary opera about a young city boy who was taught the error of his ways by simple country farmers had dragged on and on. They had left the hall afterwards to the sound of former friends muttering behind their backs.

Manxin woke the next morning before the market roosters began their hymnal. She gently untangled herself from her sisters, the mixture of their clammy sweat damp on her clothes. Even Dali was still asleep, knotted into a foetal ball on a stack of old newspapers and ragged clothes in the far corner. Only the wooden bed where their father had slept was empty.

461

'What are you doing out here? You should be resting!' she chided her father as she wandered into the kitchen.

Jinyi had balanced the splintered tabletop on two piles of broken wood from the torn-down shelves, and was sitting on a wobbly stool that she had never seen before. In front of him was a wooden bowl filled with flour, another in which sat a slab of pork attracting a horde of giddy flies, and a couple of grizzled green onions, still dusted with mud. The kettle was chugging and hiccupping on the stove. Manxin could not help noticing that the blob of meat was almost the same colour as her father's bruises.

'Sit down. I have something I want to show you.'

She approached sceptically. 'How much did all of this cost?'

He pretended not to have heard her. 'Now I want you to watch carefully — I can only do this once. We'll start with the filling: everything rests on that first bite, the hot meat warming your mouth, the soup dribbling out and tingling on your tongue, the smell —'

'Pa,' she interrupted, 'why are you making dumplings? It's not the Spring Festival for months. It's no one's birthday. Is Ma coming home today?'

He shook his head. 'I'm afraid not. It's just something you need to learn. You ought to know how to cook these things for yourself. I'll teach you, and then you can show your brother and sisters.'

'But we've made dumplings together hundreds of time! I know what to do!'

'You know how to take a pile of filling, put it in the pastry and then fold it closed. You need to see how to make it all, from scratch, so that you can do it on your own.'

'All right.' She squatted down at the other side of the tabletop, and looked at him. He huffed and wheezed as he chopped and kneaded, appearing far older than his age. She understood his reasoning — the authorities could arrive at any time and send him for re-education, just as had happened to Yuying the year before. The curls of diced green onion stung Jinyi's eyes.

'Who taught you to make dumplings then, Pa?' Manxin said, breaking his train of thought. 'Your family?'

'Ha!' His laugh sent a shot of pain through his body. 'No, not them. My parents died young, and the rest of them . . . well, the only thing they taught me is that the worst crime in the world is to forget your family. Remember that, Manxin. I've been guilty of it myself before, I'm ashamed to say, but I understand it now.'

'I know, Pa.'

'Anyhow,' he continued, trying to lighten the mood, 'we didn't have the means or the money to make dumplings in the countryside back when I was young. We could only eat whatever we found in the ground — stalks, roots, withered crops, sometimes whole fist-fuls of crumbly earth that would stick be-tween our teeth, funny-looking sprouts, salt-worms, earthworms, caterpillars —'

'I don't believe you,' she said, but he could tell that she was not sure. He laughed.

'No, it was your grandma who taught me. You kids used to call her Granny Dumpling, remember, because she inherited the dump-ling restaurants when your grandpa died, back before everything was redistributed. Well, in the old days before we had the strength and wisdom of the Chairman to guide us, I used to work in the kitchen in one of those restaurants. That's how I came to marry your mother.'

He shredded the pork with sharp flicks of his wrist, never taking his eyes from his daughter.

'But what about other types of dumplings — carrot, or lamb, or rabbit, or cabbage, or shrimp? Are you going to show me those too?' Manxin asked.

'No, we're only doing these. You'll just have to improvise with the rest.'

She flinched — the rules, edicts, speeches and exhortations of the state did all they could to restrict any chance of free opera-tion. She viewed the very idea of improvising with suspicion; it sounded intellectual, right-ist, and therefore frightening.

'That's how the original chefs, centuries back, found the recipes we use now. You'll only find out whether something works or not by giving it a go. You might stumble across a really good taste; you never know. Whatever happens, you'll learn something about yourself.'

Manxin shook her head. This conversation, she felt, was definitely veering into dangerous territory. Could it be that her father really was an enemy of the new ways, really did deserve the visit of two nights back?

'I already know everything about myself,' she said, defiantly.

Jinyi wanted to laugh and pat her shoulder, but held back, since he could just about recall being fourteen himself. 'I'm a hard-working, dedicated, honest Communist and I follow the Party with my whole heart. There is nothing else to know.'

Jinyi coughed and his body hunched in, like a waterlogged concertina. His daughter leapt up to stop him collapsing onto the precari-ously balanced work surface, but turned away abruptly when she saw the way the pain had remapped his face.

Manxin returned to the room to wake her siblings. The market catcalls and doorway anthems were flooding in through the win-dow; the day had begun. Jinyi hunched over

465

the half-finished rolls of pastry and the jiggling blobs of soft filling, listening to the fuzzy buzz and distortion of the cranked-up amplifier outside the town hall blaring out the day's first rendition of 'The East is Red', and he felt his eyes red too, stinging and tight.

As the tune rattled on, Jinyi was reminded of an old proverb about a musician, a master of the whiny *gugin,* a long seven-stringed zither made from only the finest cedar. Every day, from dawn until dusk, this musician would sit in the courtyard of his house playing his compositions. One day a wandering stranger stopped beside the house and squatted down to listen to the reeling, spindly melody shaking itself free from the belly of the box-like instrument. When the piece was finished, the stranger spoke.

'A great river, tumbling towards the sea. A woman in the countryside, waiting for a boat to return.'

The musician was amazed. 'Yes!' he exclaimed. 'That is exactly the feeling I wished to communicate. Listen to another.'

The musician again began to pluck, faster this time, the strings pulled taut and snapped again and again, the piercing music shredding the afternoon air. When he had finished that second piece, the stranger spoke once more.

'The terrible excitement of battle; the twin possibilities of death or glory.'

Once again the musician was astounded. Finally, he thought, I have found the perfect listener, someone who can really appreciate my music.

The musician and the stranger spent every day after that together, the musician playing and the stranger listening and commenting, before lapsing into a shared silence of contentment while they shared rice and wine. Yet almost exactly a year after their first meeting, the stranger died of a sudden illness. On the day of the funeral, the musician took an axe and smashed his *gugin* into a hundred shards of tinder, and threw them onto his friend's pyre. 'There is no point playing any longer,' he told the mourners, 'for no one else will understand my songs as well as he did. I am no longer a musician.'

Jinyi clutched his sides, drew breath, and listened for his children yawning and clambering out of bed. He calmed himself and made an effort to sit as patiently as he could, for what else could he do now but wait?

The Jade Emperor ran his hands over the black and white swirls of the *taijitu,* and it immediately began to glow — a strange warmth spread out across the walls, which shed their dust and smoke stains and suddenly seemed freshly built. I looked around to see that everything in the temple had been restored, complete with gold leaf and gilt and stacks of well-bound scriptures, all except for where the idol of Lao Tzu should have been.

The Jade Emperor saw my glance. 'The old sage would be far happier with a bird's nest than a caricature. Now, what can you tell me about the Way?'

I hadn't realised I was going to be examined. And besides, the old god still hadn't answered my question. Yet I shrugged and decided to play along.

'Well, of course, in the Tao Te Ching, Lao Tzu tells us "The Way that can be spoken of is not the Way." If that's true, then a humble man like me surely couldn't be expected to be able to say anything about it.'

He grinned. 'But you explain love. Surely that is just as impossible to pin down, just as difficult to define. Better to give up your quest now, Kitchen God.'

'No . . . well, maybe you're right, but . . . hey!'

I looked up to see that the Jade Emperor had disappeared, though his words remained, echoing around the little temple. All the Jade Emperor ever seemed to do was make my head ache.

9:
1974
THE YEAR OF THE TIGER

There are things people cannot hear: earthquakes before they begin to murmur beneath
the ground, volcanoes before they burst, the
turn of the wind that tells birds to flee, the
ear-piercing whistles that make dogs cower
and whine — the looping waxy tunnels leading to the human eardrum miss the high-
pitched wails and vibrations of nature calling
to its kin. There are colours the eye cannot
formulate, pixels that the flipside of the retina
cannot reassemble, blind spots that blot out
the periphery. And when all these blind spots
are totalled up, the whole world is obscured.
There are, and I think you can guess where I
am going, questions that cannot be answered.
There are universes beyond our reach.

What does this tell us? That our experience
is limited, is crowded on all sides by darkness
and fog. Even up here, looking down on all
you lot, my fellow deities and I are often
puzzled. That is probably one of the reasons
why the Jade Emperor challenged me in the

first place. Yet though our curiosity — both human and divine — our instinct and wonder may be spurred by impossible queries, these are always eventually pushed aside, for the minutiae of life continue despite our ignorance, and our questions too get subsumed in our blind spots.

Jinyi was trying to sleep. The mist rising from the paddies, snaking around the building's squat stilts and slinking in between the floorboards, however, had other ideas. His fifth winter there not yet finished, and already his bones creaked and rasped when he tossed and turned under the rancid, stinking bundle of furs. Five other men shared the room, slotted into rows of three on either side, each one fiercely protective of their marked-out part of the hard floor. The warped walls shuddered in time with their snores. Jinyi sighed, and imagined his feet, ringed with blisters and dead skin, becoming webbed from the endless hours of squelching through the paddies. The dark was absolute; even the moon seemed to have been left behind back in the city where his children were.

He turned over again and cursed himself. He was so exhausted that he could not sleep — how could that be? Not that he wanted to sleep, because when he slept he dreamt of her, and when he woke he found himself alone on the cold floor, unsure in what province his wife might be, and that was too much. He pushed the promise to the back of his mind.

In only a few hours the god-awful cycle will begin again, he thought, and then I'll be praying for rest. No, wait, I cannot let myself think like that. This is for my benefit, it is doing me good.

Jinyi had a hundred other little phrases that he told himself in order to get through the grind of minutes, hours, days, months, seasons; however long it would take until he could see his family again.

As sleep approached, his mind wandered back to the journey down there. He had spent days shoulder to shoulder with a hunched and half-blind elderly professor on one side and a handsome young dentist on the other, a dozen of them crammed into the back of an open-top wagon as it had juddered down too many dirt roads to count. Their knees had knocked together and their breath had streamed up into hopeless smoke signals as mountains dipped and sagged around them, the engine spluttering whenever the gears were changed to match the challenge of another ascent. Jinyi remembered the roar of rivers behind them; the chatter of hawks and the distant explosions of cliffs being blasted; the tribal drumming of rain against the pulled-up tarp while they had tried to sleep sitting up; heads slumping against unfamiliar bodies; the persistent smell of sweat and cigarettes; the distant snags and pockmarks of mines worked precariously into hillsides; the glares of uniformed men at endless outposts; the sound of cities carried from afar; the threatening beauty of the scenery as one province tumbled into another and then another, and the roaring silence that none of them could break.

As the landscape shook them through, Jinyi had realised from where he recognised the endless hills and plains. This is where it all comes from, he had thought to himself, the world ensnared in the scrolls and etchings that hang on the walls of a thousand rooms and restaurants I've wandered through.

Chinese painting for a long time ignored the trappings of Western art: realism and the obsession with light and space. Instead, the focus was on shadow and silhouette, on the fluidity of the dancing lines of ink. Why? One view is that the arrival of Buddhism along the Silk Road gave rise to the idea that the world is transitory, is nothing but an illusion, and thus attempts to capture it realistically were considered ridiculous, for everyone agreed that there was nothing real to be captured. Another view is that the fluidity of the lines suggested a world of continual flux, a world that has no place for permanence. Furthermore, the quick and careful brush strokes bring to mind the painstaking work of the calligrapher, suggesting that images share the same work as words: to fix and define the nature of things, and thus render the wild under our control.

The Song-dynasty landscape painters went even further, tracing line over line to create a sense of the unreachable: craggy mountains, snow-tipped gorges, vast precipices and ever-present reels of fog and mist blurring the distance. Yet one thing almost always absent from these paintings was people, as if the harmony the Taoists sought between transcendent nature and the sloppily human was always just out of reach. It was the landscape of these artists — a landscape of sublime mountains that threw unstoppable shadows, of winding paths and forking forest tracks where the future was obscured by haze and drizzle — that the truck had stuttered into. I am being taken, Jinyi had thought, into the unknown expanse of the past.

He was almost asleep when the frail wooden door was shoved open and the fat cadre came bellowing into the room.

'Get up, you lazy shits! Don't you know there's no such thing as a lie-in here? There's work to do, and if you think you're too good to do it, you're sorely mistaken. The real peasants have been up for almost an hour now — it looks like you lot have missed breakfast and are going to have to get straight to work! Come *on!*'

As he spoke he kicked over the shared chamberpot in the centre of the room, which had the desired effect of sending the men scrambling up, away from the spilt streams of steamy dark piss. Since they slept in their clothes, moth-chewed coats and all, the journey from scattered dreams to the dreary greys of the field was a short one. As soon as they were out of the door the six men, lumped together because each of them appeared to be around fifty (most of the people in the countryside, they were told, did not know their exact age), were herded into work units and set to task.

Jinyi had spent the previous day guiding the geriatric oxen to their winter graze and cover, the beasts' irritability and undignified lust sending their hapless driver sliding across the frost-dusted mud at regular intervals. Today would be more of the same, winding the oxen through the sloping paddies away from the village, toward the sustenance of the forest. Having spent his childhood in the countryside, Jinyi fared better than most of the others, bearing less of the cadre's rage and the peasants' scorn. He already knew that the thing that got to people there was not the monotony, for work was like that everywhere, but the unpredictability and sheer struggle that consumed the daylight hours.

'Wait, Jinyi — stop it, stop it! — this one's

got a mind of its own.' One of their group, a short, podgy man, whom the cadre had nicknamed Lard, was struggling with one of the shorter oxen, flinching when the animal's hot, greasy tongue lapped out at him. Lard's round face was blotchy and red, his breathing laboured and his tiny eyes screwed up in concentration.

'Grip the horn and drag. He's used to it, so he's not going to charge you. Stay calm, and he'll calm down too.' Jinyi had found himself, despite his natural inclination to slip into the background, nominated the leader of their small group.

As well as Jinyi and Lard, there was a tall, bow-backed man with wobbling jowls nicknamed Turkey. He was the newest arrival, with freshly pink stitch scars still littering his shaved head to prove it. There was also a thin boy — fifteen perhaps, give or take a year or two — who called himself Bo. Jinyi seemed to spend the days herding the men as much as the beasts, yet they followed his every word; the only time, Jinyi noted ruefully, that growing up in fields had ever bestowed more than condescension.

'It won't respect anything, it's just a . . . a great oaf. It's got that look in its eyes, like it's planning something,' Lard complained, and the others let him. Better to get it out of his system out of the earshot of the peasants. If they were to report his words to the cadre,

476

some kind of carefully crafted punishment might await the lot of them.

'You're looking at these animals the wrong way,' Jinyi said. They had reached the top of the slope and grouped in preparation for the descent among the frosted weeds and sly patches of ice. 'You're looking at them as if they're exhibits in a zoo or pets or distant specks in an old painting. You're looking at them as if they're thinking things. They're not. People here treat them like you might treat a car, or a tool, not like an unruly child. We've got to see the world through different eyes, remember — that is why we are here.'

The others let their heads slump in mute reply. They all knew why they were there. Twenty-odd oxen with matted flanks and swishing tails peered down, suspicious of starting downhill after such a laborious climb. Their destination, the slimy mulch of a forest of evergreens, was still only a blurry wave on the horizon.

Turkey took off one of his shoes and cursed. 'Stupid thing. The heel is full of holes — look! My socks are the same, the ones that aren't waterlogged, that is. My wife used to sew and darn and all that. I'm not sure I can do it on my own.'

Not wanting that kind of talk to overcome them before they had even started the difficult part of the day, Jinyi waved his arm and the four of them began to shove at the wide rear ends of the stubborn beasts.

It had taken Jinyi almost three months to build up an idea of where he was. Nothing was certain — even the length of the first journey seemed to have become confused after a few days on the road, so that by the time they had arrived he was not able to say whether they had been huddled up in the back of the truck for five days or ten, while they had taken so many turns and looping narrow passes that his inner compass had spun and buzzed as if held close to a powerful magnet.

The villagers there, meanwhile, knew only the names of their village, the village over the mountain and the closest market town. The province those might be situated in was an irrelevance, of no more importance to them than the arbitrary naming of the galaxy that their home planet happened to sit in. The endless dips and slopes and the continual undulation of forests and flats had confused Jinyi's sense of geography, though the paddies and the frequent rainfall suggested that they had limboed down closer to the Equator. Though he later found out that he had been only two provinces away from his wife, it did not matter — when you were not allowed to visit, it made no difference whether the distance was one mile or one thousand.

'Not far now. Bo, how are you doing?' Jinyi kept up the flow of talk every few minutes, in order to reassure the others and stop him from worrying about himself. The boy shrugged, pressed on.

The village squatted near the bottom of a long, stretched-out hill. It looked like a tall mountain had been splatted out by a giant fist and then the lumpy damage covered over with a smattering of trees and streams. Every week a truck passed through, with a half-trained doctor who spent most of his visits attempting to debunk the locals' superstitions and warn them away from their homemade remedies. There was no way out. The dirt road could have led anywhere, the couple of work mules looked as if they had already signed a long, drawn-out agreement with death, and the cadre always kept one eye on his rusty motorbike, even, it was whispered, while he slept.

'Are we lost?' Lard asked glumly as they struggled up into a craggy clearing, amongst juts of rock that stretched out between them and the dark greens of the wood. He was panting, sweaty despite the chill, leaning against one of the animals. They had wound round so far, dodging nettles, rocks and patches of permafrost, that it felt like they were moving in ever-widening circles. One of the oxen lowed in response to Lard's question, and Jinyi did a quick headcount.

'No, we're fine. Just leave the navigation to me. And even if we do get lost, the beasts could probably lead us back. I bet they've done the rounds a hundred times or more.'

Bo, slumped down on a low rock, and an ox began to lick at his ankles. They settled there, and Jinyi fished in his jacket pocket for a few shrivelled, dried-out corncobs, snapped in half and passed around. Turkey lit a cigarette which was passed from mouth to hungry mouth, saliva trailing from the soggy tip. 'So how does this work?' Turkey asked tentatively. 'How long are we here? A few months, a few years, what?'

'As long as it takes, I guess,' Jinyi replied.

'I see,' Turkey nodded, letting his jowls shake out. He ran his hand over his head, feeling the prickly bristle where his long mane used to be. Red Guards had shaved half to humiliate him, and he had asked his wife to do the other half to match. 'It's funny, in a way, you know, before this I used to be a —'

'No!' Lard interrupted, surprising everyone with the force of his speech. He lowered his voice. 'We don't talk about our old lives here.'

'I see.' Turkey looked to Jinyi, who sighed and began to explain.

'Three reasons. One, if the locals hear you, and report it, everyone's just going to think you prefer the old bourgeois ways to real work, and they'll make your life difficult. You'll be handpicking weeds for weeks if that happens. Two, we're supposed to be here to change, and you can't do that with one foot in the past. And three, most importantly of all, if you spend all day thinking of your wife and kids and all the other things you left behind, you'll go crazy.'

Turkey and Lard laughed, and even Bo managed a thin smile. They started up again, each man slipping between the lazy, hulking beasts, nudging them ever closer to the tall spray of gaudy greens up ahead.

Hours later, their battered shoes were still crunching and slipping on the begrudging grass, their hands fumbling at the fat bulks of the herd to keep from falling.

'Did you ever think about how peculiar words can be?' Turkey said, to split the silence. 'When I was young, my auntie used to tell us stories about hell. You know, the demons that live there, the tricks they play, the hungry ghosts — all that bullshit meant to frighten you, all the stuff the government thankfully did away with before it could cause any more harm. Anyway, it occurred to me that hell, well, what does it actually mean?'

Lard looked across at him, wiped the rivers of sweat from his face and attempted to draw in air. 'It doesn't mean anything,' he panted. 'It's was just a way of stopping people from questioning the harsh feudal world around them.'

'Yes, I know, I know, but what about the words? Hell. *Diyu*. Two characters, right?

481

What if we split them up and take them on their own. *Di:* field. *Yu:* prison.'

'It's referring to what happens under fields, Turkey,' Jinyi said. 'When you bury a body, you put it under the ground, and it's trapped there, like a prison, because it can't ever get back out. That's all.'

'Maybe. Or maybe it's telling us something. Perhaps hell is a field that is also a prison. Like when you're stuck in wide-open spaces with nowhere to turn. Does that remind you of anything?'

'You'd better stop this now,' Jinyi said sharply. 'I'm not much good at giving advice, and I'm far worse at taking it, but you've got to listen to me. I'm used to keeping myself to myself, and I've spent most of my life trying to avoid trouble, to run away from it at any cost. But here I am, and here you are, and we've all got to make the most of it. You're looking at everything back to front.'

He shifted on his heels, picking at his fingernails as he spoke. 'Listen, if I've learnt one thing in all the time I've been here, it's this: if you think something is hell, it will be hell. You've got to change how you think — when that happens, we'll all get to go back home.'

'What you're saying is that we're here to find out what it is that we have to learn.' Turkey laughed, but no one else was in the mood. It was not a joke anymore; it was the only thing they had left to cling onto.

The group reached the forest in silence, each with howling stomachs and their mouths curling involuntarily into snarls. They had heard of other groups getting into fights with each other over the smallest things; the shouts, cries, thwacks and other repercussions were measured out in fistfuls of moonlight every other night. Lard was already clutching his chest, walking slower and slower.

Jinyi clenched his fists and bit his lip; however much he tried, he could not stop himself following the thread of Turkey's speech. He remembered the kitchen-table calligraphy class, how Yuying had taught him to pick out the intricate web of the veins and arteries of each character, then hurry them into action with the tip of the brush. The sky stretched out around them, and Jinyi prayed to himself that his wife was still out there somewhere, looking at the same frayed clouds and thinking of him.

Through the first line of clustered pines they came across a covered clearing, where the ice had not yet fully spread. The four figures sank down on their haunches as the oxen grazed, each lost to their thoughts. They had been told to come to the forest, and they had come; there was no more to it than that. They had been told to return by dusk, and they would. Just as the Buddhists told us we would be reborn according to our accumulated actions, Jinyi thought as they waited out the afternoon hours, so we are now being reborn in different places, our old lives given up and new ones thrust upon us, and there is nothing we can do about it. As the light dipped toward the west, scattering between the shivering needles to tug at their shadows, Jinyi waved the others up, and they started to pull the beasts around to retrace their steps. It had hardly seemed worth the journey. Above them, the muddy winter clouds began to race across the sky, as if a pack of unwashed peasants had suddenly grown grubby wings and found the means to escape.

The cadre, meanwhile, was taking apart and meticulously checking the parts of his pistol. He made sure that he used it at least once a year, usually just loosing a single shot at the trees to scare the locals and remind them who was in charge, though he had been known to fire it at village werewolves scampering through the dark, at the blurry ghosts of people emerging from the bottom of his bottles of rice wine and at the spirit of the wild tiger which, the older families of the village told their children, still came from the forest once a year to collect its toll. The cadre took a damp cloth and ran it over the metal.

'I'm in no hurry to use you again, but you can't be too careful. Especially these days.'

He had developed a habit of talking to himself when alone in his two-room hut at the top of the village, in order to counter the quiet emptiness that threatened to envelop his rooms. He had never married, not even looked at a woman that way since the comfort women who offered themselves on the Long March, back when he still had a full head of hair and a lean stomach.

'You're still good for a while, you little bastard. Still good.'

A couple of months before, back in the middle of one of those long, sweaty summer nights that rose up from the depths of the paddies to torment everyone but the fat bumbling mosquitoes, he had led a group of men down to the forest, where he had shot one of the villagers. That was the bit he hated; not the condemned man shaking and staining his handed-down trousers, but the staring eyes of the village men, studying the cadre's every move to see if he had the balls to go through with it. Although he had stood only twenty feet back, his clammy, shaking hand had twitched and sent a bullet past the condemned man and into the tree behind him. Aware that he was losing face and authority, the cadre had marched up to the man and thrust the gun so far into his throat that the criminal's sobs and howls had suddenly become retches. Neither the cadre nor the onlookers were much impressed when, a moment later, they found their clothes stained with blood, skull, brain and other lumpy bits of crimson gunge that had come whirling and splattering from the dark blossom of the condemned man's head. Despite this, the villagers had insisted on waiting there for more than ten minutes before carrying the messy body back to its family, to see whether or not he would get up, shake himself off and scratch the itch caused by the fresh hole in his skull.

'I'm not doing that again. I wouldn't have had to, ten years ago. But now the peasants need to know their place, what with all these bourgeois come down to study them. If anyone causes any trouble round here, it will be me that gets the blame.'

The Central Committee had sent him to that particular village as it was only a hundred *li* from his hometown, and yet after all his years away with the PLA he was a foreigner to the locals, with his rules, his mannerisms, his accent and his anger. The previous summer had been so hot that the villagers had thought their clothes were on fire, and the cadre had had two rapes to deal with. Following reports of the first, he had set up a private meeting with the accused, using only the brunt of his pistol. From the way the accused had limped awkwardly from that meeting, the cadre had been sure that it would not happen again. Yet barely two months later, it did. She was asking for it though, all the local men agreed, and after they had watched the cadre shoot the rapist, they warned that his ghost would return and avenge himself on the village.

Chairman Mao smiled down from the huge picture draped across the wall — his mole blown up to the size of a peach stone — and whispered words of encouragement that no one else could hear. The cadre put down the pistol and was reaching for cigarettes when he heard the shouts carried across the fields. He grabbed the pistol and began to run, only remembering as he reached the door that he ought to rebutton his trousers.

Even the elderly dog that spent its days padding round and round the village had halted its circumnavigation to howl and wag its tail as the crowd gathered. The cadre elbowed through the ring of noisy farmers and their squawking wives, shoving his way to the arrivals from the city, who parted hastily when they saw him. He spotted Jinyi, cap in hand and bent down over a moaning man.

'Get up! Now! Get away from him.' The cadre yanked Jinyi up by his shoulder and pushed him away to reveal the outstretched body of Lard, shaking and foaming on a bed of grass and frost. The cadre stared down contemptuously, and then shook his head. 'You city lot are all the same. Wouldn't know real work if it slapped you in the face. He'll just have to get used to it, like everyone else. Now, the lot of you, get back to work!'

However, the crowd showed no sign of dispersing. 'Excuse me, sir,' Turkey said, and saw from the cadre's bared upper gums that this was perhaps a mistake. He continued nonetheless, 'I think he's having a heart attack.'

'You're new here, aren't you, Turkey?' the cadre spat back. 'Fresh from the city and thinking that you know how everything works, is that it? You're an intellectual, right? I suppose you think you know better than even Chairman Mao. Well, let me tell you something. You know nothing. China is big, and you are small. The people's will is enormous, and you will bow to it or be crushed. All of you traitors here will learn that you are nothing if you are not working for the people, with the people.'

The cadre paused and looked down at Lard to see his hair matted with sweat, his eyes rolling and air rushing noisily in and out of his flaring nostrils. 'And if you have to be broken down completely and put back together again in order to learn this, then so be it. You, Turkey, will be on night duty, cleaning the latrines.'

Lard's twitches began to lessen, his moans shrinking to mouselike rasps. The cadre turned to leave once again, but this time there were murmurs from the villagers.

'We can't leave him here.'

The cadre sighed. 'When he stops fucking around, he can get up and walk back to the dorm. Until then, he stays where he fell. No one's going to pick him up as if they were his bloody servant.'

'No.' An old man raised his hand. 'We cannot let a man die here, on the fields. The crops will stop growing, and then we'll starve. This is well known.'

Others nodded and added their voices to the protest. 'The fields will dry up and the rain will avoid this very spot — it has happened before.'

'Yes, yes, that's right. We can't let him die here.'

The cadre was beginning to feel red-faced himself. Superstition, as he well knew, was dangerous and proscribed; but there were also quotas to meet, expectations that could not be dashed.

'Fine. But he's not to be taken inside till he can get there himself — I don't care if he has to drag his fat face through the mud to do it.' And with that the cadre marched back towards his hut.

The sinewy old man bent and gripped Lard's right leg, yanking it into the air and producing a sudden moan from him.

'Come on then.' The old man encouraged the crowd, and more stepped forward; a stocky woman with a broken nose gripped an elbow, a short man hoisted up a shoulder, and a strapping teenager yanked up the left leg. Jinyi, seeing that he did not have time to argue with them or debate the merits of this idea, quickly darted forward to cradle Lard's lolling head as his body was wrenched up to waist-level.

Lard's breaths came quicker, shrill wheezes sending spittle dribbling from his tightly scrunched lips.

'Get a move on, he's too fat to lug around for long,' the old man snapped, and the group stumbled awkwardly to the left, in the direction that the old man had thrust his head. They pulled and tugged the body between them, drawing low moans as they staggered across the uneven ground, avoiding patches of ice, toe-crippling lumps of rock and the last unhardened rivulets of rainwater snaking to the paddies. Jinyi kept his hands round Lard's fleshy neck, supporting the heavy head as the body was jostled between slipping hands, and he was reminded of the way he had held each of his children, plump and pink and newborn and so fragile he had been afraid to even breathe on them.

'Wait!' the stocky woman suddenly shrieked and stopped, sending the rest of the group toppling forward, fighting to retain balance while keeping a grip on Lard, whose eyes had now closed completely. 'We're not going towards our house! Oh, no! We don't want a city spirit hanging round us, giving the jitters to all the sows. Turn him around.'

They wheeled clockwise and set off in the opposite direction. The rest of the villagers were still standing by the converted grain stores in which the bourgeois visitors from the city now slept, and were watching the wobbling procession.

'Where are we taking him?' Jinyi asked, noticing that they were moving further away from the line of stilted houses and shacks that might, if he stretched his suspension of disbelief to breaking point, have contained someone with a vague understanding of medicine or resuscitation. When he was a child, after all, there had been a blind man in a nearby village who could tell a person's ailments simply by squeezing their pulse from their wrist, and would recommend herbs and grasses accordingly.

'To the dried up riverbed in Dead Man's Valley, of course!' the old man answered impatiently, enunciating each character in the patronising tone the villagers had unanimously adopted when imparting seemingly obvious bits of wisdom to the backward strangers now working among them.

'But it's deserted down there, isn't it? There's nothing but rooks and slate. We won't find a doctor anywhere near there.'

'A doctor? He doesn't come till Sunday. A

491

doctor! Ha! You city folk haven't got a brain to share between you. Whatever next?' the stocky woman laughed.

'Wake up, boy,' the old man said, bewildering Jinyi, who had not been called boy for at least the last twenty years of his life. 'Of course it's deserted. That's where we make all the pyres these days.'

Jinyi looked down at the head clasped in his hands, and gave thanks that the eyes were completely closed. 'But he's not dead yet!' he whispered fiercely.

'Just a matter of time. You don't want to have to make two trips, do you?'

Jinyi realised that there was nothing he could do. He kept his curses firmly under his breath, and the dying man's head in his grip.

They descended in a cloud of slate dust and skidding gravel, each face whitened by the smoky spray as they fumbled quickly down the beaten path. As soon as they had side-stepped their way past tree stumps and rabbit warrens to the bottom, the group slumped the body onto the ground and squatted down around it. Jinyi felt Lard's wrists, his neck. He wanted to ask whether any of them knew his real name, but could already predict the answer: they neither knew nor cared.

It was at times like these that Jinyi did all he could to try not to think about Yuying and their children, to stop himself wondering whether he had let them all down, utterly, completely. The words of their promise echoed around his head. That's the peculiar thing about mortals, if you ask me — stick them in the shittiest place on earth, make their lives a misery, and instead of trying to cheer themselves up they'll go out of their way to make themselves feel even worse.

To calm himself Jinyi clung to his own logic: China is such a vast country, he reasoned, that everything that happens probably has a counterpoint or alternative in another town in another province. If I am suffering here, then others must be happy and content. If I am hungry, somewhere else others must be stuffed full. If I am cold, others must be warm. What other reasoning could there be for sending so many city people to the fields, for showing them the obverse of their lives, if not to prove this syllogism of opposites? For each and every action there must be an opposite action occurring in another place. If it is hell here, he thought, then that only proves that somewhere else might be heaven . . . please let it be where my wife is, where my children are.

'He's got a pulse. And I think he's still breathing,' Jinyi reported, though none of the villagers seemed interested.

'Then we wait,' the old man replied. The sun was bubbling under the line of houses at the top of the slope, the frost bristling and itching for another night in which it would consolidate its two-pronged attack, inching further down the hill and climbing further up the cracked walls.

People spend their lives waiting for things that never happen. This, though, was inevitable. Jinyi wondered how Turkey had known what to call the sudden spasm and collapse; he himself had heard the phrase 'heart attack' before, and knew what it entailed. In another century, he mused as the four villagers bent close and muttered amongst themselves, we might still have believed in the terrible fiction that there is no end — then I might have whispered in his ear, told him who to look out for. My parents, my aunt, my father-in-law, my two small sons; the corpse I saw on a dirty track somewhere between my youth and my marriage; the dead man whose face I shaved when I was still a teenager; half my friends now, gone or as good as. Better this way, though, better to keep them as memories, nothing more. You can keep memories safe, even if you cannot always control them.

'Shouldn't we try to do something?' Jinyi finally snapped, interrupting the low murmurs of the villagers.

They stopped talking to stare at him. Finally the old man reached over and cuffed him round the ear. Jinyi bit his lip till he drew blood, not wanting to enflame the situation, knowing he would be blamed for whatever happened since his name was already tarnished.

'You're here for an education, right? Well, listen up. We don't tolerate any of that intellectual crap round here. You ought to know that by now. Raising the dead, that's beyond even the power of the great Chairman, so it certainly can't be done by the likes of you.' The old man paused to hock up what sounded like a larynx full of flotsam, and spat out the ball of sticky phlegm with a look of satisfaction. 'Magic. Immortality. Those stories are dangerous, young man. Best to just keep your mouth shut.'

They sat in silence, Jinyi's ear reddening in the dusk chill. It was hard to tell exactly when Lard died, to measure out the last of the spasms, tremors and gases that the limp body expelled, to record the moment when the heart shuddered down to the slow closing beats of an ellipsis at the end of a sentence. They checked and rechecked, pressing ears to the fat man's lips and chest, until they were finally satisfied and the sour smell of death and loosened bowels assailed them, at which point they rose and shook themselves off — come on, time for bed, busy day tomorrow. Jinyi held back and, when the others were not looking, rearranged the dead man's hair into something resembling a side parting, then folded his pale hands across his defeated chest.

And if you are wondering what we gods know about death, then I am afraid I cannot tell you. I get different reports all the time, and, frankly, none are trustworthy. My own experience was of waking up and finding myself transformed into a god — this, however, is a rare occurrence and probably should not be expected by the majority of people — I do not want to be responsible for any false hope. My department has always been responsible for watching, studying and reporting, and owing to the intense rivalries between departments up here, it is hard to know what is currently happening in other, more shadowy areas. Let me just say this: life, in all its manifest forms, is complicated — why should death be any simpler?

Lard's dead eyes stared out from the hastily constructed funeral pyre the next day; strips of wood and scraps of hacked-down evergreen formed a squat bed for the impressive girth of the dead rightist. Despite not wanting to waste a day when more important jobs could be attended to, the locals had been cajoled down to the valley by the cadre and stood with their arms folded while he made a speech. Jinyi, Turkey, Bo, and the twenty others sent from distant worlds for their spirits to be stripped away and remolded, hung their heads, each aware that it might be them next.

The cadre cleared his throat. It was current

practice for the Party to pass judgment on a person's life after their death, and this was exactly what he intended to do, despite not only knowing nothing about the man's life prior to his arrival in the village seven months ago, but also not remembering his real name.

'Our comrade here has reminded us of the work we still need to do. Everywhere are imperialists, capitalists, intellectuals, followers of Liu Shaoqi. Together we can strike them down; we can change their polluted minds and set their hearts aflame with the spirit of Mao Zedong Thought. Dare to criticise, dare to fight! Though there are many men like him, clinging to the old and corrupt world, together we can kindle the flames of this Great Proletarian Cultural Revolution and transform the whole of society, the whole of our mighty country. The toll of revolution is blood and sacrifice. Each of us must work harder, do more, strive and steel ourselves — or die.'

The cadre cleared his throat once more, and pulled out a polished silver lighter, embellished with a picture of Chairman Mao, rays of light jetting out from behind his moon-shaped face. He clicked it once, twice, three times and, sparking a flame, crouched to start the fire. As his flesh began to crackle and brown, Lard became one of the lost and forgotten.

It is difficult to estimate how many people

disappeared during the Cultural Revolution, how many never made it back home. The number would have to include not only the first wave of the bourgeois, rightists, moderates, intellectuals, writers, artists, Soviet-followers, actors and politicians who had in some way aroused the envy or petty jealousy of Jiang Qing (Mao's second wife), and even Party members themselves who dared criticise the government, but also the second wave of teachers, businessmen, doctors and professionals, and finally the third wave consisting of the Red Guards themselves, finally deemed too dangerous to be allowed to form large networks and therefore dispersed to the countryside to embark on an alternative schooling. Countless numbers fell prey to dysentery, diarrhoea, flu, tetanus, TB, malaria and other germs they were not used to; heart failure, malnutrition, scurvy, broken bones, torn ligaments, sustained violence, strokes, epilepsy, breakdown, rape and suicide claimed countless more. Take Yuying's youngest sister, Chunxiang. On that very same day she collapsed in a field in Anhui, broken by sunstroke and the memory of having been raped and beaten by boys young enough to be her children. It is not known how many hundreds of thousands never found their way home from the blind spots of the map, for the majority of those who did survive the Cultural Revolution wished never again to speak of those bitter years.

At every turn, survival seemed to demand a suspension of rationality. I am reminded of Zhuxi, a renowned philosopher during the Song dynasty. Seeing his fellow philosophers and teachers worshipping the spirits of their ancestors, he came upon an idea: it is not for others, even the dead, that we cling to these primitive beliefs, but for ourselves. These spirits, he argued, do not exist; the practice of worshipping them, however, is important, as it forms an elaborate act of remembrance, a collective recognition of the unstoppable tide of history in which we struggle to swim. We make ourselves believe what we cannot fathom.

Legend has it that, late one night after returning from his work as a government official, Zhuxi sat down to write out these ideas, but as he picked up his ink brush a breeze blew out his candle. He relit the candle and rubbed the ink stick in a thin dish of water, yet as soon as he brought the darkened tip of the brush to the crinkled paper, the candle blew out once again. Zhuxi called for his servant, but no one came. As he reached down to light his candle one last time, he heard a low moaning sound, and the shuffle of feet.

When he looked up, Zhuxi was characteristically unimpressed. Though the apparition in his room appeared to be a skeleton, with reels of flayed skin and rungs of muscle hanging from the exposed bones, with red eyes staring from a misshapen, bearded head, Zhuxi, as a politician, was used to the impossible happening.

'Good evening, honourable Master Zhuxi. Your peerless learning and incomparable scholarship is renowned even in the next world. Please accept the greetings of the Lord of Ghosts.'

With that the apparition bowed to the seated philosopher. However, Zhuxi was also used to dealing with sycophants. He raised an eyebrow and said impatiently, 'I see. What business do you have here?'

'I have come to beseech you, on behalf of my people, not to write this tract,' the ghost replied hesitantly, before making another awkward bow.

'Why would you wish to do that?' Zhuxi asked.

'As I said, your wisdom is without equal, and your opinion is respected above all others throughout the country. If you were to prove that ghosts do not exist, then no one would doubt it,' the ghost stuttered.

'And this would inconvenience you, perhaps?'

'To tell you the truth, we are not sure what would happen to us. What becomes of you if no one believes in your existence? Perhaps

we will fade away completely, consumed by
the ether. Perhaps our voices will disappear,
our bodies too, while only our thoughts and
memories remain. Perhaps our entreaties to
the human world will only be met with
laughter and mockery. I cannot say. But I beg
you not to write that we do not exist.'

Zhuxi considered the question for a few
minutes, but the ghost began to grow impatient.

'Watch!' he cried, and shook his bony
hands. They both suddenly found themselves
standing outside, on the mountain that
overlooked Zhuxi's house, a lone red lantern
on the porch stirring the darkness of the valley. 'See. Our powers are great, beyond even
your great knowledge.'

'I'll grant you that. But we are of different
worlds, the yin of day and the yang of night,
and our knowledge itself is defined by its
boundaries,' Zhuxi argued.

'That is true. We are shadows that speak,
glimpses in mirrors, possibilities not yet
considered. That is why you must not destroy
us.'

'You have transported us from my house in
an instant. Tell me this: can you transport my
heart from my body, that I might understand
the workings of my own life?'

The ghost shook his misshapen head. 'Even
we are bound by certain laws.'

'Then there is hope for you yet, for everything must take its place in the great principles of nature, of which we yet know so little. Take me home, sir.'

Suddenly they were back in the dimly lit study. The ghost smiled, put his blood-stained finger to the candle and watched it leap into flame. When Zhuxi looked up from the jittery light, the apparition had disappeared.

He stirred the ink, flicked at it with the tip of his brush, then began to bite the slim wooden end as he turned over his thoughts. Finally, he began his essay: 'If you believe in something, it will be. If you do not, then it will not.'

If a whole country believed that it could rip apart four thousand years of history in an instant and begin again, then who could stop it? Temples were smashed down to splinters and firewood, mansions burnt to the ground, parents turned in by their own children. We do this not for yesterday or even for tomorrow, we do it for today, they chanted as they booted the bleeding heads of capitalist dogs; they screamed and shouted as millions of teenagers in identical shirts and caps lined up in Tiananmen Square, wetting themselves for a glimpse of an old man waving his short, dumpy hands from a shaky podium.

Yuying had been contemplating the same undulating wave of bracken for longer than she could remember. Each year she grew stronger, feeding on her experiences, scrubbing away some of the taint of her bourgeois past. She believed, in her heart, that she was becoming a better citizen, and this lessened the feeling of homesickness and the worries for her children far more than she had expected when she first arrived. They would be safe, because they were together. It was her husband she saw every time she closed her eyes, mouthing a promise again and again. She tried to push him to the back of her mind. She could not.

She bent over in the field, tugging up vegetables by the roots just as she had done when staying with her husband's aunt and uncle, and she felt the mistakes of the past slowly being shed. She found herself absent-mindedly keeping one eye on the track that descended past the fields towards one of the offshooting tributaries of the Yangtze, arching like a half-moon around the village, marking the boundary they were not allowed to cross. If she blotted out everything else she could hear its rush, the terrible force of the places it had surged through.

Yuying stooped, picked up the crammed-full wicker bag and hoisted it onto her back, then shambled carefully between the rows of carrots. Who was she now? The question rolled around and around her head, picking away at her certainties. The sum of her parents, sisters, husband, children? She found solace in the vastness of the landscape, the horizon line of flat fields and bracken broken only by the squat wooden houses and the occasional truck or horse-cart plodding down the slim, stony road to the east. It rendered her small, her past negligible. She gave in to it, let it take her over and remould her for whatever tasks the future might ask.

They were ascetics there, she had convinced herself, looking into the calm eye of duty, stripping away the self until only the country and all its mercies remained. At night, sitting around a fire in the small village square, the women reminded each other how they were changing the world for the better, and sang songs approved by the cadres. This was how it should be, this was the meaning of her life: she understood that now.

She let the bag slip down her aching back to the floor of the storeroom, then tipped the contents out for inspection.

'Bian Yuying, that is enough for today. Well done, you have been doing well. You may return to your room,' Comrade Hong said as he glanced over the scattering of carrots. His voice was clipped, his mannerisms shaky and measured, especially when compared to the gruffness of the second cadre, Comrade Lu. He waved an effete hand towards the door, his pencil moustache twitching above his tiny, pursed lips.

Yuying looked out at the pink glow where

the clouds dissolved at the edge of the sky; there was still at least an hour of workable light. 'I am happy to keep working, comrade. I want to do my fair share.'

'Of course, we all want to do our best for the revolution. But haven't you heard that your daughter has come to visit you? We must remember, Bian, that sometimes we must let our hearts have reign.' Comrade Hong was beginning to warm to the sound of his own voice, to his chosen sermon. 'It is, after all, our hearts that store the words and honourable example of Chairman Mao, and it is our hearts that stir for a better world. If we ignored our hearts, we would be like the Americans or the English, loving money and caring only for capital. Go and see your daughter, and be sure that the revolutionary zeal is burning in her heart too. I am sure she has travelled a long way.'

Yuying was dumbstruck: why would her daughter be here? Panic fluttered up through her stomach, but she pushed it back. She trod around the borders of the plots, then skirted round the back walls of the lines of houses, where old men and women were already out and tossing rice in large trays, separating the grain from the stalk. The lazy flicks of their wrists sent the grain dancing over the trays; as it jumped and fell she thought of rain and the footsteps of quick mice, the lightest of timpani, the music of sunset and hunger.

'Ma! Hey! Ma!' Yuying turned the side of a house to see her middle daughter standing awkwardly beside the stopped supplies van. Liqui's face was painted with a mixture of sweat and dust, stray hairs leaping out electrically from the confines of her long plait. She was thinner than her mother remembered, underdeveloped for her age; her faded jacket hung loosely from her scrawny shoulders. She was swinging a dirty rucksack in her hands. It was hard to keep track of time there, since the only language used was of sowing, harvesting and storing, but a quick tally of the seasons led Yuying to calculate that Liqui was now fifteen, or near enough.

'My, Hou Liqui, you've grown!' Yuying said. They stood and faced each other, both hesitant to reach out and touch. It had been three years since they had last met. An awkward silence began to develop as they studied each other, each of them too uncertain to dare step forward.

It took them ten long minutes to begin to feel comfortable in each other's company. Yuying wanted to say she was sorry, but couldn't. Liqui wanted to tell her mother to come home, but didn't.

In the end, they went inside. Liqui followed a few steps behind, watching Yuying totter toward one of the frail wooden shacks. She too was thinner than Liqui remembered, her hair knotted tightly into a bun and betraying her age with a few lone whites snaking through the blacks. Her arched back pulled her body up into a curve, her round face stretched tighter over her cheekbones.

'Is this where you sleep?' Liqui asked as they ducked under the laundry drying over the roof to enter the poky room, the floorboards divided into sleeping areas, the walls and low-jutting rafters stained with smoke and dead insects.

'This is how everyone sleeps in the commune. There are eight of us in here — all women, of course, though we're all treated exactly the same, men and women,' her mother replied, and they sank down, sitting cross-legged in the corner where Yuying slept. She reached up and brushed away a looping spider's web before wiping her fingers on her dark trousers.

'How was your journey?'

Liqui shrugged, wringing her cap in her hands. 'Fine. When I heard that some barefoot doctors from home had been posted to Hubei too, I knew that I had to come. Manxin's too busy doing your work at the factory, and Xiaojing's too young to travel on her own, so it had to be me. Luckily, a couple of the barefoot doctors refused the offer of a lift — they said they were going to walk across four provinces as proof of their conviction. So there was a bit of extra space. I had to walk for a few days to reach Xiantao after they dropped me off, but that supplies van picked me up just as I was leaving there, so I was pretty lucky.'

'Xiantao? Where is that?'

'It's the closest city to here, Ma. Only forty *li* away. Don't you know it?'

'Oh, I see. The locals just refer to it as "The City". I've never heard its name before. And nothing bad happened to you on your journey?'

She bridled at this, and wrinkled her nose. 'Of course not. They used to be Red Guards. We're all comrades, after all. Anyway, bad things don't happen to people who don't deserve them.'

Her mother nodded, then sighed. 'How is . . . everyone?'

Liqui wrapped her arms around her knees and began to rock herself forward. 'Fine.'

She did not say that she had not seen her father for a year, since he was last allowed home for the Spring Festival, when he had looked tired and gaunt and spent most of the three-day visit asleep. Neither did she mention Dali's recent stuttering and panic attacks, his tearful refusals to leave the house if there was anyone at all on the street or his reversion to bed-wetting, which terrified his younger siblings.

'Actually, Ma, there's something I have to tell you. Granny Dumpling has died. We thought you should know.'

Yuying tilted her head and opened her mouth, as if puzzling an equation that did not quite balance out. 'How? When?'

'She's been ill for years, Ma. She hadn't got out of bed since the sixties. We didn't tell you before, because, well, what would have been the use? She was old and ill, and there just wasn't any way of getting medicine. It happened while she was asleep, just like that. Yaba had been sitting with her; Manxin found him snoring in a bedside chair when she cycled round to take them both some breakfast one morning.'

'I see.'

Liqui waited for her mother to say more, but instead Yuying simply stared up at the last frail threads of sticky spider's web that her fingers had missed.

'We wanted to reach you for the funeral, but it all happened so quickly that we didn't know what to do. We sent some messages, but no one was sure if they would get to you. We couldn't wait, Ma. Sorry.'

'That's all right. You did what was best.'

'We were thinking about taking her ashes up to where Grandpa is buried, but Yaba didn't want us to. We were wondering what you thought.'

'Yaba probably knew your grandmother better than anyone, you know. Even me. She trusted him, so you should too,' Yuying said.

'You'll be happy to know that the Party

verdict at her funeral was much less severe than anyone expected. They briefly mentioned her bourgeois beginnings, of course, but said that she had served the new order well, and was a good model of the way people can reform. Isn't that great?' Liqui said.

Yuying smiled. What the Party meant was that she gave up a highly profitable restaurant empire without any fuss. 'That's wonderful. I'm not sure she would have recognised herself in that summary though — she went along with many things, but that didn't mean she fully understood them.'

'She could always tell if you were lying though.'

'Oh no, she only said that to make sure you would be good. She had a little story for everything, but none of them were true. I think that it helped her, somehow, find a place in the world. I wish she could have lived to see the results of this Great Proletarian Cultural Revolution, to see a new start, a perfect world. She was born at the wrong time. Just think, after us, no one will ever have to see a world where things are topsy-turvy, where some people have everything and others have nothing, a world of greed and poverty.' Yuying clasped her daughter's hands. 'We're changing that, now, aren't we? Your children, my grandchildren, they won't need to be re-educated, because there will be no old ways to get lost in. Everything is going to be so much better. And your grandmother would have been happy knowing that. She always wanted to help people — especially the poor or the lost, like Yaba or your father.'

Her voice began to crack when she mentioned him. She wanted to ask her daughter to tell her where Jinyi was, to describe exactly how he looked now, to repeat every word he had said when she had last seen him. But she could not. She could not burden her daughter with her longing. She could not risk looking like she had not reformed. Imagine what they might say — a woman who cares more for her husband than the revolution. Is there anything worse?

So instead Yuying and Liqui drifted into an intimate silence, a family silence, a hand-me-down silence that people grow into, until Liqui reached for her dusty rucksack. She felt around the canvas cloth for a few moments before she closed her grip on something bulging at the bottom.

'Ma, I brought something for you. Mrs Xi, from your factory, gave them to us. I saved one for you.'

Her fist emerged, wrapped around the squidgy globe of a bruised tomato. It was overgrown, a deformed apple, bulging and leering near the sunken dimple tip. It was the colour of faded lipstick, with bits of hair and crumbs and fluff stuck to it from the journey. Liqui wiped it on her sleeve, careful not to add any more soft bruises to its already considerable collection, then thrust it into her mother's hands.

'Thank you, but —'

'Go on, Ma.' Liqui pushed her mother's hands towards her mouth.

Yuying tentatively sank her teeth into the squelchy red flesh, a dribbly frogspawn of ruby seeds and juice spilling over her fingers as she did so. It tasted sour, almost fermented, but beyond that she was surprised at how juicy it was, quenching a thirst Yuying had not registered was there. She handed it back.

'Please. We'll share it,' she said, but waved it away when it was next proffered and ended up watching her famished daughter eat the whole thing, both of them with identical smiles beginning to form on their lips.

Mother and daughter sat like that as the last dregs of the day gurgled away. When the other women came slowly trailing in, Yuying introduced her daughter as tactfully as she could, knowing that some of her roommates still felt the heart-stopping pull of homesickness and longing.

Liqui's eyes were weighed down with tiredness after her journey — she had spent both nights trying not to nod off in case her head should lull down onto one of the boys' shoulders, or, even more mortifyingly, she should snore. She did not pick up many of the names or stories trotted out; instead, what stayed with her was the way that the women there wore their scars as others might armbands or nametags. Rather than attempt to hide or draw attention away from them, the women identified themselves, and one another, by their markings, studying them for meaning and solace as if they were stigmata. The woman with blotchy pink scald burns stained across her face and neck; the woman with five hammerbroken fingers which now arched out, swollen, lumpy and hooked; and the woman with the sunken eye, glazed and unseeing and bordered by stitched-up flesh. The marks left on the others were not quite so easy to see.

Liqui slumped further down the wall, ready to huddle up with her mother and retreat into her snug warmth, when one of the women turned to them.

'Where's Mingmei?' the woman with the claw-like hand asked. A quick headcount showed that there were only seven women, plus Liqui. Yuying shrugged.

'She hasn't been in here with you? We thought she was feeling sick again, like last week, and had come back for a lie down. No? Really?' she added as she scratched her cheek with her good hand, the other limp at her side.

'Should we go and look for her?' one of the

seemingly unscarred women asked.

'No, she'll come back when she's ready,' the woman with the sunken eye joined in. 'You know what Mingmei's like. She's always fluttery, strange. She clings to her thoughts, and keeps them in, letting them twist her. We told her that with Mao Zedong Thought, anything is possible. She pretends to agree, but it's clear that she hasn't given up her bourgeois past.' She seemed to be saying all of this for Liqui's benefit, pointedly listing the criticisms with an upturned nose, as if she could smell each word escaping her mouth.

There were grunts of agreement, though Liqui was not quite sure what they meant. The women's resentment of their missing roommate was clear enough, however, and Liqui knew firsthand that what people liked to do more than anything was judge. Furthermore, immorality was like lice; sheer proximity was enough to run the risk of being infested.

'She deserves those punishments. The cadre is only doing what's best for her. She'll see that someday, and stop moping about it all,' the clawed woman said.

'And she doesn't do herself any favours: never joining in the evening songs, never sewing things, never speaking to the locals. And it works out badly for the rest of us, just because people think we're all the same,' another woman added.

Liqui had expected sisterhood and shared sympathy between the women, yet this was something else; a brittle closeness founded on the common ground of their shared anger and hostility. They complained about Mingmei not because she was bringing their dorm into disrepute, but because they could not complain about anything else, least of all their current situation. They spoke about her because they had to speak about something to stop their mouths from opening into screams.

They slept. The night was warm and luscious, melting around their bodies, the smell of musty sweat and old shoes rising from the walls, and though each of them could guess how it was going to turn out, they wished only for sleep to come prowling from across the fields. The bad news could wait till morning.

At dawn the shouts came mixed in with the cock's crows. From a distance, as they flocked with the crowd of villagers towards the calls from the sodden banks of the river, Mingmei looked as if she had sprouted scales, winking like chainmail in the shifting splints of morning light. The bottoms of her trousers and her bare feet were caked with wet mud, and Yuying could not help noticing that the young woman's exposed toenails were cracked and dirty.

The murky water pulsed on regardless, twisting and sprinting as if some unseen force in its roaring depths was driving it ever stronger towards the limits of the heart's range, spray spitting at the slippery banks. Her shoes must have made it to another county by now, Yuying thought; it is the little things that outlive us. Wet twigs clung to the crooks in Mingmei's clothing, a few tangled in her hair. Her puffy face made her look as though she had just been crying.

'Her limbs had got caught up in that dam down there, a right mess if you ask me — I think I tore even more when I pulled her out. Scared all the geese and ducks and cranes away. Stones in her pocket too, though I wouldn't have thought them necessary — people from cities can't swim anyway, can they?' a middle-aged man was saying to Comrade Lu, the bulkier of the two cadres.

'Hmph,' Comrade Lu huffed in response.

'You're lucky she got caught. Most bodies disappear. But the river gave her back. It must mean something,' the middle-aged man continued.

'I suppose she must have come across the east side of the fields and thrown herself in there, before being carried around,' Comrade Hong said quietly.

'Well, yes, of course,' Comrade Lu replied,

before turning his attention to the gathered crowd, a mixture of villagers and foreigners, with Yuying at the back, clutching her daughter's clammy hand tightly in her own. 'I hope you all get a good look at this! You, you, you and you,' he punctuated the words with short thrusts of his meaty fingers into the crowd, 'take her body back up to the houses; we can't leave it down here by the road. The rest of you, it's time to get back to work.'

With that he waved them away; a quick glimpse of death before breakfast might provide a morsel of gossip for a few days, he thought, perhaps even an instructive story to scare the kids with, until she is forgotten.

'Liqui, I don't want you to think —' Yuying started as they clambered back towards the plots.

'Ma. It's all right. I'm fifteen — I know how things are. Our strength gets tested all the time. I've seen worse things than that. If it were easy, we wouldn't need to do so much now,' her daughter replied, letting go of Yuying's hand. She was too old for it, and, she secretly told herself, she knew more of the world now than her mother did.

The crowd dispersed through the fields to the menial tasks with which they tied themselves to the day. The women there had made themselves immune to death. They did not speak of it, except perhaps to mutter that Mingmei had brought it on herself. In later years the women in her dorm would revisit these times with different eyes, remembering the way each of them ignored Mingmei's tears and the couple of evenings she returned later than usual, bruised, with matted hair and dirt-stained clothes. They would think of how they told her to shut up and let them sleep, or how they had stared dismissively at the growing curve of her belly and told her that she only had herself to blame. Like the blinding fire of dying stars or burning suns, some things can only be looked at safely from a distance. To open themselves to it then was impossible, because it would have meant storming the locked attics of the mind and letting out the things that had, over a number of years, been painstakingly bundled, bound, gagged, taped, beaten, chained and locked inside.

'She's better off this way,' they heard the woman with the claw telling the others as they stooped to the picking; no one argued with her.

The 'Long River', the Yangtze, dissects the country in a horizontal squiggle, its slow dive from the Sichuan mountains to the Shanghai coast resembling the whirling nosedives and leaps of a kite the wind has tugged from a child's hands. It has more than seven hundred tributaries which irrigate a million plots, and even now trickle through ten million dreams.

It is dragon, god, king — bestowing grace or punishment on the little lives it holds tight, according to some unknown plan. Yangtze River dolphin, Yangtze porpoise, alligator, sturgeon, carp, mullet, swordfish, Chinese paddlefish and a million others.

Like those branded undesirable and exiled to the countryside, be they loose-tongued urban workers or wily Party men like Deng Xiaoping sent to be reformed through labour, Qu Yuan, wandering along the banks of another river over two thousand years earlier, would not have dared imagine the dramatic rehabilitation he would later receive. He was watching the egrets swooping over the trawl, singing some of his freshly composed verses to himself when he heard a voice behind him.

'Hey! I know you, don't I?' The speaker was an elderly fisherman; his skin wrinkled and patchily sunburnt, his frail body a marked contrast to his rippling, bulky arms. The ambling poet and scholar was, by contrast, pale and nervy, his long knotted beard speckled with premature grey.

'No, I am afraid that you must be mistaking me for someone else. I am sorry. Am I in your way?'

'Nah. Not at all.' The old fisherman grinned, showing his toothless gums, as he began to stride down the bank to where his thin boat was moored, hidden behind a strut of tall reeds. Then suddenly he turned back.

'Wait. I do know you. You're that official, aren't you? Yes, yes, I've heard all about you. You're Qu Yuan. Why, my son can even recite some of your poems, though they're a little beyond an old man like myself.'

Qu Yuan coloured a little as the old man retraced his steps to face him.

'But here's the thing, my friend. This whole county is mostly fishermen or tea-pickers or, if you're lucky, sow-breeders. Now, tell me, what's a renowned man like you doing round here, eh?'

Qu Yuan ran a hand through his beard as he considered his reply. He had until recently been a chief minister in the government of the state of Chu, and what was more had been one of the king's most trusted advisers. Yet the king had gone against his advice and attended a meeting in another state. There, a trap had been sprung and the king captured, only to die in the foreign jail before the demanded ransom could be paid. Qu Yuan had urged the king's son, who became the next monarch, to build up the army to avenge this humiliation. However, the new king had put his trust in more sycophantic ministers, who advised caution and, jealous of Qu Yuan's past favour, argued for the minister's exile. The new king had agreed; after all, he did not wish to risk humiliation himself.

When Qu Yuan spoke, his voice was hoarse and throaty, despite his careful enunciation and obvious gravitas. 'Where everyone is dirty, I alone stay clean; where everyone is drunk, I alone remain sober. That is the reason I have been banished here.'

The old man laughed. 'Don't be so stuck up! Surely a wise man like you knows that you have to move with the times. If everyone around you is getting tipsy, why not at least have a little tipple yourself? No one's perfect, you know. If you ask me, sir, you only have yourself to blame.'

'If a man had just washed his hair, you would not expect him to then put on a filthy hat; if he had just bathed, you would not expect him to then dress in dirty clothes. I would rather throw myself into the river than sully myself by rolling in the dirt with those hypocrites in the government,' Qu Yuan replied.

The old fishermen sighed and wandered back down the bank to free his boat, shaking his head as he went.

Before the sun had sunk into the flow the next day, Qu Yuan had proved himself true to his word by wading down into the water and letting the current take hold of his wandering thoughts and pull them toward the ocean. When the elderly fisherman came to tar his trusty boat, he was struck by the silence, the absence of that sonorous voice singing strange and hopeless poetry. Realising what had happened, he called together as many others as

521

he could, and they took to the river in rickety rafts, battered canoes, crammed rowboats and leaky cobbled-together crafts, to search for the body. The elderly fisherman pounded an old skin drum, sending a rattling beat between the boats and urging the rowers faster as they desperately tried to catch up to where the famous poet's body might be.

After hours of trawling oars through weeds and around the darting schools of sparky bronze fish that on other days they would have been delighted to find, the men were becoming desperate. One of their number began to sing:

Birds with golden wings and jade-scaled
    dragons
I have tied to the reins of the storm;
And as we soar above the grey and dark
I dream my restless heart will be reborn.

The elderly fisherman recalled his son singing that same verse, part of Qu Yuan's epic lament, *Sorrow in Exile,* and he finally understood. He called to the others.

'We have searched all day, and found nothing. We're not going find him now. But don't give up hope. Though we can't bring back his body for the proper funeral rites, we can still do good and show our respect. Take out the rice you brought for your lunch — come on, I know those of you with wives have had something prepared for you — good, that's it. Now chuck it in the river!'

No one moved. Eyes glanced round nervously, each man holding covetously onto his food.

'Come on! Do you want the fish to eat his body? What kind of ignoble ending would that be for such a great man? Throw your rice in and give the fish something else to eat, and then they'll leave Qu Yuan alone, and his body can at least have some rest!'

The old man then threw his own lunch, wads of sticky rice wrapped in bamboo leaves, into the river. The young man who had been singing some of the poet's verses followed suit, prompting others around him to do the same. Soon the dingy afternoon was filled with the plop and splash of food being thrown to the gathering fish. The fishermen went home that night hungry and downhearted.

Yet they did not forget Qu Yuan. People found his longing, idealistic rhymes spilling from their lips as they sailed, sowed, harvested and hoed, regardless of whether they had meant to memorise them or not. And as successive governments fell to corruption, mismanagement or military hiccups, Qu Yuan's prudence and sobriety was mourned even more. Thus the next year, on the very same day, the fishermen gathered once again to take to the river, drums and packages of rice in hand, this time joined by men and women from neighbouring villages.

Happiness is the easiest thing to lose. Sorrow, on the other hand, is impossible to forget.

It was the day before the fifth of the fifth, the Dragon Boat Festival which commerated Qu Yuan, but Jinyi could not keep track of dates. It was spring, his sixth year away, and nothing else mattered. Jinyi would not be back with his family for the Tomb Sweeping Day, Worker's Day, Double Ninth Day, the Mid-Autumn Festival or even for National Day, the only one he was certain was still being celebrated. He was allowed one visit home a year only, seven measly days including the two at either end it took to make the journey. Yet still he kept his hopes of returning to Fushun for the next year's Spring Festival held deep in his holey pockets, along with the words he always wanted to say but instead had to store up under his swelling tongue, along with his children's faces, which he called up whenever he closed his eyes.

That was why they were there: to let go of everything that they thought they knew, then remake themselves. Passing from acceptance to resentment to contentment, then veering back, Jinyi zigzagged through emotions that he thought he had tamed and caged. He had even started biting his nails again, something he had not done for close to thirty years, though he still had the willpower to make sure he only did it when he thought no one was watching.

'Coming for water?' Bo pulled him back from his trance.

Jinyi nodded and got up from the long bench in the cramped village canteen, clutching his wooden bowl tightly as he stepped around the slippery spills and spit covering the floorboards. He followed Bo and Turkey out into the dusk.

'I've got dust in my teeth; I can feel it. Dust and grit, from that bastard wind today,' Bo muttered. As he had grown older, he had become more vocal, although only around those he had spent a long time with. He had recently turned sixteen, though he had told no one. Guessing some milestone, Jinyi and Turkey had saved up their allowances to present him with a packet of cigarettes that was almost full.

'Dragon's breath,' Turkey said, thrusting his chin towards the red mop of molten cloud stretched across the dark.

'Dragon's breath? You might as well say that these dusty gales have been huge dragon farts! You two sound like my grandmother. Come on, you're not that old!' Bo said.

'We are old,' Jinyi said. 'You know when you're getting old, don't you? It's when you're stuck halfway between getting annoyed about all the things you suddenly can't remember and getting angry about all the things you can't forget. Damn it if I don't feel old too. I'm nearly halfway to a hundred.'

'Pah. Our noble Chairman is older than you and me combined, and so is Comrade Zhou Enlai, one of the greatest and fairest men this country has ever seen. They're both still going strong,' Bo countered.

Jinyi laughed. 'Ha. I reckon you could get us all in a lot of trouble if you were heard comparing us to the beneficent leaders in Beijing.'

They stopped at a long metal trough and skimmed their hands through a pool of misty starlight. Each of them scooped up a bowlful of fuggled rainwater, which they swirled around until it had mixed with some of the burnt rice stuck to the side and soaked up the bland taste of that day's dinner.

They drank. That was what the moon must taste of, bitter and thick, the sour zest of longing and leftovers.

'Drink up. We'll need the strength for tomorrow,' Jinyi warned.

He was right. By the time they ate the next meal, a late breakfast of hard buns speckled with green onion, they had passed the rocky plain and begun an ascent of a bramble-knotted hill. Six oxen (which Bo had been quick to nickname Marx, Engels, Lenin, Stalin, Bethune and Lei Feng, if only to upset

526

the delicate patriotism of his two companions) slapped their fly-squatter tails against ruddy flanks as they sauntered between the sweaty men.

'Why us?' Bo moaned as they slipped into single file around the turns of the muddy track, sandwiching the oxen between them.

'You should be happy. Nothing better than being outside on a day like this. You can't tell me you'd rather be sitting around thinking about the past than being busy. Plus, it's is an important delivery — it shows the cadre trusts us,' Jinyi said.

'Either that or he wants us to fail so as to find an excuse to punish us,' added Turkey. These days, however, the others were never sure whether Turkey's words were a product of a knowing humour or an excess of bile. His expression always hovered somewhere between smile and grimace.

Jinyi could no longer be bothered to point out the obvious: that they should not be talking like that. Yet as the months piled up, he was increasingly unsure of everything. The oxen, he reasoned at last, would not rat them out. Someone must keep them buoyant though.

'No, I don't think so,' Jinyi sighed. 'We know the oxen, we're always with them, so who else was he going to ask? And anyway, Bow Lake Village needs them, so we're doing some good by delivering them. That ought to be enough.'

'If the wind stops licking at our backs, and the spring rain holds off, then I'll agree. It beats hoeing and sowing anyway: my back doesn't take kindly to them. Not after a year's worth of bending down to scrub those stinking latrines. Hell!' Turkey replied.

They stopped for breath at the top, looking down to the geometrical order of the paddies below and behind, the fumbling lines of irrigation and the sharp, slicing paths, the type of order only man knows, imposed from the outside on the tangled wild. They then began to descend on the other side, a steep crisscross of ferns and burr. With every twist in the thin path between the greedy vegetation one of them stumbled or tripped, so they closed in until they were almost shoulder to shoulder among the animals, a chain gang of flapping tongues and bristles and blisters.

'Is this it?' shouted the Bow Lake cadre.

After a ragged afternoon and a chunk of evening, they had made it to Bow Lake Village, but the cadre there, shaking a stump where his right hand should have been, did not seem as grateful as they had imagined.

'A bit mangy, aren't they?' the one-handed cadre continued, flipping the ears of the beasts, and staring into their milky eyes. He listed their defects with a grim relish. 'This one's covered in fleas; this one's got a bit of a limp; this one's got a swollen ball bigger than my fist; this one smells worse than death; this one's got skin like a crumpled snot-rag. What's the matter, you couldn't find any that were actually dead? I'm surprised this lot survived the journey. Well, they'll have to do, I guess.'

The three men did not know how to respond to the unimpressed cadre. He finally glanced at them and sighed. 'I hope these animals have more life in them than you three. Come on, I'll show you where we eat, and then to the barn — we're a bit crowded here right now, but the straw's pretty soft, and I expect you'll be heading back early in the morning anyway.'

Jinyi cleared a space among the loose straw and dirt and surrendered himself to the lice, nits, fleas, bedbugs, earwigs, woodworms, money-spiders and ants in the ancient barn. The oxen, meanwhile, began their new life by lowing a mournful song until the moonlight finally quieted them.

The journey home was the same slipshod scenery replayed backwards, first snowball blossoms pouting on the trees, the air ripe with manure and their steps matching the accompanying percussion of the three men's rumbling stomachs. The way the wind whipped the frail branches of the shorter trees called up a shrill, reedy voice, and Jinyi pictured a eunuch singing to a deserted palace garden after his imperial masters had left for a war they were certain to lose. He picked up a stick and beat back the weeds and thorny bushes that overhung the mule track, poking for high berries and trying to become forgetful again. But though he could swipe away weeds and thistles, he could not clear the clutter of his thoughts, which returned again and again to his wife, his promise; the silly hopes he had placed in her palms.

The afternoon gave in to evening without a fight, and in a few hours darkness descended in a cloak of angry rainfall. The three of them scurried down into a small enclave between the rocks, spraying each other every time they rustled their heavy, drenched clothing.

'Where do you think it came from?' Bo said, settling down on the stony ground.

'The storm? West of here, I guess,' replied Jinyi.

'No, I mean really came from. Listen, you know a few years back the American president came here? Well, what if they were trying to trick us, and what he really wanted to do was to fiddle with our weather?'

'Don't be ridiculous. You can't just change the weather.'

'Of course you can. You've heard about all the technological things they have there.'

'He might be right,' Turkey said. 'You hear all kinds of things about what those foreigners are up to.'

'Well, even if they can, why would they want to mess around with our weather?'

'Why? Because we make them nervous. They see us and the wonders of our country, with everyone working together and living in peace and harmony, and they get jealous,' Bo replied.

'He's right again,' Turkey said. 'Remember what happened when we went to go and help out our brothers in Korea, only for America to come and split it in two and take over the south? They would have swallowed it all if it wasn't for us. And Taiwan too.'

'They love money more than people, you see,' Bo stated, as if he was a professor lecturing a particularly hopeless class. 'But I'll tell you what, if invading armies do turn up here, we'll smash them mercilessly!'

'I agree that whatshisname — Nixon, yes? — well, he might have been up to something. But if you ask me, he only came to try and find out how China has become so great, so he can copy what we've done back in America. And anyway, do you really think a couple of Americans can trick our mighty leaders? Don't be silly. Premier Zhou Enlai alone can speak six languages, so nothing could get past him!'

The others nodded, convinced.

The rain continued, and Jinyi, Turkey and Bo found themselves wondering whether they ever would return home. They could not know that it would only be a few more years until Mao died, the Gang of Four were arrested and families began to be reunited. Too many dead, too many disappeared, too many unrecognisable, too much destroyed, to be able to expect anything of tomorrow. Streams of rainwater skirted up to the entrance of the enclave, and trees whined and hawed to them from afar. Better to live in history than in your heart: this was the lesson of the countryside communes.

'In a storm like this,' Turkey ventured, 'paths might get washed away, repainted with mud and glut.'

Jinyi stared out at the grey scribbled haze and picked up the thread. 'Men out in the gales might get swept into a river and washed away.'

'Or tumble down some hill, or freeze in some cave,' Turkey said.

Bo looked at them both and shook his head. He had not followed the unspoken implication — that the three of them might wear the storm as a disguise, and escape under the veil of the assumptions it might conjure. The cadre would assume they'd died in a flash flood or hillslide, and soon forget them. They could find their homes again, their children, their wives.

Yet it was just a joke, nothing more; each village was a facsimile of the last, each new face in each new place treated with equal suspicion and contempt. It was not only geography that imprisoned them, however, but also psychology: to run would be to surrender the little parts of themselves, of their old lives, that they had spent the long seasons trying to cling to; to escape would mean that they had been prisoners all along, rather than men bettering themselves to better the country.

'There are places where it hasn't stopped raining for a thousand years, where the locals wade to work and the dogs feed on fish they catch in courtyards,' Turkey said, rubbing his eyes.

'Hmm. A thousand years, eh? We could be here a while then.'

The three of them huddled and shivered on the damp stones, drawing close for warmth and watching for signs of respite in the wash of dragged leaves and trees bent double. The far-off thunder sounded like the crackle of a transistor radio, waiting to pick up the hint of a voice. The drab stretch of hills and fields had been reimagined by a drunken Impressionist, transformed into a slur of greys and midnight blues. They sat in silence as the storm took over the night, hoping that some break in the clouds would render the world familiar again.

Instead of feeling downhearted, I only felt more determined to prove the Jade Emperor wrong. I lived inside Yuying and Jinyi's heads for weeks, months on end, returning only to my own little kitchen in heaven to reflect on the story and get some rest, for it is impossible to relax for even a second amid the hurricane of the brain's constant chemistry. The mind is a maze — though plenty of orders regularly pulse up from the heart, there are so many attics, corridors, locked doors and dead ends that some feelings inevitably become lost and never find a corresponding thought or prompt to action.

One night, after Jinyi and the other men had fallen asleep on the wooden floorboards in the little hut above the paddies, I crept outside and soon found myself staring up at the sky, remembering the poet's advice to pay attention to the little details that carry us along. Suddenly I saw a rip between the stars, and I soon made out a large trail of dust clouds and pawprints as a great lolloping dog started towards the overripe full moon.

I leapt to my feet, determined to fly up and catch the panting stray before it reached the moon. However, as soon as my feet had ascended from the ground, I felt a hand on my shoulder pulling me back down.

'He's a rascal that one — you'll never stop him!' a gruff voice said, and I turned around to see the heavy-set man whose strong grip held me back. His features looked as if they had been badly chiseled into his face as an afterthought, and he had a dark third eye set in the middle of his forehead. He was wearing an old soldier's uniform.

'I know you,' I said. 'Erlang Shen, right?'

He grunted an affirmation. Erlang Shen, nephew of the Jade Emperor and a great warrior. He had fought to subdue the Monkey King back when he was causing problems for heaven, he had ventured into hell many times on various missions, and everyone knew that it was he who controlled lightning bolts, which he directed at naughty children. His main job, however, was fighting demons and other devilish creatures, which he did with the help of his trusty black dog . . .

'Hey! That's your dog, isn't it?' I looked up, aghast to see the large hound gobbling a fat chunk out of the moon.

He laughed. 'Yeah, that's right. He does it every night, I'm afraid.'

'What do you mean? You let him take a bite

out of the moon every night? What will you do when he finishes it?' I asked in horror.

'Oh, don't you worry about that. After a couple of weeks his stomach will get so full that it will be fit to burst. He can't digest it you see, all that chalky crumbly mush. He howls and writhes about, making a right old fuss, until it occurs to him to spit it out, which he does every night until he feels comfortable. Then he'll suddenly realise his stomach is empty and feel famished, so the whole damn thing will start again. But like I said, there's no stopping him.'

'How long has this been going on?' I asked.

'Oh, a couple of billion years, give or take,' he said.

'Don't you get bored with the same thing happening every night?'

He looked at me and laughed again. 'But he always eats a different bit. There's always a bit of unexpected variation in everything; that's what keeps all of us going.'

He whistled, rattling the long lead in his fat hands, and I left him, feeling a little more confident about my task.

10:
1977
THE YEAR OF THE SNAKE

There are spirit voices, writes Marco Polo, that call travellers from their paths and lure them to disaster. When crossing the shifting deserts of the Silk Road by night, he tells us, men separated from their party often stray from the track to follow the low chatter of disembodied voices. They may hear the voices of their companions or loved ones, or else the distant chatter of drums, the frantic shouts and screams of far-off battle; anything that might drive them deeper into the unknown depths of the dunes. The men who follow these calls are never seen again. For this reason, Polo advises, stay close to those you travel with, and do not be tempted to strike away on your own, however much your senses urge. The traveller that Polo posits is someone who seeks his own reflection: he does not so much fear being lost as he fears losing himself. Take a man away from his home, from his language and from his fellow men, and how much of the man remains?

Marco Polo recorded with awe the Chinese use of paper money as a substitution for gold and jewels; the Mongols' many wives and fiery alcohol brewed from mare's milk; the great Khan's ten thousand white horses; snapping fire crackers and sparking rockets in the new capital, Beijing; the magic black stone that sustained fire; and the strange and detailed calendar used by the court. And yet the magpie eye of the traveller who never settles in one place often sees only novelty and wonder, and not the hunger and sores and scabs and turds lurking behind the carefully constructed sets. It is both the privilege and the punishment of us gods that we see everything.

What, you may ask, has this long-dead Italian got to do with Jinyi and Yuying? All three were called by spirit voices. All came close to losing themselves in the places they encountered. None returned the same as when they left.

Jinyi started wondering, as he made the long journey home, whether everything had been real or just part of his fevered imaginings. All he knew was that the only reason he had kept going when others around him had fallen in the fields was longing.

Scholars debate whether Polo ever really made it to China or not; what they forget is that, more often than not, histories are written in the heart.

The Jinyi who journeyed back to Fushun looked like a ragged, withered uncle of the one who had left. His receding black mane was sparked with white, the fringe dusted with tobacco yellow. His eyebrows now threatened to meet in the middle of his face, which managed both to pull tight around his eyes and sag limply around his cut-glass cheeks. Save for a single week each year (if he was lucky), he had not been home since the heyday of the Red Guards. His hands, wrinkled like prunes, fumbled with the stiff door handle; he was old.

Of the nine years he had been in the fields what more can be said? Imagine lying so still that grass grows up through your pores. This is how the time had passed. Now Mao had died and been gutted and pumped with preserving fluids and stuffed and boxed and shoved into a mausoleum in the centre of Tiananmen Square, where his faithful vigilantes had a decade ago gathered for a glimpse of his smile and wave; the old Chairman's wife had been blamed for the mayhem and was being prepped for the show trial of the century; and those left of the lost generation were slowly being allowed to trickle home.

Jinyi joined a ragtaggle band of emaciated workers begging for lifts from every truck, van, army car, motorbike or rusty bicycle that passed them. The huge migration mirrored the birds that had just fled the winter, seeking out some familiar warmth. Is it that I have successfully reformed, Jinyi asked himself, or have they given up on reforming people? He hitched rides through small towns decked with patchy lanterns and strings of withered red chillies, over rickety river bridges, beside dipping paddies, fields and plains, around half-logged forests, past wide-eyed villages and smoke-stack cities, and into the coal skies of the familiar north. He concluded that he did not care.

Despite having no money, trading on the kindness of strangers for a shared bowl of noodles in village rest-stops or a bite of someone's apple or *mantou* in the back of a cramped pick-up, Jinyi spent the journey home thinking about the feast that he would prepare for the Spring Festival the following month, the treats and dishes he would craft for his newly reunited family. He would cook his wife's favourite dumplings. He conjured up the smile he would see on her face, and the thought warmed him more than a hot meal might have. At crowded country canteen tables and in grubby seatless bus stations he attracted stares from the hundreds of other returning undesirables as his hands unconsciously rehearsed the action of kneading the dumpling dough, scooping in the filling and pinching tight the shell-like skin. Must have rats nibbling between his ears, onlookers muttered loud enough for him to hear. Again, did not care.

Jinyi finally managed to open the stiff door and collapsed inside, his bones chilled by the January frost, only to find that the house was empty.

'Dali? Manxin? Liqui? Xiaojing? Is anyone here?' he tried to shout, but finding his voice frozen tight in his larynx, he settled instead for a hoarse whisper. There was no reply.

As his eyes adjusted to the gloom, Jinyi registered a lopsided wooden table, evidently second-hand and poorly restored, surrounded by four mismatched chairs, each a different size and design. He sank into one, and wondered whether it was the chair or his back that creaked. A rusty kettle was slumped on the stove, talking to a wok upturned on the floor beside it. A drooping picture hung on the main wall, capturing Chairman Mao and Zhou Enlai approaching the microphone in Tiananmen in 1949, whole lifetimes ago. Great men, Jinyi thought, set to live out their next incarnations in textbooks, posters, movies, poems and watch-faces.

Suddenly he was grinning, remembering how as a child he had believed that the spirits trapped in pictures would creep out at night to do as they pleased. He had even blamed them when confronted by his enraged uncle over the bite marks in the corn bread. It must have been those tiny monks and their fat cows from that picture, he had wailed as the fist bore down. After all, his aunt had warned that boys who were naughty would get trapped in the mirror for sixty-four years, so why couldn't it work both ways? Remembering this, Jinyi almost laughed, but stopped himself. Then he reconsidered, looking around to check that there was no one near who might hear or report that Hou Jinyi was laughing. So he guffawed and giggled and hee-hawed, ten years of laughter spurting out like shaken-up cola, until he was exhausted.

The shelves had even been refitted, and both a wooden cabinet and a fuzzy brown fold-out futon had appeared. The bread factory had continued to pay his and Yuying's wages to the children each month, and Dali, Manxin and Liqui had since been allocated their own factories, making army coats, tinned foods and notebooks respectively. The factories had faces and hands and big plans; they could replace families before you could even salute.

Jinyi wandered through to the bedroom and slipped onto the still warm *kang,* content that this corner at least was the same as when he had left, a small slice of his old self hung up like a forgotten coat that twitches restlessly on the hanger, begging to be worn again. Jinyi wrapped himself in one of the girls' sheets, giving in to the deepest of sleeps from which he would later re-emerge as a father, a husband, an ordinary bread-oven man and the inconspicuous tenant of 42 Zhongshan Lu.

'Pa.' He was woken by a hand on his shoulder, shaking the dust from the long sleeves of his dreams. 'How are you feeling?' It was Manxin, her eyes peering out anxiously from under a pushed-back bob. Jinyi rubbed his eyes — at twenty-four, his eldest daughter looked startlingly like a stockier version of her mother.

'Pa, say something.' Liqui had appeared at Manxin's side, her mouth knotted into a ball of nerves as she worried her plait.

'I'm fine, I'm fine. Don't fuss,' Jinyi said.

He raised himself up as his youngest, Xiaojing, her hair cropped above her equine face, entered with a bowl of rice broth which she pushed into his hands. His three daughters were lined up in front of him like soldiers awaiting inspection.

'Where have you been?' Jinyi asked the gangly girl at the end of the line.

'At the middle school. Manxin took me to queue up to register. It's going to open again after the holidays and I can go! I am thirteen now, after all,' Xiaojing answered.

Thirteen. Jinyi nodded; he had missed more

than half her life. What had this lanky teen-ager done with the lisping little girl who used to trail a battered doll around and teach it how to make tea? Did she even recognise him?

'Of course. You all look so strong, so healthy. Daughters of steel and iron, isn't that what they say? You make me feel old.' He tried to smile.

'You're not old yet, Pa,' Manxin chided.

'So where is my son? His life is busier than even mine was at that age. Last time I came back for a visit he was working night shifts so I never saw him, and the time before he was away with a volunteer group in the country-side. I can't even remember the time before that. He can't still be at work at this hour, can he?'

The girls shuffled nervously, a row of bit lips and fidgety hands.

'Listen, Pa. We didn't tell you any of this before, because we didn't want you to worry when you were so far away, but Dali never worked nights, he never visited the countryside.'

'Then where was he? Come on,' he said, his voice rising uncontrollably. 'Where is he, dammit? A secret is like a demon trapped in a wine bottle — the longer you keep him in there, the more havoc he'll cause when he escapes.'

Yet he did not need to be told. He remem-

544

bered the last few times he had seen Dali, how his slow grunts and hunched-up shoulders had deflected any questions, how the corners of his dark eyes had danced with fire. Jinyi had, however, slept too deeply during those brief visits to hear his eldest son pacing at night, tugging greasy clumps of hair from his scalp as he frantically listed and re-listed his troubles under his breath.

'He's dead. Pa, I'm so sorry we didn't tell you.'

Jinyi managed a nod, but his head had been sent spinning from him, an unhinged comet crashing through his senses. He felt it in his stomach, in his chest. He felt it in his shaking fingers.

'How?' he stuttered at last, his hands creeping up over his chest, hugging himself tight against the shock. And Manxin tried to tell him, the words slipping and spilling out in a tearful rush, with interruptions and sniffles from her sisters, until the four of them ended up flopped on the warm *kang* in a brittle hug of shared quiet, knowing each other's stinging pain.

Under a washed-out midnight sky, Hou Dali had tiptoed from the house. It was 4 September 1974, the last sweat of the drawn-out summer still hugging his clothes. He had been waiting all day for his sisters to fall asleep. It was by then months since he had last bothered to turn up at his factory job, checking the lining and then sewing buttons onto winter army coats, his quick, slapdash stitching barely concealing his contempt for the fat-bellied officers who would tug and gripe at his handiwork. Instead he had been kept at home by his sister, forced to drink bowl after bowl of stinking herbal medicines, brewed from roots and herbs by Manxin in the same pot they used to cook rice. It was better than venturing out alone and risking more of the same: being thrown into the local toilets, dragged up flights of stairs just to be pushed down them, stripped and tripped into the shallows of the river or forced to drink the piss of former Red Guards.

Every several paces down the deserted street he had stopped and looked about him, thinking he was being followed. The banners and torn posters left on some of the walls made his lips curl, while the hundred washing lines displaying identical blue jackets, a fluttering army of bodiless fanatics, left him dizzy, disorientated. His right leg moved faster than his left, the nerves and tendons frazzled by a hot iron from the factory. He had ducked into an alley between house rows when he spotted the night soil collectors making their rounds. A slice of clear sky loomed between the brick walls as he waited, panting, a spray of stars fizzling like the flick of a dragon's scaly tail.

How, he had wondered for the hundredth time, could his sisters bear it? Perhaps Hei, the leader of one of the gangs that had been tormenting him for the last eight years, had been right when he said that Manxin was more of a man than Dali was, and that they must have got mixed up at birth. 'That is what comes of being traitors, born to imperialist scum!' Hei had sneered. Even at school he had been picked on because he preferred sitting alone with his pictures of aeroplanes to lobbing a makeshift ball against a wall or scrabbling in the mucky field in a game of tag. No, he had corrected himself as he snuck down the alley, that was wrong — he hadn't thought himself above them; he would have given anything to play with them, but he was just too scared that the wrong words would come stuttering out of his mouth.

Worse than the torments though, were the times when they did nothing. The times he would walk down the winding streets to the factory and everyone would ignore him or turn the other way. Or the way his few friends disappeared in a shroud of silence, just as his parents had. Or the vague threats he would sit up for nights on end worrying about, which never materialised. Or even his sisters who, though well-meaning, nonetheless believed in the Party and the Red Guards as much as they did in their brother's 'madness'.

He crossed the road where he had last seen

his closest friend, before he was kicked and stomped into a mass of bloody coiled springs and broken filament because of the classical poems in his journal and the spectacles beneath his oily fringe. Better to always keep your mouth shut, Dali had told himself.

Across to the food hall where his mother and a thousand others had been denounced, attacked, branded or publicly executed, and down past the high school with its shards of toothy glass in broken windows and the distorted light of small fires keeping those inside warm. He had lumbered over a fence where the plots and communes on the out-skirts began, confident that any local guard dogs would have been stolen and stewed years ago.

If I can't get them back directly, then this is the next best thing, he had thought. He slid down a short bank and his bare feet scuffled onto gravel, his mind too much of a blur to really register the scrapes and stubs on his soles.

Dali had stopped suddenly, feeling the flat wooden tracks under his feet. He gripped one hand in the other to stop it from shaking. When the power of the state extended even to the schoolyard bullies and the woman next door watching you doing your washing, where could you turn? I should have seen it coming, he had told himself; we Chinese invented the kowtow, for heaven's sake: the most humiliating form of bow imaginable, sticking your nose in the dirt and your arse in the air to show how inferior you are. Some things never change. They can do anything they want to me, but at least I can still control this.

If they had only listened to him, Dali had found himself thinking once again, they might have been the best Red Guards in the country, they might have truly transformed China into a socialist paradise instead of this hole of liars and thugs. He felt sweat bristling on his chest, welling between his buttocks. To steel himself he thought of the bruises, the cuts, the blows, the kicks, the slaps, the burns, the pinches, the clouts, the thumps, the thwacks, the shoves, the throttles, the scars, the black eyes, the breaks, the fractures, the torn ligaments, the sears, the jabs, the scrapes and, most of all, of the words and sentences and slogans and names. This then was the law of cause and effect — this was the only action he still had control over.

Fuck all of them. He had held out his arms and rushed forward, whirring and giddy, imagining he was a child again, imagining he was an aeroplane. Hou Dali did not see his life flashing back before him — he had simply run forwards, his arms stretched out and his eyes closed, straight into the unstoppable rush of the coming train, the sudden thud and crush of the collision scattering the last of his thoughts across the gravelly tracks.

'Why didn't you tell me before?' Jinyi asked.

'How could we?' Manxin sniffed back a sob. 'You already had so much to worry about. Why wash your wounds with poison? We thought if we told you, you might never come home again. There are only so many things a man can hear.'

Jinyi nodded. All this time he had been thinking it was harder to be taken away than to be left behind. All this time the whole country had been fooling itself into believing in the impossible, and so had he.

'I'm so sorry,' he whispered.

He looked at the three pairs of leaky almond eyes, the prickles of red tendril creeping into the corner of each one as they looked to him for comfort, for reassurance, for something, for anything. Jinyi was filled with the same urge he had felt some twenty-five years before for the two lost boys — hold them close, never let them out of his sight again.

Yet this was not the lapping river of grief he had felt before, when the babies were taken. This was harder, more forceful: a dart of ice freezing his tongue, scalding the tips of his fingers like a thousand nettle stings, so that he wanted to tear his burning skin from his suddenly useless body.

'Girls,' he fought through the moans welling up in his throat, 'we are in the middle of a huge storm of fog and rain. It is still almost impossible to tell right from wrong, to tell love from hate. But at least we are together now — that is all that matters.'

'But it will get better, won't it, Pa?' Liqui asked. 'The Gang of Four has been arrested, the schools are going to reopen, and you and Ma will soon be back together again.'

Jinyi stared up at them, suddenly lucid. 'Look around you. Nobody knows what will happen next. Could anyone have predicted the last ten years, the last twenty? No. This could just be a respite, a brief lapse. Be careful — you watch what you say, who you speak to, who you trust. You work hard and do not criticise anything or anyone, not even the Gang of Four, until we see what happens. That is the only way to survive. Understand?'

The girls murmured their agreement, and Jinyi slipped back into the abstract depths of that numbing feeling. He waited for something to happen — for the door to suddenly swing open, for words to be spoken, for his heart to buckle under that unbearable weight — but nothing came. He heard only the girls' unleashed sobs and, mingling into them, the voice of a man outside with a loudspeaker, hawking the evening newspaper. The past does not end, does not disappear, he thought; it always finds a way to creep back in under the door and turn the air sour. Jinyi clutched the girls closer, three heads sinking into the hollow of his chest.

By the time he pulled himself from the futon the following morning, his elder daughters had left for their factories and Xiaojing was quietly stirring a breakfast of millet porridge at the stove. He battled with the ordinary actions of washing, dressing, eating, as if they were absurd stage directions of a surreal play in which he had been cast. Yet if the last decade had taught him anything, it was the necessary primacy of performance over truth, of actions over feelings. Grief still filled him, but it was now subsumed by another worry: what he would say to Yuying.

'Pa.' His youngest daughter was speaking. 'Perhaps we could go to the hill today. We put a mound of stones there for Dali, as there were no ashes. We could go together.'

'I'm afraid I'm too busy. I'm going to go down to the bread factory. They will want to know when I'm going to start work. I can't keep them waiting, it wouldn't be right.' Though behind his flimsy excuse, what he meant was clear. I cannot, not yet, I will not let him go.

'Of course. I only thought . . .'

He swallowed hard. 'Life has to come first. Think what people would say if they heard I was sitting here moping. Anyway, what do you usually do with your time?'

'I used to be in the Red Guard Youth Movement. These days I do some cooking and cleaning here, pick up your and mother's coupons from the bread factory, and haggle in the market. Oh, sometimes I go to the tin factory with Manxin, to watch and learn, but I try not to get in the way.'

'Do you often see your friends?'

'Friends? Well . . . I guess the vegetable woman at the market is pretty friendly . . . and so is Mrs Tien next door — sometimes if I'm cooking by the window I can hear the old stories she tells to her grandson. And of course I've got my sisters.'

'And now you've got me too,' Jinyi said, and Xiaojing nodded politely, unsure of how to respond to the strange things her father was saying.

He was not the same man of her memories — he was shorter, smaller, weaker, slower; his words were a jumble of hesitant syllables, showing neither the wisdom nor the paternal authority she had imagined as her mind had reworked her earliest memories. Neither did he seem to be the same man her sisters had told stories about: the man who could conjure luxury dishes from only scraps of leftovers, who could haul two children onto his shoulders and race them around the park like a wild animal escaped from a zoo, who would sing slurred songs about demons and dragons after a cupful of rice wine. Instead he was a pale, more shrivelled version of the man in the black-and-white photo on the shelf, a man with a halfhearted smile who did not know what to do with his hands.

Jinyi pulled himself up from the table with a sigh.

'You could come with me if you want,' he said, anxious to reach out to her.

Xiaojing gestured to the pots beside the stove. 'I should do some cleaning and make lunch.'

He nodded and stepped out of the door into the morning drizzle. The new factory boss told him that he could start back as soon as the national three-day holiday for the Spring Festival had finished. However, after appraising the haggard fifty-something man in front of him, the boss suggested a move from the ovens to the packaging production line. 'Far less sweat for a man of your maturity,' as he so delicately put it. Jinyi murmured his gratitude, though the job was little more than an anchor now, stopping him from floating into space.

A quick wander around his old work station and the canteen was enough to confirm that the handful of the workers who remained from ten years before were barely recognisable, and keen not to make eye contact. Not because they ratted him out — there was no shame in that, since everyone had had to shout loudly about others to drown out the chorus of charges against their own families

— but because some things do not change. All of them there still knew even the smallest details about each other's lives, from the number of teeth each man had left to the songs he hummed under his breath. I would rather have their contempt than their pity, he told himself as he trudged back home, taking the longest, most meandering path possible.

Yuying believed in atonement and rebirth, albeit framed in terms of class dialectics. Just as the winter wiped away the tallest and strongest of the previous year's crops to make a clean slate for the spring, so she had been learning to forget who she used to be. Yet as she crossed county after county, and she measured out the seeds and nuts she had saved up for the journey, Yuying was not sure she had ever been anything except what other people had told her to be. She closed her eyes and let the juddering rhythm of the carriage tug loose the threads of her thoughts. From the frosted-up window spilt empty fields, half-built cities fanning out from spluttering cooling towers, unnamed stations where trains never stopped, dottings of slanted red brick and bonfires, hovels and boarded-up restaurants with crumbling stone lions, and huddled grubby workmen preparing for the night shift with a shared jar of rank tea.

She thought of her children. She thought of her husband. And as she did so, she felt some of the joy that had once kept her going bubble back to the surface.

The train was a zoo gone wrong. There were snarling lemurs of old women furiously elbowing their way to seats and hulking bears of men in need of a shave, lumbering through the carriages and dumping their huge tied-cloth bundles on sleeping feet or hands. There were buck-toothed and hare-lipped ticket-clickers hopping between the bodies hunched on the floor, dodging the restless legs that dangled from the luggage racks, while jabbering monkeys perched on tables or squatted between bags, gibbering and spitting and throwing playing cards, sunflower seeds and cigarette stubs at everyone around them. And at every station, just when it seemed that the train was filled to overflowing, a hundred more feral dogs with foaming mouths came barking and pushing and shoving their way onboard, sniffing out a spare inch of mucky, cluttered floor space.

The smell of cheap tobacco and black soap mingled with curdled sweat and the festering stink of the single hole-in-the-floor toilet. Yuying tried to move her feet, to wrestle them free from a tangle of travelling bags, decaying snacks and blood-crusty tissues. The rocking carriage was clamorous and shrill, the different dialects tumbling over each other and vying for loudness. Yuying slouched down in her seat, and snippets of conversations crept into her half-sleep.

'They said they'd found a pig for New Year — well, the kids have never tasted pork, though of course most of it will be given to the Party to redistribute, but just a bit of dripping, a *jin* of lard, ooh, I can almost taste it —'

'Mao Zedong may die, but Mao Zedong Thought will live forever —'

'His wife wasn't a bad woman, she just wanted to give them a good meal, and to be fair that cat had had a good life —'

'A string of a thousand bobbing red lanterns strung between the village houses, blossoming into fire —'

'We walked all the way from Hengshui, which took us nearly a week you know, and when we got there and raised our little red books and saw him waving in the distance, well, I'm not ashamed to say that tears streamed down my face and they didn't stop for hours —'

Though the conversations meandered on towards morning, Yuying soon slipped into unconsciousness as province after province rushed past the window. When she awoke, nothing would be the same.

Jinyi was contemplating the holes in his winter socks when his wife poked her head nervously round the door. Though he wanted to leap up and hug her, he was unable to move — the woman in front of him seemed to have shrunk, knotted into a tangle of crow's feet and grey streaks. He put down the socks and asked their daughters if they would go to the market to pick up some onions. As they left, they each kissed their mother on the cheek, and already she knew that something terrible had happened. Her bag slumped in the doorway, where it would be left until her daughters unpacked and folded it away hours later when they returned.

Jinyi did not remember much of what he said. He stumbled through the phlegmy, coughed-up speech, rushing towards the end so that he could be free from the words stinging his throat.

'. . . they didn't tell me either, but they were just trying to look after us, to stop the world from crashing down around us.'

'I knew,' Yuying replied, her voice wavering like a taut *pipa* string being tuned up through the octaves. She had not moved from the doorway, as if to enter the house completely would mean admitting complicity with what had happened.

'You did?' Jinyi rose hesitantly. He was unsure whether to approach her — unsure whether she would still, after all these years, want him to — and unsure of what to do with his lumbering hands.

'I knew it from the day he was born, just like with Wawa. Both of them were such perfect babies, so fragile that I thought they might shatter if someone even let a fingertip graze them. Life isn't meant for perfect things. I knew it when we were told to put making steel above common sense; I knew it when we were told to starve patriotically because the noble peasants had been huddling around homemade furnaces instead of growing food in the fields; I knew it when the whole country began to rise up to cut down the past. I felt it in the pit of my stomach all this time; I just never knew what it was until now.'

Jinyi watched as his wife's head slumped down, her hair hanging loose around her neck, and she walked unsteadily towards the bedroom, waving away his arm, outstretched to steady her. Those were the last words she would speak for a year.

The winter wind pawed at the windows and sharpened its claws on the rickety door. Jinyi had expected tears, shouts, sobs, howls, things being thrown and broken. Accusations and pointed fingers would be better than this, he thought. The sudden silence had flooded the small room and was squeezing out the air. He did not dare try the handle on the bedroom door for fear that it would be bolted. Three days left to the Spring Festival, he muttered to himself; I'd better start preparing things. And so their first hour alone together in ten long years, their first real conversation in a decade, ended with Yuying perched on the wide *kang,* her round eyes staring at a ribbon of blood left from a swatted mosquito while her tired, wiry husband pummelled his calloused fists into a clump of dough.

Yuying sat as still as she could, wondering whether her body could hold everything inside it without bursting. After an hour, perhaps longer, she heard her husband singing to himself as he cooked. It was an old song, older than the both of them put together. For a moment she was tempted to give in to it, to put aside the receding hair lines, the sagging arms and bellies and breasts, the ear-hairs and pinched faces and wheat-husk teeth that showed how far they had hardened and faltered apart from each other, open the door and hold him to her. Yet still she did not move; life, she told herself, was not like that anymore. She still loved him. More than anything. But there was something in her that felt she was being punished for daring to love; something that told her that every time the two of them drew close, history or fate or whatever you want to call it conspired to pull them apart. The maps that once lined her heart had been redrawn, written over and scribbled on so many times that the original pathways had become illegible.

'Pa, how is she?' Manxin asked later, once the turquoise evening had settled on the streets and the girls thought it safe to return.

'I honestly don't know,' Jinyi replied, not looking up from the kitchen corner where he had walled himself in, surrounded by a fat heft of dough left to rise slowly in the wintery sun, pots of chilli oil he had spent the afternoon simmering down until it tasted of flames and the bowlful of thick dark sauce in which he planned to float a blubbery cut of tofu.

'But she's your wife,' Liqui ventured.

'I know,' Jinyi sighed. 'But it's been ten years. I don't know what else to say. Let's just give her some time to get used to the news, some time to accept it. If I know your mother, she'll come out soon and be ordering everybody around in no time.' He tried to smile, but it shrivelled on his face.

'Well, I'm not going to be the first to go in,' Xiaojing said defiantly, and her sisters looked at each other.

'We'll wait, like Pa said, and give her some time,' Manxin suggested, and they slumped on the futon.

The long wooden clock hanging on the wall belted out the hours with a shrill chime, the lazy pendulum juddering through the quiet. Rescued from Granny Dumpling's place, the creaking mechanism was older than its former owner and just as stubborn. Xiaojing took the key and wound it, the teeth gnashing and squawking in the slot, as if this might hurry time along. The girls had left their books, needlework and pens and paper in the bedroom, and none of them had the courage to go in and retrieve them. Instead they slouched and stared at the scroll of a pair of cranes, a gift from Yaba to replace the one the Red Guards had torn up. The two proud birds retained something of their slender grace, their curved beaks poised to dart down to the slight ripples spilling out around their sharp-line legs. The girls had found out long before, however, that no matter how long they stared or how much they wished, the cranes would not dance for them.

'I'm going to bed,' Liqui said as soon as the clock struck ten, her words dovetailing into a yawn. 'We've got a Party inspection at the factory at six tomorrow morning, so I can't be late.'

'Take this through to your Ma, then,' Jinyi said, still sitting in the kitchen, pointing to a bowl of gloopy stewed aubergine.

It was then they realised that, despite their father having spent the whole day laboriously preparing sauces and marinades, none of them had sat down to dinner. The girls exchanged glances, and decided not to point this out — anyway, it was not the first time they had gone to bed hungry.

'Aren't you coming to bed, Pa?'

'No, no, I've got a little more to do in here. If I get most of it done now, we can spend the whole Spring Festival as a family. I'll be a little while, so I think I'll just sleep in here tonight — I don't want to barge in and wake you all up later.'

And so he kept chopping, folding and marinating until tiredness subsumed his worry, his grief and his anger, and he covered the half-finished dishes with damp cloths and piled them on the windowsill. When the girls awoke the following day, the futon would already be folded up once more and their father gone to the market.

Yuying stayed lying on the *kang* long after her elder daughters had gone to work, leaving only creases in the undersheet. Her body hummed, sighed, creaked, not used to doing nothing. This was the first day she had not slept in her clothes for years — she eyed the two blue Mao jackets, distinguishable only by the armband sewn onto one, and the two pairs of slate grey trousers crumpled like shed skins beside the bed. She reached out and shoved them as far from herself as she could, as if to wear them would be to slip back into every mistake she had ever made. She waved away her youngest daughter's offer of company, and watched her slouch off, quiet and confused.

She would only sink in my misery, Yuying thought, justifying her actions to herself; she wants a perfect mother, one who could make the world right for her, not this rag-and-bone mass of wasted years and bad decisions. Perhaps I was never made to be a mother, or a wife. Perhaps it is my own fault. Yuying resisted the urge to reach for the ball of twine or to make the bed, any action whose effects might spill out into the world. Instead she stared at the cracked ceiling, wondering how a single word — a simple 'yes' or 'no', even a nod or a shrug — might rewrite history. Words and actions escape from you and take on a life of their own, she thought, their meaning shifting and changing until they have welled up into an unstoppable tornado.

Take the elderly street cleaner who suddenly began to hum a patriotic song as he swished his brush through the dust and puddles. The skinny woman working at the noodle booth on the corner turned suddenly, the song reminding her of her recently deceased husband, and in doing so she accidentally knocked over a jar of chilli oil. She mopped up the translucent red drool from the worktop, but some had already dribbled down into the bubbling pot of noodle broth. The late-for-work engineer, using up two more minutes he did not have, gulped down a boiling bowl of noodles without waiting for his tongue to run screaming to his brain, and then set off to the behind-schedule bridge being erected further up the river to more easily connect Fushun with the provincial capital. Halfway through the day, thanks to the excess chilli in his breakfast, his belly started squealing and squelching, and he was soon sprinting for the nearest bush, his trousers barely down between his ankles before the steaming torrent erupted from his burning behind. After he had exhausted the number of secluded spots in which he could let loose his rumbling bowels, he hobbled off to find the nearest public toilet. Hours later, the foreman, thinking the engineer had finished his tasks for the day, declared the bridge ready to open. The next morning, a rickety bus full of young men returning home from the fields for the holidays plunged into the strong currents of the river when one of the supporting legs of the bridge buckled under the weight — it had not been properly safety-checked on the previous day. A local tragedy, everyone agreed.

But why stop there? One of the drowned boys' fathers was a local Party official. He vented his grief by sending the Central Authority an angry letter, which he promised to also publish in the national newspapers (all run by the Party, of course), decrying the shoddiness of a revolution that could not even ensure the building of working bridges. In return, he was publicly criticised and sent to a humiliating outpost in the freezing grasslands of Inner Mongolia. The local state-owned logging commission had been waiting years for this same official to stop vetoing their plans, and promptly bribed his greedy replacement. Within a year, the forests surrounding the city had all been uprooted; the air was thick with smoke, asthmatic children came choking to the hospital every day and the birds and foxes, denied their usual nourishment, took to scavenging from the local fields and farms, leading to another famine. Trucks filled with grain were sent from the neighbouring county, but could not cross the broken bridge. Hundreds scrambled into the river to swim across to reach the food, but were swept away by the current. Thousands more died of hunger and malnutrition, and all because of the song an elderly street cleaner chose to hum one morning.

And still I could go on. But let us return to Yuying, sinking into exhaustion. Even her imagination was turning everything sour. She spent the day sifting through her own life, half sleeping, half rummaging through her restless grief, searching for deeper roots to better explain how everything had gone wrong.

By the time she rose to find a few rice crackers to fill her stomach, Jinyi was back and pasting couplets on the front door. She listened as her daughters arrived and hovered around him while he glued the two strips of red paper over the flaking paint, angling them to cover some of the scrapes and scratches in the door.

'Pa, where did you find those?' Manxin asked. 'Didn't we throw ours out years ago?'

'Of course. These are brand new. I think. I came across them on the way home.'

'You didn't steal them, did you Pa?' Liqui asked cautiously, her knuckles raised nervously to her lips in expectance of a confirmation of her fears.

'No!' Jinyi frowned, then laughed. 'You really don't remember who I am at all, do you? Your old dad wouldn't do anything like that.'

'But Granny Dumpling told us about how one time —'

'Oh. Hmm. Yes, well, that was when everyone was starving, and the Japanese were eating for free everywhere. So in a way, by stealing food, I was making sure the Japanese soldiers had less. I was just doing my best to help end the occupation.'

'Yeah, sure,' Xiaojing snorted.

Jinyi finished and stepped back to admire his handiwork. The two strips were not quite parallel, and the gold lettering was already beginning to peel. Jinyi was too embarrassed to tell his daughters that when confronted with the piles of couplets, he had picked the first pair he saw, unable to connect the swirling characters that his wife had once taught him with the words in his mouth. He had been forced to ask the stallholder to read the couplet to him, blaming a quickly fabricated short-sightedness. Just a little out of practice, that's all, he told himself.

'Anyway, I didn't steal them; I got them from a stall outside the market, in exchange for just a single food coupon. Don't look at me like that — we've got enough inside for a feast. And don't tell me you lot wouldn't trade an apple for a whole year of good luck.'

'So we're going to celebrate?' Liqui asked.

'Of course. I've invited Yaba over, too. It'll be nice. All the family back together again. I mean, uh, well . . .' He realised his slip, and so did the girls. They stood in awkward silence.

Then Jinyi remembered the cartoon of twin red fish folded on the ground. He waved them up in the cold air before pasting them between the vertical lines of fluttering characters.

'Now, Xiaojing,' Jinyi said as he patted them on. 'We put pictures of fish on our door at Spring Festival for good luck. The word "fish", you see, sounds very similar to the word "leftover". Now, I guess most of the gods are hard of hearing, because if you have fish on your door then they'll make sure you have enough in the coming year. Enough food, enough money, enough clothes — so much, in fact, that you'll have some left over.'

'Pa. I know all of this. I may not have gone

to school yet, but I'm not stupid,' Xiaojing replied, and Jinyi suddenly remembered being thirteen himself.

'Yes, I'm sorry. It's hard for me to know what you've learnt, what you remember. I've been away for so long . . .' He fumbled with the words, and picked dirt from his fingernails. 'If you ever need my help . . .'

'We know,' Liqui said quickly, seeing the look on his face. 'So why are there two fish?' she asked, the only way she could think of to show her love.

'Erm. I'm not sure. I suppose because everything works better together than alone. People, Mandarin ducks, even fish.' Jinyi looked up, and caught his wife's eye at the window before she turned back toward the bedroom. 'Let's go inside, it's getting cold.'

While the girls were sharing tidbits of gossip at the kitchen table, passing bundles of thread and wool between them, Jinyi knocked as lightly as he could on the bedroom door.

'Yuying?' he whispered into the grain. 'Can I come in?' The question struck him as ridiculous. It was his bedroom. No, it was their bedroom. No, it was loaned to them by the state, with was led by the people — 'Why am I tying myself in knots?' he muttered to himself.

'Yuying, when we lost the boys . . .' Stupid euphemism, he thought; no one ever got lost: we knew exactly where they were. 'We survived. Together. Do you remember you once told me I was the worm in your stomach? You meant I could guess what you wanted, what you would say, even before you could yourself.'

He glanced over his shoulder to check that the girls were still giggling and talking, before pressing his face closer to the door. 'Well, I don't know what to do now, and I need your help. Yuying. I love you. I always have.' It was the first time he had said it.

The door, however, said nothing in reply, and Jinyi eventually retreated to the lumpy nudges of the futon. The cold was so thick that night that he felt he was swimming in it, twisting and fidgeting his way through the drawn-out hours till sunrise.

Spring Festival has always been my busiest time of year. As the moon hollows out at the end of the lunar year, it is time to take stock. The Jade Emperor studies a family's behaviour over the previous twelve months and assigns the next year's fortune to them accordingly. Call it karma, or divine justice, if you like. Yet in a country with a population of over one billion, people are not so arrogant as to assume that the Jade Emperor personally looks over their every dull action. They realise that he has far better things to do. Thus the job of giving a brief account of each family falls to yours truly, the Kitchen God.

Who better? After all, the kitchen is where most of the juiciest gossip, the most clandestine of whispers and the bitterest arguments can be heard. Perhaps this is why most families try to bribe me — during Spring Festival, I find sugary snacks, glutinous red-bean dumplings, homemade candy and twirls of toffee all set on my altar to ensure that my mouth is full of sweet tastes when I open it to give my report to the Jade Emperor. Well, what did you expect? This is China, a place where a bribe, a reference to a well-known uncle, a carefully chosen gift or secret handshake can get you anything. People get the gods they deserve.

Yaba arrived just before midday, lumbering in without knocking, nodding his big bald head at Jinyi and the three girls milling around the main room, before sloshing a large jar of rice wine down on the table.

Jinyi grinned. 'Where did that come from?'

Yaba simply opened his palms, as if to say that perhaps his inability to speak was not such a bad thing in the face of certain questions.

The two men — one shrunk and slightly withered, the other plumper, slower, bald — saw straight through the masks of wrinkles and scars to the younger, more familiar faces hidden beneath and fell quickly into a familiarity of old jokes and sign language. Neither felt the need to mention all the things that had happened since they had last met, and Yaba was soon lighting two cigarettes in his dry, yellow mouth, one of which he passed to his old friend.

As the three girls gathered at the table, Jinyi handed them each a small red packet. Inside was a single crumpled banknote, not enough to buy more than a couple of carrots. Only Xiaojing did not manage the obligatory smile; she was too busy studying the watermark and trying to fathom what she might do with this inky scrap of starchy paper.

'Manxin, do you want to get your mother, and then we can eat?' Jinyi asked sheepishly. His eldest daughter carefully pushed her hair back from her round face, and took a deep breath before slipping through the bedroom door, pushing it closed behind her. The distorted echoes of Manxin's pleading whispers could be heard in the main room, and Yaba scratched his chin as the rest of the family tried, and failed, to blot them out with small talk.

The table wobbled each time a new dish was piled on; the soggy dumplings, orange lotus, marinated chicken feet, steaming tofu and shredded twists of pork in a neon sauce surrounded the freshwater fish, one eye staring up at the poised chopsticks as its splintered flesh sank in a brown sizzle. Jinyi was determined to enjoy this reunion dinner, though he found his appetite ebbing away with the sheer exertion of pretending to be happy. He was about to exhort Yaba to begin when he remembered something and stumbled up to throw open the window, before searching for something to prop the front door open with. How else would they let the New Year's good luck in? Heaven knows we need it, he thought. He settled on the unscrubbed wok as a doorstop. If it were possible to sweep the last years out along with the dead skin and shoe grime and matted cobwebs, he wondered, how far back would I go?

Manxin emerged with Yuying, who slowly lowered herself into a chair. Her eyes were dream-battered moths, fighting to stay in flight. To everyone except Yaba, who still saw her as if she was a podgy little girl skipping in his footsteps, she looked unusually pale, her whiny breathing unnaturally loud, as if making up for her lack of words. Jinyi poured thimbles of liquor for himself and Yaba and they sank the first toast.

'Everything that happens today will happen for the rest of the year, that's what our ancestors believed,' Jinyi said, the sharp aftertaste scalding his tongue as he topped up the thimbles. 'To be close to my family — that is all I want for the rest of the year. Please, eat.'

'Thanks Pa, it's wonderful food. Much better than Manxin's!' Liqui said, and her elder sister playfully thumped her shoulder.

Jinyi raised his thimble, but everyone had suddenly stopped eating. They lowered their chopsticks and turned to seek the source of the metronomic pinging. It did not take long: Yuying was tapping a long fingernail against her teacup. She looked up at her husband, a sad but assertive gaze, her pupils adrift in a nexus of bloodshot circuitry.

'Er, well, of course, yes, I'm sorry.'

He leaned over and trickled a measure of rice wine into his wife's cup.

'Ma, perhaps you —' Manxin began, but as she spoke her mother picked up the teacup and knocked back the contents. Yuying rattled it back on the table, her eyes watering.

'People might *talk*,' Liqui whispered across to her mother, picking up where her sister left off. The only women seen in public smoking or drinking were usually either prostitutes or those disgraced beyond hope of rehabilitation.

'Let your mother be,' Jinyi said. 'Men and women are supposed to be equal now, aren't they? If she wants a sip, she can have one.'

'But if she drinks today, she might be hungover for the rest of the year,' Xiaojing said.

'Girls, when I was young there were old men on every corner quoting Confucian epigrams at you. Now Confucius has been banned as a corrupting influence, quite rightly of course, but that does not mean you should not still respect your elders. Your Ma can make her own choices, and you can make your own.'

'Yes, Pa,' they muttered.

Yaba clapped his hands and then raised his fingers to click his chopsticks together, and the rest of them followed his directive to stuff themselves full of food. Yet it was not long before the pinging started again. Jinyi shrugged and pushed the bottle across, allowing his wife to glug out a few fingers of liquor, which she promptly downed.

The conversation soon turned to the new tower blocks being built beside the station, how far five yuan might now stretch, the wastelands of untended weeds and bracken being bought up by newly registered companies on the outskirts of town, who had married whom and how many children they now had and, at the girls' insistence, the long dresses suddenly appearing in the windows of some of the small stores near the river. The two youngest girls teased Manxin about the man from the engine workshops that she had recently been introduced to, asking her questions about when she would next meet him and what he looked like. She soon turned bright red and Jinyi had to tell them to stop. They chattered until the dishes had dwindled to scraps and bones, and midnight arrived with a crackling burst of fireworks spitting light into the icy sky.

Hours later, squirming on the futon through the haze of tipsy sleep, Jinyi was awoken by the sound of a cawing bird. No, he thought, that cannot be right. He turned over and closed his eyes before hearing it again. A stray cat howling for a mate outside the front door? No. His ears tuned in — a noisy retching and the splatter of vomit. He heard heavy breathing, then another croaky rasp and the hissing sound of someone trying to spit out all the tastes in their mouth.

He opened the door carefully, in case it was a trick. Instead he found his wife, hunched forward on the step and vomiting into the street. He asked nothing, but reached out and gently took hold of her long hair, holding it back for her as she leaned forward once again over the step.

In February, after three weeks of Yuying's silence, Jinyi and his daughters had reached breaking point. Jinyi shouted until he felt as though he had swallowed a desert, while the girls pleaded tearfully; but none of them could make Yuying speak. Furthermore, she often refused to leave the house. As the month ground to a close, one of the new bosses from the bread factory accompanied Jinyi home. The boss, who urged people to call him Mr Peng, was so tall that he had to stoop to fit through their door, and gave the impression of having been zipped into a badly fitting body. Mr Peng stood next to the kitchen table where Yuying was sitting, and pushed his new glasses up his long nose.

'Now, Bian Yuying. My predecessor . . .' he shuffled the papers on his clipboard and fiddled with his glasses again, '. . . Mr Wang, mentioned you in a couple of his reports. Let me see. Ah, yes: "An exemplary worker, showing patriotic spirit and socialist zeal." Quite a glowing recommendation, don't you think?'

Yuying looked down at her feet.

'Don't worry,' he blustered on, 'I haven't come here to embarrass you. But we could certainly use your experience back at the factory. What do you say?'

Yuying continued to look at her feet.

'Well, I won't pressure you. Have a think about it, and when you feel better, you know where to find me.' He turned abruptly. 'Hou Jinyi, I'll see you in the morning.'

'Yes, sir. Thank you for your time, sir,' Jinyi said as Mr Peng strode away as fast as his long legs would carry him.

Jinyi made his way to the stove, slipping into a familiar routine of cooking and then cleaning. He did not mind the extra work — it gave him less time to dwell on the past or to worry about his wife. He tried to guess what she might want, what she might say if she were to choose to speak again. In this way, he created imaginary conversations, which blurred and became entwined with his daughters' voices. He pushed the gnawing sting of grief down into the deep pit of his stomach, where it knotted his intestines and needled his sides.

In April a doctor was sent by the factory to check whether Yuying was simply trying to avoid returning to work — 'which would, I'm afraid, need to be reported to the authorities,' the young doctor took Jinyi aside to say. 'Imagine what would happen if everyone decided just to stop talking, to stop working. The whole country would be in chaos. No, it wouldn't do, I'm afraid, uncle.'

The doctor's hand-me-down white coat trailed close to his feet, and its sleeves hung loosely from his shoulders. He checked Yuying's tongue and tonsils, then shone a light into her ears. He spent a long time looking suspiciously into her eyes and talking to her as though she was a badly behaved child, despite the fact that she must have been around twenty years his senior. Finally he recorded her heartbeat, temperature and blood pressure.

'Now, Mrs Bian, have you been having any, er, well, have you been feeling hot at all lately? Not, not the weather, I mean, erm . . .' The doctor lowered his voice to a whisper, '. . . *hot flushes?*'

Yuying stared him down, raising her eyebrows to show the contempt in which she held him, and then shook her head.

'No, ah, well, fine . . . fine.' He flustered with his briefcase and beckoned to Jinyi to meet him outside.

'Women's things,' the doctor said, and tapped his nose conspiratorially. 'Though she may simply be faking it.'

Jinyi cleared his throat and glanced down at the basket of fruit on the doorstep, inside which was clearly nestled a large bottle of rice wine. He pushed the box towards the young doctor with his foot, and cleared his throat again. 'Just a little gift to thank you for your help. So, umm, what are you going to write in your report?'

'Oh, emotional breakdown brought on by family tragedy, menopausal depression and so on. The factory won't be expecting her back any time soon.' The doctor picked up the fruit basket. 'Make sure she gets lots of rest and drinks plenty of water.'

When he had finally convinced himself that no one would notice, Jinyi began to wear his son's old vest beneath his work shirt, savouring the slightly sour smell, the closeness. When he chattered and joked and hummed as if nothing was wrong, it was not because he was not angry and exhausted, but because he felt he had to provide a balance, a warm and noisy yin to counter the silence and stares of Yuying's yang. If her silence was a protest, his good humour was an act. And, with all acts, if you keep it up long enough you begin to believe it yourself. Only when you slip into someone else's mind, as I have, does it become clear that the best actors are the ones who fool themselves.

In May, Liqui returned home early after work with a short man with tiny paper-cuts for eyes and tufts of grey hair. He was carrying a small wooden box. Her father was out with Manxin, chaperoning her for a meeting with the suitor from the engine workshop. Yuying was therefore sitting alone in the bedroom, arranging a handful of drooping daisies in a pen pot. Liqui led the short man in.

'Mother, this is Doctor Ma — do you remember, Granny Dumpling used to speak about him? He's come to help.'

Doctor Ma bowed and turned to Liqui. 'If we could spend a little time alone . . .' he drawled, and Liqui obliged, closing the door behind her.

'Now, the body has nine pressure points which reveal their pulses, just like our own sun, drawing nine planets into orbit. From their irregularities we may identify the source of any problem.' He held her wrist tight, counting. 'However, some problems may not be problems at all — the body is a master of tricks and disguises. I want you to concentrate on that stain on the wall for me. Can you do that?'

He turned around and fiddled with the small wooden box. Then with a sudden shriek he spun around and threw the open box at Yuying. Out leapt a wrinkled toad, which landed on Yuying's chest. Its spindly legs whirred at her stomach before it slipped down to her lap, emitting a burpy croak before throwing itself to the floor. Doctor Ma ran after it, and eventually succeeded in trapping it under the open box. He slid the lid underneath and scooped it up.

'Ah, well, I see that my surprise didn't quite work. Never mind.' He scratched his chin. 'Let's stick with the toad though. Perhaps if I coaxed it, it might give you a voice of its own to speak with, though that may cost a little extra. No? All right, all right. I see. You could of course buy the toad off me, for a much reduced price, I might add, and I would be happy to give you a secret recipe for cooking it — that would be sure to revive your spirits. No? Really? Hmm, well . . .'

The door opened and Liqui poked her head round, her plait swishing in with her.

'Is everything all right, doctor? Only I heard a clatter and —'

'Yes, yes, everything is fine. Just a little experiment. Ah, I see the sun has set. I must be going, I'm afraid — another appointment, you know how it is.' The doctor lurched

581

through the door, clutching the boxed toad tight against his chest.

'Sorry, Ma. I was just trying to help,' Liqui said. Her mother did not reply.

Before long, the days had melted into the sticky mess of summer. As much as he loved his daughters, and as much as he wanted to talk to his wife and convince her that everything was going to get better, Jinyi voluntarily took on extra hours at the factory, sweating away his time knotting plastic casing around the warm loaves. The futon was pressed back into shape and their father gone by the time the girls rose for breakfast each morning, and, on the many nights he played cards with Yaba and an assortment of factory and restaurant men on cramped dumpling-shop tables, Jinyi did not return until they were all asleep.

It wasn't that Yuying didn't try. Believe me, I was watching while everyone else was out; she would stand in front of the mirror and try and form her mouth into the correct shapes. It never looked right. So she closed her eyes and tried to force the words up from her throat. A hum, a gurgle, anything. But her tongue was barren, her mouth cracked earth.

And it wasn't that she didn't love them. On the contrary, in fact. She loved them too much. She believed she had found the demon

582

that had been following them all those years, the demon that stole their children and cut away at their happiness, the demon that had become an expert at biding its time and waiting till everything seemed perfect before tearing them apart once more. And because she loved each one of them so much, she could not bring herself to look any of them in the face and tell them what she had made herself believe — it was all her fault. She was the demon.

'Hou Jinyi?' There was a fat man in a freshly pressed uniform knocking at the door, mopping his brow with a fancy handkerchief.

Manxin opened the front door and felt the stuffy evening air rush in past her. 'He's not back from work yet, I'm afraid. But his wife and daughters are here.'

'Quite,' the fat man said as he entered the main room, forcing Manxin to stand aside. 'However, it seems that Bian Yuying will be little help if she insists on staying silent. You must be Hou Manxin.'

'Yes, that's me.' Manxin followed as the man sat himself at the kitchen table and peered over the laid-out dinner dishes. Manxin signalled to her sisters, who got up from the futon and retreated to the bedroom. The fat man eventually pawed a chicken leg and began to tear off strips of the moist flesh with his teeth, gulping them down noisily, barely chewing.

'My name is Ru Tai, assistant to the deputy magistrate of the South Fushun People's Security Bureau. Perhaps you would care to enlighten me, young lady, as to what your mother is up to. I'm sure that both of us would be very unhappy if it turned out that any anti-revolutionary activity was being engaged in on the patch that I am responsible for. Hopefully, we can sort this out ourselves. So, let me see.'

He pulled out a black leather notebook and thumbed through the pages with a greasy finger. 'Your neighbours have reported that your mother has not spoken since she returned. What have you got to say about that?'

'It's not that simple, sir. She's been unwell — a doctor from the factory where she works told us that she needs more rest.'

'Yes, I have read his report. But you do not deny that she no longer speaks?'

'No, that's true, sir.' Manxin hung her head.

'I see,' he said, helping himself to another chicken leg. 'And why do you think that is? Remember, your answer will be kept between the two of us.'

'I think she's just sad, sir. Since my brother died she —'

'Yes, yes, yes,' he said, suddenly annoyed. 'I can see that you really don't have a clue. Well, I better talk to the woman herself. Go and fetch your mother.'

Manxin did as he ordered, and re-emerged from the bedroom with Yuying. She was wearing a long dressing gown, her bunned hair pierced through with a single chopstick. The two women stood in front of the seated official.

'I shan't patronise you by asking you to answer my questions verbally,' he said, 'but I would ask you to be cooperative. It would be a shame if I had to make a report about this household, what with your daughters' precarious positions at their workplaces. So please oblige me by knocking once on the table for "yes", and twice for "no". Do you understand?'

Yuying rapped the table a single time.

'I will keep this simple. Bian Yuying, is your silence some kind of protest?'

Two knocks.

'Do you know of anyone else involved in the same activity?'

Two knocks.

'Are you an enemy of the government, a member of an illegal organisation or a capitalist-sympathiser?'

Two knocks.

'Do you blame the Party for your own petty problems and mistakes?'

A pause. Then two knocks.

'Do you intend to resume speaking in the future?'

Yuying did not answer. She and the official

stared at each other, both trying to pin intentions on the other's gaze. Finally she shrugged; how could she predict the future? The official pushed his wobbling body up from the table, wiping his fingers on his uniform.

'I'll tell you what I think. I think either you're a mad old woman, or else you're a seditious troublemaker. I'll be checking up on you — if I hear of anything else happening on this street, the police will on their way, and let me assure you, they are much less easily convinced to be lenient than myself. Goodnight.' He lumbered to the door before stopping and turning to them. 'Some people might tell you that countries are built by wars, struggles, noble actions. Perhaps they may even be right. But states, Bian Yuying, great nations, they are built on words. Do not doubt though, that these words can be rewritten. I suggest you think about that.'

After the official had waddled into the clammy evening, the two youngest girls filed out of the bedroom and hugged their mother. For the first time in months, she hugged them back; and even her eldest daughter, who stood a couple of inches taller than her, nuzzled down into the warmth of the dressing gown. When Jinyi returned from an after-work mahjong sessions with a few new colleagues who knew nothing of his past, he found the four of them asleep on the futon, heads on shoulders on knees on backs, a mound of light snores. He relished the noise, resting his face on his elbows at the table; it reminded him of the night music from the early days of his marriage, when he would lie beside his young bride and listen to her murmur in her sleep, not knowing whether or not to risk placing his hand over hers.

Autumn cantered in, curling the frazzled leaves, and the butterflies slowly evaporated. One night autumn rain dressed the city in hazy mauve, and water dribbled through a bad join in the warped roof, sprinkling down onto Jinyi's grey hair. He wrenched himself off the futon, only to find that the bedsheet around his ankles was also moist. He sighed and tiptoed into the bedroom. The girls were lined up one by one along the *kang,* so, not wanting to wake them, he slipped into the wooden bed alongside his sleeping wife. If she noticed him, then she did not show it. He fell asleep awkwardly rigid, and woke with his arm around her.

In the weeks that followed, Jinyi pressed this imagined advantage, as if planning military manoeuvres to end a protracted siege. He began to come home earlier to talk calmly to Yuying — about his day, about the local gossip, about his meandering thoughts and theories and, when he felt particularly bold, about the past — while their daughters took turns cooking and washing.

He started to bring home new clothes for her to wear, to brush and weave her hair just as he had done for their daughters when they were young, and as he did all this he felt like he was somehow tying them back together, binding a net to keep them safe from all the things that had once kept them apart. However much he wanted to, though, Jinyi was careful to never ask her to speak — he did not want to upset the precarious balance they had established. Her silence was like a stray dog that had wandered into the house, one that they had slowly come to accept as part of the scenery.

Xiaojing soon turned fourteen and came home from school accompanied by a heavy-set man with a closely cut black beard.

'This is Weiwei's father. He insisted on walking me home,' she sighed, and dropped her rucksack on the floor before skulking off outside.

'My pleasure.' He beamed at her, not picking up on the teenager's irony. 'My daughter, Weiwei, is your daughter's classmate. She let it slip — you know how girls love to chatter — about your ailment, Comrade Bian. I must say, it intrigued me. Perhaps I can be of some assistance.' Yuying stood up from the table and looked him over. 'You see, I am a dream-reader. Not full-time, of course. I also work in the ticket office at the station, but the study of dreams is my true vocation. Furthermore, I can communicate with spirits. Therefore, I lay my services at your command — please, do not think of offering me money, for those of us with gifts must use them for the good of the people. Oh yes, just because we are aware of the spirit world around us, it does not mean that we are not patriotic citizens in the earthly world. In fact, you might be surprised at how closely entwined these two worlds are. Anyway, I digress — though I must insist that we keep this meeting between ourselves, I am afraid.'

Yuying looked at her daughters, and as she did so the bearded man slipped through the open door into the bedroom. The three women quickly followed him and found him holding a photograph of the family taken during the May Holiday in 1970, his eyes scrunched closed.

'Ahh! Your son. He is calling, calling out to you. Yes, yes, speak, speak to me. He is holding an old woman's hand — his grandmother? — and she is leading him across a river of stars. Oh, it is so beautiful there, he says. He wants to tell you he is safe now, he — aaaahh!'

He screamed as Yuying tipped the bedroom chamber pot over his head. Lukewarm, bubbly urine sloshed through his hair and trickled down over his beard to darken his jacket. He spluttered and coughed, rubbed his eyes and pushed his soaked hair back from his brow, before shaking himself like a dog emerging from a river.

'Plygh! Plygh!' He spat. 'You . . . you . . . demon! May a horde of ghosts swell up your throat until you can only croak the words of death!' he shrieked as he stormed out of the house. Yuying closed the door behind him, and her daughters giggled.

It was only a few days later that Manxin arrived home from the factory, shook the rustle of crunched-up leaves from her coat and asked the whole family to sit at the table. Her moon-shaped face was lit with the wisps of a smile which she was trying to force down into a more refined expression. They all knew what she would say before she even opened her mouth — she had been meeting with the young man from the engine workshop once a month since spring, and Jinyi had even had dinner with his parents.

'Xue Jingtien and I are getting married!' she announced.

In the noisy gabble of overlapping squawks and squeals that followed — as Jinyi tried to start a passionate speech about how proud he was, as Xiaojing and Liqui shouted and laughed and teased, and Manxin gushed at the possible plans — no one heard Yuying hoarsely whispering, 'Congratulations.'

There are a number of different theories about how the world began. Some say that it came from Pan Gu, a man who emerged from the primeval chaos. Back when there was only nothingness surrounded by more nothingness, an egg formed, and in it grew Pan Gu. After thousands of years, he burst forth from the shell, and with him emerged the sky and the earth, the heavy matter sinking to his feet and the light matter rising up around his head. Some thousands of years later, he died. His eyes became the sun and the moon, his hair split and sparked up stars; his blood became rivers, his skin fields; his last words became the clouds, borne along by the winds of his last breath. From the fleas that had fed on his giant body, humans slowly evolved.

Some insist that the goddess Nuwa patted a handful of dark matter into a ball and called it earth; from the wet clay that bubbled up there she moulded men and women to populate her creation. I have also heard talk of a large explosion, which may have some measure of truth, since the gods have always enjoyed fireworks displays — the louder and more dangerous the better. Other people even talk of the world being put together in a single week, as if by builders on a tight deadline. Who said that those foreign barbarians have no sense of humour?

But it seems to me that the oldest stories are closest when they assert that there can have been no beginning, just as there will be no end. Everything is perception, even time: yesterday is only a story, a memory; the future is as yet only a collection of hopes or fears. Neither is real. Only the present moment exists. We must remember to be more careful with it.

11:
1981
THE YEAR OF THE ROOSTER

'Between here and there we must travel back a hundred years. See that old woman in the park, walking backwards? Some people think they can do it that way. They don't know the secret path we know though, do they Lian?' Jinyi said and winked.

The little girl nibbled on the deep-fried dough stick left over from breakfast and nodded. Jinyi grinned at his granddaughter, eager to display a confidence he did not feel. It was only two weeks earlier that he had found himself meandering about the park, suddenly unsure of why he was there. He had been forced to ask a stranger to help him get home, and the loss of face still upset him. But what was worse was the niggling suspicion that fate was once again snapping at his heels. He was together with his wife again and, now that they had been asked to take early retirement to make way for younger workers at the factory, now that their children had left home and their troubles slipped further into the past, they had discovered each other anew. Yet something told him that life wouldn't let him get away with happiness for long.

'Can we go back for lunch?' Lian's head was a scrag of black hair, her face as round and dimpled as a mooncake.

'Of course. Keep hold of my hand now, come on — you can't travel back in time on your own. And don't forget your grandma,' Jinyi replied, looking up at Yuying, who was a few steps behind, holding an umbrella up over their heads to stave off the late spring sun.

'What kind of nonsense is your grandpa filling your head with now, hmm?' Yuying said as she caught up. 'Yesterday he was telling you about a dog in space. What was it today? She's only three, Hou Jinyi.'

'I'm three and a half!' the little girl huffed.

'Quite right,' Jinyi chuckled. 'And there was something else, wasn't there?'

'An ape?' his wife said. She was growing used to Jinyi's words slipping into thin air. They got misplaced, along with his keys, his glasses, his chopsticks and his thoughts. Yuying had to continually poke and prod him to keep him from floating away from the present.

'Yes, yes, that's it. There was an ape in space, walking on the moon. I heard about it on the radio. They do crazy things in some of those foreign countries, let me tell you.

Anyway, I only told her we were travelling back in time, and that's the truth — just look around you.'

He was right. Their neighbourhood may have been thrust into 1981 — a few paces from their house a large new market shop had taken over the cobbler's stall, the hat shop and the long-vacated calligraphy supplies store — yet as they headed down the streets to the outskirts they found themselves retreating through the decades. The further they went, the more the new shop-fronts faded into tin roofs and shanty shacks, and the few private cars morphed into rust-crippled bicycles with ear-piercingly shrill bells. A man with a loudspeaker was sweating in the morning heat, trying to sell his stack of newspapers before the cheap print pooled into an inky smudge. Yuying fought to stop herself clutching her ears in protest. She lately found herself worrying that the smallest noises might announce the most terrible portents.

The three of them stopped at a crumbling brick shell of a building, in which an oven was panting steam over round baskets. Students were sitting on plastic chairs and feasting on cheap sloppy dumplings. They bought a small, sticky red-bean bun for Lian. A chunky radio, plugged into an uncovered socket and surrounded by a mangle of frayed wires, blared out a tune Jinyi found difficult to follow.

'What is this rubbish?' he grinned at the middle-aged woman as he handed over the coins for the snack.

'Search me.' She dipped her head toward the students. 'They tuned it, and now I can't make it play anything except this foreign crap. It sounds like just before feeding-time at the zoo, if you ask me.'

'What are they singing about?' Lian asked to distract her grandfather as she tried to subtly sneak the sweet treat from the open bag swinging against her grandmother's hip.

'I'm not sure. It sounded as though they were singing in American,' Jinyi replied.

'They speak English in America,' Yuying gently corrected him.

Ever since she decided to speak again, she had made an effort to speak only of the positive. It was not easy. She measured each word before she opened her mouth, imagining how it might ripple out away from her. There was enough bad news in the world, she had decided, enough blame and recrimination — and if we cannot alter the past then we must do our best to steer the present away from trouble. Time is a master strategist who might outwit you at any second; don't give him any opportunity to turn everything upside-down, she thought. Silence was futile — the only thing you cannot escape is yourself. What's more, this new decade, already bringing a wedding and another birth, had knitted her more firmly to the future she had once dared to imagine for her family, a future that had once seemed impossible. Each new year washed away more of the older scribbles in the sand.

'Quite right, of course. English. I was never one for languages, Lian, not like your grandmother here. If you work hard, you can be just like her.' Jinyi winked, and the little girl scrunched her nose. Why would she want to be old and wrinkled and smell like jasmine?

'In England, you know,' he continued, 'the people look like sea lions. The men all have moustaches which they keep straight with candle wax, and they wear top hats all day long, even when they go to bed. Don't look at me that way, Yuying. I saw something about it on that funny box at Yaba's flat. What do you call it?'

'A television, dear.'

'Can we get a television?' Lian asked, suddenly interested.

'One day, when you're a little older, I am sure you will have a big television in your house. A colour one too, I'm sure, not a tiny black-and-white one like Yaba's.'

The little girl was not impressed with this answer. However, they were almost there — ahead of them the road trickled out into a tractor-ripped mud track, and the barbed-wire fences of the private farm rippling up

597

over the green hill came into view. When they arrived, they would split up; Jinyi spent the mornings hunched in the smoky canteen, helping to prepare the workers' hot lunch, while Yuying strung out notepads of numbers as one of the accountant's assistants. They worked only mornings, home in time for the lunchtime nap, having retired from the bread factory in order to pass on their jobs to their two youngest daughters, who had been forced out of their old workplaces by more senior workers returning from countryside exile. State-controlled jobs were hereditary, and there were not nearly enough of them to go around, although it was better to say that as quietly as possible, and only when you were sure no one important was listening.

Jinyi looked down at his granddaughter, who was already eyeing up the brook that sliced down between the potato patches and the fruit vines. There might be a few more grandchildren to come, he reasoned, but nothing like the rowdy orchestra of relatives he had once looked forward to. One family, one child, that was the rule, though Jinyi could still remember when the government was telling everyone to have more children, to fuel the revolution in its early days. Best not to dwell on that either, he told himself, his inbuilt censor snapping into action.

An abandoned tractor was chugging at the entrance to the farm, the engine still on and pulsing hungrily against the handbrake. A middle-aged man, lazing on a rusty deckchair with his wooden leg stretched out in front of the main gate, signed them in.

'Watch out, it'll rain soon,' he said as he waved them through. This was the only thing he ever said, and he said it, without fail, every morning.

'Stay where I can see you, ok? You can go and paddle in the stream, but don't disturb anyone. When you get tired, come back to the kitchen and I'll make you something to eat,' Jinyi said to Lian, who nodded over-sincerely, the fast movement of her head threatening to bowl over her small body.

Jinyi entered the kitchen and pulled on an apron, then settled at the work station under the window, where he could watch his grand-daughter tug up the wild flowers and collect the stones that glinted at her from the onyx-streaked stream tumbling around her knees. Sly silver minnows darted past, tickling her ankles, and she bent and splashed, her pudgy fingers trying to scoop them up.

Two skinned hares, pink slips of knotted flesh, hung from a hook on the wall. Jinyi reached for a cleaver and suddenly thought of the horoscope he had got for his granddaughter.

Manxin had been pregnant for sixth months, living with her new husband in a room so small they had used their bed as a table to eat dinner on or as a seat for guests. The night before he had gone for the horoscope, Manxin had waited for her husband to start his nightshift, then packed a suitcase and turned up at her parents' house. They had opened the door to find her bob of hair ragged and wild, her face a blotchy mess of tears.

'I can't stand it any more,' Manxin had choked and wheezed. 'I can't! I'm not going back, not with that woman! I'll . . . I'll . . . I'll go to Guangzhou and start a new life. I can't live like that — why didn't you tell me I wasn't just marrying him? I've married his whole family!'

Manxin's new husband's mother was a small, crooked woman with scraped-back hair and inch-long fingernails. As soon as the honeymoon trip to Beijing — holding hands and grinning at each other as they meandered around the Summer Palace, Tiananmen Square and the new mausoleum — had finished, Manxin found that her parents-in-law would be coming to dinner every evening. 'Your new husband is our eldest son, after all, and really you should put some more salt in the soup and, oh heavens, is that really how you're going to cook that chicken and risk poisoning us all, no, no, no, you'd do better to follow my instructions, yes, and perhaps you should think about combing your hair before you go out, what will the neighbours say?'

'Come in, come in, I understand,' Yuying had sighed, sweeping her daughter into the room.

Jinyi had pottered at the stove, refrying the previous day's leftovers — 'You'll feel better after you've eaten something,' he assured his daughter. Yuying and Manxin had settled on the futon, the creaking pendulum in the clock on the wall cutting through Manxin's sniffles.

'How can I have a child there? Xue Shi will be criticising me every time I pick up the baby, every time I dare to open my mouth. Ma, I can't stand it.'

'Your old granny left her house, sixty-odd years ago, and never saw her family again. Things have changed since then, of course, but you can't expect things to come completely undone. Some people just have a strange way of showing their love. Some do it with nosy advice, some with food, some with silence, some by going to work each morning. The heart is a strange machine.'

Manxin had nodded, thinking of her husband and how the shy looks of their engagement and the sweet, giggly whispers of the four-day honeymoon had turned to unresponsive grunts between swigs of beer and stale cigarettes. She thought of the dirty shirts he threw in her direction and the derogatory comments he made about the food he wolfed

601

down before his next nightshift began. Her husband spent the nights locked in a booth at the interchange of railway tracks a few miles from the station, cranking the levers that shifted the tracks into differing slots, depending on the train's destination. So far, he had only made one mistake, sending a train hurtling past the wrong platform — luckily, the train that had been waiting there had just left. It happens to everyone, the officials had told him; why, there was a crash that killed a thousand up in Harbin only last month — ha! no, of course it wasn't in the bloody papers — so as long as you don't mention this incident to anyone, we're just going to dock your wages for a year. Xue Jingtien had then slouched off home to sulk at his pregnant wife. The next evening she had packed the suitcase.

'So I can't go back, you see!' Manxin had sobbed, looking at her parents for support. Jinyi had put a steaming plate in front of her and smiled.

'By day, a tree in our path might be a mild annoyance, something we have to walk around to reach our destination. By night, its sharp silhouette and hunched shadow make it look like a ghost hungry for flesh. Things look different in the day. Go back, think about our grandchild.'

She had looked down at the marrow curve of her belly swelling beneath her faded jacket.

'I can't live like this.'

'You have a choice. Change everything by running away, or change everything by staying,' Yuying had said.

'Listen,' Jinyi had added. 'Go back for just one more night, that's all I'm asking. Everything will be different tomorrow, I promise. Take my word for it. Go on, for your father.'

Slowly she had nodded, and, after finishing the refried leftovers and two bowls of lightly burnt rice, she had let them take her back to her room. Yuying had lifted her daughter's spirits by recounting the events of the first few months of her own marriage, transforming the nervous bickering and disappointments into well-meaning farce, complete with the resolution of a happy ending. Marriage is a type of theatre, she had whispered; for everything to work, a lot of strings need to be pulled behind the stage.

Jinyi had left his wife with their daughter at her room, where Yuying had helped her prepare the breakfast porridge for when her husband came grumbling back home. She had regaled her daughter with altered tales of her own childhood, of the fierce patriarch and the empire of restaurants, of the occupation and the civil war, but mostly of the days of arranged marriages when prepubescent girls were mutilated, disowned or sold, all to save face. Jinyi had slipped back into the warm night and, instead of going straight home, he had taken a side road, past the glass windows of late-night massage parlours filling the evening with pink fluorescent light, and crossed the river on the crumbling stone bridge. As he had scrambled down the other side, his aching limbs and panting chest reminding him of his age, he could already see the tip of the slim pagoda, dressed in the green nets and wooden poles of shoddy scaffolding. It rose above the long line of new office blocks, staring out between a sea of foreign logos.

He could hear the foreman's angry shouts from two blocks away. Nightlights were hanging from the paint-stripped temple gate, and as Jinyi had approached he caught sight of a short man slipping on the half-tiled roof, then steadying himself and carrying on. The workers had turned to look at him as he had entered, dark eyes shifting under masks of dust, patches of clean skin visible only where dribbles of sweat had washed away the weeks of dirt. They had stared, but said nothing. After he had ducked into the temple, orders were barked and the drilling had started back up, mimicking the sound of some angry god issuing proclamations.

'Please let me apologise for the workmen — they seem to be here twenty-four hours a day. Terribly noisy, but the sooner they finish the repairs the better.' A thin middle-aged man with a shaved head had looked up from where he was crouched over a tattered book. An open umbrella was suspended over his head, catching the dust raining down from the ceiling, protecting the long folds of his saffron robe.

'It's no problem,' Jinyi had said, his voice echoing in the empty hall.

'It's nearly done. Amazing, isn't it? When you think of the damage done back in the . . . erm . . . what do we call it now?'

Jinyi had shrugged. 'The Great Proletarian Cultural Revolution? A mistake, I suppose.'

The monk had nodded. 'The insides here were gutted, axes were taken to the walls, and then a fire was started. Luckily, we had the foresight to bury most of the books before the crowds arrived. I did not expect it to be so long before I dug them up though!' He gestured to the ragged book in front of him. 'But a few of them survived. The earth moves in cosmic cycles; nothing is ever a surprise. The cranes may leave but they always return eventually. Whatever changes, something always remains. Whatever remains, something always changes.'

'I see,' Jinyi had said. 'I was worried you would be closed by this time.'

'The soul is always open. May I ask if you are looking for something in particular? Only, I have a good memory for faces, illusory and deceptive though they may be, and I can't recall having seen you here before, friend.

You have faced hard times and yet more are to come — do not worry, this is no magic, just what I can see in your face. You are worried. You come here for solace, am I right?'

'Not this time. I'm . . . fine. But I need a fortune. Not for myself, for my grandchild.'

'I see. We can also calculate the most beneficent name, depending on the child's horoscope. Just tell me the sex of the child and the exact hour and date of birth and I will begin the consultation.'

Jinyi had shifted awkwardly. 'Well, the thing is, the child hasn't been born yet. I think it's due at the beginning of February. And, er, they won't tell us the sex before birth; the doctor said it's against the law. If I had to guess, though, I think it'll probably be a boy. My wife doesn't agree. But anyway, none of that is important — I just want to take a good fortune to my daughter, to reassure her that everything will be all right.'

'I understand your concern, but I can be of no assistance, except to tell you that everything will indeed be all right — the universe has a way of tying up loose ends. It's called karma. Perhaps you should talk to my brother.' The monk had stood up and reached for a small bell, which he then rang. The sound of shuffled footsteps could be heard in a nearby room. 'His view of the world is quite different from mine. As, indeed, it should be. We can only live in the universe we believe in. Goodnight.'

As he had walked away, a bigger, bulkier man had appeared through a side door. He had approached to Jinyi slowly, his bulbous bald skull glowing in the lamplight; his saffron robes faded to sackcloth brown.

'Yes?'

'I'd like a fortune, for my grandchild. I know this might —'

'Fine.' The second monk had rooted around beside a pile of books, and dug out a pot filled with thin lengths of bamboo. 'Now, here's how it usually works. You donate some money to the upkeep of the temple, and then pick a piece of bamboo. We then pull out the scroll from inside and that's your fortune. Everything is down to the vicissitudes of fate. However, as you can see, the temple needs quite a lot more work done. So, if your conscience should dictate that you must make a large donation to aid your poor brothers in their prayers, I think we could come to some kind of arrangement.'

Jinyi had pulled out his wallet and shuffled through the notes, each with the dimpled face of Mao Zedong grinning up at him. He had squinted at them for a few seconds, trying to recall each one's worth — currency values were constantly changing. In the end, he had pressed a whole week's wages into the large monk's hand.

'Make it good,' Jinyi had said. The monk

had nodded.

As the monk's oversized brush had scratched against the cheap paper, dashing out long-winded epithets, Jinyi had studied a reproduction tanka hung up on the only wall without cracks, holes, mould or smoke stains. At its centre was a Buddha floating serenely on a cloud; above and around him were various bodhisattvas in a range of acrobatic contortions, the many-handed many-eyed dancing across bright waves of sky. Beneath him were the slobbering faces of demons juggling flames, their bodies hunched and withered, yet their expressions more vivid and energetic than the drowsy enlightened above them. This is a riddle, isn't it, Jinyi had said to himself; we are not reborn in other lifetimes, but a thousand times in our own. We are not reborn in different bodies or in different places, but in different feelings. It is these we must escape if we are not to be ensnared by a single one.

'Is this one of the realms of heaven or a complete universe?' he had asked.

The monk had shrugged without looking up from his writing. 'Search me. There are whole universes living in your socks, in the winding tunnels of your ears. Now then, I'm almost finished, so if you wouldn't mind keeping it down for a few minutes . . .'

Jinyi had left the temple quarter of an hour later with one of the most impressive and bombastic fortunes ever created. This child is truly blessed, he had imagined telling his daughter, and had pictured her half-tilted smile, her dreams kindled. And, he had thought to himself, when people believe in a prophecy, they work all the more to make it come true. If he had learnt anything from his time in exile, it was that the truth was malleable, slippery.

It was not till early afternoon the next day, pacing back as fast as they could from their shifts on the farm, that Jinyi and Yuying had returned to their eldest daughter's room. Manxin had ushered them straight back out again so that they would not disturb her husband's hard-earned sleep, and the three of them had huddled on a rain-warped wooden bench outside, watching a herd of grunting bulldozers destroy a street of courtyard houses to make way for a hotel.

'I know how you must have been feeling last night,' Jinyi had begun. 'And that it must have been hard going back. It's always easier running away than sticking things out, but nothing ever gets solved like that. You did the right thing. Anyway, I've got something for you that might help make you see things differently.' He reached into his bag for the scroll. 'Now, do you remember I promised that everything would be different today?'

'I remember, and, Pa, you were so right!' Manxin had replied. 'But how could you have known? It's amazing.'

Jinyi had been confused. He had not given her the gift yet. 'What's amazing?'

'Well, this morning Jingtien came back from work and brought his parents round for breakfast. Now usually this would have made me want to cry and scream, but he was being really sweet. They had even brought the food with them so I wouldn't have to cook. Jing-tien said he had been talking to his parents about everything, and that his dad could help us. Well, his dad said that it wasn't right that I kept working in a dirty, smoky, smelly fac-tory when I had their grandchild inside me, so he offered to get me a job at the high school where he's the headteacher. Can you believe it?'

Yuying had smiled and clasped her daugh-ter's hands. Jinyi had let go of the scroll and retied the bag. Perhaps he would save it for later. 'So what will you be doing there?' he had asked. 'Will you be a janitor, or a dinner lady?'

'No! I'm going to be a teacher.'

Her parents had opened their mouths, but had not been able to think of anything to say. Jinyi had scratched his head, while Yuying had fiddled with the chopstick in her hair. She had finally settled on tact. 'He doesn't mind that you never finished high school yourself, that you never went to college?'

'No. Why would he? No one my age has

610

been to college — but that doesn't mean we're stupid. We just happened to fall into a hole in history. This is my way out.'

'What will you teach?' Jinyi had collected himself to ask.

'Well, he said it was up to me, but they had a shortage of science teachers. So I picked biology. I'm not sure why, but I spent ten years looking after my sisters, so I think I've got a good idea about how things work.'

'I think there might be a little more to it than that,' Yuying had murmured.

'Oh don't worry, he gave me a big textbook. Just cover one chapter a week, and you'll be fine, he told me. We're not allowed to mention anything outside the textbook anyway — in fact, the list of things not to talk about is longer than the list of things we can talk about. If something is not in this book, then it is not on the curriculum, which means that students shouldn't be discussing it. So all I'll have to do is read the chapter a few days before I have to teach it, and then explain it to the students. Simple really. Plus, I'll get two months off when I have the baby.'

'Congratulations. You're lucky. I thought about being a teacher once, you know, back before the revolution,' Yuying had said as she clasped her daughter's hands.

'Yes, congratulations,' Jinyi had added.

And with that Manxin had gone back to her life, managing now, with this small change, to blot out the pieces of snide advice from her mother-in-law and her husband's exaggerated demands. Jinyi did not give her the fake horoscope that day, nor the day after.

Back in the canteen kitchen he finished chopping up the meat and peered out of the window to see his granddaughter sprawled out on her back beside the stream. Whistles of steam rose from the three rice-cookers, their lids rattling, and Jinyi checked his trouser pocket — it was still there, the secret fortune, a scrunched-up scrag of mock-scroll that he no longer dared unfold. He could almost convince himself that because the real future was unknown and the phoney prediction remained unread, they shared a correspondence, that their truths were inseparable and indistinguishable. If even an interfering neighbour's few sly words about a family could divert a destiny so utterly, he thought, then why not suppose that a few written words might be able to do the same? His belief rested on the condition of the fortune never being given, and this enabled him to think of himself as its protector and, by extension, his granddaughter's most important guardian.

After gobbling down their lunch, the farm workers headed out for siestas under the shadier trees, leaving a mess of tin trays and spoons to be washed. Lian was chasing after butterflies outside, her body twirling and doubling back with a range of false starts and grabbing fingers. Jinyi scrubbed his hands with the sliver of black soap, kneading the creases and scars, wondering if there was anything left underneath. In the converted shed behind the tangled rows of vine, Yuying put away the bulky calculator which she took out each morning for show, not having had the confidence to admit to her new boss that she had no idea how to use it, preferring instead the jammed wooden abacus and her own knife-sharpened pencil.

'Are we going back now?' Lian asked as they regrouped, each of the adults stooping to more easily hold one of the little girl's small hands.

'Of course. If you stay in the past too long, you'll turn into a dinosaur,' Jinyi grinned, as his wife shook her head and sighed.

'What's a dinosaur?' Lian said.

'Er, well, a dinosaur is half dragon, half lizard. Don't worry though, they're all gone now. They were around long before even I was born!'

'In China?'

'Of course! China is the oldest country in the world. We had developed writing and building before most countries had even worked out how to start a fire.'

They carried on past a dusty building site and around the park, where toddlers on leads were being walked by slow, meandering pensioners. It was a common sight — children were expensive, and parents risked losing their jobs if they took time off, so it was up to grandparents to look after any children. That was how things have always worked here, people said; families take care of each other. Most days Lian even slept in Jinyi and Yuying's house, her cot set between the *kang* and the wooden bed where their last unmarried daughter slept.

A sour-faced street cleaner in faded neons was sweeping dust and debris from one side of the street to the other, from the east of the city to its westernmost point. The next day she would push the accumulated junk back the other way, her work a tug-of-war, in which some places were cleaned only so that others could be made more dirty — it was an example, a more eloquent official of the Public Sanitation Department might have reasoned, of eternal balance, of cosmic harmony, of yin and yang. Her brush stirred up a storm of soot, feathers, bottle tops, clumps of hair and food wrappers.

In one of the battered brown autorickshaws, a man in oversized dark glasses was picking his teeth in the side mirror. White hairs were pushed across his scalp to cover his baldness, and a faded pink scar sloped down between his right ear and his chin. A few of his fingers were missing, though this did not seem to impede his artistry with the toothpick. The man lazily tossed the toothpick onto the street, keeping his eyes on the side mirror as he spat into his fingers and adjusted the few remaining strands of his hair.

'Excuse me!' Yuying barked at him. 'What do you think you're doing? Your dirty toothpick just landed on my granddaughter's shoe, you filthy man. Perhaps you should be more careful!'

'Hey, lady, why don't you —' he swivelled round in his seat as he began to respond, but suddenly stopped, staring slack-jawed at the three of them. Unconsciously, he began to rub the stumps of his missing fingers with the few he still had left.

They started to move away, pushing Lian hurriedly in front of them as they marched onwards, but they were stopped by his shout. 'Hou Jinyi? It's me, Yangchen.' As he rose from the driver's seat, Yuying and Jinyi wheeled around. 'Ha! Didn't recognise me, did you? Well, it took me a minute too, I'll admit. And Bian Yuying, well, I still remember your dainty golden slippers. Oh yes, some things you just can't forget, no matter how hard you try. And it seems like only yesterday we were all laughing and having dinner together. You look like you haven't aged a day since then, not like myself.'

'Yangchen?' Jinyi muttered, amazed. He was not sure whether to ignore him and walk away, to vent his anger or simply act normally. In any case, he had no anger left — everyone regretted the past these days. 'Well . . . how are you?'

Yangchen slapped the bulky carriage of the auto-rickshaw. His hand left a dull print. 'Not bad. This is my new career. I'm going to get rich ferrying businessmen around town in this thing. Of course, it's early days yet. I got back a few years ago, after my sentence finished. I was surprised to find not much has changed round here. Sure, there's a lot of new things, but that's just show. All journeys away take you home, isn't that what they say?'

'Hmm. You look well,' Jinyi said, noticing that Yuying was trying to stop her lip twitching and her fists clenching.

'Ha! First off, I know you're lying, Hou Jinyi, 'cause you never were much good at it. I look rough as a dead mule, and I know it. Still, if that's the worst you can say of me after all I've been through, then I'm doing pretty well. The last twenty years haven't been kind to me, but then who have they been kind too? I'm a changed man now . . . well, aren't we all?'

Yangchen sighed, and looked at his feet. Jinyi realised that this was the nearest thing to an explanation or apology that they were likely to receive, and that in some way it was for the best. Whatever this country had been through since the revolution, however people had suffered, there was an unspoken agreement not to dwell on dark areas of the past. To do so was unpatriotic. Whatever had happened to Yangchen, he surely deserved it, Jinyi thought. Twenty years' penance is enough for anyone though, he decided, remembering the time he had spent away from home.

Jinyi and Yuying had learnt to rework their past, to focus the telescopes of their memories only upon the things that bound them together: the sum of their actions, the sum of their love — children, grandchildren, work, hopes, stories, forgotten whispers, poems, kisses. When they lay together in the warm, sleepless nights, or whispered in the early mornings before Xiaojing or Lian awoke, they spoke of the early days of their marriage, reconstructing each brick of the old house, the scent of opium and white jasmine petals, the ghosts of ancestors, the fierce Fu Lions outside the restaurants. They re-imagined the city brick by brick until it was theirs once again, reclaimed by memory. Days were for the necessary business of moving forward, for caring for their children and grandchildren, for putting food on the table and money in the bank. Nights were for the secret language of their youth, discovered among the darkness, the things that persisted. In this way, they sought to remind each other who they were, who they still might be.

'Do you want a lift? Go on, it's on me!

Least I can do. You look a little tired, sweet-heart, do you want to ride in my tuk-tuk?' Yangchen said to Lian. 'Have you ever been in one of these before?'

The little girl shook her head and hid behind her grandmother's leg, clutching tightly, afraid of what might happen if she let go.

'Ha!' Yangchen laughed. 'Never fear. Better than twenty horses this thing!' He slapped the metal roof, before yanking the door open.

Yuying refused the offer, once, then twice, but after the third insistence she knew they had to cave in to common courtesy or risk rumours of an impolite slight slipping into the vast web of gossip that spread even to the most distant reaches of the city. This is a test, she thought, to see how we fare when the past returns, to see how we handle forgive-ness. The three of them clambered into the small box-like carriage behind the driver.

As he drove, Yangchen lit up a pair of cigarettes, one of which he handed back to Jinyi through the open window separating the driver from passengers. Lian was wedged between the two adults on the thin wooden seat in the cramped carriage. She whooped every time the vehicle jolted over bumps in the half-finished roads. Twin gold medallions, one emblazed with a calm, meditative Bud-dha and the other with a grinning Chairman Mao, dangled from the ceiling, jangling into

618

each other every time Yangchen braked or accelerated.

'When did you learn to drive?' Jinyi shouted.

'Oh, I always had a knack for this kind of thing. I called in a favour with an old friend at the local transport office and he managed to sort me out a licence before I'd even bought the damn thing. Then I taught myself — it's so simple, even a monkey could do it.' He pressed his hand to the horn for half a minute to forewarn any other vehicles as he puttered round another blind corner, then turned his head around and grinned at his passengers. 'When I was a nipper you couldn't move round here without bumping into some burly figure with no top and rippling biceps dragging a rickshaw through the streets. You remember that, don't you?'

'Certainly,' Yuying called over the noise. 'My dad used to send us home in them all the time.'

'Of course, they were only used by rich folk like your father, or landlords, or the Japs. Thank god they're all gone. Anyway, there's got to be a market for that now, what with Deng Xiaoping opening up the country. It'll be filled with rich businessmen soon. And are they going to want to ride a bicycle and crease their fancy Western double-breasted suits? No, sir!'

The auto-rickshaw squeezed into a narrow

lane leading past the back entrance of the army base, then on past the adjacent military school and snack bars serving cold noodles and watermelon to soldiers flitting between the two. Above them a series of flagpoles shook out a line of matador's capes. It was then that it dawned on Jinyi that Yangchen had no idea where he was going. The city looked different through smeared windows. They turned into an alley, which turned out to be a dead end, and Yangchen began to reverse. Jinyi drew on his reserves of diplomacy to suggest a new route as subtly as he could. If they had carried on walking, they would have already been home.

'Where are we going?' Lian began to sulk. 'It smells yucky in here.'

'Jinyi, do you remember when we were working in the kitchen, we were teasing you about something, I think — we were just stupid kids back then, before I let power go to my head and ruin everything — and you said life is where the heart carries you, no more, no less?'

Jinyi tilted his head. 'I can't say I do. That doesn't sound much like me, but I'm prepared to take your word for it. Why do you still remember that?'

'I don't know. It just stuck in my mind. And I was thinking, life's more like a taxi ride. That's why I like driving. You just get thrown together with different people, different problems, and the only thing you can do is keep heading forward, keep going.' He lit another cigarette. 'It must be nice having a big family.'

Neither Jinyi nor Yuying knew what to say. Cigarette smoke blew back into their faces.

'Our youngest daughter is getting married next month. Why don't you come?' Jinyi blurted out, expecting a polite refusal.

Yuying looked at him as though he was insane, daggers in her eyes. Yangchen bit his lip and appeared to think it over.

The car stopped at the turning of the alley that led to their house, a short lane of small stone houses now dwarfed by the blocks of flats on the north and west sides that swallowed up the evening light and snipped hours from the end of the day. Yangchen wound down the window as his three passengers climbed out.

'It's a nice offer, Jinyi, and I wish your daughter good fortune and a strong husband to take care of her. But I would be a bucket of water poured on your firecrackers.' He reached into the pocket of his faded blazer. 'But here, take my business card. I can offer you rides for free, any time you want to go where the heart carries you. I know it doesn't make up for anything, but I don't have much else left.'

The auto-rickshaw pootled off down the road, beeping manically. Jinyi and Yuying looked at each other. Wherever they went, the past was never far behind.

As Yuying pottered at the stove, brewing the tea, she thought of Xiaojing's upcoming wedding to the thin, reedy man she had met in the canteen of her factory. They did not even have a matchmaker! Then again, neither had she. Yuying had heard all the tricks her friends and colleagues used to check out the family of potential suitors: listening in on private conversations with ears pressed to doors or windows, picking the intricate tiny padlocks on diaries hidden under mattresses or simply applying good old-fashioned discipline. She knew of parents who had disowned their children over their choice of partner, children who had killed themselves after their parents had insisted on an unwanted match, young men who had been thrown out of university (or, heaven forbid, high school) for having a girlfriend, and a whole army of men whose new wives had deserted them after a few months to head back to their hometowns and their own families. She had vowed she would never be like those parents, and that she would give her children what she had never had: a choice.

Still, something bothered her. If you do not have to struggle and sweat and curse and sacrifice to make a marriage work, then are you really entitled to call it love? Yuying was not sure, though she decided that it was not her place to say. Love wears thousands of disguises. She had only just learnt herself that love could creep back, could change shape, could find peace in that small knot of blood. Although Yuying knew little about anatomy, she did know that the heart was stronger than many imagined — it can survive a thousand nicks and cuts; whole chunks can be sliced off and it will continue to thump, and though there may be pain, you will at least be more aware of the stitched-up scarred parts still left.

It was June, and the fields were on fire. The yellow husks shuddered and brayed in the dancing flames. Soon the borders of the city would be marked with charred black ash, and the smell of the sweet, crisp smoke would drift over the houses, mingling with the cooling tower haze that had reduced the sky to a cataract.

Yuying was combing her hair, amazed at the number of gravel-coloured strands that caught in the comb's teeth. She had done up her dark Mao jacket and fixed a butterfly clip on her head, her one rebellious nod to modernity. She thought of Manxin's wedding, of Liqui's, and thanked her luck that this time the groom's family had agreed to host the wedding banquet.

'I was shaking with fear before we got married, and I tried to hide it by acting more arrogant and noble. I'm not sure it worked, though,' she said as Jinyi entered the bedroom and picked up a shirt to put over his long-sleeved vest.

'You fooled me. I thought you were a regal dragon. At least you didn't have to drink your father's hundred-year-old white liquor. I couldn't speak for twenty minutes after that; I had to just nod and smile. I bet all those rich merchants and officials thought I was a real simple-minded bumpkin.'

'A dragon? Hmm, aren't you going to comb your hair? Come on, make a little effort, won't you?'

'All I'll be doing is toasting the guests. By the end my hair will be as frazzled as my brain anyway. I only remember half of Liqui's wedding with all the drinking her husband initiated.'

'That is not going to happen this time. Xiaojing's husband seems even shyer than her. Besides, most of his mother's side of the family disappeared for criticising the famine after the Great Leap Forward. At least, that's what people say. Please, don't mention that today though, alright?'

They reached the groom's grandparents' house, where the celebratory dinner would be held, via a long narrow alley running close to the river. Yuying soon felt the familiar sense of shame welling up inside her: despite the ever-increasing sums they borrowed from old friends, they could not afford lavish meals and dowries for three girls on their meagre savings. Yuying pulled up her trouser legs to avoid the tawny puddles of fetid water and foamy dregs from emptied washing-up bowls.

The two of them had just reached the doorway as a spittle-thick rain began to stumble down the alley in a million tiny refractions of sharp light, the first rungs of a rainbow.

'Last one, isn't it?'

'Last what? Wedding?'

'Yes. Last of the big ones, anyway,' Jinyi said, as they settled at one of the many fold-out tables in the front rom of the old house.

'Oh, I don't know. What about Lian, and all her cousins?' Yuying smiled at him.

'Of course. I just meant that everything has gone full circle now. We've done our bit, and the girls are part of other families now. They're not ours anymore.'

'I see. So what should we do now then?' she said, teasing him.

'Oh, we're too old to do anything new. We're like birds now: our cage has been left open but we cannot quite remember how to fly.'

'So we just stay here and keep the cage clean?' Yuying laughed. The simile was ridiculous, but still she encouraged his little eccentricities; especially since these days his imaginative ramblings were often buffeted by long silences or incoherent mumbles. When he was trying out an idea on her, something he would never say to anyone else, she felt she could recognise the nervous boy coming to the big house, the young husband not knowing what to say or what to do, still not sure who he was or could be. Had that much really changed?

'No. We just do what we've always done.'

She took his hand, and they sat together listening to the sound of the groom's father stacking crates of beer in the corner.

Soon the guests arrived, lightly sprinkled from the stop-start summer showers, each with different amounts of cash stuffed in cigarette packets that would be covertly handed to the groom when each family offered him a celebratory cigarette. By the end of the afternoon, the room would be an ocean of stale smoke, letting the inebriated guests slip away under a hazy cloak.

The twelve round tables in the front room seemed to stake out different eras: the middle-aged women just beginning to mix dark jackets and trousers with colourful shoes or lipstick; the groom's lecherous great-uncles and distant cousins wearing the washed-out blues and peaked caps of the strict 1960s; a table of toddlers in red jumpers along with their fussing parents; students yawning despite the disapproving glances of elderly relatives; factory workers in stained Mao suits; new wives keeping tabs on how much their husbands drank and flirted; and a whole table of the dribbling half-dead in various degrees of decrepitude and decay. Jinyi picked up a plate and headed towards the long buffet table that had been set beside the door. In a corner, the emcee fiddled with his glasses as he rehearsed his patter.

The borrowed PA spluttered and howled into life and the emcee coughed into the microphone before he began to shout at an ear-piercing pitch. Jinyi and Yuying sat near the main door with their eldest daughters — Manxin heavy-set and relaxed with Lian on her lap, and Liqui twiddling strands of her hair beside her bored husband. Opposite them Xiaojing sat with her new family, her gangly body pressed into the dark work suit. Her short crop of hair only served to highlight her long, equine features. She was nervously fingering the tablecloth. As the emcee rattled through the obligatory greetings and adages, Yuying overheard a gaggle of young wives whispering through food-full mouths.

'I heard her dowry was pretty pathetic. As if her parents just rooted through their cupboards for cast-offs. I would have died of shame.'

'Mmm hmm, that's right, I heard it too. Just a single second-hand sewing machine. They haven't even bothered to give them a radio. She's going to get pretty bored just playing with clothes all day!'

'Well, her husband'll have to buy one himself now, or else he'll lose face just like his in-laws. My husband has already said he's going to get us a television next year.'

'No! You lucky thing! Uh, have you tasted these chicken legs? Too much garlic. Of course, we had only the neck at our wedding . . .'

They nattered on, and Yuying sighed to herself, knowing that everyone else was also assessing the dinner, the clothes and the liquor, and tolling up the expenses; she had done the same herself at similar events. After all, how do you know who you are if you don't know everything about the people around you? How else would you know your place, where you fit in, how to address others? When her sisters had got married, it was 'three wheels' that brides wanted: a sewing machine, a watch and a bicycle. By the time little Lian would get married, Yuying suspected that young brides would be demanding houses and cars.

The emcee called the new couple to the front of the room, urging them to sing a song for their guests. They nervously obliged, stumbling hesitantly through two verses of the latest ballad from Beijing as the guests clapped along, whistling and shouting encouragement and the occasional heckle.

Yuying looked across at her husband, his lips moving as he stared at his fingers, silently rehearsing his speech. His face showed that same stoic calm that he had displayed when they buried the first child, buried the second, when she had left him or when he had returned, and on that day the truck had come to take her to the fields. It had taken a few years before Yuying had learnt that it was an act, a way of measuring out his confusion. She recognised the little tics — the twitch of his left eyebrow, the picking of fingernails, the flared nostrils — that announced his uncertainty, his struggle to appear calm and collected when the world around slipped beyond his comprehension. She smiled; love is the cumulative effect of such useless knowledge.

'You will be fine. Just think of how much you will miss her,' Yuying whispered.

Jinyi nodded uncertainly as the emcee beckoned him to the front. His mouth was sticky, hot, and he ran his tongue repeatedly over his gums. 'Thank you all for coming,' he began, and looked around the room. People were picking at the dishes, bottle tops were being popped off beer bottles and a child had just started crying. What is it that I want to say? Jinyi suddenly asked himself, and panicked. What had he planned to say? Some old proverb about love and longevity, something about security and double happiness? Why was it that things resisted being put into words, he wondered, that truths suddenly seem slippery and doubtful when spoken aloud? He was sweating.

'Thank you all for coming,' he said again. He scratched his head, then, his eyes flitting across the tables, latched onto an idea. 'Thank you all for coming.'

The guests were looking nervous now, exchanging glances. Jinyi looked around for his wife, but could not quite make her out in the sea of anxious faces.

'The day of your wedding should be the happiest day of your life. I feel happy. I have a loving wife and dutiful children . . .'

His eyes searched about until he spotted Yuying smiling at him, and only then could he draw the strength to push on.

'I am proud to be the father of three daughters. Every room they enter they fill with light, with love. I wish them each several lifetimes of happiness. All my blessings, to Hou Xiaojing and . . . and . . .'

Jinyi was struggling through a fog of names. Which one was it? Dongming, Zu Fu, Qingsheng, Yangchen, Turkey, Bo? No, none of those seemed quite right. His eyes swept the room until they finally focused on the expectant face of the groom. He was mouthing something, and Jinyi took a deep, raspy breath, trying to read his lips. 'Yes, of course, to Hou Xiaojing and Fei Shuyou.'

630

Jinyi wiped his brow with his sleeve as he slunk back to his table, aware of the confused glances and indignant whispers filling the room.

Yuying took his hand and sat him down beside her. He could not keep still, staring around him, picking out the members of his family.

'Are you all right?' Yuying whispered as the emcee picked up the microphone and began introducing the groom's father.

'Where is he?' Jinyi asked.

'What?'

'Where is he?' his voice quivered.

Yuying's reply was drowned out by applause and feedback from the speakers as the father of the groom leaned too close to the microphone. Jinyi took a large slug of the rice wine set in front of him. He could not wait for the rounds of toasts.

His speech was quickly forgotten; the newlyweds returned to the front of the room to attempt to take bites from opposite sides of an apple dangled tauntingly on a string between them, and everyone cheered along. Before the cigarettes were offered, the groom was given a large bottle of beer with a chopstick inside which he had to retrieve with his mouth, leading him to gag and splutter as he downed the frothy, lukewarm brew.

When we have run out of lives, when we have lived every possible scenario, every possible pleasure and conceivable tragedy, every kind of love and every kind of death, what then? Jinyi suddenly felt as if he had run out of things that could happen to him, as though he was full. His head ached, and yet he still had to go around the tables, toasting the guests and smiling away their sceptical stares as they remembered the strangeness of his speech. He tried not to blush.

Jinyi took Yuying's hand and they rose to their feet, ready to make the rounds, to make the same toast to each of the tables, to suffer the same jokes, the same challenges to down his glass. When we have exhausted every possible moment, time starts again, and we replay each moment in a different order, with the slightest of variations serving only to underscore the similarities. By the end of the afternoon, Jinyi was no longer sure how many lives he had lived, nor which ones were really his and which only dreams.

'I hope she will be happy,' Jinyi muttered.

He and Yuying were among the last people left. Most of the guests had seen off the newlyweds in a borrowed auto-rickshaw that took a lap around the city before dropping them at the groom's parents' flat, where the marriage would be consummated on a shoddy camp-bed set up in the kitchen. Jinyi and Yuying were both tipsy, slow, not quite ready to return to an empty house.

'She will be. There is nothing more exciting than escaping all the things you thought you would never get away from, like your family,' Yuying joked.

'I'm sorry. About the speech, I mean,' her husband whispered.

'Forget it, Jinyi,' she said. 'You love her, that's all that mattered. Anyway, people will have been far more shocked at me daring to toast with you. Not very ladylike, though I'm not sure there is such a thing any more.'

'You were more like a lady than anyone else here tonight.'

'Hmm. Well, at least we gave people something to talk about, so they won't all focus on how little we spent on the wedding.'

'Yes, at least they'll have a lot to gossip over.' He laughed.

'I almost felt we should have had an extra table, for all the people who weren't here,' Yuying said, placing a hand delicately on Jinyi's knee. 'My parents, and yours, Dali, Yaba, the Lis, all those people from the factory who never came back, your mahjong friends . . . shouldn't the dead be able to celebrate?'

Jinyi thought it over. Yaba had died only eight days before Lian was born, and in the last hours before his heart splitter-splattered out into gasps, as Manxin had sat and rested her ballooning belly beside his bed in the ward, it seemed as if he mistook her for her grandmother, the pregnant woman who had changed his life some fifty years earlier.

A year before, two young men had appeared at Yaba's house one afternoon, claiming that they were the grandchildren of his father's missing brother. Yaba was amazed, and soon started to note their physical resemblances to his dead father, their shared mannerisms and accent. It might just be your mind playing tricks with you because you want to believe, Yuying had warned him; can you really remember much about a man who died more than half a century ago? Yaba had been offended. The two young men had stayed on at his house and ate the food he cooked, and, with Manxin's reluctant help, even learnt to understand much of Yaba's own invented language of gestures. However, they politely refused his offers to help them find work in Fushun. They stayed for ten months, planning a business venture which, due to its competitive nature, they could not talk about, except to ask for loans, which Yaba happily gave them. When they had finally disappeared they had left Yaba's bank account empty, his flat cleared of furniture and possessions, and his heart shot through with holes where hope had been.

Jinyi finally spoke. 'There are enough ghosts in this country. If we let them all in, we'd be swamped. And besides, there isn't enough liquor for all the ghosts we know.'

Yuying did not move. 'Sometimes I feel like the air is thick with them, like they're crowding around, determined to push us out. I used to worry about the neighbours watching us, or our colleagues noting every little thing we said, but now I wonder if it isn't something else that keeps us in check.'

'You're just used to looking over your shoulder, that's all.'

'Yes, look at me getting all soppy. Come on, let's go,' Yuying said, and reached for her husband's hand to help her up, though these days she was increasingly unsure of who was helping whom.

As they made their way carefully down the steps they clung to each other for support. The puddles in the alley had almost dried, and this time Yuying unconsciously let the bottom of her trousers scrape through the dirt. The light rain had given way to the anxious songs of cicadas, to the mellow haze of late afternoon.

The streetlamps purred. 'We've missed the rainbow,' Yuying sighed.

'There will be another,' Jinyi assured her.

Some people say that each rainbow is unique and irrefutable; this is true if we accept, as countless magicians have learnt, that each trick relies on the eyes making a fool of the brain. Some assert that our understanding of how moisture creates this spectrum of light proves that science has freed us from any need for gods with which to make sense of the world, others that the sheer beauty of the prismatic arch proves the existence of an unfathomable creator. Some maintain that the rainbow affirms the equality of all people since everyone, regardless of their country, position or wealth, sees a rainbow at some point in their lives; others argue that, since the location of the observer in relation to the sun determines the supposed position of the jet of colours, no two people see the same rainbow.

'A rainbow is a bridge,' Yuying said as they approached their own street.

'You've had too much to drink,' Jinyi sighed.

'No. Listen, a rainbow is a bridge that connects our hearts and our hopes. Where the rainbow ends is where our dream-selves wait, right? Well, I was thinking, it also teaches us something about ourselves, since it takes the burning sun and the soaking rain to create such a strange and unexpected child.'

'Yin and yang,' he said.

'Yes. Or like me and you.'

Jinyi coughed into his cupped palm. 'Does that make me a rain cloud?'

They laughed and slipped back to silence. But something in her could not stop. She thought of the bombs that had once rattled the street, she thought of burying the baby and of the stillbirth, of Jinyi abandoning her, of their arguments and fights, of her stoppered anger that had long since evaporated into acceptance, of her dead sons and dead mother, of the last ties she had with who she used to be. The rainbow was a series of incomprehensible links, a chain of colours that only made sense from a distance. Perhaps, she thought, our attempts to make sense of our lives, to tie the events together into something more than a ragbag of memories, is just as much a trick of the brain as a rainbow is a trick of the light. Her train of thought was broken as her husband stumbled and she moved to steady him.

'Anything can be a bridge,' Jinyi muttered as they reached their home. 'We just don't always see it that way. Do you remember that story about the bridge of stars?'

She shook her head.

'Well, never mind. It's too late for all that now anyway. Come on.'

He held out his hand. She grasped it tight, and they crossed the threshold together, making their way lazily towards bed.

He was referring, of course, to the story of Niu Lang. You know that old chestnut, don't you? No? Let me refresh your memory.

Like Jinyi, Niu Lang was also orphaned at an early age, and grew up in a shabby shack in the middle of nowhere with bitter relatives. Despite the beatings and petty humiliations, the frostbite and the meals of gruel or grass soup, he too developed a kindness inured against his surroundings. And there was also to be one further similarity.

Niu Lang's troubles reached a climax when his brother's wife started levelling false accusations at him, prompting her husband to throw Niu Lang out. He wandered dejectedly through a forest, searching for grubs with which to fashion a makeshift meal. Suddenly he heard a low, rumbling moan rising up from deep within the forest. Even the trees seemed to tremble, to nervously shift their weight. Niu Lang felt as though his bones had been struck with a tuning fork, yet his curiosity spurred him to follow the noise through the brambles and gorse where the rough track ended.

Ten minutes later, his bare legs stung and scratched where he had tugged up his loose-flowing *hanfu* robe, Niu Lang pushed through the last tangled thicket to reach a small clearing, in the middle of which lay a frail calf. Niu Lang approached slowly, watching as the animal's limp tongue lolled out and flies danced across its wide black eyes. Its tail thumped the ground, and it opened its mouth wider to give out a mournful low, stopping Niu Lang in his tracks. Yet there was something in its dark eyes that he recognised — the strange kind of acceptance that comes in place of fear when you are most afraid. He knelt and put his hand to the beast's sticky head.

He felt an odd affinity with the sick calf. Niu Lang suddenly leapt up and ran to the stream he had recently passed; once there he scooped up as much water as he could in a pouch made from folding over the bottom of his robe. Then he ran back to the helpless animal. Its lazy tongue lapped up the dribbles of water, and Niu Lang soon returned to the stream for more. By the time the evening fell through the trees, Niu Lang had levered his body under the young cow's bony torso, dug his heels into the earth and pushed until the animal was standing, shaky on its brittle legs.

Within a few days the calf had recovered from its illness, and, with Niu Lang's help, its veiny, sagging belly began to harden into a muscled paunch. Together they set off from the clearing, onward towards the city to look for work.

'In the city,' Niu Lang said, finding that he enjoyed talking to the docile calf, 'there are men who are fair and noble and dedicate their lives to serving the celestial emperor, and they'll realise that I am honest. They are bound to find a job for me. You'll see.'

However, when they passed the city gates and smelt the open sewers, saw the crippled and contorted beggars, the brown-toothed prostitutes and the dusty restaurants selling whatever creatures they could catch from the filth-encrusted alleyways, Niu Lang became nervous. The noblemen not only had enough slaves to do their work for free, but swore they would remove Niu Lang's eyes and tongue if he ever came dirtying their doorsteps again.

'It must be another city that everyone talks of,' Niu Lang decided, and they set off again.

They walked through fields, across slate wastelands; they waded through swamps and marshes and knee-high rivers; they hiked over hills and skidded down dykes. Yet when they arrived in the next city, they found it was the same as the first; so was the third city they reached, and the fourth. As they left the last city, defeated and depressed, the cow — for after all this travelling it was no longer a calf — suddenly turned to Niu Lang.

'I have an idea,' the cow said, in the most refined accent Niu Lang had ever heard.

Niu Lang stopped in his tracks. 'What? How long have you been able to speak?'

'Why, I have always been able to speak,' the cow replied nonchalantly. 'Everything has a voice, if you listen — though I must admit that many creatures choose to keep silent in front of your species, since they find talking causes them more trouble than acting dumb. And I would have once concurred that humans are vicious, ignorant little things. However, that was before I met you.'

Niu Lang shuffled on his feet, embarrassed.

'Oh, I see. So, erm, what's your idea?'

'Well, first, you should know that I am a heavenly cow, one of the Jade Emperor's herd. I was grazing on a stretch of cloud when I tripped and fell down to that forest, where I would certainly have died if you had not found me. Now, it so happens that we are not far from the bend in the river where many of the daughters of heaven fly down to bathe. My plan is this — we will go there and talk with them, and they will surely reward you for taking care of me.'

Niu Lang agreed and followed the cow to the bend in the river. However, they had arrived too late; the women had already stripped off their clothes and were playing in the water. The cow tugged at Niu Lang's sleeve, urging him to turn away, for if they were caught spying on the naked daughters of heaven the punishment would be dire. Yet Niu Lang was sick of wandering through shitty cities, and he was sick of eating from whatever abandoned carcasses they came across — he did not want to waste this chance. He got on his hands and knees and crawled towards the bank, his nose trailing through the mud. His heart sounded like a temple gong being pummelled in his chest, and he half expected the bathers to turn at the sound of each thumping beat. As soon as he got close enough, he grabbed hold of one of the long red silk robes then swung back and returned to the trees where the cow was hiding.

'Now we wait,' Niu Lang whispered between deep breaths.

One by one the women emerged from the water, slipped their robes over their glistening flesh and then began to rise above the trees. Finally, Niu Lang dared to look around from behind the oak. A single figure was left, searching hopelessly for her clothes at the water's edge. Niu Lang gasped, amazed at her incomprehensible beauty.

'I'm so . . . so sorry,' he stuttered as the woman stumbled backwards, trying to retreat into the water. 'I did-did-didn't mean to watch, I'm not . . . you know . . . I just erm . . . well, I have your robe.'

She giggled, and Niu Lang fought to keep his trembling legs from buckling beneath him. 'So can I have it back?'

'Only . . . only if you tell me your name,' Niu Lang said.

'Are you sure that's all you want?' She giggled again, reaching out for her clothes. 'My name is Zhi Nu.'

'Zhi Nu, would you . . . perhaps . . . care to maybe . . . walk . . . a little . . . take a little walk?' he asked, looking at the ground. 'With me, I mean.'

'I would be delighted,' she said, pulling on her robe.

The little walk became a romantic meal

beside a small bonfire, which turned into a kiss and a night lying side by side beneath the fluttering stars, which led to marriage and the birth, a couple of years later, of a boy and a girl. Niu Lang became a woodsman and built a house for them in the forest; Zhi Nu spent the days looking after their babies and the nights pressed against her husband, while the heavenly cow spent its days as before, eating grass.

Zhi Nu liked her new life down on earth; there was no pressure, no expectations, just the simple pleasure of spending time with someone who cared — no matter that he may have been a little uncouth compared to her previous suitors (who had included an eight-headed god of hell, a half-man-half-dragon and several cloud princes). At any rate, it certainly beat her old life: as one of the daughters of the Jade Emperor, she had previously spent each day and every night spinning long, silky clouds to fill the sky. Love was so much simpler.

You may have heard that time is relative. This is certainly true for gods — since we have few uses for time, it often sneaks past us. When the Jade Emperor's wife finally realised what had happened she was furious, not least because she had grown fond of those spindly wisps of cloud her daughter weaved, which smelt of jasmine and cedarwood. She shouted at her husband to do something, and he soon agreed.

The following morning, Niu Lang woke up to find the other side of the bed empty. After calling out for his wife, he decided to venture outside to see what she was up to. He did not find her. Instead, he found the cow lying broken and bloody in the garden.

'Where is Zhi Nu?' Niu Lang asked, suddenly panicking.

The cow thumped its tail, its sad eyes staring past Niu Lang. 'Closer,' it rasped.

Niu Lang sank to the ground and put his ear to the cow's dry mouth.

'There isn't much time left. They took her.'

'Who? Who took her?' Niu Lang shouted.

The cow motioned to the sky with one of its hooves. 'There isn't much time. Take my skin, please, take it, and . . . and . . . go to her.' The cow lowed its deep, rumbling low, before closing its eyes.

Niu Lang ran his hands over its cooling flank, searching for a pulse. He knew what he had to do. After retrieving a knife from the kitchen, he began to cut into the wattle of the beast's blubbery neck. He carved a jagged, bloody line down under its belly, down to its dead stump of tail, then pushed the knife in underneath the open flaps, severing the links to the gristle and cartilage beneath. Half an hour later he had ripped the fur from his friend's body, leaving it a crisscross of knotted ruby muscle.

With the two children sitting in wicker baskets suspended from a strip of wood hung over his shoulders, Niu Lang threw the skin over his head. Nothing happened. He wiped the sweat from his brow and took a deep breath. Then he started to run, breaking into an awkward canter as he tried to balance the babies and the bloody skin flailing in the morning breeze. The children began to shout and laugh, and Niu Lang suddenly noticed that his feet were no longer touching the ground. They soared above the mountains, past the clouds, and into the dark light of the cosmos.

Niu Lang landed in the heavenly kingdom, and threw the animal's damp hide to the ground. The children had spotted their mother, weaving on a giant wheel ahead of them. Zhi Nu leapt up and opened her arms, awaiting an embrace. It never came. The Jade Emperor's wife emerged from behind her and, taking a hairpin from her black mane, ripped a hole in space between them. Niu Lang fell to the floor, clutching his children, as the small hole widened into a ravine. He pulled them back from the edge as the ravine continued to push apart, driving them further away from Zhi Nu. Her hysterical shouts were soon drowned out when, with an ear-splitting roar, a river of stars flooded into the deepening valley. When he finally uncovered his eyes, Niu Lang saw that he and the children were separated from Zhi Nu by the Milky Way.

Nothing could be done, for the Jade Emperor's wife was highly stubborn. Niu Lang broke down and began to sob as his children stared in surprise. Zhi Nu also wept continuously, her tears falling into her giant spinning wheel and creating monstrous grey rain clouds which delivered mournful storms to the world below. No matter what remedy they tried, neither could stop themselves from crying.

The Jade Emperor could not bear to see his daughter like that. Yet he could hardly risk upsetting his wife by undoing her magic. Finally, he came upon a compromise. He called a flock of magpies to him and ordered that for a single day each year they should leave the earth to make a bridge across the Milky Way, on which the two lovers would be allowed to meet. And so it is that every year, on the seventh day of the seventh lunar month, all the magpies disappear and cover the Milky Way with their dark feathers. If you listen closely on that night, you may even hear husband and wife whispering to each other on that long stretch of rustling wings.

It was only in the middle of the night, woken by her urgently throbbing bladder, that Yuying worked out that this was the story Jinyi had been referring to. It was an unusual story, as it ended not in death or tragedy, but in finding comfort in the smallest things, finding hope in the narrowest of possibilities. It was a story of quiet faith and of patience. Perhaps this was his way of saying I love you, she thought, squatting over the chamberpot. She shrugged: it hardly mattered what he had meant — it was how she chose to understand it that counted.

It was not long before the Jade Emperor visited me once again, to check on my progress. I was in a deserted kitchen — he never seemed to appear when others were around. His robes were foam and flame, his eyes seeing everything without bothering to look round.

'How many earth years has it been now?' he asked.

'Too many to count,' I replied. 'But surely if I don't see the whole lifetime of the heart then my picture will be incomplete. You don't agree?'

'A day, a lifetime. Is there a difference? The heart beats thousands of times a day, flits forward and back through a thousand feelings in a matter of hours. To catalogue every small twinge and turn of the heart in one single day might take you centuries.'

He was teasing me. I tried not to rise to it. 'If I remember correctly, it was you who ordered time to be divided into years so that man could understand it.'

The Jade Emperor grinned. 'Yes, you've got

me there. I asked the rat, ox, tiger, rabbit, dragon, snake, horse, sheep, monkey, rooster, dog, pig and cat to race each other to determine the order of years. You know, the rat tricked the cat and told her the wrong time for the race, so I ended up with twelve animals and not thirteen, and the poor old cat has been getting her own back on rats and mice ever since! That rat is a wily old devil, I'll give him that — he also rode for most of the race on the ox's head, only jumping off right at the end to claim first place. You should have seen the looks on the other animals' faces! They were flabbergasted.

'But that makes no difference,' he continued. 'Why not give up now and stop wasting these glorious years on this futile undertaking? Come, join me for a banquet, and I will promote you to Lord of the Rain Dragons. What do you say?'

It was my turn to smile. 'My mother used to tell me a story when I was a boy. It was about a fool who lived at the bottom of a huge mountain. Every month he took his radishes to the market and went to collect water from the river, both on the other side of the mountain. The trip — winding up along the rocky passes and through the frosty gales before making his way carefully down the other side of the peak — took many days. Finally, the fool had an idea. He would dig a tunnel straight through the mountain, and then he would never need to make the long, tortuous journey over it ever again. For years he dug; his hands withered, his back grew bent, his eyes finally became accustomed to the darkness as he swung his pick against the rock.

'His neighbour, a renowned wise man, came to visit him one day. "What on earth are you doing?" the wise man asked. "You have been digging for close to twenty years, and you have cleared a path of barely a quarter of a *li.* Your idea is ridiculous. It would take hundreds of years for one man to make a path through this mountain. Why not go back to growing radishes and be content with your lot?"

'But the fool was not impressed with this reasoning. "Call yourself a wise man? Soon I will die, but my son will carry on this work, and his son after him. One day, my great-great-grandchildren will be able to travel straight through to the river and the market." The wise man saw that the fool was right, and left him to his work.'

By the time I had finished this story, the Jade Emperor's whiskers were twitching angrily and his eyes were the same colour as the world a few moments before an eclipse. In a second, he was gone.

12:
2000
THE YEAR OF THE DRAGON

A boy was spitting. His pinched-dough nostrils flared up, his shoulders rose as his nose rumbled and he hawked up another round of ammunition. He drew in his carp lips and tilted his head up toward the naked bulb. Then he puckered and fired — a volley of lumpy-custard phlegm was sent across the room, slipping onto the white panel floor. His grandmother was snoring beside him, her head slouching towards her gargantuan chest. The boy's legs dangled restlessly from the plastic chair that had been nailed to the floor. Then the cycle began again, as he attempted to repeat the perfect dull-edged arc of soaring spit. Jinyi stared across the waiting room at the boy, his lips moving as if in search of the word that might describe this endlessly repeated action. Yuying tutted and turned back to her book.

How long had Jinyi been watching, involuntarily moving his mouth as the boy hawked and spat? He was not sure. All that mattered to him now was describing that action. What was this small human's face-hole doing? Come on, he thought; it's on the tip of my tongue!

A number pinged up on the LED display and the boy stopped to examine his crumpled print-out. They had won. He shook his grandmother, who blinked and wiped the dribble from her chin.

'Come on then,' the fat old woman said as she wobbled to her feet. 'You be good for the doctor and I'll buy you one of those caramel-strand animals from the park, all right?'

As they waddled off down the long corridor, Jinyi turned his attention to the globs of runny-egg mucus left on the floor. Yes, I know what this is, he told himself. Something from the head-periscope, the thing from the thing. He scratched the flaky bald patch at the back of his head. Yuying noticed and closed her book, placing it back in her carrier bag with the skin-coloured lipstick, the folded wedge of cheap toilet roll, the red-bean-flavoured sweets, the half-eaten corncob and the two pairs of disposable chopsticks.

'Don't worry. We'll see the doctor soon, and he'll sort everything out.' Yuying said, placing her hand over her husband's. Both were crumpled and speckled with lines and liver spots.

'Yes, yes, yes.' He was impatient, pulling his hand from under hers. Why is it, he thought, that once you get close to seventy people start treating you as if you are seven again? Can people not count that high? I'm just a little forgetful, that's hardly the end of the . . . whatsit? . . . the thing.

Yuying smiled and looked up at the clock. She did not want to risk enraging or upsetting him. Only last week she had come back from shopping to find him shouting at the TV, shaking with rage at the unstoppable torrent of voices and pictures. He had only calmed down when she had found the remote control — inexplicably placed in the chopstick and cutlery drawer — and switched it off. That was the day before his last fall.

From the black dots on the wall display colour began to prickle up, the first light out of primordial chaos. Yuying consulted their ticket: 247, now also flashing in siren red above them. She nudged her husband, who shifted his weight forward and pushed himself up uncertainly, still too proud to reach out for support.

'Just be honest,' Yuying whispered, though Jinyi simply readjusted his stiff grey cotton suit and pretended he had not heard her.

The doctor was sitting at a white wooden table in a small room with white walls. The white sheets on the single bed were dotted with maroon patches, and the white curtain to be pulled round it was decidedly crusty. This was, however, the fifth best hospital in the city, or so the sign outside proudly claimed. It was also the second cheapest; though in theory the government should have paid back eighty per cent of any costs, since both of them were retirees of state jobs.

'Well hello,' the doctor said — a little too loudly, Jinyi thought, as though he suspected the couple was deaf. The doctor was in his early thirties, his face shining with the joys he expected to fall effortlessly into his lap, his fingers ever busy, alternating between the four red pens in his shirt pocket and his floppy fringe.

'Hou Jinyi, I would like to ask you a few questions. Is that all right?' the doctor said, after Yuying had bent close and whispered to him for a few seconds.

'Yes.'

'That's great. Now, I hear that you had a little fall last week. Is that right?'

'Well, yes, I suppose. Someone must have left . . . something on the floor, and I can't have been looking where I was going.'

'Ah ha, of course, of course.' The doctor nodded earnestly. 'So can you tell me when you were born?'

'Well, I . . .' Jinyi's words trailed off into silence.

'It's hard to say, doctor,' Yuying said, coming to his rescue. 'My husband grew up in the countryside, you see, and never saw a real calendar until he came to the city. But we celebrate his birthday in April, and we think he must be around seventy-five or seventy-six.'

'I see. Mid to late seventies, that makes sense. So, can you tell me what year it is now?'

'Yes. It's, erm, 19 . . . well, it's 1976.' Jinyi knew this was the wrong answer, but he figured it must be close enough.

'Hmm, all right, now can you tell me who the current president is?'

'It's that . . . man . . . that man with the big eye-things. You know who I mean.' Jinyi's voice was rising, unable to hide his irritation.

'Big eye-things? Ah, yes, Jiang Zemin's black spectacles are a little on the large side. Ha. Very good. I think I can see what is happening here. We will need to do a few more tests, if that is all right with you.'

'Will they be expensive?' Jinyi asked, and his wife looked at him sharply.

'Oh, I shouldn't think so. They should help us to understand the extent of your problem.'

'What is the problem, doctor?' Yuying asked hesitantly.

He took a deep breath. 'Well, the lack of spatial awareness, dizziness, memory problems, confused vocabulary and language issues — these are all signs of dementia. It's just what happens when the brain gets old, I'm afraid, once it has too much to hold. But we'll know more after the tests.'

'Where are my words?' Jinyi mumbled.

'You're just having a few problems finding them, that's all. And besides, "Nothing that can be expressed in words is worth saying." ' The doctor smiled, pleased with himself.

'Lao Tzu,' Yuying said and the doctor nodded.

'We'll know more after the tests.'

He scribbled a few indecipherable notes on a square sheet of paper, which he handed to Yuying before ushering them out of the room. They stood for a minute outside the office, buffered between people hurriedly moving through the corridors. Everything goes so fast these days, Jinyi thought. There is no time for anything.

'Come on then, let's see if we can't find where they do the tests. Upstairs, I'll bet. Perhaps they've got a lift we could use. That would be nice.' Yuying talked because she could not think of anything else to do, because the meaningless chatter was more comforting than her own thoughts.

There was no lift, only a broken escalator and a slippery set of stairs, which they negotiated hand in hand. When they reached the next floor, the corridors curled off in every direction, giving the impression that the hospital was immense, that it was akin to an endless maze from which there was little hope of escape. They passed rooms filled with incubating babies; rooms that were silent but for the tick-tock trickle of intravenous drips hanging like empty speech bubbles above the patients' heads; rooms of scattered bedpans attended by armies of insects; rooms where middle-aged men in dark suits drank liquor and smoked endless cigarettes over the beds of the comatose; rooms of rash-speckled children playing marbles; and rooms in which prosthetic limbs hung on hooks, almost beckoning. Whenever Yuying asked for help or directions, the dumpy nurses looked at them contemptuously.

'I'm sorry,' Jinyi whispered to Yuying.

'Sorry? Whatever for?' she said, shaking her head and smiling indulgently.

He did not reply. It had begun as a series of little secrets. The things that he felt confused about, the small slips and scrapes, the household projects he would start and later come across with surprise, wondering who had left the work unfinished — all the little things too trivial and embarrassing to be worth mentioning. After that it had gradu-ated into a family joke: you haven't lost the keys again, have you Jinyi? Don't worry about introducing yourself to Pa, he'll only forget your name anyway! Should I phone twice or three times to remind you about dinner? Jinyi had laughed along with the jokes, as if to say, yes, I'm getting a bit old and forgetful, but that's as bad as it gets. And as such, the slow progression meant that for the first few years it had been easy to ignore, while for the next couple of years if it was spoken of, it was only in pitying terms behind Jinyi's back.

'After all,' his daughters had all agreed, 'he has suffered enough humiliation and trouble for one lifetime. Just let him be.'

Jinyi clutched his wife's arm to make sure she did not slip on the freshly mopped floor at the end of yet another corridor. He could at least pretend that he was in control, that everything was still fine. He could still recall with perfect clarity their wedding day, the tiniest details of their earliest arguments, every turn of the river and every leafy bristle of the forests they had pushed through on their way to his aunt and uncle's house, yet he sometimes found he could not remember a single thing that had happened only the previous day. Whole days, weeks, seemed to have disappeared, been struck from the calendar. His dreams alone retained a strange clarity: the faces of his aunt, of Dongming, of his colleagues in the dumpling restaurant, of the baby boy they carried through the fields away from the fighting in the city, all returned to him at night, as if they had never left his sight. However, there were days when his new great-grandson came and climbed up onto his knee and he found himself struggling to work out who the little boy could possibly be. Again, his only recourse was to smile and avoid risking offending whoever's child it was, smile and do his best to hide his panic.

'This must be it,' Yuying announced, and they settled onto another set of plastic chairs outside another small room. A little girl in front of them in the makeshift queue was about to have her blood taken, and, when she caught sight of some of the things going on through the half-open door, she began to scream at her mother in protest.

'Oh, I must remember to buy a chicken and cook a big stew for when Xiaojing and her husband come to dinner. We'll give them the leftovers too — they need everything they can get now, what with their factory being "temporarily closed".'

'Xiaojing. Yes, she'll be home from school soon.' Jinyi latched onto a thread of his wife's daily monologue. Since they had been forced to give up the mornings on the farm, Yuying had told him what had to be done each day before they did it. It was her way of filling the time, of ordering the chaos.

'No, dear, she's much too old for that. Your daughter sells DVDs now, remember?' Yuying said, drumming her fingers on her bag.

Jinyi's eyes were half closed. In the late Tang dynasty, the Confucian poet Han Yu wrote of the mythical unicorn that its sighting is a sign of good fortune, as is made clear in the works of the classical scholars. Even small children recognise the name and know that it is lucky. However, Han Yu noted, it is also a creature which resists definition — we can only say what it is not, never what it is. Therefore, he concluded, we might be staring right at a unicorn and not know what it is. This was how Jinyi felt almost every day; the familiar things in front of him — spoons, keys, spitting boys, doctors, grandchildren — were rendered unfamiliar by his inability to match them to their name, to provide them with their definition. His world was slowly becoming populated by unicorns; a multitude of unicorns of different colours, shapes and sizes, strange beasts whose presence seemed more terrible than auspicious.

Jinyi struggled and finally forced out the words. 'Maybe we should come back tomorrow.'

'It won't be any less busy then. Don't worry, we'll be home for lunch,' Yuying said, using the reassuring but assertive tone of voice she had spent years practising on their children.

'But do we really need to know the . . . the things . . . what . . . the . . . the things?' he said.

'The more we know, the stronger we are. If the doctors know what is wrong, they can do something about it,' Yuying assured him.

Jinyi was not convinced. Experience seemed to teach that the more you knew, the more trouble you were likely to encounter. Far better to just get on with your own business and leave the answers to someone else.

When the tests were finished, Jinyi and Yuying retraced their steps through the tapering corridors, retreating past an old woman wailing at a vacant line of orange plastic seats, and a rabble of little boys taking turns racing on a rusty wheelchair. It took them half an hour to find their way out, and another half hour to walk back through town, past the dingy office blocks and the nearby fast-food neons, until they could collapse in the little bunker of a house, where they did their best to stop too much of the present from creeping in. Yuying spent the rest of the day rustling up a stew from the fuzzy vegetables and ancient spices at the back of the half-empty kitchen cupboard, having spent their monthly pension on the hospital fees, while Jinyi opened his martial-arts adventure book and spent the afternoon pretending not to worry about the results.

'I'll make you some green tea, dear, and you'll soon forget about the tests,' Yuying said from the kitchen, but quickly regretted her choice of words. She dipped a spoon into the bubbling pot to retrieve some crinkly white hairs. If she did not keep her snowy bob pinned back behind her ears, she found it moulted everywhere, just like the neighbour's yappy dog.

'What we don't know . . . is an ocean,' Jinyi

replied. His wife nodded her head, not needing to reply. And we are stranded on the evershrinking shore.

How do we fill the time while waiting for the rest of our lives to begin? This is not a new question, and there are no new answers. Jinyi did the same as he had done on his barefoot treks toward Fushun, in the fields back at his uncle's house, in the steamy restaurant and the sweaty factory, with the lazy oxen and with his wife's silence — he hid behind a docile smile. At least then he had something else to think about; now, there was nothing but the waiting, which he twisted into a penance for something he had forgotten, a staring contest with his own fears.

After a phone call from the hospital, Yuying left her husband, telling him that she was popping out to do some shopping. When she returned a few hours later, Jinyi did not notice the absence of bags; he was too busy flicking through the calendar, studying the appointments scribbled in the small boxes and trying to separate what had already happened from what was still to come.

'How are you feeling?' she asked him.

'Fine. Fine,' he replied distractedly.

It was then that Yuying decided that she would not tell him about the results of the tests — to know that the doctors predicted only slow deterioration would be of little comfort. She would go to the hospital alone whenever she could; she would keep a daily log of his behaviour, noting any problems; she would worry for both of them, and be strong for both of them. That is what women do, she told herself.

There is more than one type of demon. They are not all fang-toothed tail-swishing child-stealers. Oh, no. Jinyi had learnt that some of them are so small that they can creep into your ear while you are sleeping and, with a tiny pair of chopsticks, froth up your brain as though they were beating eggs to scramble for dinner. And where before, when he was separated from his wife and family by war zones, by work, by the whims of politics or the weight of grief, he could turn to his memories for comfort, now it was those that were being shaken off like dandruff from the shoulders of a dark suit.

Yet, in his moments of lucidity, he realised too that love also changes shape. It was no longer slim, lithe, nervous and sweaty-palmed. It was no longer sleepless, heavy, a stone weighing deep inside the chest. It was now warm, slow, soft, a tatty old blanket huddled under in the dark. It was the last embers of a promise made decades before, still glowing red though the flames had petered down.

And so, if some mornings in the first minutes after he woke he had trouble recognising the plump old woman beside him, it was not because he had forgotten her — it was because, still blurry from drawn-out dreams, he was trying his hardest to keep hold of the memories of the young lady with the shy smile and the floating vowels and the golden slippers and the strength of dragons.

Yuying was woken by her husband twitching, his legs flailing out and kicking into hers. Her first thought was for the bruises that rose up ever more easily on her limp skin. Her body was becoming foreign to her, the parts not claimed by gravity now wrinkling and hugging her muscles for comfort. Everything bruised her now — like an autumn peach, she thought. Jinyi whimpered, flailed, turned; his body was a rickety raft caught by a tsunami. She moved tighter to him, holding fast to his shoulders and scrawny arms, trying to calm him.

'Hey, hey,' she soothed. 'Wake up. Hey, what is it?'

His eyes shot open, and darted left and right. Finally he fell back, into her arms. It was a strange gift, she thought, to be belatedly granted the tenderness she had craved in the first decades of her marriage, to be given sensitivity only after she had turned hard with blisters and calluses. She stroked his thinning hair. It was matted with sweat.

She reached over and turned on the bedside

lamp. 'What was it? A nightmare? What happened? Did you see something horrible?'

'No.' His voice was small, hoarse.

'Then what was it scared you?'

'I . . . I was not scared. Just people.'

'People? What people?'

'Old.'

'Like you and me? We're not that old, you know.'

'No, no, no. People. Gone.'

She stroked his arm. It was always ghosts these days. 'Why don't I boil some water and make us some tea? How about that Fujian black dragon we've been saving, hmm? We're not going to sleep again now anyway.'

She slipped on her bobbly dressing gown and helped her husband into his. While she put some water to boil on the stove he settled on the crumbling futon, biting his nails. Might our dreams be the place where it is possible for the two worlds to meet, Yuying wondered: like a hole in the roof where the water leaks in? Or were dreams just a trick of the brain? When it came it down to it, she considered, was there actually a difference between these two theories? They reached the same conclusion — that logic is left behind at the borders of death and dreams. She slopped the water into the small clay pot and carried the tray over to Jinyi.

'Do you want to talk about it?'

He shrugged, lifting the small cup to his

nose — the first cup for smell, the second for taste. Who had told him that?

'Who did you see?' Yuying asked between sips.

'Everyone.'

'Oh. I see.' She wanted to ask, 'Were they well? What did they say? Did anyone mention me?' But she did not want to upset him, to give credence to the idea that his nightmares might be more than a sleight of hand of memory. 'Do you remember when the children were young and had bad dreams? They used to crawl into our bed, remember? Sometimes they'd all migrate across and cram in together, even though ours was much smaller than the *kang* they shared. We wouldn't get more than half an hour's sleep a whole night, and then work twelve hours or more. I wonder how we did it.' She chuckled, then looked across at her silent husband.

Jinyi kept the cup held up in front of him, an offering to some invisible residue of the dream.

She led him back to the bedroom and pulled the covers tight around his shivering body, then slipped into the ancient indents her own body had left in the bed over the years.

Yuying took out her teeth and closed her eyes. This is how life works, she thought; being given what you wanted only when you have learnt not to need it. There were a hundred questions she might have asked him with this gift of honesty and dependence, when she was sixteen, twenty, thirty even; but these days she could guess what he would say before he had even opened his mouth. She told herself it was better this way. Slowly the day's conversations at the hospital came back to her and she wondered about her husband's dreams. If he must lose everything else, his memories, our life together, even me, then at least let him keep his dreams, she mouthed to gods whose names she could not quite remember.

Perhaps, she began to think, as she lay in the bed the two of them had shared on and off for close to fifty years, this is what love is — a wilful forgetting, remembering only the best days, the little joys and the times they felt like they were flying through their lives. There was still something of that old Jinyi left, she told herself, some part of that young man who cooked her dumplings and had walked more than a thousand *li* to find her, who always had a joke to trade for a tear.

For once, as I picked through her thoughts, I felt pretty stumped. For once, I found myself wondering whether perhaps my own life had been all the better for being kept short. At least I had never got to the point where I wondered whether love had become a full-time job. And yet still it seemed that whatever was thrown at it, the heart carried on.

Jinyi, meanwhile, kept one eye open: he was on the lookout for a flicker of the blinds, a shadow from the window, anything that might announce the return of the ghosts. The thing that scared him was not that his dream was terrible or unstoppable (though it was indeed both of these), but that it was actually comforting to see all those old faces again, that the dream made more sense to him than many of his waking hours did these days.

Both of them yawned, then pretended to snore, each trying to convince the other that they were really fast asleep.

The Jade Emperor continued to appear with gifts — a handful of fireflies; a pair of scaly wings that he imagined might fit me perfectly; a mirror in which it was possible to see how things would have turned out if I had avoided all the mistakes I made in life; a perfect copy of the book of death; some tracts of celestial space where planets were yet to be born; and many other trinkets. However, these only made me more certain that I was closer to winning the bet; I turned down all his bribes.

'I am nearly done,' I finally told him.

He did not reply.

'Listen, can I ask you something?'

The Jade Emperor bowed his head forward, which I decided to take as a yes.

'Living so long in the minds of people, well, it's made me remember being human. Not much has changed since I was one. Love, of course, continues. But so do wars, dictators, tyrants, torture, disease, famine, floods, earthquakes, random acts or edicts of violence.

So . . . I just wanted to know why you don't do something about it?'

'The Taoists call it *"wu wei"*: deliberately not acting. Imagine a river; it does nothing but follow the Tao, and yet it might slowly wear down hills and mountains or carry men home. I act in accordance with nature. Many of the Taoist monks may have fled or been killed or repressed, but no one has forgotten *wu wei.* Why do you think all those people never rose up, and still do not rise up against the government, against the corruption or the terror? Why go along with the Cultural Revolution or the denunciations that accompanied it? *Wu wei* means not resisting. Even I must try to follow the Tao. The only way for life to improve is for everyone to be in harmony with the Tao, to let the world return to its natural course,' he said.

'I see. Let them get on with it down there, make their mistakes and learn from them. But they don't seem to learn from the mistakes. They keep on making the same ones, over and over again,' I said.

Once again the Jade Emperor bowed his head forward. 'If I were to stop a flood today by diverting a river, others would only suffer from arid land and famine tomorrow. Humans are fickle creatures; they do not know what is best for them. Think of happiness. Happiness is a glimpse of water to the man in the desert, and a sight of dry land to those lost at sea. As I told you before, there is only the circle, only a

670

journey that each person makes again and again. Take your precious heart. Life flows from heart to artery to capillary to vein and back to the heart. The same motion will continue again and again. This is the secret you have been looking for, one that I told you at the start of your quest. You will find no other answer but this — people carry on with their lives because they have no other choice. That is all you will learn from watching them.'

'No,' I said. 'What about love? What about doing the right thing? What about atonement and retribution?'

However, I found myself talking to a wall. The Jade Emperor had disappeared, and I realised there was nothing I could do about it, except finish the story.

13:
THE YEAR OF THE CAT

Where the gnarled peak meets the low-hanging shreds of cloud, shards of ice begin to melt, to crackle and spit, and slowly trickle down the vast slopes of Geladaindong Snow Mountain. Further down, the lower tracks of snow turn to slush and join the dribbling drips, until soon the trickle has become the smallest of streams. It pulses down through the Tanggula Range that provides the sharp spine of the border between Qinghai and Tibet, slipping down cliff faces and ravines until it has traversed the six-thousand-metre drop to sea level; until it has become the Great River, Chang Jiang, the Yangtze, the third longest in the world, set on its eight-province journey toward Shanghai and the East China Sea. It is a river that toys with life and death as if they were flotsam, driftwood.

Halfway through its journey east, where junks and sampans would once have begun loading up grain and tea leaves to carry through the Three Gorges to distant coastal

672

cities, it passes Fengdu, the City of Ghosts. Fengdu sits on top of a hillside overlooking the swelling river and, clustered on the opposite bank, the refilling cruise ships and the neon strips of seafood restaurants and office blocks of modern-day Fengdu City. One can only hope that the restless souls who make their way here, for this is where all the dead must go, are not confused as to which side of the river to alight.

It would be tedious to list the numerous demons, devils and other hellish apparitions that reside there, and what's more, it would only serve to further inflate their already gargantuan egos, so I will merely point out that it is a place of darkness and despair, a place where groups of long-dead scholars spend their time thinking up new and ingenious tortures, and yet never manage to think of as many as do the generals and presidents back in the land of the living. It is a place where the potential uses of flesh and bone are most celebrated.

After the trek up the steep hillside, after the first gates and skinny pagodas, the recently deceased will reach the Unavoidable Bridge. If the arriving soul crosses the bridge holding the hand of his or her lover in exactly nine steps, then they may progress together, their hearts safe; if they arrive alone, or cross the bridge in a step more or a step less, the soul will forget everything it ever knew of love.

There are then fearsome judgements at which the dead are given a last chance to tell the truth of their lives, to ask those they have wronged back in the land of the living for forgiveness. There are five-cloud pagodas and snake-like dragons, vampiric women and other wretched, contorted beasts that may once have been human. However, it is at the highest point on the hillside of the City of Ghosts that the most important tower stands. It is a tall, narrow structure resembling a lookout post, painted a faded blue and topped with weather-worn eaves. This is the Tower of Distant Homelands. It is one of the last stops for the dead, who must climb to the top and, from the great height, locate their former home somewhere in the distance below. Their bodies have already been broken by death; seeing for one last time the homes they can never return to serves to break the spirit. After this, the soul is unrecognisable. I shall say no more about where they go next, for I do not wish to give you nightmares.

Jinyi might be spared some of these trials, for he had already lost much of his past, his home, many of the little moments of comfort and love that sustain us, and close to a quarter of his body weight. He was propped on his side because of the bed sores that drew a dark patchwork over the sharp ridges of his back. One of his eyes was plum black and shrunk shut from where Yuying had smashed the bedside lamp into his face after she had woken one night to find him screaming and strangling her. It had been the only thing she could do to make him stop. The doctors had warned Yuying and her daughters that it would not be long before he would be making that infamous journey. Their exact words were, 'Why on earth didn't you bring him here sooner?'

There was no simple answer. The slowness of his decline had meant that they had been uncertain when to bring him in, especially since he had become increasingly afraid of venturing outside his daughter's flat. Yuying had been forced to sell the house — which she first had to buy completely from the government using borrowed money — to pay for hospital fees and cabinets full of medicines, and they had been living in their grandson's old room in Liqui's flat for the last year and a half. The family had felt that to enter the hospital permanently would be to admit two things that they did not want to acknowledge: first, that they could no longer cope with looking after him, and second, that there was little chance of him recovering. So much better to let him die peacefully in a familiar bed, surrounded by the loving faces of his family. However, his violent fits and terrors had now precluded that possibility.

Yuying traced her finger over the photograph

of her husband, his black hair wild and manic as it had been throughout that hot summer of 1946. Then she closed the album, placed it back in the drawer in her grandson's bedroom, and arranged a few winter clothes over the top. It was time to go.

She rubbed her eyes. She registered a dull numbness, an ache in her sloped back from slouching too long on the wooden chair beside her husband's hospital bed. She made her way to the kitchen and filled a plastic box with dumplings. He would miss her if she did not go back soon, she told herself.

Without him, she thought, I will only be half a person.

How do we go about dealing with death? The first emperor, Qin Shi Huang, decided that death would not stop him. When his hunt for the elixir of immortality stalled, he thought of another idea. He had perfect stone facsimiles created of his entire army, man for man, from archers and swordsmen down to the horses that trotted with them. And beside his army he replicated his court, from mandarins and musicians through to jesters and even birds. Once the likeness of every man, the moustaches and eyebrows and fish lips and dimpled chins, had been chiselled into the stone, they were to be sealed deep beneath the imperial capital of Xian, part of the emperor's giant tomb, of which only a tiny proportion has yet been rediscovered. Did he imagine, perhaps, that with an imperishable army he might conquer whatever world awaited him with the same ease with which he had proved his mastery in life? Or was he instead convinced that the relationship between a thing and its double would reveal the duplicitous nature of the fabric of the world?

It seems more likely he believed that if he might control perceptions and beliefs, he might change the world: if only a handful of people believed in the stone army, then that might be enough to animate them. This is, after all, the same emperor who started work on the Great Wall and who ordered the burning of ancient books, declaring that history began anew with him. Yuying would have said that this was unnecessary, as was the book-burning ordered by Mao, since she believed that every generation had only a short-term memory: they remembered just enough of the past few years and of their parents to measure themselves against them and resolve to be different. Surely that was the only explanation for the circular nature of revolution and capital, the reason that the new century resembled the time of her birth more than any other period in between.

Yuying walked back to the hospital, past the snaking river, past the old mansion where she had been born, past the factory where she had worked, with her thoughts buffeting her flesh like a hurricane. They tugged her, needled her, shook her through.

Both her husband and her eldest daughter were asleep, one on the rickety old bed, the other on the small wooden chair beside it. There was a small bedside cabinet topped with a few magazines, an empty bed across the opposite wall and a bedpan waiting on the cold stone floor. The rattling window looked out onto a workyard where circular saws cut through strips of metal. The bloody remains of mosquitoes dotted the flaking white walls. She woke Manxin and sent her home.

Jinyi was slick with sweat. He was asleep on his side, rasping and dribbling with his mouth open, the IV drip taped to his forehead, as it had been since he had scratched and torn it from his hands. His eyes were shut, his chest rocketing up and down. From her bag Yuying removed the box full of warm dumplings, and waited for him to wake. She would wait as long as it took.

The little parcels of dough reminded her of the previous year, when Liqui had brought home a variety of dumplings from a small café, and Jinyi, still just about able to feed himself, had wolfed all of them down as though he might never see another meal, saving only those filled with pork and green onion.

'Can I have some of those?' Yuying had

asked him.

'No!' he had shouted, and thrown his arms around the dumplings, his eyes darting round the room to catch out possible thieves.

'Please? Go on, Jinyi, share one with me,' Yuying had said.

'No! No one can touch!' he had spat. Yet a second later he had softened, his eyes sunk down, and he had whispered, 'I am saving them for my wife. This is her favourite kind.'

Yuying had not known whether to start laughing or crying. She had simply decided to eat later, waiting for her husband to either recognise her or forget about the dumplings, whichever came first. He had forgotten about the dumplings.

A few hours later, Yuying felt a hand on her shoulder, gently shaking her from her sleep. She looked up to see her youngest daughter's pinched face slowly creeping into focus above her.

'Ma, it's me. Why don't you go home and get some rest?' Xiaojing said.

'No no, I want to help,' she replied, with a light wave of her hand. Her daughter pulled up another wooden chair and sat beside her.

'You won't do much good like this, Ma. If you try and lift him or feed him yourself, you might get hurt. Liqui will come by in the morning, and then Jingchen after his night-shift, so there'll be plenty of people here,'

Xiaojing said.

'I know, I know. I'm useless now, I know.'

'No, that's not what I meant, I —'

'I know you didn't. Forgive me, I'm tired. But I can't leave, not now. I may not be able to lift him well, or clean him, or hold him down while we feed him, but he still needs me. If he wakes up and I'm not here, who knows what he'll do? Some days I'm the only one he recognises.'

'I know. Even when he's quiet, I can see that look in his eyes — as if he's trying to work out who I am and how I got here and whether I intend to hurt him or not. It scares me.'

'Your old father is still in there somewhere, deep down, don't you ever think that he's not. This illness it's . . . it just confuses the way he sees everything, that's all. It's not his fault."

'It's just hard to see that sometimes, Ma. Well, stay if you want, but there is a warm bed waiting for you back at Liqui's, and I can deal with him if he wakes before Jingchen gets here.'

'Go. If I want to rest I'll settle on that bed there — the old man who shared the room died a few days ago, so we've got it all to ourselves now.'

Xiaojing looked at the metal cot and wrinkled her nose. 'Is it clean, though?'

'Why wouldn't it be? The dead take their

diseases with them.'

'It'll bring you bad luck though, Ma, sleeping where a dead man slept.'

'Ha! I've had enough bad luck; a bit more can't hurt. And besides, we're in a hospital, dear. If you think there is a bed in here that someone hasn't died on, then you've got your head on backwards.'

Xiaojing sighed and shrugged, picking up one of the crumpled magazines that each of them had read and reread a hundred times. There were still a few hours until dawn. Each of the daughters and their husbands took different shifts depending on their work and the needs of their grandchildren, bringing in home-cooked food — the hospitals no longer provided meals — and pyjamas scrubbed clean from the daily 'accidents'. This was the pattern of their lives, a part of them praying for it to end, a part of them praying that he would hold on forever. Yuying tried to sift through those last years, to pinpoint the exact date when the nervous, screaming, flailing, child-like man in front of her came and stole her husband away, but she could not do it. She had given up counting the slips, the falls, the tantrums, the fits and shouts; they were simply part of her routine now. A good day was one in which he smiled, stayed calm and quiet; the bad days passed in a rush of activity. Only last week, a few days before he had tried to suffocate his wife, he had woken in the night and started shouting. To placate him, Liqui, taking her shift watching him while Yuying slept, had offered him food and he had mumbled something about noodles. Since there were no noodles in the house, Liqui had hurried out to find some after waking her husband and asking him to man the bedside in case Jinyi started hitting his head against the wall again. Jinyi had cried until no more tears would come, until his eyes were messy red blotches in a mask of scrunched paper. Liqui had searched the city for a twenty-four-hour shop, then bought noodles, returned home, boiled the water and finally brought the steaming bowl to the bedside. I will not eat, he had shouted, you cannot poison me! And I hate noodles!

When dawn shuffled in and the nearby workyard roared into life, an elderly nurse came in to change the drip.

'He's a tough one, isn't he?' she said, grinning at the two tired women seated beside the bed.

'How do you think he is doing?' Xiaojing asked.

'Oh, I'll bet he's survived far worse than being cooped up in here. My old husband was the same, a mere wisp of a man too, but with the strength of an ox. I wonder where it all comes from.'

'He's certainly strong when he gets angry,'

Xiaojing muttered.

'Ha, yes, that's right. He's quite a fighter, this one. If you ask me, the more of life they lose, the more they cling onto what remains. I'll be down the hall when this bag runs out — just holler for me, won't you,' the nurse said, sweeping from the room.

Everyone has advice, Yuying thought, brief words of wisdom that soon crumble to dust. Everything looks so simple, so clear-cut to them when they do not have to live it every minute of every day. Everyone is an expert on other peoples' lives. She remembered one of the earlier doctors who had tried to reason with her that Jinyi was lucky, since everyone else in the country was going out of their way to actively forget the past, while he was granted a reprieve from those terrible years. She snorted, and her daughter turned to look at her before she slumped back into her restive state.

Jinyi snuffled, coughed; his unbruised eye squeezed itself open. He looked about the room, his hands twitching at the sheet.

'Good morning, Jinyi, how are you feeling?' Yuying asked, her voice calm and clear.

He stopped twitching and stared at her quizzically.

Yuying scraped her chair closer to the bed as she answered his unasked question. 'Don't worry, we're in hospital. There is nothing to worry about. I'm here. I'm your wife, Bian

Yuying. And here's your youngest daughter, Hou Xiaojing. Would you like something to eat?'

'Nnh,' he rasped, and recoiled, shocked by the sound of his own voice.

'A drink?'

'Nnh.'

'Do you need to go to the toilet?'

'Nnh.'

'Would you like me to read to you from the newspaper then?'

'Nnh,' he grunted, and began to groan as he tried to move his aching right arm.

'Jinyi, no! Don't do that, you'll end up on your back again, or else you'll fall onto your chest and we'll have to get the nurse to help prop you up. Would you like another pillow?'

He did not reply, his eye closing to a dim slice. His mouth stayed pursed open, the dank, heavy air hissing in and out. His mind was a jigsaw into which the wrong pieces had been forced, his thoughts unaccountable relics of shipwrecks and ruins. Light flickered in from the window as the circular saws burred through scrap. Time was a series of indivisible, unlinked moments — he could no longer connect this strange series of events, order them and call them his life.

Liqui arrived with food and clean clothes, and the women greeted each other with yawns. They spotted a dark stain spreading across the front of Jinyi's pyjamas and tried to unknot the buttons without disturbing him. They slid them down and off his feet, revealing his pale, spindly legs, the sparse tufts of grey pubic hair, the coiled snail of his shrivelled penis. Yuying dug out a baby wipe and cleaned the sticky mess, carefully anointing his vein-mapped flesh. His daughters threaded his feet through a clean pair of pyjama bottoms, which they dragged up to cover him. Jinyi rasped and moaned, his eyes pressed closed, immune now to embarrassment.

'Now go, please, Ma. You need the rest. Go on, the house is empty now; you can get a good bit of sleep and come back soon,' Xiaojing said.

'No. I'm not leaving him. Not again.'

'OK. At least go and get yourself something to eat from the canteen,' Xiaojing said.

Yuying sighed and got to her feet. 'I suppose I don't have a choice if I don't want you to keep on at me. I'll be back in a minute.'

She bent close to the bed, supporting her weak frame against the metal headboard, and whispered to her husband. He did not respond. She pulled on her heavy coat, replaced her slippers with her flat black shoes, and arranged her bag on her shoulder, delaying leaving as long as possible, hoping for a sign that he had heard her before she went.

'Don't forget this,' Liqui said, thrusting a

mobile phone into her mother's hands. 'Just in case.'

Yuying nodded and wandered from the room, clutching the fold-up silver phone in her palm. Her own company frightened her — if she was not helping others, seeing herself through their eyes, then she was not sure who she was. The mobile beeped, and she fumbled with it, prising it open to see that it was low on battery and needed to be charged. She should have known that, she reminded herself. The messages she received on the phone were troubling; she could read them all right, but she was not sure how to reply, how to order the brush strokes on the numerals into a coherent sentence, and so the communication could only go one way. In fact, she considered, the whole damn beeping thing bothered her. Phones in houses were fine, the idea of buidings linked by wires tripping through the sky seemed clear to her: making a call was like completing an electrical circuit. But these disembodied gadgets seemed somehow ghostly — like storing a thousand captive voices in your pocket.

She lined up in the canteen in silence. When she remembered how she had once thought — how everyone had once thought — that by changing the way she acted she could help change the world, her lips strayed into a wry smile. Now every little thing she did, from cooking to whispering to washing to holding hands to arguing with doctors, she did to try to keep the world from changing. It was an impossible task, she thought, but that is what we Chinese are good at.

In one corner of the canteen was an old, battered television, playing out a traditional love story in the form of a soap opera. Tinny strings raced to a crescendo as the doe-eyed actors stared at each other. It was a story I'd heard a hundred times before — but then again, those are the best kind. Shall I tell it to you? After all, we can't stay moping around at Jinyi's bedside all day now, can we?

Zhu Yingtai's family were as rich as they were conservative and traditional. Thus when, at the age of twelve, Zhu Yingtai asked her father if she could go to school, the old man did not know whether to burst out laughing or to retrieve his old walking cane to beat such foolish ideas out of his daughter once and for all. After a moment's deliberation, he chose the latter. However, the bruises across the back of her legs did not deter Zhu Yingtai. Ever since she had taught herself to read, she had spent her days looking through her father's collection of classical tomes; while her sisters picked at their needlework, learnt how to prepare tea for visiting guests and attended to the silkworms, Zhu Yingtai was carefully turning crisp, inky pages, lost in the intricate brush-strokes. As was later to become tragically clear, she was not the type of person to give up her hopes without a fight.

She took a length of silk cloth and spun it tightly round her chest; she bit her nails down to the quick; she wriggled into a pair of straight trousers and pulled on a baggy jacket; she practised sneering and walking with her feet facing out and her hands swinging ape-like at her side; and she learnt how to hawk and spit. Finally, Zhu Yingtai took a deep breath and a pair of scissors and hacked off her long plait, until her hair was cropped close to her head. Then she climbed out of her bedroom window.

Yet instead of running away, she simply walked round to the front of the house and began to bang as loudly as she could at the gate. A flustered servant hauled the great wooden door open and peeked out.

'I am an acquaintance of Old Zhu. Please direct me to his chambers,' Zhu Yingtai said, as sonorously as she could.

The servant scuttled away and, on returning, beckoned her into the entrance chamber. She made an effort to sit with her legs splayed casually in front of her, and began to crack her knuckles as her father swept into the room. He stared down contemptuously at the odd-looking visitor before him.

'Is this some kind of joke?' Old Zhu asked. 'Answer me, boy! What business do you have claiming to be an acquaintance of mine? Do you have a message for me, or are you a beggar here to waste both of our time?'

'Do you not know me, then?' she asked, pitching her voice as deep as possible.

'Enough of this foolishness!' he shouted. 'I have never met you before in my life. Now get out of here before I set the guards on you!'

Zhu Yingtai began to approach Old Zhu. She cleared her throat, and spoke in her natural voice. 'Father, look more closely. It is me, Yingtai.'

The old man peered into her eyes, and was suddenly rendered speechless.

'Since I have fooled even you with my disguise, surely those who have never met me will also believe I am a boy. Therefore if you let me attend school dressed like this, there will be no risk of me bringing dishonour on the family. No one will recognise me for who I really am, and you can tell the neighbours that I am off visiting relatives in another province. What do you say, father? Please let me go to school.'

Old Zhu slumped back into one of the elaborate wooden chairs. 'If you are willing to go to so much effort and debase yourself like this just to get your way, then I see that I am powerless to stop you. I will allow you to go to school, on the condition that when you return you submit to my rules, for the good of the family. A woman should not believe that she can do anything she wants.'

Zhu Yingtai agreed and, after kissing her father's hand, ran straight to her room to begin packing for her new life. Three days later she had said goodbye to her family and was riding towards the renowned academy in Hangzhou when she spotted another rider on the plains in front of her. Squinting, she could make out that he — for the likelihood of a woman travelling unaccompanied in bandit country like that was small — also carried many bags with him, and was heading in the same direction she had marked out on her map. She broke into a canter, determined to catch up with him.

Liang Shanbo's first impression of Zhu Yingtai was not particularly favourable. As the sweaty, red-faced young boy approached, Liang Shanbo sighed to himself: great, another know-it-all runt attaching himself to him in the hope that his friendship would stop the weaker boy from getting beaten up after class. Short, gangly, not particularly athletic, decidedly effeminate and with the worst haircut this side of the Great Wall! It was just his luck to get stuck with him for the next two hundred *li*.

'Hello there, er, mate! Are you off to the Hangzhou Academy?' Zhu Yingtai said as she drew side-by-side with him.

'I am,' he answered.

'Oh, great! I'm so excited — I've already read the four classics, and I can't wait to find out more about what we'll be learning. What's your name?'

'Liang Shanbo,' he replied, still staring straight ahead. Zhu Yingtai waited for him to continue with the courtesy questions, but was met only with silence. She decided to fill it by listing all the things she was looking forward to.

Liang Shanbo began to cluck his tongue against his teeth in annoyance; yet as the plains struggled up into hills, which in turn became rough breaks of bracken and burr, he found some of the shorter boy's enthusiasm rubbing off on him. Perhaps, Liang Shanbo thought to himself, this chap is not so bad after all. By the time the rain-washed eaves of the school rose up above the cedars, the two of them had told each other everything about themselves — give or take a few vital secrets. When the scholars began the lessons later that week, they even found themselves huddling next to each other on the stone floor, sharing a slim pool of plum-dust ink in which they took turns dipping their slender brushes.

'Mix the ink stick with a little spit, and then your writing will really shine on the page,' Liang Shanbo whispered to his classmate while the elderly scholar marched about, explaining how the earth floated in a sphere of celestial water.

'Thanks,' Zhu Yingtai replied, and proceeded to show her new friend how to clean the wax from his ear with the brush's spindly tip.

Liang Shanbo and Zhu Yingtai became inseparable; they were the first out with their longbows in the morning and the last to bed during the long summer evenings when they would test each other's memory of freshly composed verses as they strolled around the lake. They developed a collection of private jokes and a habit of finishing each other's sentences. It was therefore of no surprise to any of their friends or teachers when, after a large intake of new students at the beginning of their second year led to shortage of space, they chose each other as roommates.

This new arrangement presented a few problems for Zhu Yingtai, yet she went about solving them with her usual resilience. She developed a reputation for fastidiousness where personal hygiene was concerned, performing her private ablutions daily (a stark contrast to the other boys' weekly washes), but only once everyone else had gone to bed. She was proud that, after close to three years, despite mutterings about her odd physique, no one had discovered her secret. In their windowless room, where the best friends studied together by candlelight, Liang Shanbo and Zhu Yingtai slept top-to-tail on either side of a single stone bed. And so Zhu Yingtai began to wish that her days at the academy would never end.

'Hey. Hey! Are you awake?'

Zhu Yingtai was woken by Liang Shanbos's urgent whisper. The darkness was thick and stale, as though they were lying in the depths of a dragon's stomach. She rubbed her eyes before answering.

'What's the matter? Are you all right?'

'I'm fine. I just wanted to ask you something,' Liang Shanbo replied.

'Oh. What time is it?' she yawned.

'I don't know. Anyway, I was just wondering . . . well, you know how this is our final year and all our studies will come to an end next term . . .'

'Yes, of course. What's the problem?'

'Well, I guess I feel a bit confused. You have your family business that you must go back to,' Zhu Yingtai blushed in the dark as she heard him repeat her lie, 'but what about me? What am I going to do when we leave here?'

'You should take the imperial examination,' she answered. 'You're bound to get the highest mark in the whole province. Then you'll be able to do anything.'

'I know, I know. But what's the point of having money or power or success if I haven't got my best friend near me to make fun of me and bring me back down to earth?'

Zhu Yingtai realised that this was the opportunity she had been waiting for. 'Listen, I have a sister who is close to our age and unmarried. I could arrange a union between you and her — if you two were married, our families would be entwined and we would always be able to stay in contact.'

'That sounds like a perfect idea. I will marry your sister, even if she turns out to be as ugly as you!' he joked, and rolled over to go back to sleep.

On the last day of term, after their teachers had handed them specially written scrolls and wished them well for the future, the two friends went over their plan once again. They agreed for Liang Shanbo to travel to Zhu Yingtai's house for the wedding as soon as he had taken the imperial examination. How could her father possibly refuse her marrying a mandarin? Zhu Yingtai reasoned. The only question was whether Liang Shanbo would still want to go through with the marriage when he found that his old school friend would be his bride. Their horses parted on that same plain where they had met three summers before, and each rode off with the kind of giddy smile that the malevolent gods of fate always seize upon as a provocation.

When she reached her house, Zhu Yingtai was amazed to find a red silk wedding dress already laid out on her bed.

'Are you surprised?' her father asked as her sisters stood behind him giggling.

'Very. How did you know?' she asked.

'How did I know? I arranged the whole thing. You will be married to the honourable

Ma Wencai next week. I've spared no expense — this will be the grandest wedding this village has ever seen! How's that for a coming home gift, eh?'

'What? Ma Wencai? Who the hell is Ma Wencai?' she screamed.

'Watch your words, young lady! Ma Wencai is a great gentleman, and will soon be your husband, so you'd better start showing his name some respect!' her father replied.

'I cannot marry him — I will not marry him!'

'You will! His father has already helped our family through many difficult times, and put in a good word for us with the local government to enable my promotion. How would it look if I repaid him with a humiliating spite? More importantly, you gave me your word that when you returned from your studies you would submit to my rules. Have you forgotten your promise?'

'No, father,' she sobbed.

'Then stop crying and call your maids. There is a lot of work to be done if we are to transform you in just five days from looking like a young boy to a beautiful bride. Try the dress and pick a wig, and do not disturb me. I have work to do!'

And with that her father huffed from the room, leaving Zhu Yingtai to mop at her eyes and sniffling nose with her sleeve.

True to his word, Old Zhu had planned

such a lavish and elaborate ceremony, with a guest list that stretched into thousands and was rumoured to include the local chief magistrate himself, that news of the approaching wedding soon spread throughout the entire province. So it was that, leaving the examination hall in the provincial capital and feeling quietly confident, Liang Shanbo happened to overhear two of the adjudicators mention a village whose name seemed strangely familiar to him, though he could not work out why. He therefore stopped at the steps to listen to the rest of the conversation.

'. . . and suckling pigs, and it seems that there will be some kind of lion dance too. Everyone is going. I'm surprised you weren't invited.'

'Huh. Well, it doesn't bother me. The groom's family may be all right, I suppose, but I heard that the bride hacked off all her hair in order to look like a man! Whoever heard of such a thing?'

'I'm sure there's no truth in that old rumour. Old Zhu is a well-respected official. I'm sure his daughter is —'

'Wait! I'm sorry, but did you say Old Zhu? From Chicken Claw Village?' Liang Shanbo interrupted.

The two elderly adjudicators stared at the rude young man in front of them, noting that his face was turning pale. 'Perhaps,' one of them answered. 'What is it to you, boy?'

'Just tell me!' he shouted. The old men tutted.

'Not that it is any of your business, but yes, we were talking about the wedding that will be held in three days in Chicken Claw Village, between Ma Wencai and Zhu Yingtai. You must have heard about it. Hey — steady on now, what's the matter?' The adjudicator reached forward to try to catch Liang Shanbo as his body crumpled and he toppled forward.

'Bring him to my house, quickly!' the adjudicator shouted to his nearby sedan-carriers.

However, despite the careful attentions of the servants in the adjudicator's household, Liang Shanbo did not recover. He awoke only once and, when he remembered the conversation and realised that not only had he loved a woman in disguise all this time, but that she was now going to be separated from him forever, he felt a tiny splinter, like the tip of a calligraphy brush, enter his heart and split it in two. The next morning his family arrived and carried his body into the hills, where they buried it beneath an ancient yew with howls and sobs. Word of the boy's strange death carried like smoke throughout the villages in the valley below.

Zhu Yingtai was inconsolable. She awoke on the morning of her wedding to see the sky gone sour, a downy grey mould skimming over its surface. She wriggled into her dress and combed the horsehair wig while wiping away her tears, aware that, storm or no storm, her father would not relent. Hiding her grief under layers of make-up, she joined her expectant family. Yet just as the wedding procession was about to weave up through the hills toward her new home in the Ma-family mansion, Zhu Yingtai felt her sedan being lowered to the ground and heard the servants muttering among themselves. She peeked out from behind the silk curtains, and saw what was bothering them. A great hurricane was tearing up the trees on the distant horizon, drawing them towards disaster. Yet it was not the storm that caught her attention. She saw only a solitary yew standing near the top of the hill. She tugged the long red train of her wedding dress up around her calves and pulled herself out of the sedan, squelching into the mud.

Zhu Yingtai heard the servants begin to shout in panic, but she was too fast for them. Slipping from her shoes she ran up the hill, towards the storm. Rain lashed down and her dress slopped with water, but still she dragged herself forward, until she had reached the ancient yew where Liang Shanbo had been buried. She turned to see the servants catching up with her, ready to restrain her and carry out her father's stern commands. As their panting bodies drew closer, she closed her eyes and threw herself towards the grave.

The servants stopped, confused. They rubbed their eyes, and stared at each other in disbelief. Zhu Yingtai seemed to have vanished into the very earth. Then they heard the sound of something cracking, and the soil on the grave began to shudder. As the servants turned and ran in fright, the grave split open, and out fluttered two white butterflies, united at last.

Yuying caught only the last few minutes of the film before the credits came scrolling up the screen. Her rice and aubergine from the small canteen had turned cold on the plate in front of her. What better end, she thought, than butterflies? If only she could bring herself to believe that death was just a change, a sudden righting of the mistakes of life: shadows wound into a brittle chrysalis from which we are reborn. Perhaps it was, she thought; she had been wrong so many times before, and if the world could change so utterly then why couldn't she?

She returned to Jinyi's ward, her head buzzing. She had been daughter, student, wife, farmer, mother, commune member, comrade, colleague, traitor, revolutionary, mute, grandmother, nursemaid, carer. What was left? She had shed so many skins that she was not sure that anything remained underneath. But there must be something left, she reasoned, for she had not turned into a butterfly, her story had not ended.

She sat down once more and took Jinyi's brittle hand in hers. If only all stories were as simple as the story of the Butterfly Lovers. But she knew Jinyi would not be transformed, no matter what her daughters said to try to stop her worrying. All you can do, she thought, is try to hang on to the things you love while the undertow of history tugs away all your finely made plans.

Jinyi's eyes crumpled open. He did not see the two butterlies fluttering towards him. He saw two snags of a colour he could not name in a place he did not recognise in a room that was blurring in and out of focus. He saw things. Things and other things; their names and purposes beyond him. He saw things he thought he ought to know, things he thought he should recognise but could not, no matter how hard he grasped in the darkness. Like the old woman sitting at his bedside, snoring lightly, with an open book laid across her lap. Wasn't she that . . . that . . . that. He felt nervous, and so cold that he was shivering; he felt scared, and so hot that his eyes were on fire. He felt afraid, and the fact that he was not sure what it was that was so frightening only served to make him even more terrified.

His lips were sheets of sandpaper, grating against each other. Pain slithered through his body, sinking its teeth in harder whenever it grew restless. But there was something else also, some dull, deeper ache, that was knotting his body. Perhaps if the surgeons had been able to cut in that deep, they might have found the promise that bound the coronary arteries to the thumping muscle and kept it wringing life through the broken-down body. Jinyi managed to raise his eyes once more to the old woman keeping vigil beside his bedside and, for a second, before he slumped back to his fitful sleep, felt a little less scared.

Yuying opened her bag once more and pulled out a ravel of twine and a pair of needles. She would knit. This would be enough for now, she thought. To do something useful. To knot these days into a pattern she could recognise. To keep going. That was all she had ever done, she reflected, knitted, unpicked and knitted again, turning herself into whatever she needed to be. She would tie herself to the future; after all, people were always growing out of old clothes, and new babies were always being born. She would weave herself into the fabric of their lives, so that something might remain once Jinyi and she were gone and the whole sorry last century had been forgotten. She would do what her mother had done, and what her daughters now did, and fill the time with the skipping clicks of long needles.

As soon as she began, she started to feel strangely comforted. She remembered knitting for the hoped-for baby in her father's house when the schools had shut down during the civil war and she remembered burying those knitted blankets with her first son. She remembered embroidering clothes in the shack in the country, in order to make money to buy her way out of a nightmare. She remembered knitting for a house of wailing toddlers after returning from the bread factory, while Jinyi stood at the stove waiting for dumplings to rise to the top of a bubbling pot. She remembered sewing clothes for herself and the other women being re-educated with her in the endless fields. She remembered knitting for her granddaughter Lian while Jinyi told the little girl stories about his journeys north, and how lucky she was to have a family who loved her. She remembered a thousand and one other little details that added up to make a life. She would carry on, because that was what she had always done.

Jinyi's eyes opened once more a few minutes before midnight.

'I love you,' whispered the old woman hunched at his bedside.

'Where am I?' he rasped.

'You're right here, with me. Don't worry, everything is going to be all right,' she said, and clasped his hand tight in hers.

'Who are you?'

So she told him. She started at their wedding day with the sound of the hooves clattering against the street outside the Bian mansion, and worked her way forward through the years. And as each story took flight from her tongue Yuying realised the same thing that I had long ago learnt in my bet with the Jade Emperor, that the heart survives on the tiniest details — driven by hunger, hardened by hope. Hearts are made, piece by piece, forged in the furnace of our feelings and fears and doubts and longings. Jinyi and Yuying had set their hearts against history, and they had won out. Without love, we would be lost among dreams. Truth, history, socialism, revolution — all are illusions. Love is the only thing that sustains, that keeps people moving, that ties them to the earth. This is what I would tell the Jade Emperor, and I realised that I did not care whether or not he would understand.

I left Yuying and Jinyi in the small hospital room. As I began my homeward journey, I thought of my old friend Chang Tzu, who, waking suddenly in the night, wondered whether he had dreamt that he was a butterfly or whether a butterfly was now dreaming that it was Chang Tzu.

ABOUT THE AUTHOR

Sam Meekings received his undergraduate degree in modern history and English literature from Oxford University, and his master's degree in creative writing from Edinburgh University. Originally from southern England, he now lives in China with his wife and two children. *Under Fishbone Clouds* is his first novel.